OUT OF
THIS FURNACE

OUT OF
THIS
FURNACE

BY THOMAS BELL

With an Afterword by David P. Demarest, Jr.

UNIVERSITY OF PITTSBURGH PRESS

Second printing 1976
Third printing 1977
Fourth printing 1977
Fifth printing 1979
Sixth printing 1981
Seventh printing 1985

Library of Congress Catalog Card Number 76–6657
ISBN 0–8229–3321–7 (cloth)
ISBN 0–8229–5273–4 (paper)

TEXTUAL NOTE

Out of This Furnace was originally published in 1941 by Little, Brown and Company, then reissued by the Liberty Book Club, Inc., in 1950; it has been out of print since then.

Minor textual changes were made in the 1950 edition, and it is not clear whether these alterations were initiated by the author or the second publisher. This new edition duplicates the original version.

To the Memory

of

my mother, my father and my grandfather

CONTENTS

OUT OF
THIS FURNACE

AUTHOR'S NOTE

This book is a novel, fiction, and — allowing for the obvious exceptions — the proper names used in it do not refer to actual persons who may bear the same or similar names.

With that said, this much more may be: I have been as true to the events, the people and the place as lay within my power.

Part One
KRACHA

1

GEORGE KRACHA came to America in the fall of 1881, by way of Budapest and Bremen. He left behind him in a Hungarian village a young wife, a sister and a widowed mother; it may be that he hoped he was likewise leaving behind the endless poverty and oppression which were the birthrights of a Slovak peasant in Franz Josef's empire. He was bound for the hard-coal country of northeastern Pennsylvania, where his brother-in-law had a job on a railroad section gang.

A final letter from America had contained precise instructions. Once landed in New York he was to ask his way to the New Jersey ferry and there buy a railroad ticket to Pennsylvania. It was likely that aboard ship he would meet Slovaks who were going his way or were being met in New York by relatives; their help should be his for the asking. If not, he was to ask his way by showing to any policeman the enclosed paper, on which was written in English: *Andrej Sedlar, Lehigh Railroad, White Haven, Pa.* He was to beware of strangers who tried to get friendly with him on the street, and under no circumstances should he permit anyone to handle his money.

The warnings had not been entirely necessary. Kracha knew as well as the next man those dismal tales which had drifted back to the old country — about trusting immigrants robbed and beaten their first day in America, about others who stepped off the ship and were never seen again, about husbands found in alleys with their throats cut from ear to ear while their brides of a month vanished forever into houses of prostitution. Determined that no comparable calamities should befall him, he had set out prepared to assault the first stranger who so much as bade him good day.

Unfortunately no one had thought to warn him against his own taste for whisky and against dark women who became nineteen years of age in the middle of the ocean.

He had first noticed Zuska on the pier at Bremen. Later, aboard ship, he met her and John Mihula, her husband; in the crowded steerage that took no planning. They were Slovaks from Zemplinska, the province to the northeast of Kracha's own Abavuska, and they were going to Pittsburgh, where Zuska had a married sister. Mihula was several years older than Kracha, a pleasant, quiet young man with delicately pink cheeks and blond, wavy hair. There was nothing else noteworthy about him except, possibly, his possession of a woman like Zuska.

She was as dark as her husband was fair, as lively as he was grave, a dark-skinned, compactly plump girl who missed beauty, even prettiness, by a face too broad at the cheekbones and a nose that matched. She lacked beauty, but had no need of it; the day after she boarded the ship every man on it was as keenly aware of her as if she had come among them naked. She had a throaty laugh, a provocative roll to her hips and she could warm a man to the roots of his hair with a look.

Long before the voyage ended — it lasted twelve days — Kracha had convinced himself that Zuska was a deeply passionate woman unluckily married to a husband whose abilities were hopelessly unequal to her needs. His pity for her was as profound as his own sense of frustration; in the congestion of the steerage the privacy necessary for such condolences as he felt like expressing was unthinkable.

A week or so out of Bremen, however, Zuska revealed that the day was her birthday, her nineteenth, and stirred by no clearly defined impulse Kracha bargained with a steward for two quarts of whisky and German wine in a long-necked bottle. His appearance, laden, was a triumph. The inescapable accordion player was summoned, the bottles opened, and they had a little party. They drank, danced and sang. Kracha undertook to explain why, among people who were not from Zemplinska, Mihula's way of saying he had just risen would be sure to arouse ribald laughter. He did not convince Mihula, who no more than anyone else could tolerate being told how to speak his own language, but Zuska glanced at Kracha and laughed. Encouraged, he pretended to be drunker than he was and took liberties with her person which she repulsed with surprising ferocity but without changing his opinion of her.

And that was why Kracha, who had left home with enough money to carry him from his doorstep to his destination, marched out of Castle Garden with exactly fifty-five cents in American money in his pocket and, confronting him, the necessity of getting from New York to Pennsylvania by the tedious process of putting one foot before the other.

2

THE Mihulas were still entangled with the immigration officials when he came out into the windy October sunshine. It was now well after noon. He had promised to wait for them, to say good-by before they separated, so he put his *zajda,* his bundle of clothes and things, on the ground at his feet and looked about him.

The low, neutral-colored city, its edges jagged with ships' masts and rigging, was hazy with chimney smoke. The harbor sparkled with sunlight; above him Castle Garden's flag whipped at half-mast, adding its little slap to the gulls' cries and the low rumble from the city. After Budapest and Bremen, what he saw was not overwhelmingly impressive. It was America, of course, but he would not feel himself really in America until he was in White Haven, secure in a job and a place to live.

He regretted parting from Zuska though it was because of her that he would have to walk the roads to White Haven like a gipsy instead of riding a train at his ease. He wondered what she would say if she knew and decided that she would put two and two together as swiftly as the addition had ever been made and mark him down for a fool. Which he was. He was paying a high price for a mild drunk and proof that Zuska had soft thighs.

He saw them appear in the entrance of the building and went toward them. Zuska, looking everywhere at once, was carrying two bundles; Mihula had a wooden box on his shoulder and another bundle at the end of his arm. He greeted them jovially: "I was beginning to think they had sent you back to the old country."

They put their bundles down. "I am glad to be out of there," Mihula admitted.

Kracha glanced at Zuska. "Well, what do you think of America?"

She smiled and shrugged, her eyes bright with excitement.

Mihula was watching for his cousin, who had promised to meet them. They were going to spend a few days with him before going on to Pittsburgh, and Kracha had already been urged to join them for a night at least. He had declined; the sooner he and Zuska were separated the better. Out of politeness, since he wouldn't have recognized Mihula's cousin if he'd stumbled over him, he craned his neck for five minutes; then he said, "Well, I shall say good-by now."

"Are you leaving right away?"

He nodded. "I go across the ferry and take a train there. In five, six hours I should be in White Haven."

"When we go to Pittsburgh we will have to ride all day and most of the night." It was half a boast.

"You have my sister's address," Zuska said. "Let us hear from you."

"You will."

He shook hands with Mihula, then with Zuska. "Till we meet again."

"God willing."

"Who knows? We may all be millionaires by then."

"*Ach!*"

"It has been a pleasure to know you both."

"Let me thank you again for the little party you made on my birthday."

"It was nothing." He picked up his bundle. "Take care of yourselves."

"*Ist s Bohom,*" Mihula said. "Go with God."

"*S Bohom.*"

So he left them.

By showing his paper to every policeman he encountered, he reached the ferry house without mishap. There he learned finally, for good and all, that a ticket to White Haven did indeed cost more than fifty-five cents. This last hope extinguished, he crossed to New Jersey, where a uniformed guard pounced on him as soon as he appeared and was so insistent on helping him that Kracha brought out his paper. The guard escorted him briskly to a ticket window. After a minute he escorted him, almost as briskly, away from it, his expression implying that never again would he trust a human being. Kracha eyed him sardonically and a moment later found himself on the street.

With a river at his back there was only one way to go. He walked until he was out of the city, in the countryside; by that time it was getting dark. He ate some of the bread and sausage he had left home with — steerage food was notoriously vile — drank from his bottle of water and went to sleep in a haystack.

After that he asked his way by showing his paper. Most people were kindly. Sometimes he got a lift on a wagon, but he walked ten miles for every one he rode. He avoided towns when he could. He let his beard grow, and washed his socks and feet every day but did not change his clothes. When his bread and sausage gave out he knocked on the back doors of farmhouses and begged food by gestures, an open mouth, bunched fingers.

He slept in fields, in haystacks, in barns. Sometimes the nights were bitterly cold; in the morning the fields would be hoary with frost. He had really bad weather only once, a day and a night when the rain fell steadily. He walked through the rain until he came to a small shanty and took shelter there. It was a one-time cowshed by the smell of it and a tattered County Fair poster seemed to be all that was holding it together. Next morning the sky was heavy with clouds but there was no rain, only a cold dampness in the air, mud underfoot and water dripping from the bare trees, and he was able to go on.

Signposts were few and crude but he could not read them anyway. He clung to his paper and the belief that as long as he kept going west he would not go far out of his way. He never knew where he was; his memories, afterward, were of country roads and little towns in a land settling down for the winter. The harvests were in and the shorn fields were empty of activity; there was little to see but the still earth, the sky, and sometimes a tiny figure away off in a field.

One week to the day after leaving New York, toward midafternoon, Kracha entered a small mountain village noisy with sawmills. There were few people in the street; he chose one who looked least like an American and exhibited his paper. The man, tall, bearded, lightly clothed for the weather — it was raw and windy — pushed back his cap and read with his lips moving. Then he looked at Kracha and said something while his hand moved in a gesture that took in the whole street.

Kracha blinked. "Do you mean to say this is White Haven?"

"White Haven, *ja, ja!*" He kept waving his hand.

Kracha gave it a second look and began to laugh. The other — he turned out to be a Swedish lumberjack — laughed too, his teeth gleaming in his beard, as if it was the best joke in the world that Kracha should find himself in White Haven without knowing it.

Now he was walking the railroad tracks half a mile north of the village. The tracks ran beside a little river for a while and then turned away from it up a wider valley of their own. Once a coal train passed him, going south. The ties were infernally spaced, too close together for his normal step and too far apart to be managed two at a time. The ditch alongside was worse; there he had to contend with broken stone, culverts, weeds and cattle guards.

The muscles of his legs were beginning to hurt and the afternoon had grown appreciably darker when the tracks went around a curve and he saw some shanties set on a patch of flat ground between the tracks and the hills. Two empty coal cars stood on a siding near by. Smoke, light-colored against the dark hills, was rising from one of the shanties, and a man was sitting on the doorstep of another, his white-bandaged foot conspicuous even at this distance. Someone was chopping wood, the slow, deliberate blows echoing off the hillside.

Kracha went forward, his heart beating a little faster at the thought that this was perhaps his long journey's end. The injured man watched him approach and when he was within speaking distance he said, "You look as though you had come a long way, my friend."

Kracha halted. The man had spoken with the hard accent, the solid vowels and corrugated *r*'s, of a Rusnak, but the language he used was understandably Slovak. "God be thanked!" Kracha exclaimed. "It seems like a year since I heard my own language spoken."

"Are you just over from the old country?"

"A week ago today I was still on the ship. Tell me, is this where the railroad workers live?"

"Some of them. Did the company send you?"

"No. I am looking for a man named Andrej Sedlar."

"You will find him back of the cook shack. That's him you hear chopping wood." He stared at Kracha interestedly. His name, Kracha learned later, was Joe Dubik, a Rusnak, a Greek Catholic Slovak, from Tvarosc in Sarisa. "Is it possible you're his brother-in-law?"

Kracha nodded. "I am."

"Djuro — Djuro — what was the name — Kracha?"

"Yes."

Dubik reached for his crutch. "I am going to enjoy this. Come with me."

They went down the line to the cook shack. "They had you drowned in the ocean and lying dead in a ditch," Dubik said.

"It was nothing as bad as that, as you can see."

"What happened?"

"My money was stolen in New York and I had to get here on foot."

"Devil take me, that's no Sunday stroll! Here, in this door."

The cook shack was dark inside; what light there was came from the adjoining kitchen. Benches and two long tables set with tin cups and plates filled it comfortably. The smell of frying meat was in the air and through the door at the far end Kracha saw his sister at the stove.

She heard them approach and spoke without turning, querulously: "Nah, what do you want?"

"I'm hungry. I've come a long way and I'm hungry."

"Wait for supper." But almost before she finished speaking she had turned, a puzzled look on her face.

Then she shrieked.

Andrej came running in from the yard, the ax still in his hand. In the doorway Dubik leaned on his crutch and never stopped grinning.

3

KRACHA'S story of his walk from New York was a nine days' wonder. The first time he told it he had Francka watching him, listening to every word, and he was shrewd enough to keep it simple. When he came out of Castle Garden his money was in his pocket; when he reached the ferry house and wanted to pay for his ticket it was gone. Kracha spread his hands. There it was. He had given the problem a lot of thinking without getting anywhere, his manner implied, and now he was prepared to hear their speculations.

Opinion settled eventually on the pickpocket theory, possibly because it was more dramatically satisfying. Kracha maintained an air of impartiality. If his pocket had been picked, and he wasn't saying it hadn't been, surely he would have felt the thief's fingers?

Oh, such people were clever, they were smarter than gipsies, they could pluck a hair out of a man's nose without his feeling it.

Kracha allowed himself to be convinced.

Only Dubik learned the true story behind Kracha's walk from New York. He learned it from Kracha himself one Saturday night as they walked the tracks to White Haven, a fine night with the smell of spring in the soft, damp wind. Kracha was carrying a lantern; Dubik was smoking a cigar.

"First I buy myself gloves and a shirt," Kracha said. "A piece of leather to fix my shoes. Tobacco. Matches. A dollar and a quarter should do it. Which will leave me a dollar for myself. But until I've bought what I need nobody is getting me inside a saloon."

"Good."

"After I've bought what I need, then I buy myself a drink. Whisky and beer. Hah!"

They walked in silence, Kracha almost able to taste his drink. After a while he said, "I suppose you'll be out all night again."

Dubik chuckled. "Would you have me disappoint her?"

"Maybe she has a friend and we could have a little party, the four of us."

"No friends. She is all alone in the world, poor girl, except for me. And her husband, of course."

"Ah. And where does this husband keep himself while you play games with his wife?"

"Nowhere near. I will tell you this much: he is a railroad man."

"Lehigh?"

"Yes."

Kracha grinned. "All in the family, so to speak."

"We often talk about him."

"And what is it you have that he doesn't?"

"My health." After a minute, with a barely perceptible lift of his shoulders, he added, "And my youth."

"How did you meet her?"

"If I told you you might guess who she is."

"You needn't be afraid that I'll try to steal her."

"It's not that."

"Is she American?"

"She was born here but she calls herself Dutch. Her husband is American."

"So you carry on your little affair in German?"

"German, a little English — we manage. I am teaching her Slovak."

"I can believe it. What sort of woman is she?"

"Small and dark. Plump."

"I like plump women myself," Kracha admitted.

"Her belly is like a pillow, I give you my word. And what breasts!"

Kracha pulled at his mustache. "On the boat coming over I met a dark girl. From Zemplinska."

"Married?"

Kracha sighed. "Yes. This is between ourselves, you understand."
Dubik nodded.

"I would have given every penny I had for half an hour alone
with her." Kracha hesitated. "As a matter of fact —"

"Well, go on."

"She had a birthday coming over. To celebrate I bought some
whisky and a bottle of wine. Well, the money I spent for all this,
you understand, this money was the money that — well, to be brief
it was the money —"

"That was to have paid for your railroad ticket here."

Kracha let out a deep sigh. "Yes."

"And your pocket was no more picked than mine."

"Good God, would you have had me tell Francka the truth?"
Dubik laughed.

"The devil of it was," Kracha said ruefully, "I got nothing for
my money."

"Nothing? Not even a kiss?"

"I slid my hand under her dress and she almost knocked me
down."

"*Ježiš!* Did she think you were spending money on her because
you liked the color of her eyes? She owes you a debt and if you ever
meet her again make her pay. With interest."

"She is in Pittsburgh now."

"You were too easy with her."

"Well, it's all over and done with now. But keep it to yourself. If
Francka ever found out . . ." He shuddered.

His secret was safe with Dubik. Chance had made them buddies,
sharing the same room, the same bed; time made them good friends.
They never had to learn about each other, feeling their way; as
Kracha once said, they spoke the same language. They had honestly
liked each other almost from the hour they met. In build and coloring they were much alike, with Dubik a shade the taller and thinner.
They were the same age, twenty-one, but Kracha always thought of
Dubik as younger than himself, as an extremely likable younger
brother who was too gay, too trusting, too careless of the future for

his own good. His exuberant joy in living, in things he could see and feel and taste and do, endowed him with a sort of eternal youth.

He had a sweetheart in the old country to whom he wrote regularly.

4

IN MARCH Kracha got word from the old country that Elena had borne a son. He weighed six pounds at birth and was christened Djuro, after his father. Kracha drank his first-born's health. In April a letter came: his son had died of a fever. "God be good to him," said Kracha. "I've had a son and lost him without ever laying an eye on him."

As the year advanced the priest who wrote their letters for Elena and her mother-in-law began ending them with suggestions that Kracha send for his wife as soon as possible. Her health had not been of the best since the birth of her child and it might do her more good than medicine to be with her husband again. He reminded Kracha that no house — and this particular house was a peasant's one-room hut with the naked earth for a floor — was big enough for a wife and her mother-in-law. They quarreled constantly over everything and nothing, over the money Kracha sent each month, over Elena's feather bed — the old woman had suggested that she leave it behind when she went to America, where she could no doubt buy herself another and much finer one — over housework, over who should feed Kracha's old dog, Hussar. The solutions to these problems, which Kracha dictated to Andrej, who had learned to read and write in the Army, satisfied no one in Europe or America, neither Elena nor her mother-in-law nor Francka.

In a little over a year Kracha had repaid the twenty dollars Andrej had loaned him so that he could come to America, and had put by fifteen dollars. Shortly after Christmas he borrowed another fifteen dollars from Francka and sent it all to Elena.

She arrived early in February. The mountains crackled with winter; wind was a solid cold, day after day, and the snow stayed unmelted even on the sunny slopes, with the trees and underbrush poking out of it like stubble on a man's face. A clean, frozen world. The shanties had been built of unseasoned rafting lumber which the sawmills gave away for the taking; warping, the boards spread and after a windy night Kracha would awaken with the wrinkles of his blankets filled with snow, his mustache brittle. On the job they did little but shovel snow, shim rails and keep the switches workable.

When the gang got back to camp that night Andrej called from the cook shack. "Hey Djuro! Kracha!"

The others streamed on past him to the bunkhouse, its windows a dim yellow with lamplight. His breath smoked in the frosty air as he replied. "What do you want?"

"Come here."

"Later."

Andrej swore. "Come here! I want you to meet someone."

"*Bohze moj!* Do you mean she is here?"

Heavy with clothes he jogged across the frozen ground to the cook shack. "Is it Elena?"

"What do you think?"

She was sitting in the kitchen with Francka and two other women. Her embroidered blouse and short, flaring skirt made the others look unexpectedly drab. Her uncovered hair was pale and fine with a faint wave to it, her features small and just missing delicacy. Excitement had lent a little color to her face; even so, Kracha halted in the doorway, shocked to see how thin and pale she was.

She looked around and her eyes widened. She rose. The others were silent; they might have been watching a play. As Kracha's arms went around her she began to cry. The women beamed.

He patted her shoulder. "What are you crying about? It's all over." But he felt pleased.

"They always cry," Andrej observed sagely. "No matter what happens, they cry."

"Let me have a look at you."

"But do you think Francka would cry like that over me? Not her. Not if I had been away ten years."

"Since when did you become worth crying over?"

"What have you been doing to yourself?" Kracha demanded. "You're all bones."

She winced under his fingers, drawing her thin shoulders back. "I had a bad time with the child."

"And your throat — what in God's name — "

She gave up trying to keep it hidden; her hands dropped from holding her shawl together and she let him look with something like desperate hope in her eyes. Kracha stared at her helplessly. After the birth of her child she had written that her throat was swollen but he'd thought nothing of it despite cryptic remarks from Francka. Now he recalled them, and his mother's warnings before he married. In a highland country where goiter among both men and women was common Elena's throat had always been too plump for the rest of her.

He felt dismay and pity and a little anger. If they had been alone he might have said what needed saying at that moment, the one word, the one tenderness, and so perhaps might have saved them both a world of heartache. The moment passed. A flood of pain washed the hope out of Elena's eyes and she bent her head slowly and drew her shawl over it until her throat and her face were hidden.

One of the women said helpfully, "She will have to take good care of herself for a while. She needs to build up her strength."

"Sure, sure!" Kracha agreed heartily. "In three months we'll have her as fat as a pig."

Francka made odd noises in her throat.

Elena looked up, her face in shadow. She spoke tonelessly. "You are looking very good," she said.

"Why not? All he does is eat and sleep." Francka poked the fire in the stove. "And drink."

"Listen to her. Have I missed a day's work yet?"

He had put on weight and the layers of clothing he wore, the thick, multicolored mackinaw, made him look even bulkier. His face was red from exposure. He slapped his chest. "I feel good. I eat good, sleep good, work like a horse. There is nothing the matter with me. And now that you're here there is nothing else I want."

The women were beaming again.

Kracha glanced at his sister. "Can we fix a room for ourselves tonight?"

"Tomorrow. She can sleep with me tonight."

"What good will it do her to sleep with you?" Andrej exclaimed. "Have you lost your mind? They haven't seen each other for over a year."

"They've waited this long, they can wait one more night."

Kracha slept that night with Dubik as usual. Next day men and beds were moved around and when Kracha got back from work their room was ready. He found Elena standing near the lamp, using a needle and thread on something. She looked up and as he closed the door she said, *"Vitajce u nas.* Welcome."

"So we're all settled?"

The room held an iron bed, much used, a box which supported the lamp and served as a table, Elena's large trunk and his smaller one. The floor was bare but clean. Burlap sacking was stretched across the one window in lieu of a shade, and clothes were hung from nails driven into the exposed two-by-four uprights; the house had no inner walls. Here and there patches of wood and tin had been nailed over cracks and knotholes to keep out the wind. On the bed's straw mattress was a gray blanket, two lumpy pillows and Elena's feather bed. The air in the room was clammy cold.

She waited for him to say something, the lamplight making dark hollows in her face. Kracha went around the room inspecting everything, the clothes on the nails, the sacking on the window, the feather bed.

"Marya Barana is letting me cook on her stove until we get one of our own. But we will need pots, dishes — "

"Easy, easy. You will get everything you need, all in good time."

"But you like it?"

"Sure."

"It is the best I could do." She spread her hands in a small gesture. "We have nothing."

"We have a bed to sleep in and a roof over our heads. The rest will come. Well," he went on, looking at her, "how does it feel to be with your husband again?"

She smiled slightly, her shoulder lifting in the merest suggestion of a shrug.

Her poor health, or America, had changed her; Kracha never could decide. He had left her a lively, healthy girl, cheerful as the day was long; now she seldom smiled and went about her housework listlessly. She never complained except of tiredness; when Kracha asked her, sometimes gently, sometimes not, what was wrong she invariably replied, "Nothing." And that was all he could get out of her. As a wife she was meekly dutiful. Once abed, Kracha demanded little more than consciousness from a woman, but even that little he was unable to arouse in Elena. At his gentlest she yelped more often than she sighed. For a while he put himself out to humor her, buying her things in White Haven, praising her cooking; to such attentions she responded satisfactorily yet never with enough impetus to carry over into bed. Kracha consequently felt swindled, then baffled, then angry.

When she became pregnant he ceased to bother her, returned to his whisky. He hoped vaguely that she'd resent this. So far as he could tell, she didn't.

Francka remarked, "I see you have kept your word."

"What are you talking about?"

"Your promise to make Elena fat."

He scowled at her. A suitable retort, one that would have taunted Francka with her own childlessness, did not occur to him until afterward, too late to be effective.

Dubik lost his mysterious sweetheart that summer. He no longer stayed away all night and when the gang grew jocose about it he merely smiled. He told Kracha the husband had been transferred and they had moved to Wilkes-Barre. They agreed it was just as well, now that he was sending for Dorta.

She arrived around Thanksgiving, a solidly built girl with a milkmaid's flaming red cheeks and a hearty laugh. She wore her hair in a braided halo and it became her, though her face was more pleasant than pretty. There was an air of competence and dependability about her; of her easy self-assurance there could be no doubt. Unlike most of the wives and sweethearts who came from the old country she neither simpered nor became a dumb image in the presence of strangers. Half an hour after her arrival she was perfectly at home. Dubik said, "And this is my friend Kracha," and she smiled and shook hands, saying, "I am glad to meet you at last. He was always talking about you in his letters." She made no bones about her affection for Dubik and he, grinning around the stem of his pipe, watching her every gesture, every flash of her eyes as she related some shipboard adventure, was obviously proud of her. Elena sat near by, big with child, her eyes on Dorta, her face expressionless.

They were married during a raging snowstorm three Sundays later. Dubik hired horses and a sleigh from a neighboring farmer to take them to the Irish church in White Haven and bring them back. That afternoon the wedding party in the cook shack was only well begun, with Kracha, as best man, hardly launched on the traditional exhortation — "Dearly beloved, in the life of a man there are three great happenings: when he is born and begins to live, when he dies and leaves this our earth, and when he changes his condition, his life, that is, when he enters into marriage. And this is a great and sacred . . ." — when Elena moaned.

They helped her to her room. For a while the women flew about getting this and that but it soon became evident that her time had not yet come. Dorta, whose mother was a midwife in the old country, made Francka promise to call her when the crisis approached, and the party was resumed. It was a fine wedding. Kracha got pleasantly drunk and was in bed asleep before he knew it. He learned it when Elena awoke him. "Djuro — Djuro — "

"What is it?"

"Go for Francka."

He swung his legs out of bed and reached for his trousers. "God above, what a time to pick!"

"Get Dorta too. Hurry."

"Dorta?" He was half out the door. "Dubik will never forgive you."

She named the baby Mary. The snow had stopped falling by daylight but the cold was so intense that it was three or four days before Dorta and Andrej could take the child into White Haven to be christened.

In the spring the company transferred most of the gang to the Bear Creek division, ten or fifteen miles to the north.

5

DURING the years Kracha worked for the railroad he helped build parts of it, that section northwest of Wilkes-Barre toward the sawmills at Harvey's Lake, for instance, and double-tracked the line from Mauch Chunk to Mountain Top, but mostly he was concerned with keeping in good repair what was already built. He lined and surfaced track, renewed ties, replaced rails, cleaned ditches and culverts, repaired fences, put up cattle guards. During August, before seedtime, he became a farmer again, swinging a scythe on weeds. He learned the names and uses of tools, to recognize cocked joints and broomed rails, to spot a tie that was pumping ballast, to use a Jim Crow, the U-shaped rail bender, to swing a twelve-pound sledge. He fought brush fires in dry weather and floodwaters in wet. Storms made silt of ballast, threatened trestles, uprooted trees and telegraph poles; in winter the ballast froze, the switches froze, spikes snapped like glass, snow choked the flangeways and drifted in white hills across the tracks. His wages were ten cents an hour, and when bad times came and the company cut wages, nine. It was an excellent month when he made as much as twenty-five dollars.

The company kept moving the gang from place to place, from White Haven to Bear Creek — where Kracha's second daughter, Alice, was born — from Bear Creek to Harvey's Lake, and from Harvey's Lake to Plymouth, where Elena presented him with yet a third daughter, Anna. They did the same work, lived in the same ramshackle shanties, wherever they went.

Dubik did not accompany them to Harvey's Lake. He said he had his fill of railroading and was going to try his luck in the steel mills. He wasn't the first, nor the last. The wage rates in the mills were only a penny or two higher than on the railroad but a man worked more hours per day and more days in the year. Besides, Dubik added, he had been in one place long enough; it was time for him to be moving on. Kracha, unable to finance such a venture himself, tried to persuade Dubik to stay, or at least to postpone the trip to a later date. He failed; in April Dubik and Dorta and the boy set off for Braddock, about ten miles south of Pittsburgh. Some time later he wrote that he had a job in the blast furnaces and was working seven days a week. In that letter and all those that followed he kept urging Kracha to join him.

Kracha missed him, which is to say he had to change some of his habits with Dubik gone. He found no one who was as satisfactory to talk with, no one with whom he had a good time merely sitting in the sun or walking the tracks to town. After it had become certain that Dubik was leaving. Andrej had remarked, half as a joke: "So Dubik is leaving us. And what will you do with yourself?"

Kracha had shrugged. Elena, trying to keep a squirming Alice on her lap, said: "I am sorry he is going. He has been a good friend to us both."

She had reason to regret his going. Though Kracha had ceased to hope that she would ever be the kind of a wife he wanted he was not resigned to it, and their relationship had its ugly moments. Dubik, himself as contented with what he had as a man could be, had exercised a soothing influence, counseling patience and tolerance. It wasn't all Elena's fault, he would say. She had to work hard, cooking, washing, scrubbing; and what pleasure did she ever get? Women had a hard time of it, Dubik said. Put yourself in her place. How would you like to live her life, eh?

But that was beyond Kracha's imagining and he had brushed it aside as nonsense. As well ask Elena how she would like to take his place in the gang. Since it was impossible there was no point in suggesting it. Elena was no worse off than any other woman in camp. Did Dorta live any better, have it any easier? Yet she was always lively and good-humored. Nor had Kracha ever heard Dubik complain about her behavior in bed.

Dorta, her husband replied, had her health.

All true; and it was, as Kracha saw it, likewise true that Elena was a skinny, unpretty creature whose mere lack of energy was enough to drive a man to drink. "What the devil's the matter with you?" Kracha exclaimed once, exasperated beyond endurance. "You go around here like something dug out of a grave."

She put the soup bowl on the table. "I'm tired. I washed all day."

"My fine lady is always tired. When we get rich I'll hire a girl and you can do nothing but sleep."

And once, a little the worse for whisky and the inflaming talk of the bunkhouse, he sat on the edge of the bed and as she passed to blow out the lamp he caught her wrist. "Let the lamp be."

She pulled back. "Let me go. I do not feel good."

"You never feel good."

"My back hurts."

"I have a cure for that."

"Djuro, let me go. You will wake the children."

He held her without effort while he studied her. She was wearing a petticoat and a knitted undervest which did her body no kindness. Her hair was in a braid, drawn back harshly from her face. Child-bearing had cost her several teeth; those that remained were bad. He was used to the sight of her goiter by now, but tonight it looked more disfiguring than usual, like the overstuffed crop of some obscenely unfeathered fowl. He stared at her and hated her, less for what she was than because desire drove him to her and she, unbeautiful, unresponsive, whining, made it a bitter taste in his mouth.

"Look at you." He jerked her to him and his free hand prodded her limp breasts, her skinny flanks. "You call yourself a woman? Bag of bones!"

And he pushed rather than struck her so heavily that she fell against the trunk. As she began to cry he rolled over into bed.

When the company moved them to Plymouth Francka announced that she and Andrej were moving to Homestead. She had been planning to follow Dubik to Braddock until he reported trouble in the mills there. Ten days before the previous Christmas the mill had shut down "for annual repairs" and a notice was posted announcing that all men not otherwise notified should consider themselves discharged. As time passed it became evident that Carnegie and his manager, Captain Jones, did not intend to reopen the mill until the men accepted a wage cut and a return to the twelve-hour day, changes which Carnegie insisted were made necessary by the competition of unorganized mills. The Braddock mills had been working under a union contract with the Knights of Labor. The union rejected Carnegie's offer and the mill stayed down, Carnegie's other mills taking care of its unfilled orders. It was a lockout, not a strike, Carnegie pitting his resources against the workers'. The outcome was predictable. In May, after being idle for five months, the men capitulated, and that was the end of the union and of the eight-hour day in Braddock.

Dubik wrote that it had been a bad winter and advised Andrej to go to Homestead. The mills there still had a contract with the union and though it did not cover unskilled laborers, conditions were better even for them than in nonunion mills.

Francka and Andrej went to Homestead and Kracha, almost the sole survivor of the original White Haven gang, promised to follow as soon as he could. It took him nearly a year, a rather full year, too, as it turned out. In October a train full of Irish Catholics returning from some church festival in Hazleton crashed into a similar train at Mud Run. Kracha and the rest were routed out of bed at two in the morning and spent the rest of the night extricating the living and dead from the wreckage; when Kracha got home his clothes were stiff with blood and dirt. In November President Cleveland was defeated for re-election. A bearded man named Harrison won and work was neither better nor worse because of it that winter. In February Kracha heard that Crown Prince Rudolf, Franz Josef's son, had been found dead beside his mistress in a hunting lodge at Mayerling. Everybody shook their heads over this and when they were not predicting that war would come of it entertained themselves with gossip about the splendid, immoral lives of princes.

At the end of May came news of the disastrous Johnstown flood. Half the city had been destroyed, thousands of people lost, but after Kracha learned that Johnstown was not near Braddock or Homestead he thought no more about it. Then, in July, one of the men asked him if he had a brother-in-law in Homestead and when Kracha said he had the man told him the Homestead mills were out on strike.

This was shocking news to Kracha, who had been planning to leave for Homestead almost any week now. He exclaimed, "Good God, do they strike in the steel mills every year?" and had one of the men write to Andrej. It was two weeks before he got a reply. Andrej wrote that it was true there had been a strike but it was all over now. Having broken the union in Braddock, Carnegie had tried to break it in Homestead. The union struck, and after one attempt by Carnegie to reopen the mill a new contract, satisfactory to the union, had been signed. The new contract was to run for three years — that is, until July 1, 1892.

That the mills were running was all Kracha wanted to know. The morning after the September payday he and Elena and the three children boarded a train for Harrisburg, where they changed to a train for Pittsburgh, where they changed to a train for Homestead, where Francka met them at the station. Andrej couldn't come, she said; he was working night turn.

6

UP FROM the station there were lights and store windows but Francka led them the other way, across the tracks and down into dark, badly paved streets lined with houses that looked old and shabby even at night. Children played under corner gas lamps; older people were vague, murmuring shadows on doorsteps and porches. The day had been uncomfortably warm; the evening was stuffy and windless, the air so acrid with smoke that even Kracha coughed. Elena, clearing her throat and holding the baby away from her face as she spat, asked if it was always so smoky. Francka replied that it was no worse than usual, and added, "During the strike there was no smoke. But no money, either."

"Which way is the mill?" Kracha asked.

She gestured down the street. There was little to see. At the far end of the street were a few purplish arc lights, a dim bulk, and above and beyond it a flickering yellow glow that made lazily-moving shadows of smoke and steam. He could hear intermittent whistles and the distance-muffled clash of metal on metal.

"What is that light?"

"The Bessemers."

A man wavered along the sidewalk toward them, still carrying his lunch bucket though it was long past quitting time. He was singing to himself in Slovak and it was obvious that he was drunk. He glanced at Francka's group, Kracha's bundles, and waved a hand. "Ha, greenhorns!" The rest was a mumble.

Francka exclaimed disgustedly as she passed him. The drunken one stood unsteadily and looked after them. His voice carried well. "Goom-by old country! Hooray America!"

Kracha grunted.

In the middle of the block Francka paused. "Through here." They followed her through a black, tunnel-like passageway and came out in a courtyard. All around it kitchen doors were open and as Francka led them to the lower end of the yard, Kracha got passing glimpses of lamplit interiors, a woman ironing here, a man lighting his pipe there, a lithograph of the Holy Family on the wall, a baby crawling on the floor. Doorsteps were well populated; shadowy figures asked Francka if her relations had got here at last and she assured them they had. In the yard's center was a large, roundish structure easily recognizable as the communal privy. Above the yard one could tell where the roof lines ended and the sky began by the yellow flicker of the Bessemers.

Francka dug a big key out of the folds of her handkerchief and unlocked a door. "Wait till I light the lamp."

The lamplight revealed a small, crowded room containing, among other things, a stove, a bed, a table, chairs and a closet for dishes. The wall above the bed was hung solid with clothing; the space under the bed was occupied by trunks and washtubs.

Francka bustled about. "Sit down. Put the baby on the bed. Is she dry? I suppose you're all hungry."

"I am," Mary said.

Francka glanced down at her. "Oh, you. You're always hungry. But don't think you'll eat before you've washed some of that dirt off. You all look as though you'd just come from the mill."

"Everybody on the train had their windows open," Elena said. "So much dirt and cinders! I hope it will be a long time before we ride so far again."

Kracha assured her it would be. He unfastened his ready-made tie and took off his collar. Rubbing his neck he paused in the doorway. "Which one is yours?"

"Number 4. The key is right beside you there."

"A key? What style!"

"You're not in the mountains now. Take the bucket and bring back some water."

When Kracha returned he took off his shirt and washed. Drying himself, he asked, "Have you only the one room?"

"What more do we need? Rents are high. When I move I want it to be to my own place."

"Ah," Kracha said knowingly, "Andrej must be making good money."

"He is making fourteen cents an hour," Francka said shortly, "which is what you can expect when you get a job."

"Has he spoken to his boss about me?"

"Last week, when your letter came. He was told to ask again when you got here."

"Is that all?"

"He told his boss you were coming and wanted a job. What more could he do?"

"Does he think I have a good chance?"

Francka shrugged. She picked up the washbasin and standing in the doorway threw the water into the yard. Then she poured fresh water into it. "Work is good right now. They always try for records at this time of the year. To see how much steel they can roll. Come here, Dirty Face."

"I don't want to be without work too long," Kracha said, stroking his mustache into shape. "I hear they've built a new mill at Duquesne. It might be a good idea for me to try there. Or to see Dubik. Braddock isn't far away, is it?"

"Across the river. But you just got here — *Bohze moj,* did you expect to find a job waiting for you?" She scrubbed Mary vigorously. "Nah, nah, hold still. It won't kill you."

"When does Andrej get home?"

"Tomorrow morning. Six o'clock."

Elena had opened her dress and was nursing Anna. "Have you heard of a place for us?"

Francka reached for the towel. "It's time you were weaning that one."

"I wanted to wait until we were settled here."

"Some people are moving out of the yard this week and the landlord has promised me the room." She went to the door and pointed diagonally across the yard. "That door where the man is standing."

The door, the room, was almost directly opposite the monumental privy. Kracha grunted. "I could wish that closet farther away from the table where I eat."

"If you don't like it you can look for yourself some other place. But rooms are not so easy to find."

"What rent does he want?"

"Three dollars a month."

Kracha nodded. "Well, it will do to start. We can always move later."

"What about furniture?" Elena asked.

"The Jew in the secondhand store will sell you all you can pay for."

Andrej came home in the morning, the marks of a night's labor on him but noisily glad to see them. He was pounds thinner and his face and neck bore the perpetual flush of one who worked with hot metal. He spoke a strange language: slabs, plates, shearman, heater, roller, pusher, tonnage. He ate a huge breakfast of steak and coffee and then rolled into a bed still warm from the women and children. Kracha had slept on the floor.

Andrej spoke to his pusher, a sort of sub-foreman, that night, and the following morning Kracha met him near the Fourth Avenue gate. It was only beginning to get light; the morning air was damp and cool and there was a thin fog over the mill and the town.

"Did you speak to him?"

"Yes. He will be along soon."

"What did he say?"

"Nothing. But don't worry; they're always like that. It's impossible to get a straight word out of them."

The pusher appeared. He was a heavy-set Irishman, distinguishable from ordinary workers almost solely by a cleaner face and a silver watch chain looped from his suspenders to the watch pocket of his trousers.

"This my brother-'law, boss," Andrej said.

Kracha tipped his hat. The Irishman nodded without saying anything.

"I buy drink," Kracha said. "You like?"

"I never refuse a drink," the Irishman said.

Both Kracha and Andrej laughed heartily at this confession of human weakness in a godling and the three adjourned to a near-by saloon. There Kracha ordered a round of whiskies and beers. The bartender set imported Irish whisky before the pusher without being told. He poured himself a double-header and mispronounced a Slovak toast. They drank. And at an opportune moment Andrej slipped three dollars into the Irishman's coat pocket.

Everyone felt relieved when this had been accomplished.

"My brother-'law good man," Andrej said, as though to assure the Irishman that he'd made a good bargain. "Work hard."

"Well, if he wants to stay in my gang he's got to work hard. Loafers don't last long with me."

"I work hard," Kracha said.

The Irishman finished his beer and wiped his mouth with the back of his hand. He refused another drink but accepted a ten-cent cigar. "All right. Bring him with you tonight and I'll see what I can do."

"Sure boss. I bring him. Thanks very much."

"Thanks very much," Kracha said.

The Irishman nodded, said "So long, Jim," to the bartender, and left.

"There you are," Andrej said. "You got here two days ago and tomorrow you go to work."

Nothing, Kracha agreed, could have been more smoothly managed. They had another beer to celebrate and then went home with the good news.

7

IT WAS no use, Andrej said, to expect a visit from Dubik. The blast furnaces worked seven days a week and if Kracha wanted to see his friend he'd have to go to Braddock. They went there the last Sunday of the month, the Sunday after Kracha got his first pay, crossing the river by rowboat ferry to Keating and then walking south through Rankin and Braddock, about three miles. The afternoon was windy, overcast and cool, a good day for walking.

Dubik was living in Hand's Court, a group of small frame houses at Tenth Street and the B. and O. Railroad. They found Dorta, a six months old baby in her arms, gossiping with some women in the yard. She had grown a little fatter; her hips and bosom were generously maternal. But there was no change in the way she talked and smiled.

"He will be so glad to see you," she chattered, leading them to her own door. "Every Sunday he has been saying, 'I bet today Djuro shows up.' Or else wondering how he could get over to Homestead himself. But it's such a walk after a day's work. And he didn't know how you were working."

They entered the kitchen, as clean and tidy as Dorta's kitchens always were. "You say he is sleeping?"

Dorta nodded. "But go wake him. It's time he was getting up anyway. Go on."

Kracha went upstairs. The blinds were down, the small bedroom in twilight. There was an empty cradle at the foot of the bed. Dubik lay on his side, asleep. He had lost weight and even in sleep he looked exhausted. The boisterous shouts Kracha had meant to awaken him with died in his throat.

He shook him gently. "Get up, lazy bum. You have company."

Dubik opened his eyes. Then he grinned slowly, without moving his head on the pillow, and it was the old Dubik. "Where the devil did you come from?"

"Where do you think? From Homestead."

Dubik sat up and they shook hands, grinning at each other. "By God, Djuro, I'm glad to see you."

Kracha slapped him affectionately on the back. "But the trip to Homestead is too much for you, eh? Your best friend is only three miles away, you haven't seen him in two years — "

"Devil take you, you know I have no time." He scratched his head and yawned. "Since the mill went on two turns I'm forgetting what it's like to live. Did you come alone?"

"With Sedlar."

"Give me a minute to put on my pants." He slid out of bed and looked around the room. Then, "Dorta! Dorta!"

"What do you want?"

"My pants."

They heard her say something to Andrej and then she came upstairs. She smiled at them as she entered. "Well, what do you think of your company?"

"Fine company. Full of complaints because I haven't been to Homestead."

She got a pair of blue serge trousers from the closet. "He's only joking. He knows how you have to work. Here."

"What — my best pants?"

"It's Sunday, and you have company."

"My work pants are good enough for such company."

"Put them on, put them on!"

"Good God," Dubik grumbled, "one would think these Krachas and Sedlars were grand dukes at least."

In the kitchen Dubik brought out a bottle of whisky and they drank and talked until a freight train whose heavy roars had been steadily growing louder swept past, headed north toward Pittsburgh, and ordinary conversation became impossible. Dubik rose, got his pipe and tobacco and sat down again. Most of the cars were loaded with coal and coke. They went past rumbling, clanking, filling all space with sound; then the caboose scuttered by, dust and paper in its wake, and the air cleared, their eardrums relaxed.

"Were you around when this Captain Jones was killed?" Andrej asked. Carnegie's General Superintendent had been fatally injured in an accident that week.

"No, that happened on *C* Furnace and I work on *H*. By the time we heard about it he was on the way to the hospital."

"What happened?"

"They were tapping the furnace and the iron burst out and splashed over him. Last Thursday night. He died yesterday."

Kracha grunted. "There are pleasanter ways to die."

"They say he was a hard man," Andrej said.

Dubik shrugged. "He was a boss. In his place maybe you and I would be no different. Still — " Dubik relit his pipe and then said what he thought, not only of the late Captain Jones but of the living Carnegie as well.

Dorta murmured, "You should not speak like that of the dead."

For a while no one said anything. Children played noisily in the yard; from the mill at Thirteenth Street came a faint, low murmur.

"Did you have much trouble getting work?"

Kracha explained how that had been managed, while Andrej looked smug. Dubik nodded. "They do that here too. But at least you have your Sundays off. Here the work never stops. The furnaces are going day and night, seven days a week, all the year round. I work, eat, sleep, work, eat, sleep, until there are times when I couldn't tell you my own name. And every other Sunday the long turn, twenty-four hours straight in the mill. *Ježiš*, what a life!" He smiled at his wife. "Dorta has only half a husband."

"Have you heard me complain?"

"I bet sometimes you wish you were back on the railroad," Kracha said.

"If the railroad paid as well as the mill I would go back tomorrow.

But no man with a family can live on what they pay. Even here it is not so easy."

"I want to rent a larger place and take in a few boarders," Dorta said. "But it's so hard to find a house. And not everyone will rent to our people."

"We've lived this long without boarders," Dubik said, "and we can live a little longer."

"Pooh! You have nothing to say about it." She turned to Andrej. "Has Francka got boarders yet?"

He shook his head. "One week she is all for renting a house and taking boarders; the next week she is adding a thousand figures together and saying it might be better to wait until we can buy a house with a piece of ground for chickens and a garden. I'm through arguing with her or trying to find out what her plans are. Let her do what she likes."

"There's the kind of husband I should have," Dorta said, looking at Dubik accusingly.

He spread his hands. "I give her my whole pay, I drink only on paydays, I beat her no oftener than twice a week and still she complains."

There was, Kracha admitted, no satisfying some women.

"A house is a nice thing to own," Dubik went on, stretching his legs out in front of him and crossing his ankles. "But do you know what I'd like to do? Buy a little farm back in the hills somewhere."

"What would you use for money?"

"It wouldn't take much." His face had brightened and Dorta was watching him without saying anything, an odd expression in her eyes. "A small house with a piece of good ground around it, a few chickens, pigs, maybe a horse and a cow. Then you could tell the mill to go to hell."

"Not for me," Kracha said. "I got my fill of farming in the old country."

"You will get your fill of the mills, too."

They stayed for supper, and towards seven o'clock they left. It was nearly dark by then; church bells were a lonely sound in the quiet evening air. Dubik walked with them part of the way and showed them the library Carnegie had given the town earlier that year. No, he'd never been inside but he'd heard it was very fine. "When do I have the time for such things? Since they cut wages and put us on twelve hours I've even stopped going to church. I was going to learn English, take out my first papers, try to educate myself a little. After all, my children will be Americans, real Americans. But I've had to give all that up."

A thin rain began falling as they waited on the old barge at Keating for the ferryman to return. He was a cheery old pot with a cap tilted over one ear and a clay pipe stuck in his mouth but women disliked riding with him because he was always forgetting to button his fly. Tonight, however, he was wearing oilskins. He took their nickels and rowed them across, commenting in a thick Scotch brogue on the girls he assumed Kracha and Andrej had visited that afternoon. They had no idea what he was saying. The blast furnaces at Rankin flared intermittently through the rain, like half-smothered fires; on the Homestead side a Bessemer converter vomited yellow flames toward the low-hanging clouds and cast a sheen on the river. There were similar, if fainter, pulsations in the sky to the north and south as far as the eye could see. The valley of steel was stirring out of its Sabbath lull. Kracha huddled in the stern of the rowboat and contemplated the dark waters, the restless fires, the unnatural sky; and for the first time since he'd set foot in America, felt himself in a strange land.

8

THEY buried Captain Jones in the cemetery back of the hills above Braddock, erected a tall monument over his grave, and renamed the upper portion of Library Street "Jones Avenue" in his honor. Schwab, who had been in charge of the Homestead mills under him, succeeded the late Captain as General Superintendent of both plants; and Mike Dobrejcak, eldest son of the carpenter in Dubik's native village, wrote he was coming to America and expressed the hope that Dubik would help him find work and a place to live. "The Irish are moving out of that house on Washington next to the shoemaker, you know the one I mean," Dorta said thoughtfully. She had rented it by the time Dubik got home from work the next day, and when Kracha visited them at Christmas she had three boarders besides young Mike and was looking none the worse for it.

Mike was a lean, drawling, rather too grave boy, his cheeks still rosy with youth and country living. Dorta mothered him shamelessly and her older boy followed him around like a puppy. His father had died the previous winter under notable circumstances. Idling in the village tavern, he had bet someone a liter of the native whisky that he could build a table, carry it to a neighboring village, and come back, all in one day. He won the bet, but — the mountains were knee-deep in snow — he caught pneumonia and died before the week was out, leaving a widow and three sons, the youngest of them four months old. He also left a set of carpenter's tools, a one-room hut built in the mountain style of logs chinked with clay, and about three acres of ground in two separated plots. He had been one of the more comfortably situated Slovaks in the village; unlike the great majority he could read and write, and for a time he had been the village *notar,* a sort of secretary to the Mayor.

Mike was approaching the age when he would have been called for military service, and it was partly to escape this that he had come to America. The steamship agent from whom he and his companions purchased their steamship tickets laid out a route for them and made arrangements for getting them across international borders without bothering the guards, and with half a dozen young men from various villages, all as poor, all as eager to get to America, he crossed central Europe on foot, walking the roads to Bremen. The journey took about three weeks. They had trouble only once,

Mike said, on a country road in Poland. An officer of some kind stopped them and asked them where they were going. "To America," they replied, which seemed to amuse the officer extravagantly. He had a better place for them, he said. What he meant Mike had no idea; perhaps a jail, perhaps the Russian Army, perhaps forced labor on some lord's estate. The travelers hinted that it would take more than the officer to keep them from America, and he said he could get all the help he needed. "Where?" "Over the hill." "That is all we want to know." They pushed past him and ran up the road and along the edge of a rise; they looked back at the gesticulating officer and lifted their arms. "Go get your help. By the time you return we'll be in Germany."

They had no trouble after that. On the ship an officer picked Mike out of the crowd and put him to work in the First Class kitchen. He carried coal for the cookstoves, bags of flour for the baker, washed dishes, scrubbed floors, polished brass. From morning till night. But he ate, he said, like a king. The best of foods, the finest of liquors, were his for the taking. He could have been drunk every night if he wished. And when the ship reached New York the officer gave him ten dollars.

"Ten dollars? What for?" Kracha asked.

"For my work."

"Think of that."

"It wouldn't have bought half what I ate and drank."

"Maybe you should have asked him for a steady job."

"He offered me one without my asking, but I told him I had to get to Braddock, I had people waiting for me."

"He got here in the morning, while it was still dark," Dorta said. "Joe was working night turn. You can imagine how I felt when I was awakened by a strange voice calling me from the yard, 'Mrs. Dubik, Mrs. Dubik . . .' "

Kracha stroked his mustache. "Did you ever tell him how I walked from New York to White Haven when I first came to America?"

They had. "But Mike expected to walk all the way to Braddock,"

Dorta said. "It was only because the officer gave him that ten dollars that he was able to take the train. Besides," she added, as though it were nothing, "you were only a few days on the road."

Indignantly, "A few days? A week! A full week! And I was alone!"

Dorta shrugged. "Well," she said illogically, "it was partly your own fault."

Kracha stared at her and then, suspiciously, at Dubik. Dubik shook his head. "Djuro, I swear I've been as silent as the grave."

"What are you talking about?" Dorta asked.

They didn't tell her.

Misfortune struck Dubik some months later. On the last day of July, fire swept the First Ward and before the hand pumps of the volunteer fire company brought it under control it had destroyed about forty houses in Willow Way and Washington Street. Kracha found Dubik and his family back in Hand's Court, staying with some friends there. He offered what help he could. "I have a little money saved," he said. "I brought it with me and it's yours if you want it."

Dubik smiled. "Dorta, what did I tell you would be the first words out of Djuro's mouth?" He slapped Kracha on the back. "Thank you, my friend, but we don't need the money. We were able to save most of our clothes and furniture; what we need is a place of our own. It was bad enough to find rooms before but it is worse than ever now."

Kracha, having gaped and sniffed at the ruins in Washington Street and washed the taste of them out of his mouth in Wold's saloon, repeated his offer once more and then took his money and a sense of well-being back to Homestead; Dubik made shift to find new living quarters. Joe Wold, real-estate dealer and proprietor of the First Ward's most popular saloon, had lost several houses in the fire. He announced that he would rebuild at once and meanwhile would loan money to any of the homeless who needed it. Wold was a Slovak Jew and a growing power in the First Ward. It was said that the mill sent him to Europe regularly to persuade people to come to America, which was one reason there were so many Slovaks in Braddock from Wold's — and Dubik's, and Mike Dobrejcak's — native Sarisa. Dubik finally settled in the new house the company erected almost overnight on the cinder dump, the stretch of filled-in ground between the P. and L. E. railroad tracks and the river — a bleak, wooden row of the kind found oftener around coal mines than in steel towns. A small soap factory, stables and nondescript shanties were its nearest neighbors.

Work slackened more than seasonally the following summer. That was the year the Roman Catholic Slovaks in Braddock took over the First Baptist Church at the head of Eleventh Street and dedicated it as St. Michael's. It was the year, too, that the first street-cars appeared in Braddock, running along Main Street from the mill at Thirteenth to Rankin station, and that Francka bought a house. She found it in the deeper reaches of Munhall Hollow, a winding, unlovely gorge that extended back into the hills south of Homestead. Its one street, unpaved, disputed the Hollow's floor with a shallow creek which in places made footbridges necessary between street and houses. Francka's house, a three-room structure with about an acre of eroded hillside back of it, was one of these. The hills rose steep and ugly, almost bare of vegetation, on either side. The house was a good twenty minutes' walk from the mill.

A few months after they moved into the new house Francka became pregnant.

She refused to believe it at first; she had been fooled too often before. But the symptoms became so marked that she went to a doctor. He said there could be no doubt about it. Whatever the cause, whether it was her prayers, the water from the well of the new house, the air in the hollow or some change in Andrej or herself, it was impossible to say; the fact remained that after twelve years she was with child.

The baby, a boy she named Victor, was born in April. The previous February Frick, Carnegie's new partner and General Manager, had begun negotiations for a new contract with the Homestead locals by demanding a cut in tonnage rates.

9

FRICK had smashed the unions in his coke ovens at Connellsville and some people said he meant to do a similar job in Homestead, that Carnegie had taken him in as much for that as because his blast furnaces needed Frick's coke. These were the same people who snorted disrespectfully when they were reminded that in books and speeches Carnegie had uttered some impressive sounds about democracy and workers' rights. Their suspicions were strengthened in May. While negotiations were still ostensibly in progress Frick had a tall fence built around the mill and erected searchlight platforms in the mill yard — hardly a peaceful gesture. The union men promptly nicknamed the mill Fort Frick. Going home one morning Kracha passed a group of carpenters working on the fence and heard a rougher call to one of them, "Do a good job on that fence, Charlie." The carpenter replied, "Ain't it a hell of a note? Like asking a man to dig his own grave."

June drew to an end, the days filled with rumor. Kracha heard something different every day and had no way of knowing what was true, what false. There were, of course, no Slovaks or unskilled workers in the union. Andrej, who had been through the short, victorious strike of 1889, was confident. "If Frick doesn't give them what they want there will be a strike. It will be 1889 all over again."

"That means everybody will have to stop work."

"Sure."

Kracha sighed. What made him unhappy, what he resented, was less the prospect of a strike than perception of a slowly emerging rhythm which, ever since he'd come to America, seemed to be becoming the controlling factor in his life. He worked and saved and then something happened and he was back where he'd started. Good times were invariably followed by bad, a period of comparative prosperity by a period of slow work and reduced wages which consumed all he'd been able to accumulate.

"If there's a strike how long do you think it will last?"

"Not long. Carnegie can't afford to have his mills shut down long."

"For that matter neither can I."

"What are you talking about? While you're losing a dollar Carnegie will be losing thousands. And these millionaires love a dollar more than you or I. Take a penny from them and they bleed."

"I understand our wages won't be changed one way or another, it's only the tonnage men who are getting cut."

"Don't fool yourself. If the union lets Frick have his way it will be the finish for everybody. Ask Dubik what happened in Braddock when the union lost."

Dubik had already had his say: "Carnegie is out to smash the union in every mill he owns. What he did in Braddock he is going to try again in Homestead. I hope the union beats him. They would be in a better position today if they had helped us in Braddock four years ago. But if they lose — well, I suppose Carnegie will give them a library. And much good may it do them."

Frick delivered his ultimatum, laying down terms which would have meant the end of the union in Homestead, and shut down the mill two days before the contract expired. The "Homestead Strike" began as a lockout, not a strike. Frick shut down the mill; it was the workers who kept it shut. When a dozen deputies came from Pittsburgh union men met them at the station, showed them that the mill was guarded and unharmed, and shipped them back to Pittsburgh on the next train. There was no violence, no disorder, until the morning of July 6, when the Pinkerton men came and Kracha was awakened by the powerhouse whistle blowing in the mill. It had an alarmed, frantic sound. He got out of bed and went to the window.

It was still dark, the cooler part of the night. The street was empty but windows were sliding up, doors opening.

"What's wrong?"

"Who knows? I just got up this minute."

"Could it be a fire?"

"Not the way that whistle is blowing."

"Something may be wrong in the mill."

"If it's the mill, let the Irish take care of it. I want no trouble."

A few men, some in trousers and slippers, walked to the corner, stood there looking up the street for a moment and then apparently decided to investigate further. While Kracha was debating whether to follow their example the whistle stopped blowing and the question of who had started it blowing, and why, became at once a good deal less exciting and important. He lingered a while longer, trying to see more of his neighbor's wife (a Mrs. Lupcha, a plump young pigeon of a bride) as she leaned out of a near-by window, then went back to bed.

By the time he rose again the historic battle on the riverfront was several hours old. He breakfasted and then hurried to the upper end of the mill. Not far from the mill's general office building and nearly in line with the open end of Munhall Hollow, a roadway went down between the ten-inch mill and the boiler house to a dock at the foot of the pumping station where excursion boats docked in summer. Here, Kracha was told, two bargeloads of Pinkertons had tried to land and take possession of the mill. They were still there, effectively kept from landing by the union men barricaded on shore, and unable to leave because their tugboat had gone back to Pittsburgh.

The sidewalks were crowded except in front of the general office building; people were hanging out of bedroom windows, standing on porch roofs, climbing the hillsides. All were looking toward the mill yet there was nothing to see but Frick's whitewashed fence, and beyond it the familiar buildings and track-tangled yards. Only the very hopeful continued to insist that, through the nearer turmoil of arguing voices, the shrieks of barelegged children, the chant of a hokeypokey man, they could hear gunfire. An upriver train stopped at Munhall station, under the overpass that led into the mill, discharged about as many passengers as it took on, and chuffed off to Duquesne, the conductor and brakeman looking back at the crowds as though they'd never seen the like before. Union men were patrolling the overpass and making some effort to keep people from entering the mill. Kracha was turned back after a half-hearted attempt to pass. Only a little disappointed — he felt neither like shooting nor like being shot at — he went in search of Andrej.

He failed to find him but on the way he picked up bits of news: dozens had been killed and wounded, the union men had appropriated a small cannon from the local G.A.R. post and were loading it with powder and scrap iron, attempts to set fire to the barges and to dynamite them had both failed so far.

Around noon, hot and hungry, Kracha trudged up the hollow. He found Francka, her apron full, bargaining with a huckster in the road. She said Andrej had gone to see what was wrong in the mill, and she seemed annoyed — it was her day for ironing — when Kracha indicated that he expected to be fed.

He was still there, leaning over the footbridge and spitting into the creek while he discussed wall-building with Andrej's neighbor — the spring floods had undermined walls and dislodged bridges up and down the hollow — when Andrej returned with news that the battle was over. The Pinkertons had surrendered and had been marched to the Opera House in Homestead, since the jail was too small to hold them all. There were nearly three hundred of them. On the way, despite the union leaders' promises of safe conduct, they had been unmercifully mishandled by infuriated steelworkers and their womenfolk. But the provocation had been great. Ten men were dead, seven of them steelworkers, and sixty wounded. Andrej asked Kracha if he knew a John Sappo. "He boarded somewhere near you, I understand." He was one of the dead. He left a wife and children in the old country. Kracha didn't know him.

The first of the dead was buried the next day. The mill was still down, the union men still in control. But on the Monday following the battle, General Snowden came to Homestead with ten carloads of soldiers and camped on Carnegie Hill. The Homestead union leaders were arrested, charged with murder, riot and conspiracy. A notice was put up giving the men ten days to return to work, on the company's terms. Very few accepted the offer. The company sent eviction notices to all "striking" tenants of company houses, and began erecting bunkhouses for the accommodation of "blacksheep" — scabs — at the Munhall end of the mill. In Pittsburgh, on the last Saturday of the month, an anarchist named Berkman waited in Frick's office for his return from lunch, and when he appeared, shot him. Frick lived. One of General Snowden's soldiers, a private named W. L. Iames, expressed regret that Berkman's aim had not been truer. He was ordered by his superior officer to be strung up by the thumbs for half an hour, half his hair and mustache were shaved off and he was then dishonorably discharged. Soldiers assigned, for no obvious reason, to duty in Braddock were lectured by the local newspaper for annoying women in the street. Schwab was brought back to Homestead and the mills slowly resumed production.

The union's leaders were in jail or out on bail, the union itself shattered, and hunger and suffering were stalking the streets of Homestead. "Do not think we will ever have any serious labor trouble again," the triumphant Frick cabled to Carnegie in Italy. "We had to teach our employees a lesson and we have taught them one that they will never forget." Carnegie replied with a congratulatory message beginning, "Life worth living again . . ."

Long before this edifying exchange took place Kracha had gone to Braddock for a talk with Dubik. A few mornings later he met him at Thirteenth Street and as George Lupcha, Dubik's cousin just over from the old country, he bought a stove-gang foreman a drink in Wold's saloon. Money was passed unobtrusively and Kracha returned home to tell Elena he had a new job and they were moving to Braddock. He worked there nearly a month, however, before Dorta found them two rooms in the company houses on the

cinder dump. Dorta herself had recently moved across the tracks
to a new brick row on River Street.

Dubik proved an excellent prophet. Homestead got its library,
an even larger and finer one than Braddock. Carnegie built it on
the hill where the soldiers had camped, and next to it he put up a
huge mansion for the mill Superintendent.

Meanwhile, bad times had settled like a pall over the steel towns,
and many things happened — Cleveland was elected president a
second time, the Columbian Exposition opened in Chicago, the
mill moved the bed of Turtle Creek a thousand feet east to clear a
site for new foundries, Coxey's Army marched on Washington, the
Pullman strike developed into a great railroad strike which was
duly broken by Federal troops, and Elena rented the two rooms
next door and took in boarders — before times got good again.

10

IN HOMESTEAD Kracha had helped produce steel plates from
red-hot slabs; in Braddock he helped produce the metal from the
raw ore. He was a very minor factor in the extensive, highly involved process of supplying a nation with steel, though it cannot
be said that he ever thought of himself in just that way. Mills existed to provide men with jobs and men worked in mills because
they had to work somewhere. Kracha did what he was told and
was paid for it every two weeks; his interest ended there. There
was little about his work to make him feel it was important or
necessary; on the contrary, the company lost no opportunity to im-
press upon him that his services could be dispensed with at any
time, that it was really doing him an enormous favor by letting
him work at all.

Day turn or night turn he left home at five-thirty. All over the First Ward, all over Braddock and in every steel town in the valley, men were putting on their coats and picking up their lunch buckets and going off to work — out of the houses, down through the mean streets and alleys to the mill. Twice a day, morning and evening, the First Ward was lively with men going to work or coming home. To that rhythm the life of the steel towns was set.

As a rule Dubik was waiting for him in front of Wold's saloon, at the corner of Washington and Thirteenth where the town ended and the mill began. He was waiting this spring evening, his clean face contrasting, like Kracha's own, with the shapeless, work-stained clothes and heavy shoes. They had a quick beer and then crossed Thirteenth Street, climbed the cindery slope of a railway embankment and at once left the town, the ordinary, human world, behind. They went across the black, lifeless plain of the mill yard toward the blast furnaces, looming huge in the early dusk. Rushing flame, oddly soundless, leaped out of their tops at regular intervals as charges were dumped inside, were extinguished as if by a giant breath as the furnace top closed. Farther to the left, past the tall stacks and iron rooftops, the Bessemers' flames lit up the eroded hillsides of North Braddock.

There were men ahead of them and behind, a straggling, silent procession. They stumbled over tracks, waited while a dinkey pushed smoking ladles of slag toward the river, then went on. Purple arc lights sputtered through a haze that was three parts soft-coal smoke and one part dust. A young man changing carbons in a lamp clung like a monkey to his high perch and yelled to Dubik as he passed. Dubik waved back and the youth threw a piece of carbon after him. "Steve Bodnar," Dubik explained. "He and young Dobrejcak go around together."

At *H* Furnace they separated, Kracha going on to *F*. There he climbed rickety iron stairs and entered the cast-house, the covered space around the base of the furnace. It was a low-roofed, murky place, warm with heat from the furnace, its floor marked with ditches that led from the furnace to the edge of the platform, below which empty ladles and cinder buggies waited. The furnace itself, giving no hint of the structure that towered eighty feet above the cast-house roof, was a gross, big-bellied affair pierced with small holes which were dazzlingly bright with the glare of molten metal. McKenzie, the furnace keeper, was peering into one of the holes as Kracha crossed the cast-house to a little shanty where he left his bucket. More men kept arriving, going into the shanty, coming out. From the direction of the stoves came a low, deep hum; the skip hoist ground and rattled outside. They would be tapping soon, Kracha reflected. The cast-house had a clean, ready look, from the hot furnace to the waiting ladles.

Kracha and Dubik were front men, as distinguished from the men who worked at the back of the furnace, in the underground stockyard. There men loaded ore, coke and crushed limestone into skips which were then pulled onto the skip hoist, a vertical elevator with open sides which lifted them level with the top of the furnace. This was, of course, before the introduction of the inclined automatic skip hoist and of the double bell, a device for keeping the top of the furnace closed during charging and thus preventing the escape of valuable gas. At the top of the hoist two men called "top fillers" pulled the skip over a lofty little bridge to the furnace and dumped its contents into the bell, the conical stopper set, point-up, into the top of the furnace. The men then retreated with the empty skip, signaled the engineman, and the bell was lowered a few feet, permitting the charge to slide into the furnace. Each time the bell was lowered gas escaped, igniting to make a flame thirty or forty feet high which was extinguished with magical suddenness when the bell was lifted into place again. There were times when the front men could take it easy, but the men in the stockyards and on top of the furnaces worked without pause from whistle to whistle. Charging had to be continuous.

Dubik had been put to work in the stockyard when he first came to Braddock, "pulling buggies like a mule in a mine" for a year before he got a better job in a yard gang, and when Kracha announced his intention of abandoning Homestead before everyone else got the same idea, Dubik had assured him a job in front of the furnace was worth whatever bribe the pusher demanded. But front or back the work was hard, exhausting and always dangerous. The steel mills, like the mines and the railroads, had an appallingly bad accident record. In Braddock it was an exceptional month which didn't see a man crippled or killed outright. American industry, for all its boasting, was still crude and wasteful in its methods; and part of the cost of its education, — of that technique it was, in time, to consider, somewhat smugly, as a uniquely American heritage, a gift of God to the corporations of America, — was the lives and bodies of thousands of its workers.

Kracha worked from six to six, seven days a week, one week on day turn, one week on night. The constant shifting of turns made settlement into an energy-saving routine impossible; just when he was getting used to sleeping at night he had to learn to sleep during the day. At the end of each day-turn week came the long turn of twenty-four hours, when he went into the mill Sunday morning at six and worked continuously until Monday morning. Then home to wash, eat and sleep until five that afternoon, when he got up and returned to the mill to begin his night-turn week. The long turn was bad but this first night turn coming on its heels was worse. Tempers flared easily; men fought over a shovel or a look and it was fatally easy to be careless, to blunder.

When work was good, when one full week followed another with little besides paydays to break their monotony, Kracha lived only during his day-turn weeks. Night-turn weeks were periods of mental fog; he went back and forth to the mill in half a daze which lasted until the end of his turn Sunday morning, when he was given twenty-four hours to himself. Sometimes he went to early mass; other times he went directly home and rolled into bed. When he rose late that afternoon there was little time to do anything. Usually he got drunk. Only whisky could pierce the shell of his weariness, warm him, make him think well of himself and his world again.

Hope sustained him, as it sustained them all; hope and the human tendency to feel that, dreadful though one's circumstances might be at the moment, there were depths of misfortune still unplumbed beneath one, there were people much worse off; in fact, what with a steady job in the blast furnaces, a cozy home on the cinder dump, a friend like Dubik here and a dollar to slap down on Wold's bar of a Saturday night, one was as well-favored a man as could be found in the First Ward. And there was always hope, the hope of saving enough money to go back in triumph to the old country, of buying a farm back in the hills, of going into business for one's self.

For a few their hopes were not in vain. To others work and hope alike came to a sudden, unreasonable end when they were carried — if machinery or molten metal had left anything to be carried — out of the mill feet-first. The greater part went on from day to day feeling that all this was only temporary since such things couldn't last, that just before human flesh and blood could stand no more something would happen to change everything for the better.

But it never did. When human flesh and blood could stand no more it got up at five in the morning as usual and put on its work clothes and went into the mill; and when the whistle blew it came home.

11

AUGUST'S rich heat baked the First Ward relentlessly, one hot, clear-skied day after another. Kracha, sprawled on a bed that grew sticky with his sweat, gasped for air and in wakeful sleep kept confusing the buzzing of flies with sounds from the mill. Freight trains shook the house with the rhythmic double thump of their trucks over a cocked joint some thirty feet from his pillow; cinders rattled against the window, smoke and dust sifted through the curtains. Anna, suffering from prickly heat, whimpered end-lessly in the kitchen.

More stupefied than rested, it was almost with a sense of relief that he heard Elena start up the stairs to call him, to tell him it was time to go to work.

The two boarders who were also working night turn that week had already left when Kracha stepped out of the house. Elena followed him, wiping her hands on her apron. She asked a child playing near by if she'd seen Alice and the child said no, she hadn't, but Mary was over by the stables. Elena lifted her head and yelled, and down by the soap factory and the stables a dark-dressed, black-stockinged figure stopped running. Her voice reached them as from a great distance. "What do you want?"

"Go to the store."

"I can't go now. Make Alice go."

"Come here!"

"I can't. I'm It."

"Stop yelling your lungs out," Kracha said. "What does the brat mean, she is it?"

"Some game they play."

Beside them the house was a row of windows and doorways stretching off on either side in diminishing perspective, washtubs hanging beside every other door. From within came the common household sounds, men and women talking, babies crying. The barren, filled-in ground on which the house stood seemed lifted above the river by its sheer drop to the water's edge where the company had built up the bank by pouring molten slag. The hill on the other side of the river was a dusty green. A rowboat was crossing from the direction of Kenny's Grove. Over to the right, past the comparatively new wire works, the sun was sliding toward the hills back of Homestead. The smoke and dust there would turn it into an enormous crimson disk.

"Well. *S Bohom.*"

"*S Bohom.*"

He had a beer, generously salted, before Dubik arrived, and

then another to keep Dubik company. Neither had much to say as they went across the yard. The sun was hot on their backs; ahead of them the mass of red smoke above the furnaces looked motionless, the recurring flames pale and hot. Top fillers were tiny figures pulling toy carts over the lofty little bridges. The cindery ground of the yard was black and dust-dry. Only the river and the hill looked cool, and the river made Kracha think of the boy who had drowned while in swimming. "Have they found Novotny's boy yet?"

"Not as far as I know."

"Just when he was getting old enough to be some help to them. That's one worry I'm saved with my girls. I don't have to worry about them hopping freights or going swimming in the river."

Dubik smiled faintly. "They'll make up for it when they start going out. Clothes, sweethearts — they'll make you wish you had boys."

Kracha grunted. Then, "I told you we're moving to Cherry Alley?"

"Yes."

"The rent's higher but it will be worth it to get off that damned cinder dump."

"When are you moving?"

"Next week. Monday, I think. The last of the month."

They parted near *H* Furnace. "Don't forget," Kracha said. "Payday tomorrow."

Dubik promised not to. When working night turn they usually went for their pay early in the afternoon so they wouldn't have to carry money into the mill.

Kracha went on to *F*. His beers were already drying in his mouth.

A light rain fell for a while around midnight. Half an hour after it stopped the ground was as dry, the air as close, as ever. They tapped at four, the worst hour.

When Kracha could pause to look around him again the sky was pale with dawn and the yard outside the cast-house, all night a smoky darkness flecked with lamps, was now washed gray, revealing the familiar pattern of buildings and railroad tracks. It looked like another hot day. He scooped a dipperful of brackish oatmeal water from the bucket and drank slowly. One hour to go.

He felt the earth shake under him; and then came a terrible deep boom, like the roar of an explosion underground. Someone yelled, "Christ, what was that?" and Kracha jerked around, half expecting to see the furnace crumpling, molten brightness spurting through the cracks. But it stood solid and unmoved, efficiently digesting its bellyful of iron and flame. Kracha splashed the dipper into the bucket and ran for the open.

Above *H* Furnace an immense cloud of red smoke was rising gracefully into the morning air. It looked a mile high and its base was a leaping flame. The iron canopy above the furnace top had been torn loose from its fastenings and hung over one edge like a cap sliding off a man's head.

Kracha ran.

As he approached he could hear the roar of that rushing flame and the rattle of things falling on iron roofs, the coke and stock blown out of the furnace by the explosion. The furnace itself, except for its majestic plume and its rakishly tilted canopy, looked unchanged, undamaged. Red dust began powdering his face and hands.

The running men converged around the back of the furnace, by the stockyard. Kracha pushed through and scrambled down the iron stairs. In the cavelike stockroom the skip hoist had just been lowered. A few of the men on it could still stand. Some of the others were so horribly burned that Kracha could only hope they were already dead.

Then he saw Dubik. He was being helped off the hoist. His eyes were closed, his face burned, his clothes in shreds. Kracha clawed his way to him. "Joe! Joe! It's me, Djuro." He spoke to the men who were leading him by the arms. "This my friend. I take him. Please."

"All right. Take him down to the stables. The doctors will be there right away. Stables, you furshtay?"

"I furshtay, I furshtay."

They let him have Dubik and turned to the others. Kracha led his friend up the stairs, through the crowd outside. Foremen and straw bosses were already bustling about, ordering the men back on their jobs. Nobody was paying any attention to them. The crowd parted when they saw Dubik.

Kracha led him across the tracks, across the yard. The stables where the mill officials kept their horses were near the river, not far from Thirteenth Street. Halfway there Dubik fell to his knees. Kracha dropped beside him. "Joe. Don't try to walk any more."

Dubik's head was hanging low between his shoulders. "Djuro?" When he spoke his scorched skin cracked pink.

"Don't talk."

"Am I badly hurt?"

"A little burned, that's all."

"I'm afraid to open my eyes."

"Keep them shut."

"Don't take me home. If Dorta saw me looking like this —"

"Sure, sure. I'm taking you to the stables. The doctors will be there and they'll fix you up right away. Now don't talk any more."

He grasped Dubik's wrist to help him up and felt the skin slide under his fingers like a wet label on a bottle. His breath hissed.

He bent over Dubik. "Joe, you hear me? I'm right beside you. Here. I want you to climb on my back."

Somehow he got Dubik's arms over his shoulders, his own body under his friend's. He was heavier than Kracha had expected. Grunting, his hands and knees scraping cruelly against the cinders, he got one foot against the ground, put his hands under Dubik's thighs, and rose. The muscles of his belly stayed tight for a minute after. "So." His knees were trembling.

The sun had come up; the hills on the other side of the river were bright with it.

Men were running toward him. They seemed anxious to help, but there was nothing they could do and Kracha shook his head at them and went on, his feet sinking deep into the cindery ground.

Dubik's arms dangled before him, and over his shoulder Dubik's head, like a tired child's, moved gently with each step. Kracha could smell burnt skin. People came up over the embankment at Thirteenth Street, seeming to come up out of the ground, and advanced like a wave toward the furnaces, the clamor of their hysteria preceding them. Some of them were women.

And one of them was Dorta.

She made him bring Dubik home to the house on River Street. They laid him on a mattress thrown on the kitchen floor and Kracha went in search of a doctor. But they had all been summoned to the mill. Raging, he returned to the house. Dorta, her face like death, was sitting on the floor beside Dubik. He was shiny with oil.

She said dully, "His eyes are burned."

A stranger pushed through the whispering women and awestruck children outside the door. He had just come from the stables. He said the doctors were angry because Dubik had been taken home. He said he had been sent to take Dubik to the B. and O. station where he would be put on the next train and sent to the hospital in Pittsburgh. He said he had a horse and wagon out on the street.

They carried the mattress out through the narrow passageway to the street and laid it in the bed of a commandeered junk wagon. Then Dorta and Kracha got in and, cowbell clanking, they drove to the station at Ninth Street. Several wagons and buggies bearing injured men were already there. While they were waiting for the train the mill whistle blew. Six o'clock. End of the turn.

When the train arrived they put the injured men in the baggage car. People stuck their heads out of car windows to watch. Dorta refused to leave Dubik's side and the baggage clerk, glancing at Dubik and swallowing hard, let her stay. "Elena will look after the boys," Kracha said. He patted her hand and then watched the train pull out.

Dubik died two days later, blind and unconscious. The doctors had filled him with drugs to ease his pain and he died without knowing that Dorta was beside him.

It had been known that night that the furnace was "hanging." This was a not uncommon occurrence. The mass of stock which filled the furnace almost to its top would, for one reason or another, cease to settle to the bottom, and as the melting process at the base continued a gap would form between the pool of molten iron and the raw stock suspended above it. Usually, when this was discovered, the furnace keeper would order the blast lowered or shut off entirely and the stock would slip down harmlessly. But this was, as it turned out, a bad hang, and when the slip took place the result was disaster.

Ordinarily there were only two men, the top fillers, on top of the furnace at a time. But some minutes before the explosion they had sent down word that an ore buggy had slipped over the edge into the bell. Since it weighed well over half a ton they needed help to pull it out. A dozen laborers, Dubik among them, were thereupon sent up on the skip hoist.

The explosion blew out the top of the furnace. Three men were killed instantly and eleven injured, three of them fatally. Dubik was one of these, and the luckiest; he died early. Another died two weeks after the accident; the third lingered for nearly a month.

Officially, it was put down as an accident, impossible to foresee or prevent, its horror accentuated by a grim coincidence. In a larger sense it was the result of greed, and part of the education of the American steel industry. The steel companies were using ever larger percentages of the earthy Mesabi ores, which were cheaper to mine and handle than the massive rock ores but which demanded — as the ironmakers were learning — a variation in technique to prevent choking the furnaces.

The company contributed seventy-five dollars toward Dubik's funeral expenses.

12

SOME weeks after the funeral, toward the end of September, Kracha, Dorta and Mike Dobrejcak were in the kitchen of the house on River Street. Mike was propped on the doorstep, a favorite spot with him; the others sat at the table, the lamp between them.

Kracha had come with something on his mind, and in time he got around to it.

"I want to get out of the mill," he said. "I can't work there any more."

Dorta glanced at him but said nothing.

"Not because of what happened," Kracha went on. "Anyhow, not only because of that. I'm no more afraid now than I've ever been. God knows there is always danger; a man never knows going in if he'll come out on his own two feet. But what good does it do to worry? When your time comes to go, you go; it's up to God."

They waited for him to go on.

He pressed the ash of his pipe down with his thumb and then wiped his thumb on his pants. "I'll tell you exactly what I have in mind. I don't need to ask you to keep it to yourselves."

He paused. Then, "I'm thinking of going into business."

Dorta could not repress a faint smile. "Again, Djuro?"

"This time I mean it."

"Joe with his farm — you with your business — " She shook her head in quiet amusement.

"I know, I know. We always talked and never did anything. And now Joe is in his grave. That's what started me thinking."

Dorta had lowered her face. Kracha said, "Dorta. Please."

"I'm not crying." She looked up as though to prove it. "I have no tears left. It was remembering how you and he used to talk . . ."

Kracha shrugged. "It was all we could do. Talk."

"He got pleasure even from that. How much land, how many fruit trees, how many pigs and chickens. You remember."

"Yes. He loved the country."

"Sometimes I think it wasn't that he loved the country but that he hated the mills. He never complained to me but I know how he felt. Work gave him no time to live."

"I know."

"Coming to Braddock changed him. You remember how he used to be, always lively, always making jokes. But afterward he was always too tired."

Kracha let her talk; it did her good. She had lost weight in the past few weeks and her manner, her speech and gestures, were noticeably subdued; but that was only to be expected. There were rumors that the company was going to give, or had already given, lump sums of money to the families of the dead; some estimates went as high as six hundred dollars. How true this was Kracha didn't know. Dorta said nothing and he forbore asking her. She had thanked him when he'd asked her if she needed money; she had, she said, enough. As for the future, her older boy would be old enough to go to work in a few years; meanwhile she intended to go on as usual, keeping boarders.

"It never mattered much to me where we lived," she was saying. "One place or another it was all the same to me. But he had feelings about such things. He wanted to live well, to live in a nice house away from the mill, and to give his boys a good education so they wouldn't have to work with shovel and wheelbarrow like their father. He used to say, what was the use of coming to America if not to live better than we lived in the old country?"

After a while she said, "I remember while he was still in the old country, before he left for America, how he used to talk, the plans he made . . ."

Slightly uncomfortable, Kracha got up and went to the bucket, drank a dipperful of water he didn't really want, and then sat down again.

Dorta gestured deprecatingly. "Why do you let me gab like this? Tell me about your business."

He didn't need coaxing. "Well," he said.

"You're really serious about it this time?"

"I am."

He relit his pipe carefully. "I've been thinking it over and I've decided the time has come to do something more than talk. I'm still a young man. I have a little money put by. Not much, but enough, I think." He brushed his mustache away from his mouth with his pipestem. "Mrs. Miller wants to sell. She's been talking about it ever since her husband died but now I think she will listen to reason."

"Mrs. Miller? You mean the one who has the butcher shop on Washington?"

He nodded.

"So that's what you're thinking of, the butcher business?"

"Why not?"

He could see that Dorta, after her first surprise, was impressed.

"I know meat," he said. "Who did all the butchering and sausage making while we were on the railroad? Give me two weeks behind the counter and I'll be as good a butcher as any in Braddock." He raised a hand. "I know, I know. There's more to running a butcher shop than wrapping up a pound of pork chops. I know that. But tell me something. Is Mrs. Miller a businessman? She counts the money, she pays the bills, but who really runs the business? The two men who worked for her husband; or to put it more exactly, one man, that Willie Behrman."

"I wonder why he doesn't buy her out himself."

"Because he spends every penny he makes in Wold's saloon."

"Would you keep him on? I know the women like him."

"As long as he tends to business he can stay. I'll need someone who knows how to keep books. And as you say, the women like him."

"You talk like a businessman already."

Kracha gestured self-consciously. Then: "I'm going to see her after the first of the month. She'll be paying her bills then and maybe that will make her more reasonable. I said to myself, if you owned a business when would you feel most like selling out? Why when you had to be laying out good money to pay bills, of course. A smart idea, eh?"

Dorta smiled. Mike frowned, as though he would need time to properly evaluate it.

"Oh, I have some good ideas. Zeok and Sabol are too old-fashioned. Wait till I show them how to bring in business. Kramer I'm not worrying about at all."

"He sells good meat."

"Sure, first class, but how many around here can afford to buy it? Do you? Well then. And I have ideas about getting my meat cheaper. Why should I pay the slaughterhouse a profit? I can go back in the hills with a wagon and buy direct from the farmers, do my own butchering. I can make my own boloney, smoke my own hams and bacon. Old-country style. That's the way to make money; sell something nobody else has and sell it cheap."

"I can see you have been thinking about it."

"And the more I think the better it looks."

"Well, I can only wish you luck. Will you let me be your first customer?"

"I promise to give you the best in the house."

She smiled. "Then Zeok has lost one customer already. How much do you think she will ask?"

"Who knows? If I don't have enough I think I can get her to take my note. But after all, what has she to sell? She rents the store. She owns a horse and wagon, a few knives and cleavers. The icebox I think she rents. How much can she ask?"

"Would you have to take over her bills?"

"We would have to make some arrangement about the bills and what the customers owe on their books."

Mike spoke from the doorway. "How about a job for me, Djuro? I'm getting tired of working in the mill."

"If you're smart you'll stay where you are. I may be looking for a job myself in a few months."

"*Ach!*" Dorta said. "People always have to eat."

"But they don't always have the money to buy meat, or to pay their bills. Remember that."

"What does Elena think about it?"

Kracha shrugged and limply waved his hand back and forth in the air. "She's like that. If I make money she'll be pleased, if I lose everything she won't be surprised."

"Will she still keep boarders?"

"Yes. Of course, if everything goes well — "

"Let us hope it does."

"What would you do if you made a lot of money?" Mike asked. "Go back to the old country?"

Kracha stared at the floor. "Elena thinks she would like to go back. Since coming to America she's had a bad time of it, what with one thing and another. She remembers what it was like when she was a girl and thinks it would be the same again. But it would take money, lots of money. What good would it do to go back with empty pockets? Still, suppose I was lucky, suppose I made a lot of money. By that time the girls would be big. They were all born here, they went to school here, they're more American than anything else. Braddock is no paradise, I'll admit, but have you forgotten how we had to live in the old country?"

Dorta nodded. "It wouldn't be fair to the girls. At least we never knew any better."

"Elena would rather I bought a farm, but I got all I wanted of farming in the old country. And even here in America you can own a farm and still go around with no seat in your pants. When I walked from New York to White Haven let me tell you I saw more than one farm where I knew better than to ask for a bite to eat. There's no money in farming. The way to get rich in America is to go into business. Buy cheap, sell dear. There's your fortune in four words."

He struck a match and tried to relight his pipe but there were only ashes in it. He got up and knocked it empty against a lump of coal in the scuttle, then blew it clear and put it in his pocket. He stood with his back to the stove.

"What it comes to," he said, "is that working in the mill I get nowhere. It would be the same with any job I could get for they all pay the same and a man can't make enough working alone to keep a family. Sometimes I think they got together and figured it out to the last penny, the sonnomabitch bastards. And you know what it's been like ever since we came to America. Good times, bad times, good times, bad times, one after the other. What we save in good times we have to spend to keep alive in bad. Where can we get at that rate? Nowhere. The poorhouse. Well, I have a little money put by, more than I may ever have again because as the girls get older it will be harder and harder to save. And I'm not getting any younger myself. So."

Dorta nodded slowly.

"At worst," Kracha said, "I can only lose the little I have and have to go back to the mill."

"I hope not," Dorta said.

Kracha hoped so too.

A month later he signed papers and became a businessman. That was in October, 1895. A little over a year later he owned two horses and wagons, had a man and two boys working for him, and in a steel box in the trunk in his bedroom he had nearly one thousand dollars in cash.

13

HIS shop was a one-story frame building, old and weather-beaten, on the west side of Washington Street about midway between Thirteenth and Twelfth. It had a false front, a waist-high window with his name on it in brown paint, *George Kracha, Meat Market,* and at one side of the window a door which one reached by mounting two wooden steps from the sidewalk. Inside the shop — it was hardly larger than an ordinary room, six customers crowded it — was a counter, a chopping block, two hanging scales and a rack of hooks hung, in cold weather, with ham, sausage and assorted meats. There was also a sausage-making machine and a meat grinder with a big flywheel painted red and decorated with gold roses. At the rear of the shop was a large, varnished icebox and behind the icebox a little room that was used partly as an office and partly as a storeroom for paper and sawdust.

He was successful and he enjoyed it. He liked having storekeepers and saloonkeepers accept him as not so much an equal as a fellow businessman, of a class apart. He liked wearing his good clothes every day and bossing his employees and always having a pocketful of money. He liked having people envy him his good fortune, though when they congratulated him he always pulled a long face and assured them it wasn't all soup and noodles. There were times, he said with a sigh, when he wished he was back in the mill. What worries, after all, did a millworker have? He had one boss to please; Kracha had a hundred. He worked his twelve hours, he got his pay every two weeks and that was the end of it. But Kracha — Kracha had rent to pay, wages to pay, bills to pay. Feed, shoes and harness for the horse. Repairs to the wagon. Taxes. Ice. Sawdust. Paper. Licenses for this, permits for that. The money went out as fast as it came in, and when work in the mill was slow it went faster. It was a wonder he ever had a penny left at the end of a week.

But he wouldn't have traded places with the General Superintendent.

Three times a day the mill whistle, the men going to work and coming home, reminded him that he didn't have to work in the mill any more, and each time it was almost like the first time. That particular joy never staled, and the fear of losing it tended to keep him humble. Publicly, he accepted success as the natural fruit of his own worth and shrewdness, and he would have denied as indignantly as any businessman in America that luck and rising immigration had most to do with it. But he never really got used to the idea that a business, a business he owned, could make money as well as lose it, and occasionally he would wonder how long his luck would last.

They still lived in Cherry Alley, and much as they had always lived, though Elena no longer kept boarders. Good times and a spell of sickness in bed, which the doctor blamed on premature change of life, — Elena was thirty-three and looked a dozen years older, — had put an end to the boarders. Kracha had bought new furniture and the room adjoining the kitchen, where the girls had slept, was now a parlor. Its chief glories were a tasseled couch, a matching chair with an ingenious footrest that slid out like a drawer from inside the chair itself, and an immense oil lamp suspended from the ceiling by gilt chains. The lampshade was made of pieces of colored glass leaded together like a church window; it seemed to fill the room and was one of the most impressive objects Cherry Alley had ever seen. On the walls were colored lithographs in elaborate gilt frames of the Holy Family and of the Virgin with a dagger through her exposed heart. Drying ribbons of Easter palm were stuck behind them. On the floor was flowered oilcloth.

Francka, who had attended Dubik's funeral big with a second child — it proved to be another boy, whom she named Andy — came to visit Elena while she was still in bed, and cheered her a little. For Kracha, she wore a chip on her shoulder. In September word had come from the old country that their mother had died. The surviving sister, Borka, had written that she was coming to America, and Francka wanted it understood that she was not taking Borka into her house. She could have saved her breath; in her letter Borka had made it plain that she wanted no part of Francka. Kracha made the best of it. Borka could help Elena around the house and it was probable that she would find a husband almost as easily as her letter indicated that she expected to.

Francka's attitude toward his shop, his success, made him chuckle grimly. Confronted with a fact whose sheer possibility was, by her logic, inadmissible, Francka did not hesitate. She ignored it. Not a word did she say to Kracha about the shop; he had to tell her, unasked, that business was good.

"Oh, your butcher shop," Francka said, as though she was wondering why he mentioned it.

His irony was broad. "You know I'm in business for myself, don't you?"

"Humph! The way you talk a person would think you had a hundred men working for you."

"And how many have you?"

Francka looked bored.

"But give me time. I've been in business hardly a year. As it is my wagon goes all over, Braddock, North Braddock, Port Perry, Turtle Creek. When they finish the new bridge you may yet see it in Munhall and Homestead."

"At least you have big ideas. Maybe too big."

"You wait. I'm making money." He slapped his pants pocket. "And I'm going to make more."

"I wish you luck."

"Big money." Kracha's gaze became not unintentionally abstracted, as though his eyes were seeing things not visible to ordinary mortals. He said gravely, "Never until I went into business for myself did I realize how true it is that money makes money. There are thousands to be made right here in Braddock. And not by selling meat. All it takes is a little cash — and knowing what to do with it. I could take you out now and show you — " Kracha paused and shook his head, overwhelmed.

Francka would have given an eye to know how much of what he was saying wasn't nonsense, but it was obvious Kracha was only waiting for her to ask, so she didn't. "Just remember," she said, her lips curling, "that better men than you have lost their money faster than they could make it."

He let her have the last word. He could afford to. He gave her a small ham to take home.

After she got up from sickbed Elena seemed to withdraw more and more into herself. She took to going to church every morning, a thin, round-shouldered little woman in black, a shawl over her head, hands clasping a rosary. About her there was now more than ever a frightened, beaten look. Mary, a gawky and unpredictable thirteen — her latest exploit, upon the opening of the new school term, had been an attempt to persuade her new teacher that her name was really Marie — told him once that Mamma would go upstairs and cry in bed almost every day. The girl was obviously frightened. Kracha spoke to Elena about it. What was the matter? If she was sick, call the doctor. Crying wouldn't help.

She said nothing, made no effort to explain; and Mary reported no more such incidents. When Kracha remembered to ask if her mother still had crying spells she was so volubly evasive that it was clear Elena had spoken to her. Kracha shrugged and put it down to the change Elena was going through. At such times women were apt to be more erratic than usual.

What she was thinking or feeling, what emotions were consuming her mind, her worn body, Kracha didn't know and didn't much care, though afterward he was to wonder. Now and then he'd look at her and notice how changed she was, feel stirrings of pity for what life had done to her, to the lively girl he'd married and the young wife who had come to him in White Haven. But he didn't look at her or think about her often. In his thoughts and emotions she no longer figured as a woman.

He never discussed his shop with her; Dorta knew much more about it than Elena. She didn't know how much money he had and he didn't tell her. She took care of the house and the children and he looked after the shop; and he at least was satisfied to have it that way.

14

WORK in the mill was slow during the summer, and it was an election year. Like most of his customers Kracha was not an American citizen and took little interest in politics, though he enjoyed the parades and the excitement of barroom arguments. Like them, too, he had brought to America a conviction that the less one had to do with governments the better. Locally, the Republicans dominated all; as a rule, the only uncertain thing about an election in Braddock was the weather.

But that year politics was in the air, nurtured by bad times. Mike Dobrejcak, who had come of age and promptly applied for his first papers, was full of impassioned opinions about Bryan, McKinley, sixteen-to-one and such matters. Kracha understood none of it and suspected that Mike understood little more. The only thing he said which made sense was that Bryan was for the workingmen and McKinley for the rich. Mike was, of course, for Bryan, so passionately that Kracha felt sorry for him. To Kracha's way of thinking a little man could logically be for little men, but by his very success in getting nominated Bryan had ceased to be a little man. And the big man who was for the little man didn't exist, never had and never would. Kracha's distrust of big men, rich men, rulers, was profound.

He tried to explain a little of this to Mike, to prepare him for the ultimate, certain disillusion. It was no use. Listening to him Kracha reflected absently that he talked like Dubik in his younger days; and he agreed to take the McKinley poster out of his window and replace it with one of Bryan.

The Bryan poster stayed in the window for two days. When Mike noticed its disappearance on the third, he asked questions.

Kracha shrugged. "I was advised to take it out. You know as well as I that they don't like Bryan in Braddock."

"They? You mean the company?"

Kracha shrugged again.

"Who told you to take it out?"

"Never mind. I want no trouble. And I advise you not to talk too much yourself. Think what you like but keep your mouth shut. What the devil, you can't even vote. Why must you mix in such matters?"

"I'm going to be a citizen soon. I'm going to have the right to vote in a few years."

"Much good it will do you. I've been watching men vote ever since I came to America and may I be damned if it ever made ten cents' worth of difference who was president and who wasn't. Let me tell you — "

He put up a hand. "I know, I know. You can speak English, you read the Pittsburgh papers and know everything that's going on while I'm still no better than a greenhorn. Devil take you, let me finish!"

Mike's gesture was saved from impertinence by its absurdity. "Go on, then," he said, heroically patient.

They were in the cluttered little room back of the icebox. Out in the shop Willie Behrman was sharpening a knife and whistling lugubriously. It was just after six of a crisp fall day; Mike, coming home from work, had missed the Bryan poster and come right in to investigate. He was in his work clothes, an oval, two-storied lunch bucket tucked under his arm.

Kracha relit his stogie; he seldom smoked a pipe nowadays. "You listen to me," he said. "There are men in that mill who were born here, whose fathers and grandfathers were born here. They know more English than you'll ever learn. And what good is their vote doing them? They have to work in the mill and eat dirt like any greenhorn. Let me tell you, I've been in America long enough to learn that it's run just like any other country. In Europe your emperors and grand dukes own everything and over here it's your millionaires and your trusts. They run the country to suit themselves, and don't think they're going to let you interfere every few years with your miserable vote. Get that into your head. Your vote means nothing. The company man always wins. If he isn't a company man to start with he becomes one afterward; the millionaires see to that."

"But Bryan — "

"*Prebač, prebač,*" Kracha said. "Permit me. Your Bryan may be all you say he is but I warn you, don't expect too much. Something happens to the best of men once they get high up and start going around with millionaires and politicians. Such beautiful promises before they're elected! And afterward not a peep out of them. I've never seen it to fail. And even if your Bryan should be elected, which I doubt, you will still have to work for a living, remember that. I tell you all this now though I know you won't believe it until you've seen it happen before your own eyes. And more than once. Meanwhile, keep your mouth shut. Think what you like but keep your mouth shut."

He wouldn't tell who had advised him to remove the poster, though Mike could guess. Joe Wold almost certainly; his connections with the company were well known. Or it may have been Joe Perovsky, also a saloonkeeper, dabbler in First Ward real estate and politically ambitious. Neither would have needed to go out of his way to speak to Kracha; he could be found leaning against one bar or the other every night.

Bryan lost.

Mike said, "Next time. They beat us this time, but next time — "

"All right, all right," Kracha said. "Now come on, I buy you a drink. The world hasn't come to an end."

The suggestion about the poster had come, as a matter of fact, from Perovsky. He had been extremely casual about it, putting it up to Kracha himself. Leaving the Bryan poster where it was might do no harm, he had admitted, but it would certainly do him no great good. And after all, how many voters were there along Washington? And what was Bryan to them? Or McKinley either, for that matter? So Kracha had removed the poster and made a little gesture toward Mike and his own conscience by not putting McKinley back. The local Republican candidates for Burgess and Councilman were, of course, something else again.

It was Perovsky, too, who now suggested that Kracha get his hands on some Halket Avenue property if he had a little money lying around. The B. and O.'s main line ran through Braddock along Halket, and recently there had been talk that the railroad was preparing to lay two additional tracks and put up a new station. The streetcar company's new bridge across the river at the other, the Rankin, end of town and a rumor that a bridge would also be built at Thirteenth Street had already caused one flurry of speculation in real estate during the summer, and Kracha was believed to be one of the few who had actually made money out of it. (It was to this that he had referred in his talk with Francka.) The truth was he had at that time neither invested nor made a dollar, but he had let the report go undenied — it did his credit and his reputation no harm.

There was no certainty, Perovsky admitted, that the railroad would start laying tracks this spring, or next either. There had been talk of new tracks in other years too. But that was the risk one took. On the other hand, hard times had to end sooner or later and property was always good, it didn't run away or wear out. If Kracha didn't sell to the railroad there would be other buyers, or he could build. All in all, the likelihood of any loss was small; and if the railroad did start laying tracks it would need Kracha's property and he could ask his own price. Double, triple what he had paid.

Kracha was torn between caution and cupidity but in the end he bought five thousand dollars' worth of unimproved property along the north side of Halket between Sixth and Seventh, putting down one thousand, nearly all the ready cash he had, and carrying the rest on short-term mortgages.

Borka arrived a little before Christmas, a younger, plumper and no less homely edition of Francka. Braddock's dirt appalled her and she was inexpressibly shocked to see how Elena had changed. It was probable that she was the first, after the doctor, to guess that Elena was dying. She took charge of the house and the children like a born manager, and Kracha, who had merely hoped that she and Elena would get along, was relieved to discover there would be no trouble. Unlike Francka, Borka found his butcher shop, his eminence as a businessman, impressive, and she didn't need to have it pointed out to her that keeping on good terms with such a brother would be no handicap in finding a husband.

15

THE Monday after Greek Easter — Greek Catholics like Dorta and Mike Dobrejcak had had their own church for some months now, the former First Presbyterian Church on George Street, near the Pennsylvania railroad tracks, having been dedicated as St. Peter and St. Paul's the previous autumn — Kracha was waiting on a woman customer. He was otherwise alone; it was mid-morning and Willie Behrman was out with the wagon. The woman's four-year-old boy, having driven the cat into the back room by throwing sawdust at her, was now standing with his nose smeared against the glass of the door. Kracha had warned him away from it once without effect; his conscience clear, he waited hopefully for someone to open the door and knock the brat unconscious. Washington Street, this April morning, was wet, gray and vacant.

Kracha put a pound of pork steak on the scale, steadied it with one hand as he looked up at the dial. "Twelve cents."

"So much?"

In addition to being the brat's mother she was slow pay and had a weak, tearful voice which invited persecution. Kracha did not

Out of This Furnace

come down even a penny. The woman sighed and ordered half a pound of ham boloney.

While he sliced and wrapped she said hesitantly, "I will try and pay most of my book tomorrow." The next day was payday. "My man has not been getting many turns lately."

"All right, all right. Pay what you can."

"I wonder if times will ever be good again."

"Sure. Something else?"

"No, that will be all today. How is your wife?"

"As well as can be expected."

He was marking the total, fifteen cents, in her book with indelible pencil when the door opened. There was a bump, a thump and then a rising wail.

Highly pleased, Kracha watched while the mother gathered up her stricken one and the woman who had opened the door expressed her regrets. "I told him to get away from that door," Kracha said. No one paid any attention to him. He gave the brat a slice of boloney to shut his mouth and watched them depart.

"I didn't see him until I had pushed the door," the newcomer explained. "His mother should have kept him away from it."

"His mother has no more good sense than he." He turned to her, warm with good feeling. "Well, what can I do for you?"

"Two pounds of soup meat. Plate. And give me some good bones."

Kracha was staring at her, his face slowly screwing up with concentration. She had let her shawl fall off her head a little.

"I know you," he said at last.

She smiled. "Do you?"

"I'm sure of it. Let me think." He pushed his straw hat back off his forehead and rapped his temple with his knuckles. Then, incredulously, "Is it possible?"

"Is what possible?"

"God bless me!"

She continued to smile.

"Zuska — Zuska Mihula! Am I right? But of course I am!"

"So you remember me?"

"Where in God's name have you come from?"

"It's been a long time since we last saw each other."

"Fifteen years. More. Well, well!"

He reached across the counter and shook her hand. "Of all the people in the world to walk in here!"

"Did I surprise you?"

"The Pope himself couldn't have surprised me more. What are you doing in Braddock?"

"I moved here Saturday. My husband died last year — "

Kracha murmured condolences.

"He is better off, poor soul. He was sick for a long time. Lung trouble. I had nobody in Pittsburgh so — " She shrugged slightly.

"Do you intend to stay here?"

"For a while. What plans can I make? A widow with two young children — "

"Oh, you shouldn't have any trouble finding another husband — a woman like you! Right here in Braddock I know at least a dozen men who are looking for wives."

"It's not time to think of that yet."

"Two children, you say?"

"Two boys. One is twelve, the other nine."

"I have three girls myself. My oldest is thirteen."

"All girls?"

"We had a boy but he died. Tell me, have you been living in Pittsburgh all this time?"

She said she had, ever since coming to America. On or in the neighborhood of Second Avenue, near the Jones and Laughlin mill, where her husband had worked.

"Think of that. I didn't go to Pittsburgh often but whenever I did I always wondered if you were still around."

"If I could believe that."

"*Na moj' pravdu.* Did you think I had forgotten you?"

"Why should you remember me? It wasn't as though I was the only woman on the boat."

"Never mind. I forgot all the others but I remembered you. How does it happen you've never been in Braddock before?"

She laughed. "But I've been here many times. My sister has lived here for five years and I often came to see her."

"Your sister?"

"Mrs. Rokosh."

"The one who lives in Pine Way? But I know her very well; she's one of my best customers." This was a lie. She dealt with whoever would give her two weeks credit and was even worse pay than the woman who had just left. "So she's your sister? How is it she's never said anything about you?"

"Did you ever ask her?"

"Why should I? I didn't even know she had a sister. So you've been coming to Braddock for the last five years?"

"Yes."

Kracha found it unbelievable. But it was true. Wonders would never cease.

"Did you know I was living in Braddock?"

"Never, until this morning. My sister told me to go to the butcher and mentioned your name. I remembered it, and what she told me about you made me feel sure you were the same Kracha I had met on the boat."

"Were you surprised?"

"Of course."

"I hope your sister had nothing bad to say about me."

"What could she say? Except that you were in business for yourself now and doing well." Zuska looked around the little shop approvingly.

"I manage to pay my rent," Kracha said modestly.

"Better than that, I hope." She faced him again. "How is your wife?"

"A little better, thank God. She has had more than her share of sickness this past year."

"My sister told me. I am sorry to hear it."

Kracha leaned back against the ledge, under the rack of hooks with their pendant meats, butchers' saws and weaponlike steels. He relit his stogie and folded his arms across his apron; because it was a Monday the apron was still clean.

"After all these years," he said. "I can't get over it."

She was conscious of his gaze. "Have I changed much?"

The counter was between them; what part of her was visible to Kracha above it she seemed almost to push forward for his inspection. She had put on weight, her hips and bosom were generously proportioned, but her figure retained its look of compact solidity. Her hair was as black as ever; her skin seemed darker than he remembered it. As a girl her face had been oddly striking, not pretty but with something about it that caught the eye; maturity had thickened its features, given it the smooth, vaguely Asiatic cast more common among Russians and Balkan Slavs than among Slovaks.

"Well?" Her lower lip was pushed out.

"A little older — a little fatter — but not enough to keep me from knowing you."

"You're still the same. A little older, a little fatter. I would have recognized you even if my sister hadn't told me about you. Men are lucky; they don't change."

"Were you anxious to see me?"

"I was wondering if you'd know me."

"No more than that? Pah! I'm disappointed in you."

She smiled and adjusted her shawl. "Well, give me my soup meat and let me go. My sister will be wondering what you are doing to me."

"I? What would I be doing?"

She didn't say.

He gave her a generous measure of meat and bones and waved away the proffered book. "This time it will cost you nothing."

She looked him full in the eyes. "You were always generous," she said.

He went with her to the door. Her skirt brushed his knuckles as they stood there. "We must get to know each other again," he said.

"But I thought we were old friends?"

He laughed and without thinking patted her behind. She was well covered. Before he could regret the gesture her head had jerked in a quick glance. "Is that how you treat all your women customers?"

"Upon my soul, no."

She smiled at him disbelievingly, and left.

Kracha stood by the door staring after her, his thoughts active.

16

THOUGH his life with Elena would have explained, if not justified, experiments with other women, Kracha was still a technically faithful husband. He was only partly responsible for this himself. Extramarital adventures were not easily managed in an environment where one couldn't put on a new shirt without being noticed. And until he became a businessman opportunities were rare; what had a blast furnace laborer to offer another blast furnace laborer's wife which would lure her into adultery? Moreover, a man who worked his eighty-four or ninety-six hours a week in the mill had enough to do fulfilling his obligations at home without prancing after other women.

Lastly, and this had been perhaps the determining factor, women were scarce. There were simply not enough of them to go around even for legitimate purposes; for a long time the First Ward must have contained three or four men to every woman. No girl or widow needed to stay unmarried a day longer than she chose; Dorta, for instance, began receiving offers three months after Dubik was in his grave. (She took her time and settled on Steve Radilla, a big, solemn widower only a year or so older than she herself.) Men were driven into marriage not only by sex but by economics; a man with a wife who kept boarders was better off than any single man, whether he hoarded his money like a miser or flung it around the whore houses of Pittsburgh's South Side.

In short, Kracha had always found adultery too risky and too much trouble to do more than think about. Whisky was a safer, cheaper and in time almost completely satisfactory substitute for the excitement and release of fornication.

Zuska's surprising reappearance put a different face on the matter. He continued to see her, though only in his shop or on the street, and to think about her, and as the weeks passed the burden of his thoughts was in his muttered, "I bet you I could have her like that. Like that." There was real satisfaction in the certainty he felt. Yet apart from the risk, and it was considerable, the question was, did he want her?

So much had fifteen years done. Not only were they both older and Zuska less desirable; their positions were now exactly reversed. Fifteen years ago it was Kracha who had wanted, Zuska who had withheld. Fifteen years ago it was Zuska who had had most to give, Kracha who had stood to gain. Today — well, as between a penniless widow and a prosperous businessman Kracha knew which would have the last word. There was satisfaction in that, too.

Secure in his knowledge, Kracha waited confidently for Zuska to make the first move. If she did he failed to recognize it. Even when she found him alone, and as a rule she did her shopping in the morning, when the wagon was out, her behavior was irreproachable. She smiled, she chatted, she departed, leaving Kracha frowning after her.

Dorta married Steve Radilla in June. Kracha got drunker than usual at the wedding and added little to the festivities by recalling Dorta's marriage to Dubik in the railroad camp so many years before; how they had ridden to White Haven in a snowstorm, how the wedding night had been broken into by Elena's inopportune baby. Now — he babbled — Dubik was dead, Dorta was a bride again, he was in business for himself, the rest of that first wedding company was scattered God knew where — who would have thought it then? He went on in this vein until Francka told him to stop making a fool of himself. Andrej averted a quarrel by pulling Kracha outside, where several men had locked a woman into the outhouse and were pretending to misunderstand her yells and door-shaking.

When he next saw Zuska she said, "So your friend's widow was a bride again."

Kracha nodded, busy with knife and saw.

"I hear she had a fine wedding."

"As fine as most." He glanced at her. "I suppose you'll be next."

"Me? I'm getting almost too old to think of marrying again."

Kracha picked up a steel and began swinging his knife against it rhythmically. "I predict you'll be married inside a year."

"What makes you say that?"

"You're not the kind of woman who can be happy without a husband."

"Where did you learn so much about me?"

"I have two eyes."

"Maybe you have a husband already picked out for me."

"Why should I do anything like that? You're old enough to pick your own."

Then another customer entered.

The day before the Fourth of July Zuska's sister, a fat slattern forever pregnant, came into the shop. She ordered a larger than usual quantity of ham and boloney and volunteered the information that they were going to a picnic at Kenny's Grove the next day. Zuska was even now at home finishing a new dress for the occasion. Mrs. Rokosh further disclosed that one of her boarders, a certain John Gruzba, was coming with them; and she added — first cautioning Kracha to keep it to himself — that it wouldn't surprise her if Zuska married him.

Kracha didn't see Zuska for several days after the picnic. When he did he asked her if she had enjoyed herself.

She had. "I met your sister there," she added.

"The girls wanted to go and I had Borka take them. Elena wasn't feeling well."

"Why didn't you come?"

"What do I want with picnics? I watched the parade and then walked over the new bridge." It had been dedicated that day. One could now board a streetcar in Braddock and in, comparatively speaking, the twinkling of an eye, get off in Munhall or Homestead, or go all the way into Pittsburgh. It was putting all the ferries out of business.

Zuska leaned against the counter, its edge seeming to sink into her thigh. She had her arms folded under a light shawl. "Your oldest girl — is her name Mary? — has a pretty face. You'll be losing her in a few years."

"I'm in no hurry. My daughters won't have to take the first man who asks them if I can help it. You said wienies?"

"Five pounds."

He busied himself.

"Your sister doesn't look like you," Zuska said.

"They both take after our mother."

"You have another in Homestead?"

"Munhall. She owns a house there."

Zuska said the Krachas seemed to have done well for themselves in America and Kracha didn't deny it. He wrapped the frank-furters in slippery butcher paper.

Zuska gave him her book. "Your sister told me something about you I didn't know before."

"What was that?"

"That when you came to America you had to walk from New York to some place in Pennsylvania."

"White Haven." He stared at her. "Did she tell you why?"

"She said you lost your money in New York."

"Yes."

"Do you mean to say that after you left us you lost your money and had to walk?"

"Yes. I slept that night in a haystack."

"You were so foolish. Why didn't you come back to Castle Garden? We were there for three hours after you left. My husband's cousin had trouble getting off from work."

"How was I to know that?"

"You could have tried. My husband's people would have taken you in until your brother-in-law sent you the railroad fare. It would have been better than walking the roads alone and sleeping in the fields."

"I was too worried to think clearly. When I saw that my money was gone for good my only thought was to be on my way."

Zuska picked up her package. "I'm glad I didn't know then what you were going through. I would have felt very bad."

"You would?"

"Of course. Well, I must be getting back."

That night at supper he mentioned Zuska as casually as he could. Borka admitted meeting her at the picnic and made it plain that she hadn't sought her company. Kracha pricked up his ears at hearing Borka call her *Čarna Zuska,* Black Susan.

"Is that your own name for her?"

"Everybody calls her that. They say her brother-in-law gave her the name. They don't get along."

Kracha rolled it over on his tongue. "*Čarna Zuska.*"

"Because she's so dark, almost like a gipsy."

It fitted.

"They don't call her that to her face?"

"No, but she knows it."

"You don't seem to like her."

"And I'm not the only one."

"Why not?"

Borka shrugged. "I don't like her ways."

Kracha would have liked to ask questions but decided it was best not to seem too curious.

Though Zuska had not made a secret of the fact that she and Kracha had come to America on the same ship, she had not yet, apparently, mentioned the little party he had given for her. The possibility that she might do so disturbed him. It was a long time ago but not too long for Dorta and Francka to put two and two together. Especially Francka. And he had no stomach for ridicule. He wondered how to go about warning her and saw equal disadvantages in speaking and in keeping still.

Toward the end of August came the second anniversary of Dubik's death. Dorta had a mass said for him, which Kracha attended. Afterward they walked down Eleventh Street together. Dorta had little to say. She seemed happy with Radilla, though to Kracha he would never be anything but one of Dorta's boarders. Though she was no longer a girl, it was more than years, Kracha reflected, that had aged and matured her. Something had gone out of both their lives when Dubik died. They waited at the B. and O. crossing for a freight to pass.

"Did you hear what they're doing on F Furnace?" he asked.

Dorta glanced eastward, toward Thirteenth, where the swaying, loose-jointed line of cars was coming out of the mill. "Steve told me. Some new machinery to do away with the top fillers?"

"Yes. It takes less men and the work goes faster. I understand they're going to put them on all the furnaces."

Dorta put into words what they were both thinking. "If they had had something like that two years ago Joe might be alive today."

"Yes."

"Well, if it keeps others from getting killed — "

The caboose rattled by, seeming like all cabooses to be having a hard time keeping up with the rest of the train, and they went on down Eleventh Street.

The new automatic skip hoists and the equally new double-bell closure device were to make a great change in the blast furnaces. The ironwork shafts, topped by little shanties, of the old vertical skip hoists gave way to the inclined tracks, the cables and crawling

buggies, of the automatic hoists; and the double bells put an end
to the intermittent flames from the furnace tops. When the changes
were made the furnaces looked incomplete without the vertical
shafts beside them. People missed the periodic bursts of flame most
of all. They'd glance at the mill and wait for the flame and nothing
happened. The furnaces didn't look right, didn't look as though
they were really working. At night it was as though lights had
been put out.

17

ABOUT the time the children were starting back to school
Zuska left her sister's house, moved to a single room of her own
in Willow Way, the other side of Eleventh Street. She had been
making a few dollars sewing — she was said to be a good dress-
maker — and Borka said she hoped to make a living by it. Borka
wasn't optimistic; too many women disliked Zuska. She also revealed that Zuska hadn't moved voluntarily; her brother-in-law
had all but thrown her out. He was tired of keeping her, Borka
said, and besides she had been causing trouble among the boarders.
What kind of trouble? Well, what kind of trouble was a widow
likely to cause among seven or eight unattached men?

"I heard something about her marrying one of them," Kracha said
negligently. "Gruzba I think the name was."

Borka sniffed. "They say that was one reason her brother-in-law
told her to get out. Gruzba was ready to marry her and she refused. So her brother-in-law threw her out. When she moved in
with them the understanding was she'd stay only until she found
another husband."

Kracha poked Mary in the back with the handle of his fork.

Perhaps to minimize her growing breasts she had taken to round-ing her shoulders forward. "Sit up straight. Do you want to be a hunchback?"

"Let her alone," Elena said.

Mary straightened a little and kept her eyes on her plate.

"Why do you suppose she refused him?" Kracha asked.

Borka's expression was acidly disdainful. "Oh, she hopes to do better. She as much as said that a man who works in the mill isn't good enough for her. God knows where she gets such ideas. If she was young," Borka went on, speaking like the sister of a pros-perous butcher, "or if she had something to offer — "

Kracha grunted.

The next time he saw Zuska he grinned at her. "So."

"What, so?"

"You have boarders fighting over you now."

"Boarders fighting over me? What are you talking about?"

"Never mind."

"Is that what they're saying about me? *Bohze moj!*" There was, genuine or not, more amazement than indignation in her voice.

"Then it's not true?"

"What's the difference, if you believe it?"

"I didn't say I did."

"I'd rather not talk about it. Give me a pound of soup meat. That is if my credit is still good with you."

"Have I asked you for your book?"

"I hope you won't be too hard on me if I have trouble paying you sometimes. It's not as though I had a husband bringing home money every two weeks."

Kracha went into the icebox without replying. When he came out, a chunk of meat in his hand, Zuska said, "What did you hear about me?"

"I thought you didn't want to talk about it."

"Tell me what you heard, Djuro."

"Oh, it's Djuro again, is it? And just a moment ago it was a pound of soup meat, butcher, and no nonsense."

She smiled apologetically. "I was angry. But not at you. Tell me what you heard."

"What I said. That Rokosh's boarders were breaking one another's heads over which you liked best."

"And you believed it?"

"So, since the man you really liked was not even a boarder there you moved to prevent a war."

"Oh, I like some man, do I?"

"Sure."

"And who might he be?"

Boldly, "Me."

"Indeed?"

He grinned at her. Zuska smiled and lowered her eyes. And then, as so often before, there was an interruption. Willie pulled up to the curb with the wagon. Kracha swore under his breath.

He swore again after Zuska had gone. What the devil was he thinking of to say such things to her? And what was happening to him? For a moment there his heart had started beating and his knees had gone weak, as though he were a boy with his first woman. Was he losing his wits?

Awakened to his danger he determined to ignore her, to be the impersonal shopkeeper waiting on a customer. His resolution held good each time he made it until the next time he saw her.

"Well, Djuro," she said, "have you heard any more about me?"

"I have no time to listen to gossip."

"Even when it's about me?"

Impatiently, "*Ach!*"

She watched him for a moment. Then, "I want you to know the truth. I don't care what other people think or say but I want you to know the truth. I left my sister's house because it was too crowded. Did you know I had to sleep on a mattress on the kitchen floor? I was only waiting until I could get a place of my own."

"All right, all right," he said, as if the subject bored him.

She hesitated. "It's true there was a little trouble with one of the boarders."

Kracha looked up. "What happened?"

"As I told you, I slept in the kitchen. It wasn't what I would have liked but what could I do? There was never any trouble until this one boarder came in late one night. He was drunk but not so drunk he didn't know what he was doing. So many men think they can fool people," she said, while Kracha winced, "by pretending to be drunk. He tried to get into my bed."

"And did he?"

"I wish you wouldn't joke about it. It wasn't pleasant for me."

"Maybe you were partly to blame yourself."

"Djuro, how can you say that? Do you think I go around inviting men to get into bed with me?"

"No, but since you had to sleep in the kitchen and the boarders had to pass through it when they came home," Kracha said, "a change in your sleeping habits would have been only wise. Not to speak of modesty." He kept his eyes on her. "That is, if what they say is true about you. That you sleep naked."

"Good God, don't people here have anything to do but talk about me?"

"It's true, isn't it?"

She made no bones about admitting it. "I always have, in summer. And that kitchen was like an oven."

He would have liked to dwell on the subject longer but she refused to answer his questions or smile at his jokes. Annoyed, he gave her her chuck steak and let her go.

She continued in that mood for about a week, coming and going with hardly a greeting for him. He tried to match his mood to hers but she was better at it than he. Then he tried coarseness, loudness, trying to pierce her inexplicable reserve with broad jokes and double meanings, using the plainest words. Once she noticed how the cat rubbed herself against his legs. "The cat seems to like you."

Kracha glanced down, pushed the cat away with his foot. "She's in heat," he said bluntly.

Zuska said nothing.

"She's a damned nuisance. I would get rid of her but that crazy Willie likes her. He's named her Katarina, after some Russian Czarina, he says. Do you think she'll go out into the alleys like any other cat? Not her. Willie has to bring a *mizhu* to her here. Then he sits in the back room and watches them, laughing like a fool."

"I don't think that's funny."

"Neither do the cats, I suppose."

The day after the second payday in September, when accounts were ordinarily settled, she was able to give him only two dollars. "I will have to ask you to wait," she said. "I have some money due me but I'm having trouble collecting it."

"Like me," Kracha suggested.

"I'll pay you as soon as I can. Every penny."

"All right. I won't close up if you don't."

"I'm having a hard time, Djuro. This world isn't an easy place for a poor widow with two children."

For a second he thought she was going to cry. But she had raised the corner of her shawl only to wipe her mouth. It was this, a feeling of pity for her, an effort to cheer her a little, that made him say what he said next. This, and all that had gone before.

"Do you know," he said heartily, "you've had your own place for over a month now and you still haven't invited me to visit you?"

She looked startled. "Would you come?"

"I might."

"You're joking."

"Ask me and see."

"I have so little to make it pleasant for you."

"Do you have two chairs and a lamp?"

"Yes, of course."

"What more do we need to sit and talk?"

She smiled. "It would make me happy to have you come. I don't know many people here and sometimes it gets lonely. I would have asked you before, but as I say — "

"No more of that."

"When would you like to come?"

"Will you be home tonight?"

"I'm always home."

"Tonight, then. But I may be late."

"I'll wait for you."

She gave him a quick smile and left.

She had hardly gone when he began questioning the wisdom of seeing her at all, and by evening he was regretting his promise as keenly as ever a man regretted rash, foolish speech. He spent the evening in Wold's; by ten-thirty he had made up his mind not to see her. No. He would even offer to wipe what she owed him off the books if only she agreed to deal with some other butcher. It would be worth it. The less they saw of each other the better. She had caused him trouble before; she would infallibly cause him trouble again, if he let her. But he wasn't going to let her. He was going to put his foot down. Beginning now. He stared at himself in the saloon's big mirror approvingly, feeling virtuous and safe, good common sense like an iron rod in his hand.

At eleven he was knocking softly on Zuska's door. The alley was pitch-dark and he was sure no one had seen him.

She opened the door without asking who it was. She whispered, "Come in, Djuro. Don't make any noise or you'll awake the boys."

He hesitated, and she may have thought he was drunk. She put out a bare arm and drew him inside, closed the door and locked it.

The lamp on the table was turned low, the green shade on the one window pulled all the way down. By the faint light he could see the stove, the bed with its covers tossed back, the gleam of dishes in the closet. The younger boy was asleep on the bed, next to the wall; the older one sprawled on a cot at the foot of the bed. The two doors, one to the cellar and one to the stairs that led to the upper floor, were both closed.

She stood near him, shorter than usual because she was in her bare feet. "What made you so late?" she asked. "I waited and waited — then I went to bed."

"Did you think I wasn't coming?"

"It made me feel very bad."

She was wearing a striped petticoat and a thin, sleeveless vest; her arms and shoulders were bare. He stared at a wisp of hair caught among the creases of her underarm. "I thought you always slept naked."

"Oh — not when the boys — "

"They're asleep now. Come here."

He pulled her to him. She was so plump and soft that his fingers seemed to sink into her flesh.

18

A MONTH after his first visit Zuska moved to two rooms deeper in the same row, the same alley. Kracha had found the inconvenience and danger of her single room nerve-wracking. The necessity of keeping quiet had been especially irksome. He couldn't talk, he couldn't laugh, he hardly dared move a leg for fear of awakening the boys or the suspicions of the neighbors. Once, thoughtlessly, he gave Zuska a hearty smack on the behind and the sound of it was like a thunderclap. It was the kind of sound, furthermore, that a widow living alone would have had a hard time explaining. Another night her younger boy — she had put him on the cot with his brother — awakened, and only God knew how long he had been sitting up, watching them, before he began to bawl. They had the devil's own time convincing him that Kracha hadn't been beating his mother. The last time, Zuska's neighbor, who had the adjoining kitchen and the two upstairs bedrooms, had knocked on the door, the one that led upstairs, which Zuska usually kept locked. "Mrs. Mihula!"

They held their breaths.

"Mrs. Mihula! Are you still up?" She rattled the knob.

Kracha cursed her silently. Then they heard her mutter to herself and go slowly up the stairs.

Kracha drew the sleeve of his shirt across his face. "You'll have to move. There was a time when I might have enjoyed this but I'm not as young as I used to be."

Afterward they learned that the woman had merely wanted to check her alarm clock with Zuska's.

Even after she moved he visited her only late at night and seldom oftener than twice a week. He gave her money regularly — she made a show of refusing it at first — and never regretted a penny of it. It could be said for Zuska that she always gave good value. What the end would be, what they would do if the affair became public knowledge, Kracha didn't know. He deliberately refused to think about it when he was away from her, and while he was with her it didn't seem important. Zuska herself never mentioned it.

But he knew, or he should have known, that it was impossible to keep their new relationship a secret. Zuska, moving, may have drawn attention to herself by this evidence of unexplained prosperity. Or the boys may have said something that started a neighbor thinking. Or, as was most likely, Kracha himself had been seen coming or leaving. At any rate, by Thanksgiving Day most of the First Ward knew that Kracha and Zuska were considerably more than good friends.

She probably realized it before Kracha. He had only begun to wonder if there was something in the air; several of his women customers had a queer glint in their eyes when they looked at him, and Borka's manner, her obscure remarks on mornings after he had come home especially late, had him glancing at her speculatively. From Elena there was never a word; like a quiet wraith she moved between the church and the rooms in Cherry Alley, content to let Borka manage things, drawing ever farther apart from the lives of those around her. She asserted herself only when she intervened, a soft-voiced peacemaker, between Borka and the girls, to Borka's outspoken annoyance. It was as though Borka was their mother and Elena a too-tolerant maiden aunt.

And then Francka came out of Munhall like a rolling thundercloud.

She wasn't in the house an hour that gray Sunday when the storm burst. She chased the girls out and shut the door and confronted Kracha, dark with resolution. Kracha had a bottle of whisky on the table next to him and was in the middle of a drink and an imaginative recital of the misfortunes which awaited Max Spetz, a new competitor. No one was listening.

Elena was sitting near the stove, a shawl around her shoulders. She said apprehensively, "Francka — "

"I will not keep still," Francka exclaimed. "It's time someone knocked some sense into this thick head. Old fool! Who does he think he is?"

Kracha stared at her. "What's got into you?"

"Never mind about me! You know what without my telling you."

"What the devil are you talking about?"

"You know what I'm talking about! Don't gape at me like an old goat and pretend you don't know! *Kurvas!* Adulterer! Whoremonger!" She fairly spat the words at him.

So it had come. He said, "Have you gone crazy?"

"Crazy! You're the one who is crazy! Did you think nobody had eyes? Did you think she was so black the night would hide her? You know who I mean. Your black one, your whore!"

"Watch your tongue."

"Oh, you defend her! That slut! That bitch in heat! Your poor wife works herself to the bone making a home for you, washing your dirty drawers, bearing your children, and now when she could hope for a little peace you cover her with shame! Animal!"

Kracha held her blazing eyes for a moment, then sat back, relaxed but watchful. "I know better than you what kind of wife Elena has been to me. And so does she." He glanced at Elena; her face was bowed, nearly hidden by her shawl. "It has not been all her fault, perhaps, but neither has it been all mine. In any case, I am letting no one tell me what I may or may not do. You above all."

"I'll say what needs to be said and you won't stop me. Your wife may be afraid to open her mouth but I'm not. Have you lost your mind?"

"No. I am simply getting from another woman what my wife has never been able to give me."

Elena began to cry softly.

"When you're in hell I hope you remember what you've just said," Francka said bitterly. "What will happen to your family? What will happen to your business? Do you think you can set yourself above everybody like a Czar? Is your brain softening so that you go wherever your member leads you, slobbering like a mongrel after a — "

"Shut up. It is none of your business what I do. Now shut your mouth before I — "

"What will you do? Blessed God! If you so much as lay a hand on me I'll break your head open!"

"Francka, I warn you."

She was trembling with fury. "Do you think I'm afraid of you? Do you think I'm like your wife there, who is too sick to defend herself? Shame! Shame! That she should have to hide her head in shame when she goes out because of your — your wallowings with that black slut!"

He started to rise. "Francka, keep quiet before I throw you out of my house."

"Your house! Your house! This is no longer your house! You don't belong here any more! Go to her! That's where you belong! Go to your whore!"

"Francka — "

"My fine gallant! Look at you! Red nose, beer belly, stupid face! How much do you pay her to say she loves you? Have you kissed her behind yet? Does she smell sweet? Faugh!"

"Francka — "

"Fool! Fool! God should have struck you dead before — "

Kracha rose and took a step forward and swung his arm. Francka moved but not quickly enough; the slap made her eyeballs swim and knocked her, half-stunned, against the dish cupboard. She screamed and grabbed the lid-lifter off the stove and hurled it at him. He ducked and plunged toward her as she sprang to get the poker out of the coalscuttle. His arms closed around her. She kicked and twisted, her teeth showing, letting out scream after scream. Borka was tugging at his arms. Elena never moved; afterward he wasn't sure that she had even lifted her head. Holding Francka with one arm he began slapping her face methodically. "Shut up. Shut up. Sonnomabitch, shut up!"

Francka burst into tears and her body went limp. Kracha threw her into a corner and she lay there wailing. Her hair had come undone. Borka bent over the fallen one. Elena was crying softly into her shawl, rocking from side to side. Kracha stood in the room's center, breathing hard. "God-damned women!"

He put on his hat and overcoat and went out, slamming the door. Neighbors were standing in the yard, drawn out of their kitchens by the uproar. They watched Kracha as he crossed the yard to the passageway that led to Washington Street but no one spoke to him.

Francka and the others no doubt assumed that he went directly to Zuska. But Kracha was, for the time being, heartily sick of women. The saloons were closed; the only places allowed to sell liquor on Sunday were social clubs, so Kracha went to Turner Hall. He stayed in the basement barroom, drinking steadily, until the place closed. Then he went home and fell asleep in his clothes on the tasseled parlor couch.

19

THE world, as Kracha was fond of saying, hadn't come to an end; and though it looked none too good after Francka's departure it seemed likely to last a while longer. He didn't see Zuska until the end of the week; then he told her what had happened.

"What are you going to do?" she asked.

He shrugged. "Nothing. What is there to do?"

"You won't stop coming here?"

"Do you want me to?"

"No, but if it makes trouble — "

"I think the worst is over."

If Zuska thought otherwise she didn't say so. Kracha himself, as the days passed, began to think he might have spoken too soon. At home the atmosphere stayed uncomfortably strained; even the children felt it and Borka was so torn between an instinctive disapproval of Kracha the erring husband and the advantages of keeping on good terms with Kracha the prosperous butcher that for a week nothing she cooked tasted right. There was no change in Elena's manner. He spent as little time as possible in Cherry Alley, but he never stayed away all night; morning was sure to find him on the parlor couch.

One night he was pulling the blanket over himself when Elena appeared in the doorway, wearing a flannel nightgown, her hair in a braid. She said, "Djuro, come to bed. You can't get your proper sleep there."

He looked at her without saying anything.

She came into the room and began gathering up his clothes. One arm laden with his shirt and trousers, she stooped, wadded his socks into his shoes and picked them up. "Come to bed. You'll sleep better."

After a while he followed her upstairs.

The affair cost him several good customers. Stubbornly, he called it good riddance. He was there to sell meat and that was all his customers had a right to expect from him; what he did outside the shop was no business of theirs. But he had most of the vociferously respectable housewives against him — Dorta stayed faithful — and those he lost made their absence felt. Some of them bought for ten or twelve boarders. He could have borne the loss more easily if Spetz hadn't so obviously gained by it. This Spetz was a Hungarian Jew who had come out of nowhere and opened a butcher shop a few doors down the street from Kracha's place. Before this Kracha had lost few customers to him, some slow payers, some not, and had predicted he wouldn't last a month. He was still there.

Trouble loomed in still another quarter. Kracha had long since regretted his investment in Halket Avenue's future. The railroad hadn't done anything about new tracks the previous spring and after a summer of dwindling hope gave no sign of even thinking about them. Early in the fall Kracha received a tentative offer to buy for what he had paid, which would have meant an actual loss of the interest, taxes and incidental expenses the lots had so far cost him; about three hundred dollars. While he hesitated the agent withdrew the offer; the short-term mortgages, he said, had frightened off his client.

Then, shortly before the December interest payment came due, Kracha was notified that the bank wanted the principal of the first mortgage reduced by five hundred dollars. Worried and angry, he went to see Joe Perovsky. He found him discussing the Cuban situation in his saloon. They retired to the quiet end of the bar, where Perovsky read the bank's letter and looked grave.

"Have they the right?" Kracha asked.

Perovsky nodded. He was a solid, not unhandsome man, always well dressed, with a presence, a gift for moving easily among men and accepting their respect as his right. One could tell from his bearing that he, unlike Kracha, had never been surprised by his own success. He was known to be on the inside of things, with a finger in every pie. He was a saloonkeeper and a coming Republican ward heeler but he could have been as successfully a confidence man, a priest or an actor.

"You can be sure they have the right to do anything they like," he said. "They saw to that when they wrote the mortgage."

"Sonnomabitch. God-damn' sonnomabitch."

Perovsky took a pretzel from a bowl at his elbow and chewed on it. "If you have the money I advise you to pay."

"Of course I have the money!" Kracha wasn't going to let Perovsky or anyone else know he didn't have it. "It isn't the money. But why should I pay them? What good is a mortgage if they can ask for money whenever they feel like it?"

"You knew what kind of mortgage it was."

"Sure, but I didn't expect to have the damned lots still on my hands a year later. That hell-begotten railroad — "

"Do you think you're the only one?" Perovsky carefully adjusted his starched, detachable cuffs. "I advise you to go to the bank and have a talk with them. Explain that you want to keep the property and see what kind of arrangement you can make."

"If I could get back what I've put into it," Kracha said broodingly, "I'd sell tomorrow. No profit. I'd be satisfied to get my money back."

"Why do that? The lots are good. If I had the money to spare I'd take them off your hands myself."

"If *you* had the money? I wish I had half what you can put your hands on right now."

"In confidence, Kracha, I wish I had it myself."

Kracha laughed hollowly. That's the way it was, he reflected. If you had money you could pretend to be poor and people only multiplied your wealth.

"The railroad is bound to build sooner or later," Perovsky said. "And when it does you can ask your own price."

"I'm sorry I ever bought them."

"You may think differently next spring."

"Yes, and I've heard that before, too."

Perovsky began to look bored. "Well, if that's how you feel maybe you better sell. I think it would be foolish unless you got a good profit. But first of all go to the bank and have a talk with them. Ask for a renewal."

"Would I have to give them the five hundred dollars?"

"No. They simply extend the mortgage as it is for six months or a year. It will cost you something — "

"I should have known that. When you deal with a banker it costs money merely to breathe in the same room with him. How much?"

"I don't know. Maybe fifty dollars."

"For what? Just for waiting six months?"

Perovsky shrugged. "That's how banks make their money."

"Bastards. I would enjoy throwing the whole business back in their faces. I'd lose by it but it would almost be worth it."

"You think they would mind? As long as they got paid for it you could spit at them."

Kracha went to the bank and got a six months' renewal. It cost him seventy-five dollars and the bank made it obvious that they were doing him an unprecedented favor. Kracha had never liked or trusted banks and he liked and trusted them even less now. Good business, he reflected grimly: seventy-five dollars for no more than filling out another paper. On the way home he stopped in Squire Holman's real estate office on Eighth Street and put the lots on sale with him for five thousand dollars. The Squire was not too optimistic and Kracha went back to the shop in a sultry mood. If the lots hadn't been out of his way it would have given him pleasure to stop by and throw stones at them. Merely thinking about them made him gag.

Zuska found him poor company that night. He finally told off his roll of troubles, poor business, Spetz, the bank, and she became so alarmed, so insistent that he get rid of the lots as soon as he could, that in sheer self-defense he had to assure her the world wasn't coming to an end, he knew what he was doing, he was no greenhorn.

20

A WEEK after New Year's Elena took to her bed again. She had gone to church as usual though the weather was bad; on her return she hovered about the stove, complaining of an inability to get warm. Borka put her to bed. She seemed to get neither worse nor better; for days she lay quiet, hardly saying a word. Borka had the doctor in and he did what he could but he was pessimistic from the first. He may have guessed how little will to live there was left in her.

She went to bed on a Monday. Friday evening Kracha was eating supper in the kitchen when Borka called from the head of the stairs. "Djuro."

"Yes."

"Come here."

He cautioned Mary to see that Anna didn't choke to death on *pirohi* and went upstairs. The bedroom smelled of sickness; the lamp was turned low. One window was open a little and letting in cold, damp air.

Borka had her hands clasped tightly in front of her, a worried look in her eyes. "She's worse. I think we should call the doctor."

He glanced at the bed. Elena, her eyes closed, her face thin and bony with sickness, was lying perfectly still. Her breathing was regular but labored.

"What makes you think she is worse?"

"I can't get her to take her medicine. She doesn't seem to hear me."

"Get the doctor."

Borka started away, then paused. "Do you think we should call the priest?"

For a moment they stared at each other. Then Kracha said, "The doctor first. It may be nothing."

Borka went downstairs. He could hear her warning the girls to behave; then she went out.

Kracha approached the bed, bent over it. "Elena. Elena."

She didn't move.

He touched her forehead. It seemed no warmer than usual.

"Elena. You hear me? It's me, Djuro."

Her eyes opened slowly, the eyes of a sick, tired creature. He wondered if she knew him.

Her lips moved. "Water."

He poured some into a glass, then put an arm under her, lifted her a little. Under her nightgown she was all bones and heat. A warm, sweetish smell rose from beneath the covers. She swallowed a mouthful of water, then moved her head. He let her down. He was used to the sight of her goiter but now it seemed like an evil thing destroying her to keep itself alive. He drew the covers up, hid it.

He was still there when Borka returned. "The rain has stopped," she said. "How is she?"

"Just the same. She took a little water."

"The doctor wasn't home but his wife said she would send him as soon as he got back."

The doctor came, felt Elena's pulse and listened to her heart. He didn't have much to say. He was an old, bearded German with thick fingers, a vast expanse of waistcoat always dusty with cigar ash, and enough Slovak to make himself understood in the First Ward. "Keep her warm," he said, "and keep giving her the medicine. I'll be back in the morning."

Borka asked him if he thought they should call the priest. He scratched his cheek and shrugged. "It may frighten her and that wouldn't do her any good. But perhaps you had better call him."

After the doctor had gone Borka returned to the bedroom. "I'm going for Kazincy."

Kracha nodded.

Awed by the solemnity of their elders the girls protested only out of habit when Borka told them to clean up the dishes and be quiet about it. After she left, however, an argument started — neither Mary nor Alice wanted to wash — and Kracha went downstairs to settle it.

When he came back Elena turned her head and looked at him. He hurried to the bedside. "Do you want something?"

She shook her head ever so slightly. "Where are the girls?" Her voice was unexpectedly clear.

"Downstairs. Borka told them to do the dishes and they started to fight over who should wash."

Her cheek moved in only the beginning of a smile. After a pause she said, "Is it still raining?"

"Not any more."

"What time is it?"

"A little after eight."

She let her head roll to one side but kept her eyes open, as though she was thinking of something.

"Djuro."

"Yes?"

"There is something I want to tell you."

"Some other time. You'll only tire yourself by talking now."

"Djuro, I'm sorry I could not be the kind of wife you wanted. It wasn't all my fault. Don't you think I would have liked to be pretty? You thought I was, once. But after the boy was born I couldn't get healthy and strong no matter what I did."

"Now, now. This is no time for that."

"I didn't want to come to America when you sent for me. I was afraid of what you would say when you saw my throat."

"Never mind that now."

"But inside I was still the same, Djuro, inside I never changed."

"We'll talk about it some other time, when you feel better. We have a lot of things to straighten out, eh?" He patted the covers by her shoulder. "Would you like something to eat? Borka made some broth with barley — you always liked that — "

"Djuro, didn't you hear me?"

"Sure, sure." Not once since she'd started speaking had he met her eyes. "But you need to rest now, Elena, you need to build up your strength. Don't excite yourself by talking too much. I'll get you some of that broth."

But when he returned she was lying with her eyes closed, and when he spoke to her she merely moved her head a little.

He put the soup on the table and settled into a chair.

Outside in the alley, almost under the open window, a neighbor's girl, Anna Pavlik, was talking with a young man. Kracha, the tip of his tongue prying shreds of fried cabbage from between his teeth, was trying at the same time to catch what they were saying — the girl giggled frequently — but their voices were blurred. A little more and he might have moved closer to the window, but Mrs. Pavlik's voice burst suddenly over everything and put an end to romance. A door closed and there was quiet except for rain water dripping off the eaves.

And then Kracha noticed how really quiet it was.

When Borka returned, without Father Kazincy — he would be along presently — Kracha had drawn the covers over Elena's face. Borka looked at the bed and then at him. She said, "Djuro, no."

He nodded. "She went quietly," he said. "She didn't move or make a sound. She simply stopped breathing. God give me no worse a death."

Borka crossed herself; in a moment she was sniffling.

"Be quiet. The girls will hear you."

"They will have to be told."

"You will make it no easier for them by bawling."

He wished she had stayed away a few minutes longer. Sitting quietly beside his dead he had felt no grief; more than anything he had felt pity. Pity and regret. Life had not been kind to that cooling flesh; and the vain wish that he himself had been a little kinder was now a tightness in his throat.

After a while he went downstairs, leaving Borka on her knees beside the bed. The two girls were still at the dishes, Mary washing. He had settled it that Alice should wash.

He put on his hat and coat, then faced his children. "I don't want you to cry," he said. "Your mother is dead. Be good girls and don't make any noise. You understand?"

They nodded, wide-eyed.

He went out to notify the undertaker. When he returned the young priest had come and gone. There were two neighbor women in the kitchen who had seen him arrive, and Borka had herself and the children well on the way to hysteria. Kracha felt like kicking her. He shrugged instead.

They buried Elena in the Irish cemetery, up the hill a piece from Dubik. A light snow was falling. She had a splendid funeral, one of the most lavish the First Ward had witnessed in years. There were ten carriages and once in the hearse the gray casket was buried out of sight under wreaths. During the three days wake the mourners consumed about thirty-five dollars' worth of food, whisky, beer and pop.

Francka and Andrej came over with their two boys the day after Elena died and stayed until she was buried. They brought a suitcase containing clean clothes for the boys and a change of shirts for Andrej. For both men and women a funeral, like a wedding or a christening, provided a holiday and a feast, an opportunity to visit, to talk, to refresh old acquaintances and make new ones. Andrej was burning with curiosity about Zuska but Kracha pretended not to understand his innuendoes and he had to be satisfied with staring at Kracha enviously and calling him an old devil (*stary fras*) a dozen times a day. Zuska did not put in an appearance, of course, but at one time or another she was in everybody's thoughts and no doubt on their tongues. Francka maintained a cold reserve. Borka informed her brother that nothing about the funeral arrangements pleased Francka, chiefly because she had been allowed no hand in them. Dorta came every day and had a place in the third carriage. At one time during the wake Kracha put his arm around her and told the crowded kitchen, "In two years I have lost my wife, my

mother and my best friend." Until he said it the idea hadn't occurred to him. It was so well received that he repeated it at every
opportunity.

The family quarrel without which no wedding or funeral was
complete took place after the return from the cemetery. There was
more eating and drinking and then the mourners began leaving.
Francka and Andrej were the last to go. As Borka was helping get
the boys into sweaters and coats she said, "I think it would have
done Elena good to see what a nice funeral she had." So many
people, she rambled on. Father Kazincy had said some beautiful
things. Everyone had praised the way she had been laid out, and
nobody could say there hadn't been enough to eat and drink. By
all this Borka was perhaps asking for no more credit than she
deserved; she had worked hard.

Francka pushed her younger son's arm into a sleeve in a way
that threatened to snap it. "At least that other one had the decency
not to show her face while Elena was lying here."

Andrej, anxious for information, proved to be anything but a
peacemaker. He learned little more, however, than that Zuska was
black and lustful, that whether Kracha proposed to marry her was
nobody's business but his own, and that on some previous occasion
Francka had had her face slapped. This last astonished and delighted him. He herded Francka out of the house with, "Let us go;
I have work tomorrow. Go, go, before you get your face slapped
again."

"You'd let him, I suppose?" Francka demanded.

Andrej replied, "I know better than to interfere in these family
quarrels," and choked with laughter at his own wit. "Go on, go on!
Devil take me, you're old enough to know when to keep your
mouth shut! Good-by, Djuro. Good-by, Borka."

The dead was in her grave and the living were picking up where
they had left off.

21

HE MISSED Elena, but not as a husband misses a beloved wife — that was hardly to be expected. She had long since ceased to be a large part of his life, and her part had never been larger than during the bitter years when he was learning that she could never be the kind of wife he wanted. He had learned it and made shift to accept it. It was accomplished at a cost to them both greater than could be made up in a single lifetime but such tragedies were too common for even those involved to feel unfairly put upon. In short, Kracha was a widower long before Elena died.

He could never bring himself to face all the implications of what she had said, what she had tried to tell him, that last evening. He did his best to forget even her words, the look on her face. That beneath her unprepossessing exterior there had been all along the girl who still remembered being told how pretty he'd thought her, the girl he could recall laughing beside him in a field beyond Ochvar with the wind in her dress, the sunshine on her hair, the girl whose feelings he had once known as well as he knew his own — this had seemed too terrible to be borne even for a moment. So he had refused to listen to her, had all but shut her off before she demolished his world, a simple, orderly world in which black was black, white, white, and Elena skinny, disfigured, cranky and frigid because she was too downright mean and contrary to be anything else. And she had closed her eyes and when he spoke to her she had merely shaken her head, as one done with speech for good and all, trapped and alone to the last.

A few of his women customers were for a while given to the conventional heavings and reflections on human mortality; his response was as conventional. He was not one to play the incon-

solable widower and custom did not ask him to. The wish that he
had been kinder to her, an emotion in which his affair with Zuska
did not figure at all, stayed with him longest. It troubled him and
he went to the priest, who reproached and comforted him and
suggested prayer, masses for the dead and charity to the poor.
After that Kracha felt better. He wore a black sleeve-band and
on Sundays when the weather was fine he took the girls to the
cemetery. During the week he behaved and drank with circum-
spection.

He resumed his visits to Zuska toward the end of February, a
month after the funeral. Francka and Borka never doubted that a
woman could get any man if she stooped low enough — a common
belief among women — but it was beyond their understanding how
he could be held by such methods. They called Zuska a slut and
appeared to think that should be enough to make Kracha wash his
hands of her. They were, of course, mistaken.

If the idea ever occurred to him to break with Zuska it never
survived his next visit to her. Kracha was, for the first time in his
life, getting from a woman what he had always wanted. Long
afterward he put Zuska into three words: she was fat, hairy and
passionate. She was several other things besides, but these were
what held him. Stripped of her clothes she was even by indulgent
standards far from beautiful, but Kracha wasn't looking for beauty.
The years with Elena, thin, bony, scantily endowed, had starved
him for sheer flesh. He wanted a woman who looked and felt like
a woman and the more there was of her the better. He wanted
something he could fill his hands with, and that Zuska gave him:
big breasts, big hips, thick legs, a belly loosened by childbearing,
a layer of softening fat over all.

Nor was that all she gave him. She made it plain that she enjoyed
going to bed with him and before he left it she never failed to express her gratitude, as though he had done her the greatest of
favors. The first time she suggested as much Kracha thought she
was joking. It had never occurred to him that a woman might thank
a man for doing her this particular service. But Zuska did, and

appeared to mean it. As a not unnatural consequence Kracha's admiration of her, as well as his own self-esteem, mounted by the day.

Since there was nothing more to hide he came and went openly, though still only at night. If there was gossip or disapproval it did not reach his ears. He would have paid no attention to it anyway; he had other, more pressing, troubles.

Business refused to improve, and blaming Spetz, nosy women and the Cuban situation did no good. Elena's funeral had taken all his ready cash and put him in debt to the undertaker; he kept putting off ordering a gravestone from week to week. Zuska's household was costing him almost as much as his own. And in June he could expect to hear from the bank again.

Late one April night, some weeks after the *Maine* blew up in Havana harbor and while the country was marching excitedly to war, as to a picnic, he groped his way down the alley to Zuska's door and rattled the knob until she opened it. The boys were asleep in the kitchen. They went upstairs. In the lamplit bedroom Kracha took off his coat and loosened his collar and lay back on the bed, sighing wearily.

Zuska stood looking down at him for a moment; then she stooped and began to unlace his shoes. "Did you work hard today?"

"Work? I don't mind work. There are worse things than work."

She didn't ask him what they were.

"Is there any more news about Cuba?"

"Nothing new."

She pulled off his shoe, thick-soled, bulbous-toed, greasy from the shop, and began on the other one. "Do you think there will be a war?"

"There is enough talk about it, God knows. The price of meat has started going up already."

"I hope they don't start a war."

"We have nothing to say about it. What I'm thinking is that if there is a war the railroad won't build this spring either, devil take them."

She dropped the other shoe to the floor and straightened, wiping

her hands against her apron. Her feet were bare but she was otherwise fully clothed. "It was a bad day when you bought those lots,
Djuro."

"It's too late to be sorry now."

"Have you asked Perovsky —"

"I'm through asking him. He knows too much about my business
already." Kracha cursed him softly. "He could take them off my
hands now without feeling it but do you think he will? Sonnomabitch. But I should have known better than to go into something
I knew nothing about. If I had stuck to minding my shop —"

"What about Squire Holman — has he found a buyer yet?"

'Sure — for three thousand dollars. He's the buyer himself, I bet.
Three thousand dollars — think of it!"

"Maybe it would be better to sell even though you lost a little."

"Sell! Sell! How the devil can I sell at that price? Do you realize
that I'd have to give the bank a thousand dollars before I could
sell?"

"A thousand dollars? But why?"

"Because I owe them four thousand. Not only would I lose the
lots but I'd have to pay the bank a thousand of my own money
before I could get rid of them. A crazy business, eh? That's what
a man gets himself into when he signs a banker's paper."

"Don't talk so loud, Djuro." There was a worried look on her
face. "Well, don't worry too much about it. Maybe it will turn out
all right. Would you like something to eat? I have some *halushki*
on the back of the stove."

"Nothing."

"Just a little. It will do you good."

"I'm not hungry."

For a while neither spoke. Kracha lay with his arm across his
eyes.

"If only you hadn't bought those lots," Zuska said slowly. "You
were doing so well."

"The lots are all right. If I had some cash I could make an
arrangement with the bank and keep them until I got my own

price. But I need cash. I'm getting as bad as my own customers; the only time I ever have money now is on payday."

"How much would you need?"

He lifted his arm an inch to peer at her. "A thousand dollars. Maybe only five hundred. Have you that much hidden in your stocking?"

She ignored his pleasantry. "Do you mean you don't have even five hundred dollars saved?"

"Where would I get five hundred dollars? Or even one hundred? The funeral cost me a fortune. I owe the undertaker. I owe the slaughterhouse. Borka asks me for money, you ask me for money. As fast as it comes in out it goes."

"Djuro, that's very bad. I didn't think things were so bad with you."

"Well, you know now."

She reflected for a moment. "Djuro, tell me something. Is there some way you could have the bank take the lots back so you would be free and clear — give them the lots for what you owe — "

"And lose all the money I've put into them?"

"But if they should want money in June — "

"They will, never fear."

" — and you don't have it, they may make trouble."

He grunted.

"Could they take you to court?"

"Perhaps."

She looked down at him. "Djuro, you would be in danger of losing everything."

"Who says so?"

"I am only asking."

"Before that happens I'd do something, by God."

"What would you do?"

"I don't know yet. Something." He gestured impatiently. "Don't talk about it any more."

"Djuro, I'm worried."

"Your worrying won't help."

She was silent. Kracha closed his eyes. After a while he opened them. "Why are you standing there? Lie down." He patted the bed beside him and closed his eyes again.

She undressed and got into bed. When his hand touched her nakedness he turned his head and smiled at her. "You didn't need to undress tonight, the way I feel." He patted her leg. "Cover yourself before you catch cold."

There was a long silence.

"Djuro, are you asleep?"

"No."

"I have something to tell you."

"Well?"

"*Soma druha,*" she said. Or, in English, "I am with another."

Unconsciously his eyes sought her belly, as though expecting to find a change there. "Are you sure?"

She nodded. "I guessed it last month but I didn't want to tell you until I was sure."

"So." He stared at the ceiling. "Well, what do we do now?"

"Whatever you say, Djuro."

He sighed. "Why the devil did it have to happen at a time like this?"

She had no reply to that.

"I can imagine how they'll talk. One wife not yet cold in her grave and he takes himself another."

"Let them talk."

"You can be sure they won't ask our permission."

He rubbed his hand over his face. "Zuska, how did I get myself into so much trouble? I feel like a man in a foreign country. Little by little I've managed to mix myself in things that are too much for me. Trouble — I can stand trouble. But now I never know what to do next. Maybe I should have stayed in the mill. That's where I belong. And if things don't take a turn for the better soon that is where I'll end up."

"Don't talk like that. When we're married maybe I'll bring you luck."

"I hope so."

"Do you think Kazincy will try to make trouble?"

"He'll pull a long face, but he'll marry us."

"When, Djuro?"

"Oh, soon. Whenever you like." He was silent for a while. "Zuska, do you remember when we were on the boat? Who would have thought then that someday you and I — well, that someday you'd be lying beside me like this?"

"What did you think of me?"

"I wanted then what I have now." He patted her lightly. "I think I showed that plainly enough. You remember that little party I gave you?"

"Of course."

"I've told this only to one man and he is dead. God give him rest and peace but I might have done better if he had lived. Well, your little party was the reason I had to walk from New York to White Haven."

"I guessed that, Djuro, after your sister told me."

"Oh, you guessed it, did you? And what did you think of me — a fine damn fool that Kracha, I suppose?"

"*Ach!*"

"Well, keep it to yourself. If Francka ever found out I would never hear the end of it." He chuckled. "I'd like to see her face when she hears we're married."

The United States declared war on Spain on a Monday, and perhaps with a faint hope that the First Ward would be too busy talking about the war to have time for anything else — it wasn't — Kracha married Zuska the following Saturday.

After that, events moved swiftly. Even long afterward Kracha was unable to remember all that happened that memorable summer, possibly because during its two most crowded months he was continuously drunk. The war began near the end of April; when the armistice came in mid-August Kracha was serving ten days in jail for disorderly conduct; specifically, for beating his wife. In one sweeping avalanche of disaster he had lost the Halket Avenue property, lost his business, lost his home; and when they let him out of jail he discovered that he had lost his wife too. After the sheriff's sale Zuska had taken her two boys and left Braddock and nobody, not even her sister, knew where she had gone.

22

THEY came out of the police station on Main Street and for a moment Kracha stood blinking at the late afternoon sunshine. It was a fine day, with small white clouds in a sky that was blue everywhere except at the lower end of town, above the mill; there it was dirty and colorless. The street was hot; stores had their awnings down and men going to work walked leisurely, their coats slung over their arms.

Mary, who had brought him clean clothes in which to face the world again, touched his sleeve. "Come on, Papa," she said in English. She didn't look at him.

"Is today Saturday?" Kracha asked.

"No, Thursday."

"Somehow it seems like Saturday to me."

They went slowly toward Eleventh Street. The air above the street was bright with flags and bunting.

"So the war is over."

Mary nodded.

"It didn't last long, did it? They don't have real wars nowadays."

Mary didn't say anything.

"How are your sisters?"

"All right." Alice and Anna — and, less happily, Borka — were staying with Francka, Mary herself with Dorta. It was to Dorta's house they were going now.

Kracha glanced at his eldest daughter and sensed her discomfort. She kept her eyes lowered; her small face, delicately profiled, bore a strained look. "And you?" he asked.

She said she was all right too.

He tried to think of something to say. Awkwardly, he tapped her spine. "Straighten up; do you want to become a hunchback?" He tried to make a joke of it.

She pulled her shoulders back without replying.

On Washington and on River Street people he knew glanced at him as he passed but didn't speak. Their expressions seemed more curious than disapproving. Mary kept walking too fast, getting ahead of him and then having to wait until he caught up.

They turned into the tunnel-like passageway and came out in the back yard, its barren earth, brick house-walls and kitchen doors baking in the hot sun. Two men, dressed for work, were sitting on a bench against the warm wall; a baby slept in a carriage under a cloud of cheesecloth. The men on the bench stopped talking and looked at Kracha as he went into Dorta's kitchen.

She was packing lunch buckets. "Well, Djuro, already? I didn't expect to see you until after six o'clock."

"I could have left an hour ago," Kracha said slowly. "The policeman said it was payday and they would need the room. For a joke, I suppose."

"It's payday, all right, so that part was no joke. Sit down, sit down."

He put his bundle of dirty clothes on the floor and sat down by the table. It was set for three. Mary settled onto a low stool in one corner.

"Are you hungry?"

"Thank you, no."

"Would you like a drink?"

He hesitated, then shook his head.

Dorta did not urge it on him. She finished packing the buckets, glanced at the clock and went to the door that led upstairs. "Mike! Anton! It's getting late!"

Unintelligible rumbles from above answered her. She muttered, "'Yes, right away, right away.' Right away you'll have no jobs to go to." She went to the yard door. "Andrej, come and eat."

The younger of the two men on the bench nodded. After a moment he said something to the other one and rose, stretching lazily, as though he had all the time in the world. His companion made some remark and they both laughed softly. Dorta put a platter of steaks, cut thin and fried till they resembled shoe leather, on the table. Kracha got up and found another seat as the boarder Andrej darkened the doorway.

Dorta went to the foot of the stairs again. "Mike! It's nearly half-past five!"

Andrej was on his second steak when they came down, noisily, Mike Dobrejcak and another. Mike said, "Hello, Djuro." The other took his place with only a nod.

"Must I yell my lungs out to get you downstairs?" Dorta asked. "What were you doing that was so important?"

"He was writing a letter for me," Anton said.

"To your sweetheart, I suppose."

Mike said, his lips greasy, "Sure. He wanted me to tell her that he wasn't going to send for her until she learned to cook as good as you."

"*Ach!* Instead of thinking up lies you'd do better to think about getting to work on time. Don't think I'll feed you if you lose your job." She added sententiously, in English, "No work, no pork, no money, no boloney." It was a common saying.

The baby whimpered outside and a woman appeared in the doorway and spoke to it, chidingly. The mill was a low, metallic murmur. The railroad tracks gleamed hot in the sun; beyond them diapers flapped windily on a line near the company houses, where still other men were eating, getting ready for a night of work. The long, flat-sided hill on the other shore of the river was a solid green except where the streetcar company's new roadway was a straight, yellow scar. There was to be no bridge at Thirteenth Street after all, and no cars passing prosperously through Braddock on their way from Pittsburgh to Duquesne and McKeesport.

The men drank their coffee and got up, wiping their mouths on their sleeves. For a while there was a good deal of moving around; they filled their pipes, remembered matches, got their coats and caps, noisily sucked shreds of food out of their teeth. Mike was wearing new work shoes that squeaked. Then they picked up their buckets and were on their way. Andrej put his head into the next kitchen and waited a few minutes; then he and his friend too went out through the passageway to the street.

It was good, Kracha thought, to eat heartily, to joke with one's boarding missus, to go off to work with a friend.

Dorta began clearing the table and setting out clean plates for the boarders who would be home as soon as the whistle blew. A coke train went past on the railroad and two small children plunged out of a doorway and stood at the edge of the yard; when the caboose came by they waved and yelled and jumped in the air. The brakemen in the high little window waved back.

Kracha said, "I hear Spetz bought my shop."

"Yes. He's moved everything out. The place is still empty but I saw the landlord scraping the window the other day so maybe he's rented it already."

"And the house — the furniture?"

"They tell me that dealer from Sixth Street bought most of it. I didn't go to the sale myself."

"They took everything?"

"Everything but clothes."

Kracha, his head sunk between his shoulders, sighed deeply.

"And what's that for?" Dorta asked. "Sitting there and sighing like an old woman won't do any good."

"Dorta, if someone had told me a year ago — "

She didn't reply at once. She went down to the cellar and came back with a platter of raw steaks. "Do you know what you were doing a year ago today?" she asked.

He looked at her. "A year ago today?"

"You went to church with me in the morning." She laid out a steak on a board. "And then we walked down Eleventh Street together."

"This is the day?"

"Yes."

"Three years since he died," Kracha murmured. "It seems like a hundred."

Dorta picked up a wooden potato masher and began to pound the steak mercilessly.

When the dishes stopped dancing on the closet shelves and the echoes ceased reverberating and the house settled back on its foundations — when, in short, it was possible to be heard again — Kracha said, "Dorta, I've said it before and I say it again: I would be better off today if he had lived."

"You wouldn't have listened to him, either. Nobody could talk to you."

"Don't say that. You know me better."

"I thought so once."

"It's all finished now and there's no use crying about it, but I tell you, Dorta, to this day I can't see what I did that was wrong."

Dorta made no comment.

"I know what you're thinking," Kracha said.

"Mary, go and find the boys and tell them to come home."

The girl rose and went out silently.

"It was good of you to take her in," Kracha said.

"I'm glad to have her. She's a fine girl and she can stay with me as long as she likes."

Dorta picked up her potato masher again.

When the hellish noise ended Kracha said, "I suppose this hasn't been pleasant for her."

"What did you expect? But she's young and she'll get over it. The best thing you could do is give her and the others a home again."

"I don't want to stay in Braddock."

"Where will you go?"

"I don't know. Homestead, Duquesne — I don't know yet what I'll do."

"The sooner you make up your mind the better. Mary wants to stay in Braddock. She has the promise of a job when the summer's over."

"A job? What kind of job?"

"Looking after a small boy for some American family. They live up near Corey Avenue somewhere. They're away for the summer now. Dexter the name is, I think. She'd get a dollar-fifty a week and her keep, which is better than most. She's asked my advice and I've told her to take the job if she can get it."

Whatever comment Kracha may have felt like making was discouraged as Dorta began to pound again. When he could, he said, "If she wants to take it I won't stop her."

"It will do her no harm. She'll be fifteen in December and it's time she was going to work. I asked Dr. Schirmer about them and he says they're a good family."

Kracha pulled absently at his mustache. "What are they saying about me around here?"

Dorta shrugged. "I have no time to listen to gossip. For that matter, you're not the first man to get drunk and give his wife a beating, or be taken off to jail for it."

"I wasn't thinking about that."

"What could they say? You owed money and couldn't pay. Some were sorry for you, some were not. I don't think many of them were surprised. You know how you've been acting these last few months."

"And you? What do you think?"

She shrugged again and picked up the potato masher. "I'm sorry for you, I wish it hadn't happened. But it's not my place to tell you what you should have done."

When she finished with the last of the steaks she put them on the platter, covered them against flies with a rag and glanced at the clock. Then she sat down near the door, wiping her face on her apron.

Kracha said, "I made my greatest mistake when I let Perovsky talk me into buying those lots. Yet there was nothing wrong in that. Others bought and are no worse off than they were before. And then the funeral, of course; that took a lot of money. I was doing a good business but not good enough to take care of so many extra expenses. You see how it was; no one thing but a lot of little things together."

Dorta made a little shrugging motion, her head to one side, while she fanned herself with her apron. The air coming in from the yard was hot, but the air in the kitchen was hotter.

"At one time, Dorta, I give you my word it seemed to me as if the world were standing on its head. Nothing would go right for me. And all the time I had this feeling that it didn't have to end badly, there was something to be done that would make it turn out all right, if only I knew what it was. A man like Perovsky or Joe Wold wouldn't have had to think twice, he would have known exactly what to do and come out of it with his pockets full. They do it all the time. They know about such things, they know how to talk to people, they know what to do. But I — I wasn't in my own country, as they say. I was caught in things I knew nothing about."

After a while Dorta said, "Djuro, tell me something. If you will. Is it true she was taking your money?"

He looked up. "Where did you hear that?"

"They say that was all you could talk about in the saloon that night. And later, when the policeman was taking you away."

"I had forgotten. Yes, it's true."

"But why? How?"

He shrugged. "I can tell you what I remember her telling me. When I accused her of stealing from me, if a wife can be said to steal from her husband, she didn't deny it. She said she had to look out for herself and her children, since it was plain I couldn't."

"And your children?" Dorta asked. "Who was going to look out for them?"

"When she saw how badly things were going for me she began stealing, and so made everything that much worse. I would come home with money from the shop and in the morning most of it would be gone. Payday nights when my customers cleaned up their books I would have sometimes two, two-hundred-fifty dollars on me. At first I thought I had lost it or it had been stolen out of my pocket in the saloon. That was what she said when I first accused her of taking it."

"You should have kept your money somewhere else."

"Where? But I was too drunk to think. You can see what happened. She was taking the money I needed to pay my bills. As though I didn't have enough trouble without that."

"How much do you think she took?"

Kracha shrugged.

"Five hundred dollars?"

"Oh, more, much more. I didn't pay a bill for two months."

"Think of it."

The six o'clock whistle blew. Dorta glanced at her clock; it was three minutes fast. "They will be here soon," she murmured, and got up. She poked the fire in the stove and then slid an immense black skillet over the opening. In a moment the kitchen was full of the sound and smell of frying meat.

"Well," Dorta said, "I suppose you're well rid of her."

"She is still my wife."

She turned and stared at him. "Would you take her back?"

He ignored her question. "Why is it you women never liked her?"

"What are you talking about? I neither liked nor disliked her. I spoke to her maybe three times in my life."

Kracha's eyes shifted to the open doorway. "As you say, I may be well rid of her. But until she began taking my money she was as good a wife to me as a man could want, and better than most ever get."

"You'd take her back tomorrow," Dorta said flatly.

"How do you know what I'd do?"

"You'd take her back. If she came back you'd take her in as though nothing had ever happened." And Dorta shook her head wonderingly.

Kracha didn't reply. He stared out at the cinder dump, the heat-hazed vista of railroad tracks and wire works and Homestead's distant murk. And after a while he said, half to himself, "I always felt good when I was with her."

The first of the boarders came home from work. He nodded to Kracha as he gave his lunch bucket to Dorta, and went upstairs. He came down a few minutes later stripped to the waist, his reddened neck and forearms contrasting startlingly with his pale torso. He was washing himself over a basin in the yard when Dorta's husband arrived, escorted by Mary and the boys.

Kracha went to Munhall the next day but it was nearly a month before he got back in the mill. He went to board with a family in Homestead and gave Francka a little each payday for looking after the girls. This was understood to be a temporary arrangement, a mere stopgap until Kracha got around to opening another butcher shop, or at least until he rented a house of his own. Mary went to work for the Dexters in September. Of Zuska there was never a word.

It wasn't until nearly a year after the night of his arrest, the night his world collapsed, that Kracha saw his shop, the building, again. On his visits to Braddock he had managed to avoid passing it; this time however he started up Washington from Wold's saloon without thinking, and when he realized where he was going he shrugged and kept on. Some widow had taken it over for a candy store; her name was on the window in pale blue letters. He went inside, a bell tinkling as he opened the door. He recognized nothing, the walls, the floor, the ceiling, nothing. It didn't even smell the same. His shop had been wiped out of existence so thoroughly that it was hard for him to believe it had ever existed.

He bought a packet of Five Brothers and went out. Thereafter he was able to think about his shop and remember how pleasant it had been to be a businessman with diminishing self-pity and regret;

but it was years before he could think of Zuska without pain. When time had dulled the poignant heartlessness of the wrong she'd done him and desire had faded and his hands no longer ached with the unforgettable feel of her flesh, he still remembered how much more clever and gallant and unselfish he had been with her than with anyone else. She'd had a gift for making a man think well of himself.

Part Two
MIKE DOBREJCAK

1

IN DECEMBER of 1900, when people were saying, "Well, the first year of the twentieth century is almost over," and a few were stubbornly reviving the old argument that the twentieth century had yet to begin — "If a century is 100 years, then nineteen centuries are 1900 years and the twentieth doesn't begin until January 1, 1901" — Mike Dobrejcak was twenty-five years old, a quiet, slow-speaking, dry-humored young man whose eyes crinkled before he smiled, who smiled more often than he laughed. He had been in America eleven years, and for ten of them he had worked in the blast furnaces, first as a water boy and then as a laborer. He was still a laborer but Keogh, the furnace keeper on his turn, had taken a liking to him and made him one of his two helpers. Though his wages, fourteen cents an hour, stayed unchanged, he was raised a little out of the anonymity of the labor gangs, he took orders only from Keogh and the work was — comparatively — lighter. Of the two thousand or so men working in the mill a good half were Slovaks or other non-English-speaking foreigners, and of that half not one had a skilled job. Departmental heads did their own hiring, and, whether American, English or Irish, tended to favor their own kind.

The twelve-hour turn left even the very young with little energy to do more than lean against a bar, or sleep, but when an English class for foreigners was started in the schoolhouse on Eleventh Street, Mike attended more faithfully than most. He learned to read and write English and was exposed to those figures and folk tales of American history — Plymouth Rock, the Boston Tea Party and Gettysburg; George Washington and Abraham Lincoln — which his teachers assumed were most potently Americanizing.

Among other matters, Mike learned that Braddock had been named after a General George Braddock. A long time ago, he was told, when all this was still a wilderness, there had been a battle. In this battle General Braddock was killed and George Washington, whose presence was no doubt responsible for Mike's incorrect but persisting impression that the battle was an incident of the Revolution, had several horses shot out from under him. They named a street after Washington, in this exhibiting, it seemed to Mike, a nice sense of proportion.

What the fighting was about Mike had no idea. He knew the Civil War was fought to free the slaves, and that the Revolution started when the British put a tax on postage stamps and tried to make the Pilgrims drink tea with every meal; but what General Braddock and George Washington were doing in these Pennsylvania backwoods was never made clear. Fort Duquesne, which added to the confusion by being in Pittsburgh, was involved somehow, as were the French Army and a horde of Indians, ignorant savages who disregarded the rules of civilized warfare by ambushing General Braddock's troops in a deep ravine and shooting at them from behind rocks and trees, exactly as George Washington had said they would. But General Braddock wouldn't listen to him; and that to Mike was like a sudden flash of light, illuminating the basic, irreconcilable differences between things British and American. George Washington had been so obviously right that perceiving it made Mike feel himself already half an American, and the Revolution inevitable.

The exact site of this battle was obscure. A deep ravine was called for and Braddock itself was anything but a ravine. Set inside a bend of the Monongahela it was flat from the river to Main Street, whence it rose progressively steeper until the streets and back yards of North Braddock raveled out against the treeless, eroded hills. The only likely ravine Mike knew was Dooker's Hollow, an abysmal gorge in the hills to the east of Braddock, up near the foundries — its sewerlike entrance a black tunnel under the Pennsylvania tracks, its single street lined with shabby houses, the bare hills lifting steeply on either side, and, stalking from one height to another, the Bell Avenue bridge, from whose aging timbers fear-rigid boys were periodically rescued by the Fire Department. As a ravine it should have made an ambushing Indian grunt with pleasure.

Historians decided that the Indians had preferred the vicinity of what was now upper Sixth Street but for Mike it was in Dooker's Hollow, a Dooker's Hollow with no houses, no tipsy coal sheds, no forty-five-degree–angle back yards, that General Braddock — shaking his fist at the invisible enemy, daring them to come out and fight like eighteenth-century Englishmen — was ingloriously shot, while George Washington leaped acrobatically from one horse to another.

They buried General Braddock on the mountains above Uniontown; George Washington went on to the historically more remunerative business of Valley Forge and crossing the Delaware and posing — apparently in a cloud of steam — for those grim-lipped portraits; and Braddock wasn't mentioned in the history books again.

But, after the soldiers, came the settlers — more and more of them all the time. They cut down the trees and built houses and laid out their dreary, unimaginative pattern of streets and alleys, beginning at the river's edge and working back toward the hills: River Street, Willow Way, Washington Street, Cherry Alley, Talbot. And then, after a long interval, Andrew Carnegie thought there was money in Bessemer steel rails and he bought a hundred acres of riverside farmland from the McKinney brothers and put up two five-ton converters and a three-high, twenty-three-inch hook-and-tong rail mill; and when the prices of blooms and pig iron began to cut into his profits he picked up a secondhand blast furnace in Escanaba and brought it to Braddock in sections: *A* Furnace, this was, with a bricked-in skip hoist, the one the Slovaks called the *mala fana,* the little furnace, with an output of some fifty tons a day. So the mills came to Braddock, stripping the hills bare of vegetation, poisoning the river, blackening heaven and earth and the lungs of the workers, who were in the beginning mostly American and English. When the Irish came the Americans and English, to whom sheer precedence as much as anything else now gave a near monopoly of the skilled jobs and best wages, moved to the streets above Main and into North Braddock. The First Ward was taken over by the Irish. But the forces that had brought the Irish to Braddock were still at work. New mills and furnaces were built, new supplies of labor found. The Slovaks came; and once more there was a general displacement. The Irish began to invade the better parts of town, while those Americans and English who could afford it fled into Pittsburgh's suburbs.

All this was a long time happening, and was not accomplished without bitterness and conflict; but none of it ever got into the history books.

Immigrants continued to pour into the valley, taking over whole sections — invariably the worst sections, nearest the river and the mills — of the steel towns. Braddock got its share of the newcomers; in ten years its population nearly doubled. The First Ward became almost solidly Slovak, though even on Washington Street there were still people who wouldn't rent to foreigners. But the pressure was growing steadily; house by house, street by street, the Slovaks pushed out from center, which might be put at the corner of Eleventh and Washington. Real-estate speculators put up the houses that became so characteristic of the steel towns, long, ugly rows like cell blocks, two rooms high and two deep, without water, gas or conveniences of any kind, nothing but the walls and the roofs: Zeok's Row on Halket, Veroskey's Row along the P. and L. E. railroad, Mullen's double row on Willow Way, were typical. They were filled as soon as they were finished and made no apparent impression on the housing shortage or the rent level.

What few English-speaking people remained in the First Ward clung to its fringes, west of Ninth, above Main. They were for the most part Irish, the common laborer of an earlier day. It was with the Irish that the Slovaks as a whole came into most intimate contact, in town as neighbors and in the mill as pushers and gang foremen, and to this must be ascribed much of the subsequent bitterness between them. The Americans and English were equally contemptuous of the newer immigrants, with an even lordlier air than that they reserved for one another, but there were fewer of them.

In the old country the Slovaks had been an oppressed minority from the beginning of time, a simple, religious, unwarlike people, a nation of peasants and shepherds whom the centuries had taught patience and humility. In America they were all this and more, foreigners in a strange land, ignorant of its language and customs, fearful of authority in whatever guise. Arrived in America they were thrust — peasants and shepherds that they were — into the blast furnaces and rolling mills, and many of them paid with their lives for their unfamiliarity with machinery and the English language. Even more bewildering were the hostility and contempt of their neighbors, the men they worked with.

That hostility, that contempt, epitomized in the epithet "Hunky," was the most profound and lasting influence on their personal lives the Slovaks of the steel towns encountered in America. In a large, cosmopolitan city they might perhaps have had an easier time of it, but the steel towns were American small towns, provincial and intolerant. Economically there was no reason why a laborer named, say, Mickey, should dislike a laborer named, say, Mihal; the Mihals did not lower the wage rates of the only kind of jobs they were able to get. Nor did they take others' jobs away from them; the steel industry was in its period of greatest expansion, building new mills and furnaces and hiring new men by the hundred. That the company openly preferred foreigners as laborers, that immigration from western Europe had fallen off, that the hours were long, the work hard and the opportunities for advancement rare, helped explain why the unskilled labor force was predominantly foreign by the beginning of the new century. For the English-speaking peoples' unconcealed racial prejudice, their attitude that it was a disgrace to work on a level with Hunkies, there was no rational excuse. But it was a fact, a large and not pretty fact which marked, stunted and embittered whole generations.

The firstcomers, Kracha's generation, never suffered the full effects of it, partly for the same reason that a prisoner who does not try to escape is not shot at. Few could read or write even their own language; Austria-Hungary had never encouraged, to put it mildly, minority cultures. They lived to themselves of necessity, speaking their own tongue, retaining their old customs. Their lack of curiosity about America, the country, the civilization, was more apparent than real; they had few opportunities to learn and experience taught them that curiosity was not admired. Company men were everywhere, working beside one in the mill, drinking a beer at one's elbow in the saloons, and an interest in politics was almost as suspect as an interest in labor unions. Kracha's advice to Mike on his exciting discovery of American politics during the first Bryan campaign was generally observed: Think what you like but keep your mouth shut.

They had come to America to find work, to make a living. It was their good fortune, perhaps, to come unburdened with many illusions about a land of freedom, a land where all men were equal. They were glad to take whatever jobs were assigned them; they realized that bosses were the same everywhere, and when the epithet Hunky was hurled at them they shrugged. It was hardly pleasant but there was nothing one could do about it. The implied denial of social and racial equality seldom troubled them; as Kracha once said, he had come to America to find work and save money, not to make friends with the Irish.

This ability to shrug, to live to themselves, was the property of that generation and could not be handed on. Their children were born outside the walls, and there was no going back.

When his younger brother, Joe, came to Braddock in the spring of 1901, Mike told him what he could expect. It was quite probable that Joe didn't understand the full implications of what Mike told him, but he learned. They all did.

Years of country living and his service in the Army had made Joe a bigger and heavier man than his brother, but the two were still like enough almost to be twins, with the same broad shoulders, the same fair coloring and regular features and clear gray eyes. Good-looking men. Mike's was the livelier intelligence; he was interested in everything, read newspapers and loved to argue; Joe's was the shorter temper and the drier throat. Joe had left a wife in the old country; Mike was still single.

Joe got a job in the blast furnaces and as a matter of course went to board with Dorta. Mike had been with her so long that many people thought they were close relations, and Dorta's own attitude toward him did much to strengthen that impression. From the time he'd come to her as a boy of fifteen she had seen to it that he got enough sleep, saved his money, went to church and didn't marry the wrong girl. She was passionately interested in his more sentimental adventurings and seemed perpetually torn between a desire to attend his wedding and a conviction that his current girl friend was the last he should even think of taking for a wife.

It was certainly time, she would say, that he was getting married. His best friend, Steve Bodnar, was getting married in a few months. And look at his own brother, two years younger than he and already married over a year. He really should get married. But to a nice girl, one who would make him a good wife, not this Whatever-her-name-was he was going around with now. It was nothing to her, of course, whom he married, whether he married at all or died a lonely old bachelor, doing his own cooking and living like a pig. Why should she worry her head about him? She had enough troubles of her own. But if he expected to get married someday —

And Mike would grin and say, "Sure, when I meet the right girl." He hadn't, he said, met her yet.

2

$\mathcal{A}$S a matter of fact he had known her for years but he really saw her, really looked at her for the first time, that Sunday afternoon in Dorta's kitchen. She had put up her hair and let down her skirts long before he noticed the change. When her father's troubles reached their dismal climax he'd felt sorry for her, even then thinking of her more as a child than as the young woman she was. After she went to work for her American family he seldom saw her; now and then one of her visits to Dorta would find him passing in or out. He would nod to her, noting absently that she was "dressed up," and go on about his business.

During the summer of 1901 he didn't see her at all. The Dexters' cook had left to have a baby or look after her old mother or both, Dorta wasn't sure, and Mary had been installed in her place, her wages raised to two dollars and a half a week. Her younger sister, Alice, a pretty, scatterbrained girl, mad about boys and dancing, took over Mary's duties as upstairs girl and part-time nursemaid. When the Dexters left Braddock for the summer they took Mary with them. Occasionally Dorta would receive a letter or a postcard and pass on to Mike her reports of the wonders of the Atlantic Ocean and Bethany Beach. Mike listened with half an ear and less interest; blast furnaces in July made summers by the sea too unreal even for envy.

That was the summer Carnegie sold his steel company, including the mills in Homestead, Duquesne and Braddock, to J. P. Morgan, who had organized the United States Steel Corporation. In the mill every flat surface — shop walls, crane cabs, ladles — was smeared with stenciled signs proclaiming the birth of America's first billion-dollar corporation. In August about one hundred men were fired in Homestead for trying to revive the union, and the following month sixty were fired in Duquesne for the same reason. The new corporation was giving notice that it planned no innovations in the steel masters' traditional methods of dealing with labor. That was the summer, too, that McKinley was shot in Buffalo and Anna Kovac, whose father owned a small grocery store on Talbot Avenue, began going around saying that Mike Dobrejcak wanted her to go steady with him.

When Dorta asked him if it was true he didn't deny it, partly because it gave Dorta something to talk about. All he'd said to Anna was, "Would you go steady with me if I asked you?" She had replied coyly that she didn't know. Perhaps she'd expected him to go on and ask her. He hadn't, just then; later on, in spite of Dorta and her stories about the rats on Anna's head and the bugs in her father's flour, he might. He was twenty-seven, long past the age when most Slovak young men married, and Anna was as suitable as most of the girls he knew. She was attractive, young enough to excuse some vanity, and her father did have a nice little business. He could do worse. As it turned out, he might just as well have asked her, for within a week Anna had convinced even her own family that he had.

The Dexters returned to Braddock in September, and the Sunday following, while the country was waiting for McKinley to live or die, Mary came to see Dorta.

It was one of Mike's two Sundays off each month; that is, he had come home from the mill that morning and was off until Monday morning. He slept until midafternoon, then rose and dressed, the clean clothes feeling good against his skin. He could hear Dorta talking in the kitchen. River Street was quiet with heat and the Sabbath; in the mill yard a dinkey screeched like an angry midget. Mike strolled downstairs, rolling up the sleeves of his shirt.

She was sitting by the table, her back to the window that looked out on the railroad tracks and the river. She was all in white. He noticed that first, her white dress with its little ruffles at the throat and spilling down her bosom, the full skirt flowing over her crossed leg, the white buttoned shoes. She had taken off her hat and put it on the table beside her; it was white too, wide-brimmed and trimmed with white flowers. A white parasol leaned against her thigh.

She was quite the prettiest and most splendidly dressed young woman he had ever seen.

"Why," he said, "it's Mary Kracha."

"Who did you think it was?" Dorta asked.

"I hardly knew her."

Mary's face was lightly tanned; her teeth flashed when she smiled. "Have I changed so much in one summer?"

"You don't look the same." He stared at her. "You look more like an American girl now."

"Why shouldn't she look like an American girl?" Dorta demanded. "Wasn't she born here? Didn't she go to school here?"

"I think he means my dress," Mary said. "He never saw me in it before."

"What does he know about dresses?"

Mike wasn't sure what he meant. Here was a girl who looked as though she had stepped out of a magazine advertisement, lovely and cool and strange; and the girl was Mary Kracha, whom he had never before looked at twice. The transformation was bewildering. Common sense and his own dignity urged him to be as casual and lordly as one should be with a neighbor's girl, one of dozens; but what his eyes saw made that impossible. Nor did it help to have Dorta watching him.

"Well," he said at last, "I think I'll have a bottle of beer. Would you like some?"

Dorta said she would, though he hadn't asked her. Mary said, "No, thank you."

He went down to the cellar and fished around in a tub of water for two bottles. Dorta was smiling at Mary when he returned. He opened the bottles and took one with him to the doorstep. "Did you have a good time while you were away?"

Her face brightened. "Oh, the best time I ever had in my life. At first I was homesick and the noise of the ocean kept me awake but that didn't last long. When the time came to come back I hated to leave."

"It's a lot different from Braddock, I bet."

Mary gestured; the difference was too great for words. "I was telling Dorta, you have no idea how hot and dirty Braddock looked when we came back. I never noticed the smoke and dirt so much before. After seeing nothing but the ocean and white sandy beaches all summer, the clean air — " She gestured again.

He stared outside, trying to see the back yard and the railroad tracks and the cinder dump as they must have looked to her, after that ocean and that white beach. But it was a Sunday afternoon in summer and everything had its resting, Sunday look, no clotheslines, no dirty children, no hucksters yelling in River Street, no freights on the railroad. It looked like Sunday and it looked good to him, as good as it ever could.

He tilted his bottle. "Just the same," he said, "I bet you were glad to get back."

Mary smiled and shrugged.

Dorta belched.

"Good beer," Mike said.

"*Ach!*"

Mary glanced at the clock. "I really must be going, Dorta. They may get back early." She began to gather her things together.

"How do you go, by streetcar?" Mike asked.

"No, I walk. It's not far; to Fifth Street and then up the hill a block."

"That's far enough, especially on a hot day."

"I don't mind it."

"The streetcar would be better."

"Listen to him," Dorta exclaimed. "Instead of telling her how to get there you'd show more politeness if you offered to take her home."

Mary had risen and was putting on her hat, using the little mirror beside the door that the men shaved by. Her skirt brushed Mike's arm. "Oh no," she said. "Why should he walk all that distance?"

"It won't kill him."

"I'd have to put on a collar and tie," Mike said.

"Indeed? I expected you to go in your undershirt."

He ignored Dorta's inexplicable irony and sought Mary's eyes but she was very busy, her hat seemed to be giving her trouble. He had never noticed before how much grace a girl could put into such a simple task. He glanced at Dorta. She was making faces at him, jerking her head urgently, her lips soundlessly forming the words, "Go on, go on!" He stared at her, his mouth open. Dorta sighed hopelessly and rolled her eyes.

"All right, I will." He scrambled to his feet. "I'll be down in a minute."

Walking beside her along Washington he noticed how heads turned as they passed. When they met people he knew he tipped his hat gravely. Two young men leaning against Perovsky's saloon on the corner of Eleventh said, "Hello, Mike," and then stared at Mary. He could tell they were wondering who she was.

When he saw Anna Kovac it was too late to avoid her. She was standing in front of the schoolhouse at Talbot talking with a girl friend. She was dressed for Sunday but not all in white, she had no parasol and her kid brother was pestering her into a temper. As they approached she gave him a push and exclaimed, "If you don't stop bothering me I'll smack you!" And then she saw Mike, with Mary on his arm.

He tipped his hat to her without missing a step. Anna's mouth opened but she didn't say anything; once past her he could feel her eyes burning into his back until they'd crossed the B. and O. tracks. He heard the girl friend say, "Isn't that Mike Dobrejcak?" just as though she didn't know. Anna's reply didn't reach him, but a sudden howl from her kid brother did. Mary apparently hadn't even seen Anna; she'd gone by her like a lady, like a ship under full sail, her parasol dangling from her wrist, a fold of skirt gathered up in one hand.

They made conversation. He said it was a shame about President McKinley, Republican or no Republican, and she thought it was too. He asked her if she'd seen her father or her sisters since her return; she replied that she was going to Munhall on her next Sunday off. She got two Sundays off a month, and one afternoon and evening each week. Thursdays. He said it was hot; she agreed. No, she didn't want any ice cream. Yes, she liked it. She liked sodas better than sundaes. Chocolate sodas.

Even on Main Street people looked at her a second time.

Her street was a street of big houses, striped awnings, tree-shaded lawns, hitching posts, and a woman playing croquet with a small child on cool-looking grass. It was as far and as different from River Street as anything could be, and he was profoundly relieved when she stopped on the corner and said she'd go the rest of the way herself. Even in his Sunday suit, even beside her, he wouldn't have felt comfortable walking down that street.

"Which is your house?" he asked.

"That one there, the red brick one." It was a big, handsome house, probably the biggest and handsomest there. "It's the one you can see from Main Street. You know."

"Oh, that one." He looked at it again. The Dexters' lawn took up half the block but most of it was back of the house, where the ground sloped steeply to a retaining wall along Main Street, here still predominantly residential. Seen from Main Street the house, sitting on the crest of its green hill, was even more handsome and impressive than at close range. He had often wondered who lived in it.

"I bet it's like a palace inside."

"It's very nice."

"How many rooms has it?"

"Twelve. And a big attic."

"And how many people live there?"

"Four, not counting me and Alice."

"Four people in twelve rooms. Dorta has eleven in four, in three if you don't count the kitchen. What it is to have money!"

"Mr. Dexter would laugh if he heard you. He doesn't think of himself as rich. He has cousins in Philadelphia who are millionaires."

"Millionaires?"

She nodded. "Real millionaires. Bankers."

Mike could only shake his head. "I could do without twelve rooms and cousins in Philadelphia, but I'd like to live on a street like this." He sniffed. "By God, when you have money you can even breathe better air than other people."

She smiled; and Mike smiled back and then watched a young man wearing white trousers clamped untidily to his ankles and a girl wearing a white skirt, both on bicycles, wheeling and turning under the trees. He wondered what the young man did for a living and how much money he made.

"Well," Mary said, "I don't want to keep you."

He took out his watch; he wanted her to see it. "It's not half-past four yet."

"They will be back soon, and I have to change my dress and get supper started. It was nice of you to come with me."

"When are you coming to see Dorta again?"

"I don't know. Maybe next week."

He made a face. "I'm working night turn next week. But this week I'm on day turn," he said hopefully.

She lowered her eyes and twirled her parasol and said, "Are you?"

"Are you going anywhere Thursday night?"

"Thursday night? No, I'm not going anywhere. At least I don't think so."

"Well if I should be on this corner here, this very spot, at seven or maybe a few minutes after — "

She looked up and smiled and held out her hand. "Maybe. Good-by."

"No maybe. I'll be expecting you. And think how glad Dorta will be to see you."

This time she laughed, her face framed by her hair and the wide-brimmed hat.

"Is it a promise?"

"All right. Anything, if only you'll let me go." She pulled her hand free. "Good-by."

"Till Thursday."

He tipped his hat and she smiled at him and went down the street, a graceful white figure under the big trees. He watched until she had gone through the gate; then he went back to River Street.

Dorta was getting supper ready and packing lunch buckets to be taken into the mill to the men who were working the long turn. "Well," she said, "did you get her home all right?"

"Sure. What did you think, we'd lose the way?"

"You may be interested to know that I have already been asked if that was Mary Kracha you were seen walking with."

He started upstairs. "What of it?"

"I said that it was," Dorta called after him, "and that you were old friends. Which you are."

He halted in mid-flight, came back and stuck his head around the doorjamb. "Dorta, tell me something. Where does she get the money to buy such fine clothes?"

"Oh, you noticed her clothes, did you? Well, don't worry your head about it. They don't cost her a penny. Not a penny. The lady she works for gives her all her old clothes and Mary fixes them up to suit herself. She sews very well. And she must be a good cook," Dorta added somewhat irrelevantly, "or they wouldn't have kept her this long. She's a smart girl; she could get married tomorrow if she liked."

"Is she going steady?"

"Not yet, but they keep asking her."

"Who?"

"How should I remember all their names?"

He frowned at her suspiciously and then went upstairs, leaving Dorta looking highly pleased with herself.

3

HE was waiting on the corner for her Thursday night, not as sure that she'd really meet him as he would have liked to be. The street was quiet, heavy with dusk; he remembered afterward the glow of lamplit windows and the lingering, melancholy fragrance of burning leaves. When she appeared, her coming heralded by the rustle of her feet among the fallen leaves, he almost failed to recognize her. She was wearing a dark dress and coat and he'd got used to thinking of her in white. She said, "Good evening, Mike," and slipped her hand through his arm as though she had been doing it for years. As they fell into step she said, "Did you wait long?" and he knew that everything was going to be all right. "Since Sunday," he said. "I've been waiting since Sunday."

The next Thursday but one he took her for a walk through the First Ward, a public, almost formal, declaration that he and Anna Kovac were finished with each other. Anna's girl friend had prepared the way by spreading word of the little incident in front of the schoolhouse and an accidental encounter with Anna completed the business. Coming out of a Main Street store on a Saturday night he bumped into the Kovacs, mother, daughter and untamed son. Mike tipped his hat, Anna nodded coldly and Mrs.

Kovac, a pleasant, dumpy woman, looked bewildered and burst into rapid Slovak as her daughter drew her away.

Walking with Mary he told her that Anna had never meant anything to him, which was hardly true. But Mary didn't seem to care. They took the route favored by young couples of an evening, along Washington to Eleventh, up Eleventh to Halket, along Halket to Thirteenth and down Thirteenth to Washington again. Along Washington there were stores, lights and people; they said "hello" to people they knew, they stopped to gossip, they looked and were looked at. On Halket they kept to the north side of the B. and O. tracks, where there were still some fine houses and old trees, relics of the days when Halket had been a pleasant street in a quiet river town. Here the couples walked more slowly and talked in whispers as they moved through the deep shadows and the smell of grass and trees; and only as they approached Thirteenth did the blast furnaces and rail mills become too insistent to be ignored. It was the nearest thing to a lovers' lane in the First Ward.

They saw each other every other week when Mike was working day turn, on Thursday nights, and for a few hours on Sunday if the Dexters had gone out for the afternoon. Her Sunday off Mary usually spent in Munhall. Anna was still with Francka. Borka had married one of Francka's boarders the year before and was expecting a baby in December. Kracha still boarded in Homestead. Of Zuska there was no word or sign; her sister continued to insist that she didn't know what had become of her. There were vague rumors that she had been seen in Johnstown and that she was living with a storekeeper in Gary.

Mike no longer waited on the corner; Thursday nights he went around to the kitchen door and knocked and was welcomed in. One by one he had met Mrs. Dexter and her husband and Mrs. Hillis, her mother, an old, sickly woman, and the boy whose nursemaid Mary had been. He was seven or eight, a clean, bright boy who asked Mike questions about the mill and liked to display the few Slovak phrases Mary had taught him. Mike was in-

finitely more impressed by the boy's good manners; he would have
given a month of his life to be able to say "I beg your pardon"
and "Excuse me" as naturally. His name was Lawrence Allan
Dexter but everyone called him Lad, after his initials. Mr. Dexter
owned a small factory on Corey Avenue that manufactured electric lamps; Mary said he had about fifteen men working for
him.

The Dexters' was the first private house Mike had ever set foot
in which was wired for electricity. For that matter it was the first
private house he'd ever been in that had a bathroom, a telephone,
steam heat, and in the kitchen a magnificent icebox with a back
door cut right through the wall of the house so the iceman could
fill it without coming into the kitchen at all.

Mary showed him through the house one Sunday afternoon;
the Dexters had taken Mrs. Hillis for a buggy ride to Kennywood — as Kenny's Grove, with the embellishments of merry-go-
rounds, roller coasters and such devices, was now called. Mike's
interest in houses, in house furnishings, was no greater than most
young men's; he had used beds, chairs and forks all his life without ever really noticing them. But in the Dexters' dining room, in
their parlor and bedrooms, he saw furniture, dishes, silverware
which were desirable and beautiful in themselves and not merely
as articles of use. For the first time he perceived how graceful
the business of eating and sleeping and entertaining one's friends
could be, and how one could be proud of one's possessions, the
way one lived.

Standing in the parlor he said after a long pause, "This is the
way a man should live."

"It is beautiful, isn't it?" Mary said proudly, almost as though it
were her own.

"When a man has this much what more can he want?"

Unconsciously he had slipped into Slovak, though usually they
spoke to each other in English so that Mike could improve his
speech.

Mary smiled. "You think so? Well, Mr. Dexter would like to

have a bigger factory, and he is always talking about getting an automobile. Mrs. Dexter will stay here as long as her mother lives but she says Braddock is getting too dirty to live in, she would rather live in Squirrel Hill, where it's more stylish. You see? No matter how much you get you always want more."

"I think I could make shift to be satisfied if I had no more than this house just as it stands," Mike said. "But I suppose what I make in a week wouldn't keep it running for even a day." He looked around. "Maybe it would have been better for me if I'd never seen it."

"Now you're talking foolishness."

He grinned. "All right. But what you don't know you don't miss." He put an arm around her waist. "Do you think we'll ever have anything like this?"

"Mihal, where would we get it?"

"Well, who knows what may happen?"

She stared at him, but instead of taking it lightly her mouth had become tremulous, as though she was afraid to think he might be serious; and it occurred to him that she could believe even such feats were not beyond his accomplishing, he, her chosen one.

He sobered. "*Ach!* What would we want with such a fancy house! No one would come to see us; we'd lose all our friends." He smiled at her, squeezing her waist, her corset a stiff fabric under his hand. "But just the same, *mila moja,* we're not going to be like so many others. We're not greenhorns just off the boat. I know English pretty good. I'm still young. I mean to keep my eyes open and use my head. One of these days I'm going to get a good job and then — well, we shall see."

Mary leaned against him, her eyes dreamy. "We'll get it, Mihal. I'll help you all I can."

"Sure you will. We'll work hard, save our money — you watch. You'll never be sorry you married me."

"What a thing to say!"

He smiled into her eyes, and kissed her. "I want a good life for us, Marcha. For you, for me, for our children."

She stayed close to him.

Then they heard hoofbeats in the street and she stooped to glance out the window. It was late autumn in the street. The day's last sunlight, hard and cold, seeped through the bare trees, lay motionless on the dry lawns, on the quiet houses, glinted icily off the clean glass of lace-curtained windows.

They were married in the spring, from Dorta's house. The company was building two new blast furnaces, closer to Thirteenth Street than any of the others, and there were times when the music of the gipsies' beribboned fiddles was drowned out by the riveters' iron clamor. But nobody minded.

4

THE first of the new furnaces, *K,* was blown in early in December, always a great occasion in a steel mill. Mike was of course too unimportant to share in the festivities but he heard from Keogh about the big officials from Pittsburgh and New York, the free cigars, the photographers, the girl — some official's daughter — who started the furnace on its long task by holding a blowtorch against the kerosene-soaked kindling packed in the cinder notch. The officials aroused Keogh's scorn. "By God," he said, chewing his cigar, "I'll bet half of them never saw the inside of a steel mill. And them's the kind that tell you and me what to do." It was lucky no company man overheard him. Joe benefited; men were drawn off the other furnaces to make a crew for the new one and he found himself promoted to front man, and his turn changed.

The second furnace, *J,* was blown in in February of the new year; in March Mary gave birth to a seven-pound boy.

The midwife stayed with her all night. None of them got much sleep; at five in the morning the child had not yet been born and the midwife, Mrs. Simchak, a large, bony, unfeminine-looking woman, told Mike there was no reason why he should lose a day's pay, there was nothing he could do, he'd only be in the way. So he got into his work clothes as quietly as he could. Mary, her loosely braided hair framing her face, was lying with her eyes closed, her body tensed. Now and then she moaned softly.

Dressed, he bent over her. "Marcha. I'm going now."

She opened her eyes and tried to smile.

"I'll stay if you want me."

"No." Her voice was a breathless gasp between pains. "You go. I'll be all right."

"I wish there were something I could do."

"I know."

"Dorta said she would be over this morning as soon as she could."

Mary nodded and closed her eyes, biting her lips. Mike watched her, feeling helpless. When she looked at him again her face was wet with perspiration.

He wiped her face dry and pushed her hair back from her forehead. Mrs. Simchak called from the foot of the stairs. "Dobrejcak! It's getting late."

He kissed Mary. "I'll be praying for you."

Her baby was born at eight o'clock that morning, at about the same time, Mike reckoned, that he and the rest were sweating over the day's first cast. Keogh, himself a father three times over, was sympathetic. "I know how you feel," he said. "I used to think it was only the first time but be damned if it is. You still worry even after she's proved she can do it."

"My wife little woman," Mike explained. "Little bones."

"Well, don't worry too much about it."

He was unable to leave the mill at noon — a tuyère started to burn through and they had an exciting half-hour changing it — so it wasn't until he got home that night that he learned he was the father of a son. Anna left meat frying on the stove to show him the baby in its wickerwork clothesbasket, and while he was looking at it Mrs. Simchak came in, plainly disappointed to find him already home. She said it was one of the prettiest babies she'd ever seen, and Mike wondered what a really homely baby must look like. But he was more concerned about Mary. He saw she was sleeping; somewhat grudgingly the midwife assured him she was doing fine. No complications; it had been a very ordinary birth.

Later that evening the midwife awoke her. Mary opened sleepy eyes. "I was having such a good sleep." Then she saw Mike and smiled. "Hello, Mihal."

"Hello, Marcha."

"Have you seen him?"

He nodded. "I told you it would be a boy. The Dobrejcaks run to boys. How do you feel?"

"I could sleep for a week. I don't want to do anything but sleep." Her eyes moved from him to the bundle in the midwife's arms. "Is he hungry again?"

"Why do you think I woke you? Here, take him."

Mike watched as she put him to her breast, murmuring endearments. The midwife said, "I have some soup for you as soon as you've finished with him," and went downstairs.

"Well," Mary said, "what do you think of your son?"

"He sounds hungry. Listen to him."

"Little pig. Have you seen his eyes? So blue. And look at his little hands, the little fingernails, so perfect — " She kissed the tiny fist. "Mrs. Simchak says he'll bring us good luck because his chest sticks out. He has a big chest and even lying down he sticks it out as though he owned the world."

Mike smiled, and then they were silent for a while. Downstairs Mrs. Simchak was talking. Some girl had burst in — "Oh Mrs. Simchak, I went to your house and they said you were over here, my sister wants you to come right away, she says it's hurting again" — and the midwife was telling her she'd be over later. "And tell your sister not to get so excited, she won't be ready for hours."

Mary glanced at Mike. "Poor Mrs. Vasha. She still has it all ahead of her." She looked down at her own baby and tightened her arm around it.

"How does it feel to be a mother?"

She smiled. "How does it feel to be a father?"

"I don't know." He stared at the bald little head. "Mostly I'm glad it's all over and that you're all right. I'm too tired to feel anything, I guess. I didn't get much sleep last night, and in the morning I start the long turn."

"Is today Saturday? I've even forgotten what day it is."

"Saturday March seven, nineteen-o-three. Which reminds me."

He got out his Bible, a great, gilt-edged volume with deeply embossed covers and metal clasps which he'd bought on installments from a door-to-door salesman. He had it open to the page marked *Births* — the page opposite was marked, in the same elaborate lettering, *Deaths* — and was testing his pen on a scrap of paper when he heard Sophie, Joe's wife, asking about Mary. "A boy? God bless us!" She started up the stairs. Within the next half hour Dorta and Alice also arrived, and Mike was pushed, not unwillingly, into the background.

They named the child John Joseph, after Mike's father; if it had been a girl Mary had planned to name it Pauline. She didn't like her own name; every girl you met was named Mary, she said, and had a sister named Anna.

The month ended tragically. On its last day, the Tuesday after the christening, *I* Furnace slipped. The force of the explosion, failing to dislodge the double bell at the top of the furnace, was diverted into the downcomer, the fat pipe clinging to the outside of the furnace which drew off gases and dust. It blew out the dust-catcher at the base of the furnace and fourteen men were caught in the blast of searing gas and hot dust. Nine were killed — they were literally baked alive — and five badly burned.

Mike heard the dull boom of the explosion while he was still in bed, sleepily wondering if it was time to get up, but paid no attention to it; there was always something rumbling or clanking in the mill. While he was having breakfast Mrs. Perlak, their landlady, burst into the kitchen carrying a tin milk pail and a loaf of Vienna bread. "Oh Mrs. Dobrejcak, Mrs. Dobrejcak!" She'd just come from the store, she said. There had been an explosion in one of the furnaces and heaven only knew how many had been killed.

Mary's hand went to her cheek. "Good God!"

"What furnace?" Mike asked, thinking of Joe.

She didn't know.

Mike went to the door. It was still quite dark; the spring air was sharply cool. There was nothing to see; the mill was only a few lights at the end of the street, a distant murmur in the ear. Washington Street was spotted with the dingy, gaslit windows of saloons and grocery stores, its sidewalks deserted, the footprints of early pedestrians and wheeltracks in the roadway plain marks in the mill dust that had settled during the night. A baker's wagon rattled past. Everything looked as it always did, yet even while he stood there he could feel the news spreading. A man came out on a porch across the street and looked toward the mill, still chewing part of his breakfast; in some backyard a woman's excited voice was calling another woman's name, "Mrs. Martinek, Mrs. Martinek — "

A man came out of Perovsky's saloon on the corner and turned up the street, toward Mike. He recognized a neighbor and called to him as he approached. "I hear there's been an accident in the mill."

The man on the porch listened too; their voices were clear in the quiet street.

The man in the street replied without stopping. "A slip. They don't know yet how many have been killed."

"What furnace?"

"*1*." He was already past.

Joe worked on *D*. Mike closed the door.

It was remarked afterward that, like the disaster of 1895 in which Joe Dubik, among others, had met his death, this too occurred on a Tuesday and at the same hour of the morning, just before five, almost to the minute. "In another hour they would have been safe at home." The same number of men, fourteen, were involved, but in 1895 only six had died.

One of the dead, a man named Skotak, had been in America only two weeks, had not yet drawn his first pay; he left a wife and six children in Poland. Another left a wife and four children in Austria. More dreadful was the news that two pairs of brothers were among the dead. One pair, whom Mike did not know, had been in America a month. The other pair he knew very well; they had boarded with Dorta's neighbor, Mrs. Novotny. The elder of the brothers had come to Braddock the previous summer, when a strike had shut down the hard-coal mines in the eastern part of the state, a squat, stoop-shouldered man whom Mike remembered chiefly for a strike song he used to sing: "Me Johnny Mitchell man."

Mary's eyes were frightened when Mike left for work that morning. "Take care of yourself, Mihal."

"Sure. Don't worry about me."

"How can I help it?"

He was filling his pipe. "I know how to take care of myself."

"Much good that does when something like this happens."

"Now, now. I know how you feel but what good does it do to worry? After all, I've been working eleven years and nothing has happened to me yet." He struck a match. "Besides, when you worry it only makes it harder for me. And I have to work, we have to eat."

He put on his overcoat and cap, his clean hands and face making them look even older and dirtier than they were. "My bucket?"

She handed him his lunch bucket, oval-shaped, mottled blue enamel, promisingly heavy. "You will be careful, Mihal?" She smiled not very successfully. "Remember you have a family now."

"Do you think I ever forget it?" He kissed her. "*S Bohom.*"

"*S Bohom.*"

At Eleventh he turned and waved a hand. Mary, standing in the doorway, waved back. Then he went on toward the mill.

The first of the dead were buried the next day, the mill, as was its custom, contributing seventy-five dollars toward the cost of each funeral. Father Kazincy was in bed with a broken leg — he had been thrown by a horse, he was fond of horseback riding, much to the scandal of his more conservative parishioners — and a priest was called over from Duquesne to conduct the services.

5

THEY moved in May. "One bride moves out and another moves in," Mrs. Perlak commented sentimentally. "I only hope my son and his wife will get along as well as you two." Mary hated to leave, not only because their new home, Dzmura's houses on Willow Way, was a considerably less attractive place in which to live. "As long as we stayed in Mrs. Perlak's house I could feel like a bride," she told Mike with a rueful smile. "Now I'm just another old married woman."

Mike liked living in the alley even less than Mary, but they had been unable to rent anywhere else. Their two rooms were at the Twelfth Street end of the row, facing the alley, which of course had no sidewalks and was so narrow that Mary could buy from hucksters' wagons without moving off her own doorstep. The rent was five dollars a month, one dollar less than they had been paying Mrs. Perlak. They shared the cellar and the stairs to the bedrooms with a Mrs. Marga, whose rooms faced the courtyard, overshadowed by the high brick rear of Dzmura's hotel on Washington and forever hung with wash.

The mill got a new General Superintendent, a man named Dinkey, who had been the former Superintendent's assistant. His promotion revived arguments, never settled, as to whether the small, soprano-whistled yard locomotives had been named after him. In July the new road to Turtle Creek was opened; heretofore Main

Street traffic had followed the old township road, around which the mill had grown solidly, and streetcar passengers had been carried within toasting distance of red-hot ingots standing outside the rail mill. The new road curved sharply to the left just beyond Thirteenth Street, keeping outside the mill altogether. Mrs. Hillis, Mrs. Dexter's mother, died. In September the new First Ward school was opened, a big handsome building with electric lights and inside toilets. Mike's interest in it was proprietary; it would be his son's school in a few years.

But more important than any of these matters was the fact that work in the mills slowed down during the summer, and instead of picking up in the fall, grew steadily worse.

By November Mike was getting only three turns a week, and the first of the year the company announced a wage cut. It brought the wages of unskilled labor down to thirteen-and-a-half cents an hour, the lowest in fifteen years, and convinced many people that the company's offer of United States Steel stock to its employees had been exactly what they suspected, a device to find out how much money the workers could save on the wages they were getting, how much less they could be paid and still keep alive.

That was a hard winter. It gave way to a spring bringing little more than proof to Mary that she was going to have another baby. The expected upturn failed to appear. The mills stayed on part time and people said with grim humor that even the saloonkeepers were beginning to complain. The drop in immigration was noticeable, though the steamship companies cut steerage rates drastically; one could cross the Atlantic that summer for ten dollars, in quarters which compared favorably with the holds of old-time slave ships.

Mary's second baby — a girl she named Pauline — was born in November, and Mike cast his first vote that same month. He voted for Roosevelt; Bryan had not been nominated. A candidate in whom the First Ward took a more personal interest was Joe Perovsky, who ran for council. He was backed by the local Republican machine and Joe Wold, and won handily. His temerity had awed the First Ward; his victory spread jubilation. The Slovaks were certainly getting ahead when one of them, scarcely twenty years in America, could be elected to public office. Perovsky's own prestige and business in his saloon increased tremendously.

Conditions improved during the winter. In the spring, about the time the wage cut was restored, Alice eloped to Cleveland with a certain Frank Koval and Mrs. Dexter gave Anna a job as upstairs girl. As she said herself, she had almost no choice; all the Kracha girls were destined to work for her.

Work was steady again and full pays were the rule, but bad times didn't let themselves be forgotten in a day. Mike was in debt to the landlord, the butcher, the grocer. Both he and Mary needed new clothes, new things for the house. The months of slow work had done dreadful things to his savings account; he now had less than fifty dollars in the bank on Main Street. "As far as money in the bank goes," he said, "I'm exactly where I was ten years ago. Another ten years like this and I'll be back on the cinder dump."

Mary was at her machine, sewing. Before long she'd have to start cooking supper and packing Mike's lunch bucket. The kitchen door was open. Dusty sunshine fell past the roof lines into the alley where a neighbor's girl was jumping rope while Johnny watched from the doorstep and Pauline slept in her carriage. From farther down the alley a huckster sent his chant echoing between the houses. A Jew, he cried his wares in bad Slovak and a minor key.

"I never knew you lived on the cinder dump," Mary said.

"Sure. Dorta was one of the first to move there, after the fire. You don't remember that, do you?"

"Only from hearing people talk about it."

"That would be — I came in '89 — lived with Dorta on Washington about a year — then we got burned out — about 1890 or '91."

"We were still living in Homestead. We didn't come to Braddock until after the strike."

The company houses on the cinder dump, the stables and soap factory, had been torn down several years before. The company was using the land to store scrap and pig iron.

Mary bit off a length of thread. "I hated Braddock," she said. She wet the end of the thread and aimed it at her needle's eye.

"Mostly on account of school. I didn't know anybody and the American girls were always making fun of us. I remember in the toilets the boys would holler from their side that they could see us; you remember the outside toilets they had then. The girls were just as bad; they'd pick up our dresses and make fun of us because we didn't wear drawers. I was never so ashamed in my life. I cried and told my mother I wouldn't go to school any more unless she bought me drawers."

Mike grinned. "Girls don't wear drawers in the old country. Dorta has been here a long time and still has to put on her first pair."

In the alley the neighbor's girl had stopped jumping rope. She and Johnny were contemplating another child who, with exquisite deliberation, was biting the little colored candy buttons off a licorice strap.

"If someone had told me then that I was going to marry Kracha's little girl, that screeching, dirty-faced brat over there — "

"Are you sorry?"

"No." He stretched out his legs and crossed his bare ankles. "If I'm sorry about anything it's that we don't seem to be getting anywhere."

"We will. It isn't as though you didn't want to work or spent your whole pay in the saloons. Everybody goes through things like this. Do you think we're the only ones?"

"That doesn't make it any easier to bear. Besides, is that all we can expect? To be like everybody else? I had hoped for more than that."

She turned to look at him. "Something is bothering you."

"Nothing. Can't a man talk?"

The neighbor's girl was saying, "I don't like likrish. It makes me vomit." Johnny, too young for such dissimulation, was bent forward, hands locked between his knees and all but dribbling at the mouth.

"I'll tell you what's bothering me," Mike said. He gestured toward the bright doorway. "It's a fine day — and I have to go to work. I'll be thirty years old in a few months — and I have no more money in the bank than I had ten years ago. There you have it."

"Don't joke with me, Mihal. If something is bothering you tell me what it is and maybe we can do something about it."

"I have told you."

"Are you beginning to wish you were single again?"

"*Ach!*"

"What is it? Tell me."

"I feel restless. I want things I can't have — a house with a front porch and a garden instead of this dirty alley — a good job — more money in my pocket — more time for myself, time to live — " He moved his hand expressively.

Mary kept her eyes on him. "Don't think too much about such things, Mihal. That only makes it worse."

"Do you ever think about them?"

She shrugged.

"When Anna comes here do you ever wish you were still working for Mrs. Dexter?"

"Why should I wish a thing like that?"

"You know why. So you could be at the seashore now instead of here in Braddock. So you could have lots of clothes, money in your pocket, nothing to worry about."

Mary sniffed. "I'd rather have my husband and children and my own home. Don't think Anna has it so easy. Mrs. Dexter makes her work for everything she gets."

"I hope you mean what you say."

"Of course I mean it. Mihal, sometimes I wonder what kind of woman you think I am."

Mary glanced at the clock and turned back to her sewing. She ran the machine — an old secondhand model with a hood and a sluggish treadle — to the end of the seam and then piled the material in her lap, began pulling out basting threads. "Don't get discouraged, Mihal," she said. "If we do our best and trust in God everything will come out all right."

The licorice eater said, very clearly, "Sticks and stones will break my bones but names will never hurt me. Nyah!"

"Mihal."

"What?"

"Now that the mills are working steady again don't you think it would be a good idea — even Dorta says it would be a good idea to get four rooms and — "

"I don't care what Dorta says."

"We have to do something, Mihal. If you say no boarders, all right. But Mrs. Marga is going to move to Halket and take in boarders and we could have her rooms."

"Since when has Mrs. Marga been moving?"

"She only mentioned it the other day. She asked me if we were thinking of moving and I said no. She has to do something, poor woman. You know how her husband has been ever since the accident. He's not much good in the mills any more and pretty soon they won't let him work at all."

"Well, if she wants to move let her move."

"I could keep her kitchen and make this our bedroom. The boarders upstairs. We could get beds secondhand. And the extra money would certainly be a big help."

"We are eating every day, aren't we?"

Her voice was gently rebuking. "Mihal, is that a way to talk? Sure we're eating every day. But look at what we owe. We need clothes. We need things for the house. And instead of getting ahead we can't even keep up-to-date, every payday we slide back a little more."

She was telling him nothing he didn't already know and she may have suspected that he was fighting against admitting he couldn't support his family as much as against an invasion of his home, his privacy. She said, "I think you're making a mountain out of nothing. It's no disgrace to take in boarders. Your own brother — "

"What Joe does is his own business. If he should take it into his head to jump in the river does that mean I would have to do the same?"

She smiled at such childishness. "Mihal."

"Marcha, listen to me. It's all very well to say the extra work won't kill you. But I didn't marry to have my wife take in boarders. Do you think I'd enjoy seeing you cooking and washing for strangers? I married to have my own home. And I know what it's like when a couple takes in boarders. The woman becomes nothing but a drudge and the husband finds himself little more than one of his wife's boarders. What the devil kind of way to live is that?"

"Don't talk so loud, Mihal." She added, rising — the neighbor's girl and Johnny had closed in on the licorice eater simultaneously and the alley was hideous with his bawling — "Well, whatever you say. I want you to be happy in your own home."

So did he; but facing them was the inescapable fact that even with work good and the wage cut restored they couldn't live on what he made; or rather, they could just keep alive. A full week of seven days, eighty-four hours — ninety-six in the weeks he worked the long turn — brought him about thirteen dollars. Two people, if they were thrifty, their wants simple, could manage on that. Two people with debts and growing children could not.

There was only one thing to do, and by the time Anna returned to Braddock, tanned and handsomely gowned and inclined to stress the vast superiority of Bethany Beach to the First Ward, Mary had taken over Mrs. Marga's rooms and acquired six boarders, hand-picked by Mike himself.

6

"KEEPING boarders" had recognized customs, a code of behavior for landladies and boarders of which no one who lived in the First Ward was ignorant. Dorta needed to teach Mary very little. The secret of being a successful boarding missus, she said, was to make the boarders understand from the beginning that she was boss. "Don't be afraid to yell at them," Dorta said. "The more you yell the easier you make it for yourself. If they don't like the way you run your house let them go somewhere else. But I don't think you'll have any trouble. The men who know Mike all respect him and he's not the kind who will stand for any monkey business. The only thing I'm afraid of is that you'll try to work yourself to death."

"*Ach!*"

"Never mind, *ach*. I know your kind. You worry and try to do too much. That's why I tell you, don't try to keep your house as though for your own family. Don't worry yourself sick if something goes wrong. You're running a business now, remember that. Give them what they pay for and no more. No foolishness like making *pirohi* for them on Fridays. *Halushki* are good enough."

Mike added his own warning, when Mary reported what Dorta had told her. "She is right. And if I see it becoming too much for you, out they go."

He had no complaint until the first washday. He came home from a night in the mill to find the kitchen floor hip-deep with dirty clothes — their own, the children's, the boarders'. Appalled — Mary herself looked rather dazed — he made her get a neighbor to help, paying her fifty cents.

None of the boarders was a complete stranger to Mike but for a while he was stiffly self-conscious, almost truculent, in their presence. As time passed they got to know one another better; the boarders became individual human beings rather than invading strangers, ordinary men who worked in the mill and had the common troubles, the common pleasures. They came and went, to the mill and back, eating, sleeping, shaving, sitting around the yard talking. Mike found his position as head of the house never questioned; on the contrary, his years in America, his ability to read and write English, his citizenship paper, earned him their respect. His opinions were listened to, his judgment on nearly anything American accepted as final.

The boarders added about thirty dollars a month clear to their income. By spring they were clear of debt and Mike was putting something into the bank almost every payday. Mary bought things for the house, new oilcloth for the bedroom — the old was put in the kitchen — new curtains, a larger stove. She yearned for a parlor, a set of silverware and a kitchen cabinet. They bought new clothes, a suit and shoes for Mike, a whole new outfit, dress, coat, hat and shoes, for Mary; and that winter, for the first time since Johnny was born, they were able to attend an occasional ball at Turner Hall.

These were held — on Friday nights, usually, so that the festivities could continue after midnight — by one or another Slovak society, and were the most important social affairs in the First Ward. Each was looked forward to for weeks ahead, and when the great night arrived and they turned up Penn Way toward the hall, saw the lights above the doorway, the people standing around or pushing in and out, Mary squeezed his arm with excitement. The cold darkness outside and the bright lights within, the beer flowing copiously in the basement barroom and the gipsies making music upstairs, the pretty girls in their party dresses, the jokes and laughter and gossip with old friends who looked strange in their best clothes and company manners, the very children skating across the floor between dances — everything combined to make a man feel good, feel pleasure in merely being present. Dancing with Mary, her cheeks flushed, her eyes bright, was like old times, like being young and in love again. It was even worth having it end at last, and remembering as they walked home through the quiet, foggy streets, that he had to get up and go to work tomorrow. No, today.

For Christmas, made more than ordinarily merry by an announcement that unskilled labor would be raised to sixteen-and-a-half cents an hour, there was a tree in the bedroom, a tricycle for Johnny, a set of furs for Mary, and for Mike something he had long wanted: a combination bookcase and desk. The bookcase part had a tall, narrow door of curved glass, not flat but billowing outward in a smooth, shiny, obviously expensive curve. A slanting leaf, rich with carving, pulled down to make a writing table and revealed interesting cubbyholes and drawers inside. The children were made to understand that breaking the curved glass would mean little less than the end of the world, and every visitor was taken into the bedroom and allowed to admire it and to be impressed by Mike's collection of books, the great Bible and a dozen or so other volumes, most of which the secondhand dealer had thrown in while they were bargaining for the stove.

Mary cooked and baked and the boarders shared in the Christmas feast at no extra cost, though they gave small presents to the children. Mike, home from the mill — ordinary millworkers had two holidays a year, Christmas and the Fourth of July, but blast furnace workers had none at all — made a half-speech, half-prayer, at the table:

"We give thanks for our health and for the happiness this past year has brought us. May the coming year bring us all good fortune, good health and happiness. Yet if worse comes, may we have the strength and courage to bear it. God's will be done."

Mary and the boarders murmured, "Amen."

Johnny got tipsy on a mouthful of Tokay.

7

THERE was a flood in March. The mills had filled in the shore line for miles up and down the river, destroying trees, obliterating little streams and the pebbly beaches where as recently as the turn of the century campers had set up tents in summer, burying the clean earth under tons of cinder and molten slag. The banks no longer sloped naturally to the water's edge but dropped vertically, twenty-foot walls of cold slag pierced at intervals with steaming outlets and marked by dribbling stains.

Between its lifeless banks the river was for most of the year a sluggish, unnoticed stream, one-third water, one-third mud and one-third human and industrial sewage; but every spring the rains, the melting snows of the West Virginia mountains, lifted it to flood stage. Then it seemed to race by, its current visible, its surface littered with every imaginable kind of floating matter. There were headlines in the newspapers, mill officials scurried about excited and futile, and people went down to the foot of Eleventh Street, or one of the other places (there weren't many) where mills and factories didn't completely block off the river from the town, and stood there looking at it, at the river. Someone was forever seeing a dead body, and there were the usual arguments; and nearly always there would be a young fellow puttering around a rowboat drawn up on the shore, laconic and preoccupied but obviously prepared to brave the raging torrent without hesitation if a mother and child, say, or a lovely girl with most of her clothes torn off her (as in that lithograph of the Johnstown flood in Gyurik's saloon) came floating by on a chicken coop. None ever did; still, the possibility alone was exciting.

Some years, though, the rains and snows had been really heavy and there were even fewer trees standing on the mountains than had stood there the year before. Then the river came up over its banks so many remorseless inches an hour, invaded the railroad tracks, the mill, the alleys and cellars of the First Ward. That was bad. After a while it retreated, leaving a dreadful smelling muck behind. That was, almost, worse.

The Fire Department came down with its hoses and flushed the streets clean; the First Ward scrubbed itself and dried out in the sun and stopped boiling its drinking water. Johnny watched the firemen cleaning Twelfth Street — with his nose flattened against the kitchen window and his neck swollen with mumps. Mary blamed the dampness. The waters had splashed against their doorstep, filled the cellar and floated the outhouse off its foundation — *there* was a mess — but their house, their furniture, had not suffered any damage.

While people were still welcoming visitors for the pleasure of displaying high-water marks on the cellar steps, President Corey, of the United States Steel Corporation and the North Braddock Coreys, married an actress and went to Paris on his honeymoon; and while people were still talking about that Kracha came to visit Mike and Mary and was hardly inside the door before he was exclaiming, "What the devil are they doing on Halket Avenue?"

"Building new tracks."

"Good God, I worked on the railroad long enough to know new tracks when I see them! Nobody has to tell me." He sat down, looking thoroughly upset. "So they got around to it at last, God damn them. It was like a slap in the face when I saw it."

"They started in the spring, right after the flood." His face lathered, Mike continued to strop his razor. "It's a shame how they're tearing down all those fine houses and big trees. That used to be a nice place to walk in the summer. A pity. I understand they intend to build a new station the other side of Eighth Street. No more Ninth Street station."

"I could hardly believe my eyes. I got off the car and came down Eleventh Street and there it was, looking like another San Francisco earthquake. By God, I'd like five minutes with Joe Perovsky, that sonnomabitch."

"They say he made a good piece of money out of some property he sold the railroad."

"He'd make money in hell. Do you know it was on his advice that I bought three lots on Halket ten years ago? They helped me lose my butcher shop, those accursed lots. Perovsky said the railroad was going to build new tracks and I could ask my own price. Ten years ago!"

Mike knew the story. "Comfort yourself, you were simply ahead of your time," he said, grinning. He pinged his razor with his thumbnail and examined his face in the mirror with a probably unintentional air of quiet satisfaction. "Did you notice what they're doing on Thirteenth Street?"

"Thirteenth Street? Don't tell me they're building a bridge to Kennywood. That would be too much."

"A bridge? No. The mill is building a wall where the cinder slope used to be, with a tunnel at Washington for the men to go through."

"I suppose Perovsky made something out of that, too."

Mike doubted it.

Kracha grumbled unintelligibly to himself. Then, "Have you some schnapps around? I could use a drink."

"In the desk in the bedroom. Be careful how you close that door; I don't want the glass broken."

Kracha went into the bedroom and came back with a quart bottle of whisky, half full. "Who scratched your desk?"

"Johnny, with his bicycle."

"Well, now it's christened you don't have to worry about it, nothing will happen to it any more. Have you ever noticed? No matter what you buy it's like that." Under cover of talk Kracha poured himself a drink and drank it; now, somewhat more deliberately, he poured another. "It's a fancy piece of furniture but I still think you could have found a better use for the money. What the devil do you want with a desk? You don't write two letters a month."

Mike wiped his razor on a scrap of paper. "I wanted it so I got it."

"If you had to show off why didn't you get a talking machine, like my boarding missus? Then at least you'd have some pleasure for your money. But a desk." Kracha snorted. "Shall I pour you one?"

"No. And put the bottle back; I have thirsty boarders."

Kracha drank and smoothed out his mustache. "Where is Mary?"

"Out with the children. I think she went to see Sophie. You know she had another boy?"

Kracha didn't. But he knew that Alice was pregnant again; he'd stopped there on his way to Mike's and Frank had failed to offer him a drink. And he'd already heard that Dorta's elder son, Joie, was marrying in a month.

"Did you work last night?"

Mike nodded. "I got out of bed ten minutes ago." He scraped noisily. "Have you seen Anna?"

"Not since Easter."

"She doesn't come around so often since they moved to Squirrel Hill." Mrs. Dexter had sold her house and ground — after much heart-searching, Anna reported, much wondering if her mother would have approved — to a committee which turned it into a hospital, Braddock's first. Mrs. Dexter had received thirty thousand dollars. The hospital was already inadequate.

Kracha stared out at the yard. It was in shade but the high back of Dzmura's hotel, all windows, fire escapes and yellow brick, was hot and bright with sunshine; Sunday sunshine, which was always hotter and brighter than any other. "I wonder how much he made out of it?"

"Who? Oh, Perovsky." Mike shrugged. "More than you and I make in a year."

"And we work for it. That sonnomabitch. I bet if I met him on the street he wouldn't even speak to me. And I can remember when he all but kissed you if you spent five cents in his pigsty of a saloon. But now he's a big man, a politician. Much good his being a councilman has done anyone."

"He's put our people on the streetcleaners and down the waterworks."

"*Ach!*"

"It's something. Before him it was all Irish."

"I suppose you voted for him."

Mike, shaving his upper lip, grunted.

"More fool you."

The doorway darkened. Steve Bodnar, large and hearty in his shirtsleeves, greeted them noisily. Then, "God bless me, is that a bottle of whisky I see on the table?"

Mike groaned. "I told you to put it back!"

"Listen to him. Have I asked you for a drink?"

"I buy whisky to give my boarders a drink when they pay their board and every bum for miles around knows it at once."

"Well, since you insist, one drink. I don't want to hurt your feelings."

"Never mind my feelings."

Bodnar sat down across the table from Kracha and poured. "Well, Djuro, how's everything in Homestead?"

"Not too good."

"Ah. I thought it was only in Braddock they were slowing down."

"So far," Kracha said, "I've worked pretty steady. But the plate mills are beginning to lay them off, and you know what that means. When they stop, everything stops."

"You hear that, Mike? They're laying them off in the plate mills."

Mike had put away his razor and was pouring water into the washbasin. "Maybe they're making too much money. I read in the paper not long ago that the company made last year — how much do you suppose?" He bent over the basin, doused his face and then sought a usable patch on the roller towel. "One hundred and sixty million dollars. Clear profit. Gary himself said so."

"A hundred and sixty million," Kracha said. "Think of that."

"We work for a big company," Bodnar said. "Maybe the biggest in the world."

"A hundred and sixty million," Kracha repeated, and shook his head slowly. It was impossible to imagine that much money.

"If they're making such big profits why are they slowing down?" Bodnar asked.

Mike shrugged.

Bodnar picked up his glass. "*Bohze daj zdrave,*" he said, and drank. "Well," he went on, wiping his mouth on the back of his hand, "maybe it's only summer slack."

It wasn't.

8

THE rail mills, the industry's most sensitive barometer, went on part time. The other departments, the converters, blooming mills, foundries and repair shops, followed suit of necessity. The blast furnaces couldn't be easily shut down but the pace of their operations could be slackened, and was; even so, half the metal they produced, instead of being sent to the mixer and thence through the rolling mills, was poured into the pig machine and then stored in great, rusting hills along the riverfront. Nor did it end there; each falling block knocked down the next. What was happening in the steel towns, itself an effect, caused men to be laid off in the West Virginia coal mines, in the Connellsville coke ovens, in the Minnesota iron mines, on the ships and railroads which had less coke, coal and iron ore to move, in the stores which had fewer customers for their stocks of clothing and furniture.

Bad times had come again, as so often before.

"When they raised wages without being asked I knew it wasn't right," Mary said. "I knew it was too good to last."

Like practically every other man in the mill Mike at first almost welcomed layoffs. To sleep late, stay up late, have whole days to himself, was a luxury a blast furnace worker could appreciate more than most men. As the panic deepened, as men were laid off for increasingly longer periods, he began to worry. His greatest fear became that he'd lose his job as Keogh's helper, be put in one of the labor gangs, the stove gang most likely, and rather than submit to that he was prepared to quit. He told Keogh, "Mr. Keogh, I want to keep this job. If they put me in other gang, all right, job is a job, but if they put me in stove gang I quit first."

"Why, Mike," Keogh said dryly, "you know Hughie would be tickled pink to get you in his gang."

"Sure, I know. But I quit first."

This Hughie, a stove gang boss, was a skinny, tight-faced Irishman with a fouler tongue than most; and in Slovak opinion the outstanding Irish characteristic was a dirty mouth. He was a bad man to work under, not so much because he drove his men hard — all bosses did that — as because he made the worker-boss relationship an unpleasantly personal one. Working under him was less a matter of doing one's work well than of pleasing him, of allowing for his prejudices, flattering him, noting whether he was in good humor, laughing at his insults, letting him take the credit for good work, and at all times building up his self-esteem by fearing him. He didn't like Mike. He once told him, "You're a smart Hunky and I don't like smart Hunkies. Furshtay?"

By December Mike was getting only three turns a week. Times were the worst in memory. Even cash money disappeared. In November the mill had started paying the men with Clearinghouse scrip and a stricken wail went up from the First Ward. "What's the world coming to? They don't even pay with real money any more. We work and work and they pay us with paper." One couldn't even get one's own money from the bank.

Scrip pays continued for three months; then — what it had given one year it took away the next — the company cut wages and resumed paying in cash. It was a long while before times were good again. It was as though the country had been beaten to its knees and could rise again only a little at a time, as its strength returned.

That was an election year, and the company spread word that if the Republicans won, and more particularly the Penrose men — local option had become a threat to the machine — the mills might resume full-time operations. It did more. During the May primaries a number of departmental bosses prominent in the local option movement were called into the General Superintendent's office and ordered to support the Penrose candidates, who were of course identified with the liquor interests. They were told their first duty was to the company and the company needed Penrose in the Senate and, therefore, Penrose men in the State Legislature; popular election of Senators was still five years in the future. And the summoned ones obeyed, bosses though they were, while from Duquesne came the usual reports of men fired for refusing to vote as the company wished.

Mike had, like most Slovak males, little respect for the temperance movement and no faith whatever in company promises. He and Joe, who was voting for the first time, voted the straight Republican ticket out of prudence as much as out of admiration for Roosevelt, who had been attacking the trusts, including the sacrosanct steel trust itself, with a great deal of sound and fury.

Roosevelt's choice, Taft, won, Penrose won, Joe Perovsky won. It made no immediate difference. Mike did some figuring and reckoned that he had earned two hundred and eighty dollars during the year. Without the boarders they would have been, as many were, on the edge of destitution, sunk in debt. Only the boarders, Mary's work, had brought them through without disaster. And Mary was pregnant again.

Her baby, a boy they named after his father, was born on Decoration Day, a Sunday, though Mary had been hoping it would be born nearer, even on, her seventh wedding anniversary. She was in bed for three weeks. Pregnant or not the housework had had to be done, the boarders fed; and the strain had told.

Johnny started going to school that September. The first of the year the company raised the wages of unskilled labor to seventeen-and-a-half cents an hour and announced an accident and compensation plan. And that spring, while Halley's Comet flared portentously across the sky, Anna won a cakewalk at Turner Hall with a young man whom she described as the freshest fellow she had ever known; and with whom, by the summer's end, she was going steady.

His name was John Baraj, which he had Anglicized into Barry

on joining the Army. When the panic of 1907 eased him out of a job he and several others had enlisted. On the theory that riding was better than walking he had joined the cavalry, and had spent three dreary years in Kansas, learning to sit on a horse, cleaning stables and drinking bootleg beer. Nothing so impressed the First Ward with the horrors of prohibition as his stories of paying fifty cents for a bottle of beer. He was now driving a wagon for a bottler of pop and soda waters but he talked of getting a job as a bartender as soon as he saved enough money to join the union.

9

GOOD things. Foggy mornings with gray mist filling all the spaces between the furnaces, the iron sheds, and veiling their harsh ugliness, feeling good against his face as he came out of the cast-house and giving the air a clean taste, though Steve Bodnar coughed dramatically. "Devil take this fog! I need a drink to wash it out of my lungs." "It's as good an excuse as any." They went across the yard, their heavy shoes crunching in the cinders. The fog filled the valley, softening distance, streaking rooftops with dampness. Chimneys were smoking with breakfast fires. A snug, ordered world — the mill here, home yonder; work, and after work, rest. "Do you remember the mornings in the old country when the fields were white with frost?" "If it rains before Sunday I'm going for mushrooms. Will you come?" "If it rains."

When it rained the streets emptied; the rain beat against the windows and the wind blew down the chimney, forcing puffs of smoke out of the stove. He buttoned his coat to his chin. "Somehow I don't mind going to work on rainy days."

"Take the umbrella."

"I have a whole furnace to dry out by. Besides, the rain is never as wet during working hours."

"What kind of talk is that?"

"*Na moj' pravdu.* But you never had an outside job."

On rainy days it was permissible to stop for a drink in Gyurik's or Wold's, shaking off the rain as one entered, leaving the little glass of whisky standing before one on the bar until the last minute, prolonging anticipation while one commented on the weather, on work and the war in the Balkans. On rainy days everything in the mill steamed, cinders, ladles, pig iron, ingots. Puddles of water in the wrong places took on explosive qualities; wet ore and limestone were a nuisance in the stockyard, the hot blast man went around cursing the enginehouse and the furnace keepers nagged them all. Water lines usually chose wet days to make trouble, as though the world wasn't damp enough already. But after rain the sky was clean for a while even above the mill.

On clear nights, with the first taste of spring in the air, there were few stars visible once he was inside the mill. Looking up he saw the furnaces and stoves, piled one behind the other into the distance, small lights, and over beyond the rail mill the wavering glow of the Bessemers. A steel mill at night made a man feel small as he trudged into its pile of structures, its shadows. A cast-house filled suddenly with illumination as the furnace was tapped and the bright glare of the molten metal was like a conflagration around the end of an alleyway, silhouetting waiting ladles, the corner of an enginehouse, skeleton beams. Smoke swirled lazily through angular shadows. Passing, he felt the heat of the ladles; up in the cast-house hardly more of the men than their faces could be seen across the metal's glare. The dinkey's engineer sat motionless in the cab, thinking his own thoughts.

Keogh and the new stove gang boss were in the furnace keeper's shanty talking about the blast furnace boss who had lost his mind, a big, stolid-looking Irishman, the last person in the world one would have expected to do such a thing. People said he'd gone crazy trying to invent a new kind of horseshoe, one that didn't need nailing or something like that, which — if true — made him a grotesque, pathetic figure to stand beside the more fortunate craftsmen the Braddock plant had given to steelmaking: Morrison with his double bells, Gayley with his bronze cooling plates for blast furnace walls and the dry-air blast, and Captain Jones who with his famous Jones mixer, his apparatus for compressing ingots while casting, his hot beds for bending rails, and a score of other devices might almost be said to have single-handedly invented the American steel industry.

Mike left his bucket in the shanty and went out; and a moment later Keogh and the new stove gang boss came out too. The old stove gang boss, Hughes, had been fired for taking graft. Every payday the men in his gang had paid a dollar each into a fund of which Hughes was treasurer, ostensibly buying a chance on a new suit. It was understood, of course, that no one ever actually won a suit. With a newcomer to the gang, however, Hughes overreached himself. The newcomer, a Lithuanian, had paid his dollar every payday no more grudgingly than most, but when the better job in another gang which Hughes had promised to get him — for ten dollars cash, paid in advance — failed to materialize, he complained to the company's chief of detectives. Hughes confessed, was discharged and wisely disappeared from Braddock.

Keogh said, "He didn't lose any time getting out of town, did he? Not that I blame him, considering how many people were looking for him. I guess you ain't sorry he's gone, hey Mike?"

"He bad man, Mr. Keogh. I don't like nobody to lose job, but he bad man."

Keogh's lips moved, pursed and spat. "Well," he said, "I always thought Hunkies were pretty dumb but damned if I ever thought anybody could be dumb enough to pay money to work in Hughie's gang."

Mike shrugged. "Hughie the boss, Mr. Keogh. They need job. They no speak good English. They afraid to say anything."

"Yeah, I know. But just the same — "

His free use of the word Hunky rankled, as always. "Mr. Keogh,

if you tell me sometimes, Mike, pay me one dollar every payday
or you no work for me, what you think I do? I no like, but I need
job. Is right? Or if Mr. Hooker come to you and say you have to
pay him or lose job. What you do?"

"In the first place he wouldn't. And in the second place if he
did I'd tell him to go kiss my royal American." Keogh scratched a
bristly jaw. "I hope."

It was much better with Hughes gone.

The furnace purred as he ate at midnight, facing the cast-house,
his back against the shanty. Taking the lid off his bucket he always
thought of Mary. Keogh came out of the shanty eating an apple
and went slowly from one peephole to another. He could find no
fault. A dinkey pushed ladles under the edge of the platform and
departed, fussily ridiculous as always. Keogh strolled back. Mike
said, "Everything all right, hey Mr. Keogh?"

"Did you tell him more coke?"

"Just now, before I eat."

Keogh went into the shanty. Mike chewed food and stared contentedly at the furnace. They knew how to handle her.

Things went wrong more easily on day turns, perhaps because
there were more bosses around. Even the head blower tightened one's
nerves, while when the General Superintendent entered the cast-
house, well dressed, papers in hand, coldly inscrutable of counte-
nance, it was like God appearing on earth and produced a comparable
chaos. Lesser bosses went into a hysteria of activity over a barrow-
ful of cinders or a splash of metal on the tracks, hovered around
him in taut, eager servility. For this was not a man like other men;
this was the General Superintendent, the godlike dispenser of jobs
and layoffs, life and death. Mike would glance cautiously at him
from time to time. His clothes were of wool, his shoes of leather,
and by an effort Mike could imagine him eating, lying with a woman
or even laughing. But what he thought and felt, what it was that
made him think and feel as he did — this was inconceivable, and
it was this that set him apart. Mike could guess how it must feel
to be a boss, looking busy and worried, ordering men around, en-

joying their fear; but the General Superintendent wasn't an ordinary man set a little above others much like himself. He was of a different species altogether, partaking of the company's inhuman incomprehensibility and like the company going his way, doing this, doing that, hiring, firing, shutting down, cutting wages, raising them, and giving no reasons, maintaining throughout a cold impassibility before which a man felt himself divested of humanity, to which it was impossible to appeal or reason with, one's love and hate alike unnoticed, unfelt, unwanted.

More subtly, his presence disturbed the rhythm, the relationship, between worker and job. With his appearance the furnace and the men became separate. It was now his furnace and they its servants, and his; for its well-being they were responsible now not to the furnace and to themselves, their pride in knowing how to handle her, but to him. He took it away from them. They ceased to be men of skill and knowledge, ironmakers, and were degraded to the status of employees who did what they were told for a wage, whose feelings didn't matter, not even their feelings for the tools, the machines, they worked with, or for the work they did.

When the whistle blew at the end of the day they went home, dusk heavy in the valley, heavier over the mill, lamps pale against the evening sky, a day's work done but the furnaces, the rolling mills, going on; men might tire but they didn't, no matter how much work was done it was never enough. A river boat pushed empty barges toward the locks at Port Perry, its wheel white with water; on the B. and O. a Pittsburgh-bound train swept its yellow-windowed cars through the mill, its whistle seeming to come for a long distance through the gathering twilight and making him restless, calling up memories of evenings in town, the echoing station at the foot of Smithfield Street, the stores, the theaters and crowds. Saturday night was certainly a fine night to dress up and go out.

On Saturday nights, especially if it was a Saturday after payday, he and Mary went up street. People who lived in North Braddock said "down street" and sounded funny. Mary had only so much money to spend and so many things to buy, but it cost nothing to look at store windows and the pictures in front of the Crystal Theater, to enjoy the excitement of lights and crowded sidewalks. Clutching her purse she would linger before Schmidt's window, not to admire the watches and rings but to see what pattern of silverware was on display. Leisurely, carefully, they shopped for the needed underwear and dress goods and what not, remembered to stop in the five-and-ten for a bag of candy for the children and then strolled back to Washington, which on pay Saturdays was almost as crowded and lively as Main Street itself.

Home, Mary paid off the neighbor's girl with a handful of chicken corn candy for watching the children and had a second, reassuring look at the dress goods even before she took off her hat. "You can't tell what a thing really looks like until you get it home." Mike coughed. "Well, I think I'll go down to Wold's for an hour." "Don't stay out too late, Mihal." He seldom did; it wasn't wise for a man who had a long turn starting in the morning.

The first twelve hours were much like any day turn except that sometimes, through a break in the mill's rumble, he could hear church bells. If his hands were free he tipped his hat. The second twelve hours were like nothing else in life. Exhaustion slowly numbed his body, mercifully fogged his mind; he ceased to be a human being, became a mere appendage to the furnace, a lost, damned creature. "At three o'clock in the morning of a long turn a man could die without knowing it."

"And go right on working till the whistle blew. *Pravdu maš, pravdu.*"

There were men, young and lusty, who could go swinging home at the end but after a man passed thirty he plodded like the oldest, shoulders slumped, legs heavy, bloodshot eyes burning in a blackened face. When a man was young he could work all day and then go to Turner Hall and dance away half the night; when a man was young he could read a newspaper or study to be a citizen or argue with his friends, delighting in the sharpness and agility of his wit; but after a man passed thirty he was satisfied to go home in the evening and change into clean clothes and just sit, his very hands weary, the thoughts of his mind like the mumble of an old man in a chimney corner, as unintelligible as they were unimportant.

Mike got pleasure out of his children, out of watching them, listening to them — the way they babbled in English delighted him as though they had been uniquely blessed by heaven — marveling at their ability to live in a world of their own and at rare intervals recapturing a sense of his own childhood; groping, almost painful, moments. There were definite limits to the intimacy they permitted, and after a few awkward attempts to meet them on their own level, which seemed to embarrass them acutely, he was content to watch and listen. Joking with them, he discovered, was an unsatisfactory business, curiously like a boss in the mill condescending to joke with one of his men; the man laughed but not comfortably and on the whole would have preferred the boss to keep his place. Mary seemed closer to them, which was only natural. She appeared to make no allowances for their immaturity but addressed them as equals, without nonsense, and as an equal they accepted her. Beside her Mike felt clumsy, and against his own inclination — it was as if they had entered into a conspiracy — he found himself cast in the role of Papa, solemn, preoccupied and not to be lightly bothered.

A man never stopped growing older.

By nine the children were in bed and his own eyes growing heavy. "Mihal, go to bed. You can hardly keep your eyes open."

"And you?"

"As soon as I've sprinkled these clothes. I want to begin ironing in the morning."

"Let it go. You've done enough for one day." Rising stiffly, he relit his pipe against the privy's smell and went outside. The yard was dark; cracks of light from behind lowered blinds only made it darker. Dzmura's cash register clashed faintly.

Mike returned to the kitchen's coziness. "Has Dzmura said anything about the closet?"

"No."

"What is he waiting for, another flood?"

Mary shrugged. Mike said, "Well, come to bed."

"As soon as I finish."

They undressed in the crowded little bedroom, Johnny and Pauline asleep in the crib, Mikie in the cradle, the lamp's shadows swooping across the walls as they moved around, the curved glass of the desk reflecting an attenuated Mary as she braided her hair, as she blew out the lamp.

She lay with her back to him, their bodies curved comfortably to each other.

"I had a beautiful dream last night."

"Oh, you did. Who did you dream about, some girl?"

"Why should I dream about some other woman when I have you in bed beside me? Though this nightgown is almost reason enough."

"Oh, my nightgown. Ten minutes ago you couldn't keep your eyes open."

"Not me."

"You saw me putting it on. Why didn't you say something?"

"Must you always be told? Don't you ever think of such things yourself?"

"No."

No woman ever did. Apparently God had left that faculty out of Eve when he created her.

"I suppose you'd like me to become another Zuska, going to bed every night in my skin."

"You could do worse."

"Crazy."

"I wonder what's become of her."

Nobody knew.

"What did you dream about, Mihal?"

"Oh. Well, I was in the mill and talking to Mr. Hooker about the furnace. But in perfect English, you understand. It seems to me that I had a pretty good job or he was thinking of giving me a good job, and I was talking to him, one word after another as though I had been born here and gone to college. He was nodding his head and I could tell he was surprised I knew so much."

"Dorta could tell me what it means. Maybe you'll be getting a good job soon. I'll ask her tomorrow."

"You ought to know better than to believe such nonsense."

"Never mind. You remember I told you about the sparrow that flew into Mrs. Koval's kitchen. And a week later Karl was dead."

"*Ach!*"

They fell silent as a boarder returned and went upstairs. Mike's hand slid caressingly up and down the smooth, hard ridge of Mary's hip.

She murmured, "Mihal, I don't want to get with child again."

"Has it happened yet?"

"But you can never be sure — "

"Oh, all right, all right." He removed his hand and turned away from her.

"Mihal, please. You know it's not only for my sake."

"Why talk about it? Go to sleep."

"Mihal."

"Am I forcing myself on you? You say no, all right. It won't kill me."

She sighed. "You always put me in the wrong."

After a while she sat up, pulled the nightgown over her head and lay back again.

His Sundays off he went to church. Sometimes he stayed up when he got home from the mill and went to high mass, but he liked the evening service better. He was rested then and it was pleasant to stroll through the vacant streets, to stand before the church for a moment gossiping in the quiet evening air. There were a few old people, the kind who went to church every day and twice on Sundays, and many more young couples, young men and girls for whom vespers was an irreproachable excuse to be together and cheaper than a trip to Kennywood. Others kept turning up the hill from Main Street, dark with stores shut for the

Sabbath. Inside the church they were lighting the candles on the altar.

"Well, let us go in."

It was a cool, echoing church at night, with more empty pews than full ones, lamplight gleaming on varnished wood, giggles in the choir, the stained glass windows, no longer translucent, shutting out darkness. At high mass God was the thundering, awe-inspiring Lord of the Universe in vestments of white and gold, but at evening service He was a friend whom one dropped in to visit, God still but God at ease, His shoes and trousers showing below His robes. It was to this God that Mike prayed for Mary, for the children, for himself. About hell's fires and heaven's harps he had opinions of his own, but that God would look after a man who worked hard, took care of his family and always did his best — this could not be doubted. So Mike prayed, and God listened. To One more powerful than steel corporations and General Superintendents Mike spoke in prayer and was sure of a hearing, for in this place he was not a check number or a Hunky laborer, but a man. Into this place, as into the head blower's office, he entered removing his hat, but there the similarity ended. Here he was welcome, here he belonged. Here he spoke in his own tongue; and without fear, without awkwardness, he spoke of himself, his hopes, his troubles, his need of help. And God heard him out. For God knew him by name, knew about Mary and the children, understood how it was with all of them and had a pretty good idea what kind of person, behind his laborer's clothes and poor English, Mike really was. God, in short, liked him.

The world was always a less unfriendly place and he nearly always walked a little straighter, heartened, protected, when he came out.

10

EARLY in January Mary told Mike that she was going to have another baby. Like husbands, men, from the beginning of time, he asked her if she was sure and she said she was. She appeared to be accepting it placidly, though ever since she had weaned Mikie her half-fear of pregnancy had been a source of irritation between them. Not that Mike had wanted more children.

He stared at her. "How do you feel?"

"All right. How should I feel?"

"You know what the doctor said."

"Oh, the doctor! If people listened to everything doctors say nobody would feel like living." She had sifted a little heap of flour on her board; now she made a depression in its peak, like the crater of a volcano, and — first smelling each — broke two eggs into it. She was making dough for *halushki*. "He only said it to scare me, so I'd stay in bed."

Mike was not so sure.

"Are you sorry?" she asked.

"God forbid. There are things we need more than another child but if we must, we must."

"You know what Mrs. Marga used to say. The good God sends them and the good God will provide for them."

"I never liked that saying, for some reason." He shifted Mikie, who was contentedly dismembering a Christmas Teddy bear, on his knee. "When do you expect it?"

"In August or September."

"That means you'll be carrying it through the hottest months."

"Oh, you think of that now, do you? But every time *I* said anything you'd get mad or ask me what good was it to be married if

a man couldn't curl up against his own wife on a cold night."
He grunted.

The flour was now dough, a smooth, solid mass which her fingers,
the heels of her hands, were kneading masterfully.

"Well, all I ask is that you take care of yourself."

"I've had babies before." She added, "I hope it's a girl. That
will give us two of each, and in just the right order. But no more,
Mihal." There was a smile in her eyes as she glanced at him. "No
matter how cold it gets."

Four, he agreed, were enough.

A week or so after Anna's own baby was christened, with July's
heat baking the streets and courtyards of the First Ward, Mary
pushed the iron off one of Mike's good shirts, drew her hand
across her eyes in a vague gesture and then crumpled to the floor.
Pauline's scream — "Papa, Papa, come quick! Something's happened to Mamma!" — lifted Mike out of bed and brought Mrs.
Slema running in from the yard, her arms still foamy with soap-
suds.

Dr. Kralik was summoned. He said there was no danger of a
miscarriage but Mary would have to rest in bed for a few days.
"And when you get up I want you to take care of yourself. Don't
work too hard. The most important thing is not to force yourself.
During the day when you feel like sitting down, sit down. Try
to rest in bed for a while every day."

Mary stared up at him. With six boarders, three children and a
husband to look after, meals to cook, clothes to wash, her hours
were from four-thirty in the morning to nine at night, seven
days a week. And he was telling her to sit down whenever she
felt like it, to rest in bed for a while every day!

"But Doctor," she said gently, "I have my house to take care of."

"Take care of it. But don't work too hard, don't force yourself."

Force herself? How did he suppose she would ever get anything done if she didn't force herself? Did he think people got
out of bed at four-thirty in the morning because they wanted to?

"Are you still keeping boarders?"

"Only six."

The doctor looked grave. He was an American-born-and-educated Slovak, a plump, dapper little man with a stubby mustache and a perfect mania for washing his hands. Before a woman summoned him, she always got out her best towels.

"Mrs. Dobrejcak, if you were big and strong like most of our women six boarders would be nothing. But you know yourself how sick you were with your last baby. And now this fainting. I know, I know. It's only the heat. But it's a warning. You need to build up your strength. Do you eat well?"

"She could eat better," Mike said.

"It's only when I'm tired that I don't seem to have an appetite."

"I'll give you a tonic, and if you eat well and get your proper rest we should have no trouble. There's nothing the matter with you. Food and rest are your best medicine."

While he was scrawling a prescription he asked, "How is your sister?"

"Oh, she's fine. You mean Mrs. Barry, the one who just had the baby?"

"No, the other one, Mrs. Koval."

"Oh, she's fine. It was such a shame about her brother-in-law, wasn't it? So big and fat and then to die so quick."

"In pneumonia, Mrs. Dobrejcak, it's not always good to be big and fat." He handed the prescription to Mike. "A tablespoon in a glass of water after every meal. I'll be around later in the week." He shook his fountain pen at Mary. "And don't let me find you out of bed."

"If I have to tie her," Mike said. "You think she'll be all right, Doctor?"

"God bless us, of course she'll be all right! A little run-down, but if all my patients were as healthy as she I'd be looking for a job in the mill."

He got his laugh.

While he was washing his hands in the kitchen — Mary had all but got out of bed to make sure Mike gave him the right towel — he said, "Dobrejcak, can you get a girl to help your wife with her work? At least until the baby is born."

Mike said slowly, "I suppose it would be even better if we got rid of the boarders altogether."

"It's not my place to tell you how to run your house. I know you're not keeping boarders because you like their company. But your wife has been working too hard."

He spoke excellent Slovak, correct and precise, with hardly a trace of the peasant guttural; it was a pleasure merely to listen to him, though coming from anyone but a doctor or a priest such faultlessness would have aroused resentment.

"They say work never killed anyone. I know better, my friend. I have filled out my share of death certificates, and many times I've put down pneumonia or consumption or heart failure when it would have been more honest to write overwork. And poverty." He shook out the towel Mike gave him. "Another thing. There aren't many men in that mill who work harder than their wives. Cooking, scrubbing, looking after the children — that's hard work, make no mistake about it. No days off when the mill shuts down. And every year another baby. But try to tell that to some of our people." He slipped easily into the rich, vulgar, peasant speech, the words, the accent, the very gestures. " '*Ach,* she's always complaining. Give her her way and she'd do nothing but sit on her behind and gossip.' You've heard them yourself."

Mike smiled worriedly.

He escorted the doctor to the street. The sunshine was blinding; heat shimmered off the sidewalk. "Such heat!" the doctor exclaimed. "I pity the men in the mill. Are you working?"

Mike nodded. "Night turn. It's not as bad at night."

"Give me winter. At least there aren't so many flies. And sick babies. Well, I'll be back Friday."

He walked briskly toward River Street.

Mike sent Johnny — how could the boy walk those hot sidewalks in his bare feet? — to Hollander's with the prescription and returned to the bedroom.

Mary was talking to Mrs. Slema. "I was going to have steak. I think I need coffee; will you look? You know where the book is. Send Pauline; the butcher knows her. But what about your own boarders, Katarina?"

"I'll get my sister; she has nothing to do anyway since her people went to the seashore. Well, Dobrejcak, what do you think of your wife? You'd think she was old enough to have more sense, wouldn't you?"

Mary smiled self-consciously. The color was returning to her face.

"Thank God it was nothing worse than a fainting spell. When I heard Pauline scream I ran in expecting to see God only knows what." Here Mrs. Slema seemed to remember something and stopped abruptly. She glanced at Mike and appeared to choke. "Well, my wash is still waiting, and if your boarders are going to eat — " She bustled out.

Mike sat down beside the bed. "I sent Johnny for the medicine."

"Mihal, lie down and try to get some sleep. You have a night's work ahead of you."

"I couldn't sleep any more. I'd be getting up soon anyway."

"Poor Mihal. Even he has to suffer on account of me."

"*Ach!*"

"I don't know what ever made me do such a thing," Mary said, as though it were something to be ashamed of. "I felt dizzy and I thought to myself, I'll bet I'm going to faint. I had enough sense to take the iron off your good shirt. Then the next thing I knew I was in bed and you were telling me to drink some water. But Mihal — " She eyed him slyly. "Do you realize you had nothing on but your undershirt? And Mrs. Slema standing right beside you?"

He smiled. "Do you think I was going to stop to put on my pants? When the child screamed — "

He took her hand between his. "Marcha, I could beat you. How do you think I would have felt if something had happened to you, something really bad?"

"It was only the heat."

"It's been hot before without making you faint. No, Marcha — "
He fell silent.

When he spoke again the words came reluctantly. "We have to
get rid of the boarders. The doctor himself said as much."

He waited.

Perhaps it was too much to have expected her to protest, then
and there. In his heart he knew he would have let her convince
him that they couldn't think of letting the boarders go, that she
would be as good as ever in a few days — and in his heart he
knew the thought to be unworthy.

Mary avoided his eyes. "Mihal, I know I should argue with you,
but I can't. Maybe because I feel so tired. I know as well as you
how much we need the boarders, but when I think of my house
without them, only you and the children — " She sighed. "You
decide, Mihal. Whatever you say will be all right. Don't ask me.
I don't want you to blame me afterward if — "

"Be still!"

He looked down at the hand he held, red, roughened, the nails
broken, and patted it gently. "I'm ashamed to tell you what I was
thinking. Eh, we should know each other by now, you and I."

After a while she said, "Will we be able to manage, Mihal?"

"We have a little saved."

"I was thinking I might make a little extra sewing."

"You'll have enough to do taking care of your family."

"Oh, I will, I will. I'll be able to do so much now that I never
had the time for before." She sighed. "It will be so nice by ourselves again."

Her baby was born toward the end of September, a girl as
Mary had hoped. She named her Agnes.

One of their original boarders, now several years married, paid
them enough for their extra furniture and dishes, the over-size pots
and pans, and for the privilege of moving in after them, to pay
for Mary's doctor's bill and the christening. Then they moved to
three rooms on Washington not far from Mrs. Perlak's house,
where they had spent the first year of their married life. Mrs.

Perlak was dead but her son and his wife, with a houseful of children and boarders, were still living in it.

Mike had got unused to privacy, to eating supper with only his own around the table, to having the household revolve around him, his comings and goings. He found it pleasant. Mary bloomed. "It's so nice to be alone again. I can do so many things and the house stays clean so much longer. During the day I catch myself telling the children not to make so much noise before I remember that we haven't any boarders sleeping upstairs any more. And I have to learn to cook all over again, I keep making too much." She sighed. "I hope we never have to take in boarders again. When I think how I used to work I wonder how I ever did it."

But the boarders made their absence felt on paydays, too. For what had been true years before, that even when work was good a man could earn just about enough to keep his family alive, was still true. But work wasn't good. Like a sick man whom the doctors pronounced cured yet who still dragged his feet when he walked, from whom pleasure in living had gone out, the country had never fully recovered from the panic times of 1907. Only for short periods since then had Mike drawn full pays. While the boarders were around to help that hadn't mattered seriously. It did now. Rents were higher, prices were higher, growing children consumed appalling quantities of food — Mike hoped Johnny's incredible appetite would never be anything but amusing — and outgrew the clothes they didn't wear to threads.

Mike began making regular trips to the bank.

11

IN the twilight the men of the day shift were coming out of the mill, pouring out of the tunnel into Thirteenth Street, where they scattered. A mill cop leaned against a safety poster and watched them, a toothpick twitching between his lips; clustered in the street just outside the gate, swept by the raw light and jagged shadows of a swaying arc lamp, were the usual payday beggars, men crippled or blinded in the mill, the usual children, the usual shawled women come to escort their husband's pay envelopes past Washington Street's saloons. The October evening was cold and bleak enough to make the windows of those saloons more than ordinarily inviting.

"A drink, Mike?"

Mike shook his head. Farther up the street, in front of Gyurik's saloon, Bodnar paused again. "Come on, Mike. One drink."

"Not now. I'll meet you after supper if you like."

"Well, all right."

They parted at Twelfth Street, Bodnar crossing to thread his way through a maze of passageways and courtyards to Talbot Avenue, Mike continuing down Washington.

Mary was pouring noodles into a colander, holding her head to one side, away from the steam, as he entered. The kitchen was rich with the smell of soup. "Good evening, Marcha."

"Good evening, Mihal." She rinsed the noodles with cold water and set them in a pot to drain. "I didn't expect you home so soon tonight."

"Bodnar wanted to buy me a drink but I told him to keep it until after supper." He kissed her. Pauline was playing on the floor with Mikie; the baby was asleep in her cradle.

Mike took off his coat, stiff with age and dirt, and hung it on the door. Along the door's upper edge were still visible the letters the priest had chalked there when he'd blessed the house at last Epiphany, the initials of the three Magi and the year, thus: 19——G M B——12. "Well, I'm finished for this week."

Mary made no comment; that was an old story.

He washed and shaved and changed into clean clothes, and then they sat down to the table, a great steaming bowl of soup in the center. "Ah, this smells good. There's nothing I like better on a cold night than soup and noodles." He filled his plate. The soup was golden with fat, flecked with bits of parsley and tomato. "I bet Rockefeller would give more than a million dollars to be able to eat a plate of soup like this."

"I made him give me knucklebones this time," Mary said, beaming. "Last time I sent Pauline he gave her veal bones. I was so mad."

She filled the children's plates and then her own. Mikie, his chin barely showing above the edge of the table, indignantly refused help and began shoveling soup, noodles and breadcrust into his mouth with more gusto than elegance.

"Pig!" Mary exclaimed. "You're getting more on your bib than into your mouth. Hold your spoon right. And don't be in such a hurry, the house isn't on fire. *Ach!*"

"At least he eats better than that one did at his age," Mike said. He looked at Pauline, who stopped eating and waited expectantly for further attention. She was a very thin, big-eyed child. "I bet you don't remember the tricks your mother had to play on you to make you eat, do you?"

"On me?"

"Yes, you. She used to put water in a basin near the window so the sunshine would dance on the ceiling. Then she'd tell you, Look up there, Pauline, and when you looked up you always opened your mouth and pop! she filled it for you."

Pauline grinned fatuously.

"So much trouble to make her eat."

"I eat good now," Pauline said, in English.

"Yes, like a sparrow." Mary stared at her daughter. "Francka says she's the picture of me at her age."

"Nobody has to tell me to eat," Johnny said. He had a tooth missing in front. "Boy, I bet I could eat ten times a day."

"Oh, you. There's no bottom to your stomach."

"I can't help it if I get hungry, can I?"

"Eat and don't talk so much."

They ate; and after supper Johnny and Pauline went out to play, rich with payday pennies and warned to come home as soon as the quarter-to-nine curfew whistle blew, and Mike pushed back his chair and began filling his pipe.

"Did you see Mrs. What's-her-name about the highchair?"

"Mrs. Muha. I went there today and she said she had already promised it to a friend. I told her I would have been glad to give her something but she had already promised it."

"Then we'll have to get a new one."

"It would be a big help," Mary admitted. "But to pay out two or three dollars for a highchair now — "

"If you have to have it you have to have it. A pity the other one couldn't have lasted a little longer." He cocked an eye at her. "We may have to have more children to get our money's worth out of the new one."

"*Ach!* If I didn't know you were joking. . . . Anna got herself a beautiful one, all white with a shelf underneath for the pot. Did I tell you Mrs. Muha's sister got her new cradle today? You never saw anything like it. You wind it up and it rocks by itself and a music box plays."

Mike grunted.

"I said to Mrs. Muha, what won't they think of next?"

Mike got up to light his pipe, holding a twist of paper against the stove grate. "How much do we owe this time?"

"The books are in the calendar."

He brought them back to the table. Mary was silent while he examined them; talk about money was always a grave, rather uncomfortable business.

They owed the butcher about eight dollars, the grocer about thirteen dollars.

"What's this one dollar nineteen in the store book?"

Mary studied the page frowning. "Oh. The dollar part is what I borrowed to pay the insurance that time. You remember."

"I wish you wouldn't ask him for money. It's bad enough to owe him for the food we eat."

"The agent said we were a month behind and unless I paid something we might lose the policies. You remember, I told you about it when you came home. What else could I do? I could have asked Mrs. Fecik for it but — "

"It's better not to start that."

He put the books aside and got out his pay envelope. He tore off the end and spilled the contents into his palm. He had put in nine turns out of a possible fifteen and there was exactly eighteen dollars and ninety cents to show for it. He shook the envelope and peered into it. "No more. Eighteen-ninety is all there is."

"You'll be forgetting what a full pay is if things don't get better soon."

"How much have you put aside for the rent?"

"Seven dollars. Seven dollars and some change." She got an earless cup from the cupboard.

Mike began figuring. "Five dollars to the rent. Three to the butcher. Five to the store." He looked up. "Have they been saying anything?"

Mary shrugged. "As long as I give them a little every payday they seem satisfied. What can they say? They know I'd pay if you were working steady. And we're not the only ones." She took the breadknife away from Mikie and set him on the floor. "We need coal. You remember I told you — "

"Can we let it go until next payday?"

She shook her head reluctantly. "We'll need another load by the end of the month. I've tried to be careful but you know how cold it has been. So early in the winter too."

"Two-fifty for coal. How much does that leave us?" He figured, moving his lips. "Fifteen-fifty. And fifteen-fifty from eighteen-ninety — three-forty."

Mary looked down at her hands. "Mihal, I want to have our picture taken. All together, the whole family. You said yourself it would be nice. We wouldn't have to get many right away — just so it was taken. Please, Mihal."

"Marcha, be reasonable. There's your answer." He moved his hand at the books and the money on the table.

"You could go to the bank." She continued hurriedly, "We wouldn't have to get many right away. Just three. That would cost only two-fifty and we could have more made later; he would keep the plate if we asked him."

"If I keep going to the bank pretty soon there won't be anything to go there for."

"But it would be so nice to have a picture of all of us, while the children are small. You could send one to your mother."

"She'd thank me more for a five-dollar bill. I told you about the letter Sophie got from her sister?"

Mary nodded. Mike's mother and her second husband, both approaching sixty, were behaving badly. Apparently each had become so afraid that the other would benefit unduly from their joint labors that neither did his full share and the little farm, Sophie's sister reported, was going to rack and ruin. Which one first thought of secretly digging up potatoes out of season and bartering them for whisky in the village Sophie's sister didn't know; at any rate, when harvest time came there was so little left to sell or carry them through the winter that they were facing actual hunger. Mike had no money to send them; Joe, who had fought with his stepfather from the moment they met, refused to send any.

"Maybe you think it's easy for me to go to the bank and take out money," Mike said slowly. "But when I think how much it cost us, how long it took to save — *Jeziš!* Every dollar I draw is like seeing a week of my life destroyed, like losing blood from my veins. When it's all gone what will we have to show for our years of work?"

"It would be worse if you didn't have it, Mihal."

He stared at her; plainly she hadn't understood what he was trying to say. He sighed. "Well, if it will make you happy. Is there anything else?"

"We'll have to give Sophie's baby something."

"When does she expect it?"

"Next month. Late."

"Well, by next month — "

"Johnny needs new shoes, and he is growing out of his overcoat. But he can wait. You need more heavy underwear."

"What I have will have to do. Is that all?"

Mary reflected soberly. Their eyes met and held for a moment, and then Mike grinned crookedly.

Mary smiled too.

"Funny, eh? But that's what it is not to have money."

"It won't always be like this."

He grunted. "I'm beginning to wonder. The way times are — and nobody seems to know what is wrong or what should be done. They keep saying next month, next year — always it's next month or next year and nothing ever happens."

"Times have been bad before, Mihal, and they always got better."

"Yes, but meanwhile? I work hard. I work like a horse sometimes. And I have less every payday. What good is all my work if they won't pay me enough to keep my family? What in God's name must a man do to make a living in this world?"

Soothingly, "Now, Mihal. When they finish the open hearth maybe you'll get a good job."

He shook his head. "An open hearth isn't a blast furnace." He sucked on his dead pipe with a soft smacking of the lips. "There was a time when I thought I'd surely get a good job sometime. I worked hard. I did what I was told and more. And I've seen them hire Irish, Johnny Bulls, Scotties, just off the boat and knowing no more about a steel mill than Mikie there, and in a year they're giving me orders. Not once or twice but many times. And I've been working in those furnaces over twenty years. I know my job, Marcha. I could take over that furnace tomorrow and make as good iron as Keogh ever did. But I'm a Hunky and they don't give good jobs to Hunkies. God damn their souls to hell."

Mary was silent.

He got up to relight his pipe, dropped the taper into the coal-scuttle and watched it burn out. "If I could make a living I wouldn't mind so much, they could keep their good jobs and welcome. But they won't give me a good job, and they won't pay me enough to live on in the only job they will give me. Son of a bitch, is that a way to treat a man? What am I, an animal without sense or feelings?"

Mikie had glanced up, startled; he stared at his father for a moment, then returned to playing with a roller skate that had two wheels missing. Mary's face was sad. "It's not good to think about such things, Mihal. It only makes you feel worse. If you could do something —"

"We can do nothing. Nothing. We can't even open our mouths. Even a dog is allowed to howl when he's kicked, but we? We have to carry it inside ourselves until it tastes so bitter we want to vomit. But blessed God, a man can hold only so much and one of these days they'll learn it. Someday, Marcha —" He held out a clenched fist.

"Mihal —"

He noticed her now; and what he saw in her eyes made him go to her and pat her shoulder. "Now, now, let me talk. You'd think the world was coming to an end to hear me, eh? But it's not that bad, not yet."

"Mihal, I feel all right now. I've had a good rest. We could move to a larger house and —"

He gestured in mock despair. "There's a wife for you. I complain a little and right away she thinks she should take in boarders again.

Marcha, if you're going to be like that I'll be afraid to say anything even in my own house. And God knows I can't open my mouth anywhere else."

"But everything you said was true, Mihal."

"I could say other things just as true, that I have a nice home and a healthy family and a better wife than most. Can't a man grumble a little?" He tweaked her ear. "Let me hear no more nonsense about boarders."

He glanced at the clock and sat down to change from slippers to shoes. The money was still on the table. "Here you are, missus. All yours."

Mary began to gather it up, handling it like one who gets little money to touch, smoothening the bills carefully, folding them, putting them into the cup with the loose change to weight them down. She left a half-dollar on the table. Hesitantly, as though she was ashamed because it was so little, she pushed it toward him. "You can't go out with nothing in your pocket."

"I have some change."

"Where did you get it?"

"Don't you believe me?"

"No."

"What a wife!" He felt in his pockets elaborately. "I must have left it in my other pants."

"A fine story. Here, take it."

She held the cup clasped in her hands, in her lap. "I remember once when we were living in Cherry Alley and my father still had his butcher shop he took me upstairs and showed me the money he had in his trunk. The top tray was full of silver, more money than I had ever imagined there was in the world. What was I, thirteen, fourteen. He made me lay my two arms in it and then covered them with money so I could say afterward that I had had my arms in silver up to my elbows."

"He must have been drunk."

"I don't remember."

"We would have less to worry about now if he had been able to hold on to it. Look at Spetz. A saloon, houses, money — " Mike rose, stamping his feet. "Well, there's no use thinking about it."

"Don't get home too late, Mihal."

He picked up the half-dollar and looked at it, and then at Mary, and grinned.

12

THE Democrats had swept the mid-term elections. Roosevelt split the Republican Party down the middle and with his Bull Moose emblem confused people who had always identified him with Teddy bears. The company backed Taft. Bulletin boards flowered with Republican campaign posters and cartoons depicting closed factories and black-bearded anarchists looming over the Capitol at Washington; sample ballots were distributed with pay envelopes. Washington Street rang with political argument. There were more citizens in the First Ward than ever before, times were bad, and Roosevelt's rebellion provided timorous voters with a unique opportunity to get passionate about politics without having their Republicanism impugned. Gyurik's bartender bet Finish the grocer that Roosevelt would win, the loser to parade down Washington with a bass drum on his back, the winner thumping it; another wager pledged the loser to pull the winner from Eleventh Street to Thirteenth in a two-wheeled buggy. Perovsky, seeking votes from all, went around with a glazed look in his eyes. That a college professor named Woodrow Wilson was preaching something he called "the New Freedom" was seldom mentioned.

On election day Hooker, the head blower, came into the casthouse and said he'd take over while Keogh went to vote. "How many men you got?"

"Five or six."

"Round them up."

Mike proved to be the only Slovak in the group. Hooker stared at him. "You a citizen?" he asked. He always did.

"Yessir. Pretty soon ten years."

"Humph. Well, I just want to remind you men that it's the company that pays your wages, not some politician in Harrisburg or Washington. Anything that hurts the company hurts you, remember that. And the company hasn't got much use for a man that can't be loyal. Just keep that in mind when you vote. Take these along; it's all right to take them into the booth with you." He passed out sample ballots marked with a vote for a straight Republican ticket. "Everybody got one? All right. Get goin'."

They went across the yard toward Thirteenth Street, Mike keeping a little behind the others. They didn't talk much even among themselves. It was a cool, cloudy day; the mill's smoke hung low, and between the iron buildings the air was like fog, gray and softening. Steam stayed white a long time before it disappeared.

In the schoolhouse basement, its floor littered with papers, the air smoky, there was a steady murmur of voices, a steady coming and going as foremen and pushers brought in their men, lined them up to vote. Several mill bosses, including Byrnes, the blast furnace superintendent, stood to one side, their presence implying what the lesser bosses used plain words to say: "If you know what's good for you, vote right." Some of the waiting men ventured a "Hello, Mr. Byrnes," or a "Hello, Mr. Clarke," and having received a curt nod turned back to their companions, their good-fellowship too obvious, their voices too loud, like self-conscious children showing off before the teacher after school was out.

Perovsky, handsome, well-dressed, nervously active, was talking with a Slovak voter. He spied Mike, slapped his man on the back and came over. "Your brother just left," he said.

Mike nodded.

"Well, how's everything with you?"

"It could be better."

Perovsky laughed tolerantly. "You'll never change; always the same Dobrejcak."

He lowered his voice, though they were talking in Slovak. "But seriously, Mike. Don't do anything foolish. You understand me? I know how you feel about some things but why make trouble for yourself? After all, what the devil does it matter to you who gets elected? It's more important to you and your family that you have a job and steady work. Am I right? Sure!"

"I'm not looking for trouble."

"Good God, nobody wants trouble! But you know how things are, especially this year with Roosevelt doing such crazy things. Between you and me, the company has its plans all made, and if Roosevelt should win —" Perovsky didn't finish, only shook his head portentously.

"You can be sure I won't vote for Roosevelt or Wilson," Mike said.

"Did I ask you, Mike? How you vote is your own business." He slapped him on the back, apparently not minding Mike's dirty clothes. "If you'd like a mouthful of schnapps go across the street to the tailor shop, tell them I sent you. And come into my place tonight. No matter who wins."

Mike watched him greet another Slovak with the same smile, the same confidential lowering of the voice, the same portentous shake of the head. He was a born politician, there was no doubt about it. One could hardly help admiring him; as a Slovak one could even feel a little proud of him. It was unfortunate that his way of looking at things coincided so neatly with the company's way; perhaps when one was lifted a little above ordinary men that was natural, just as it was natural for such men to have better manners and to use better grammar. Still, there were times — as now — when he seemed little more than an errand boy, working busily while the bosses watched.

Mike had registered as a Republican — anything else would have been suicidal — but had determined to vote for Eugene Debs, the Socialist. He knew the risk. Should he be found out — and that the company had ways of learning how a man had voted nobody in Braddock doubted — he would be fired. Aided by an assumed name and the obtuseness which had led more than one English-speaking man to say that all Hunkies looked alike to him, he might be able to get a job in Homestead or Duquesne. And then again, he might not.

In the booth he had a last moment of indecision. He hadn't said anything to Mary. If he was fired she would suffer. "Yet God forgive me," he thought, "I must or feel myself no more a man." And to the injustices that had been for so long a bitter taste in his mouth was now added a dull rage at the forces which drove him almost against his will to do this thing, to risk so much. His hand trembled as he flattened out the ballot, as he pulled up the dangling pencil.

When he came out of the booth it seemed to him that he was walking unsteadily and that everyone could guess what he had done. But he slid the ballot into the box unchallenged and then joined the others outside, on the cobblestone ramp down which wagons brought coal for the school's boilers. Keogh and the others had also been told about the tailor shop.

Wilson won. Debs got seventeen votes in the First Ward. And nothing happened. All that week Mike waited for the blow to fall, for Hooker or Keogh to approach him with a strange look on his face and tell him he was through. On payday he felt his envelope anxiously — it seemed thicker than usual — and opened it before he got home, half-expecting to find all the money due him and a discharge slip. But it held only his regular wages.

For a while he went around happy that he hadn't been found out. He worked eagerly and the complete normality of everything, his tasks, Keogh's grumbling pessimism, Hooker's officiousness, were as nearly a pleasure as such things could be. Only as time passed did he sense a subtle irony. Flinger of pebbles against a fortress, his impunity was the measure of his impotence.

13

BODNAR'S legs were comparatively the firmer so he was making a show of supporting Mike as they rolled out of Wold's saloon, but they were both quite drunk. A few drinks made each gay; then their moods diverged. Like another Mikolaj, the First Ward's singing drunkard, Mike sang one song after another, the sadder the better, though unlike Mikolaj he didn't sing them at the top of his voice, or in the middle of the street, or pulling at one ear. (The First Ward's other famous sot had been nicknamed Mike Nation because he liked to break windows.) Bodnar, on the other hand, grew hot with lust.

So now Bodnar was betting a million dollars that this time nothing would stop him, this time he'd give her what she longed for, that sweet, plump bitch, while Mike crooned his favorite song, the ribald and more popular version of *"A ja zo Sarisa,"* the tuneful lament of a young girl married to an old husband.

The door swung to behind them, closed on the saloon's glittering mirrors and hissing gas lamps; its rich and juicy atmosphere gave place to the cool, smoke-scented air of the street. A little German band was tootling and grumping under the corner lamp, its audience mostly dirty-faced children who should have been in bed hours before. Across the way a mill cop watched by the tunnel gate. The spring night was pleasantly crisp.

They staggered determinedly up Thirteenth Street. At night it was hardly more than an alley, a passageway, with the mill wall on one side and a façade of old, ramshackle houses on the other. Here and there a lamp hung in the smoky haze and seemed to splash the street with shadows rather than with light. The miserable rookeries were dark, the sidewalk barely wide enough for two to walk abreast and badly paved. Over the wall—it was built of great blocks of stone and a week after it was finished it had looked a hundred years old—the mill rumbled on, efficient and sober and not to be swerved from its tasks.

Mike stumbled. "Excuse me, my friend."

Bodnar didn't reply.

Huddled on doorsteps, motionless in the black frames of passageways, women waited, shawled, quiet, patient. They watched the two men approach until each was sure neither was the man she waited for. At one Mike waved a limp hand. "Go to bed, Mrs. Grancik, go to bed."

Her face was a mere blur in the darkness but her voice was clear. "Have you seen my old one?"

"He wasn't in Wold's when we left," Bodnar said.

They went on.

Mike stumbled again and put out a hand to brace himself against a housefront. He lowered his head.

Bodnar exclaimed, "Devil take you, not here on somebody's doorstep!" and jerked him across the narrow street and propped him against the mill wall.

Mike vomited. Bodnar caught his hat as it slid toward the ground. After a while he drew his sleeve across his mouth, his sweaty face. "*Ježiš!* I don't think I have a gut left."

"Wold's whisky," Bodnar observed with a sort of judicious regret, "is not what it used to be. Nor are we."

Mike said, "I'm tired," and began to slide down the wall.

"Well don't lie down in your own vomit!" Bodnar jammed Mike's hat back on his head and pulled him to the sidewalk and dropped him on a convenient doorstep. "And don't go to sleep or upon my soul I'll leave you here in the street."

"I won't sleep." He rested his arms on his knees and let his head drop.

How long he sat thus he didn't know but when he raised his head he felt better, almost sober. He was weak and tired but his mind was clear. Bodnar had made himself comfortable on the doorstep beside him and was trying to fill his pipe. Mike looked around. The mill wall shut in the street so that the eye sought to escape. At Washington the light above the gate rocked in the wind; the wall was even higher there, rising as Thirteenth Street sloped toward the river. In the other direction, at Halket, there was a wide gap in the wall where the B. and O. tracks entered the mill, and one could see inside. A few lights made gray smears across the dirty windows of the few visible buildings, repair shops mostly. There was a brighter light, green-shaded, in the watchman's shanty. Overhead, the sky was restless with soiled clouds.

"What are we doing on Thirteenth Street?" Mike asked. "Don't tell me we were going to call on your sister-in-law again?"

Bodnar refused to answer and Mike smiled faintly. Bodnar's life was cheered by the conviction that his wife's sister entertained a secret passion for him, and each time he got drunk he felt he must keep her pining no longer. Few husbands were without such a private, seldom-consummated project in benevolent adultery.

Bodnar struck a match and lit his pipe, the little flame illuminating his face, his knuckly, hard-skinned fingers. In his face the face of the light-hearted young man with whom Mike had shared his youth was blurred under the lines and hollows and thickenings of maturity. We're getting old, Mike thought. Bodnar blew out the match and said, "Mike you've been doing too much talking lately. You know what I mean."

"I suppose I have."

"Oh, you admit it? Well, that's something."

"But I think Joe's boarder has cured me of it."

"What the devil has anybody's boarders to do with it? All I wanted to say was that you've been doing too much talking out of the wrong side of your mouth. Blessed God, you've lived in Braddock long enough to know there are some things it's better to keep to yourself. But no. Not you. You have to drop a word here, another there, twist no matter what's being talked about into politics or worse. What's got into you?"

"It was something I learned."

"Eh?"

"Nobody can help us but ourselves, and if anything is to be done we will have to do it ourselves. That's what I learned. God pity me, sometimes I wish I could have gone along without learning it, gone on talking and making plans but inside me feeling that maybe it wasn't really true and if it was I was somehow excepted. Inside me hoping that somehow things would change by themselves or that other people would do what was necessary and I'd never have to risk the little I have."

Bodnar recognized a word in the sentences rolling past him and grasped at it. "That's what I mean," he said. "The risk. I'm glad you realize what you've been doing. I know how you feel. I feel like that myself more than you might think. But after all, Mike! It isn't as though your talking could change things."

"It seemed the only thing to do. I thought there must be others who felt like me but were afraid to show themselves. I thought if even one man took a chance and spoke out it would encourage the rest, we could find one another."

"Sure. And one of these fine days the company hears a word too many about you and then where are you? Out on your behind. Use your head, Mike. You have a job, you have a fine wife and family — why go out of your way to make trouble for yourself?"

"No more. No more, I promise you. They thought I was trying to get them to talk about unions and politics so I could report them to the company."

"Report who? What are you talking about?"

"One of Joe's boarders passed a remark. Never mind. I'm finished, finished."

He sat with his head bowed, his hands hanging limply from his wrists. The street was quiet except for the mill's rumble and the music of the German band, softened by distance. They were playing "In the Good Old Summertime," and some young people on the corner of Talbot were singing the words.

"What are they doing to us? I can remember when people weren't afraid. Now fear is everywhere, spreading suspicion and bitterness, draining every man's heart of courage and making honesty a sin against his family's bread. Don't they fear God's anger, these misusers of men? Then let them beware ours. More than coke and ore is going into those furnaces of theirs."

Bodnar was silent.

"I can't say what I want, I can't do what I want, I can't even hope any more that some day things will be better for me. Marcha laughs when I show her how gray I'm getting but just the same I can't work as hard or move as quickly as I did ten years ago. And you know what that means. Slow down and out you go. And then what will become of us?"

He lifted his head. "I don't mind work. I've never been afraid of work. But what have I to show for all my years of work? There's so much that is beautiful and pleasant in the world; why must only poverty and meanness be our portion?"

A Talbot Avenue streetcar, waiting to begin its long trip through the sleeping towns, the lonely streets, to Pittsburgh, made a yellow glow for the young people to sing by. The voice of the mill was harsher than theirs. It came over the wall like the breathing of a giant at work, like the throb of an engine buried deep in the earth. In it were the piping of whistles and the clash of metal on metal; the chuffing of yard locomotives, the rattle of electric cranes and skip hoists, the bump-bump-bump of a train of cars getting into motion; the wide-mouthed blow of the Bessemers, the thud of five-ton ingots dropping six inches as they were stripped of their moulds, the clean, tenpin crack of billets dropping from a magnet, the solid, unhurried grind of the ore dumper, lifting a whole railroad gondola of iron ore and emptying it, delicately; the high whine of the powerhouse dynamos, the brute growl of the limestone and dolomite crushers, the jolting blows of the steam hammers in the blacksmith shop, the distant, earth-shaking thunder of the blooming mill's giant rolls. A hundred discords merged into harmony, the harsh, triumphant song of iron and flame.

"Listen to it," Mike said. "When I remember that men built that it makes me proud I'm a man. If they'd let me I could love that mill like something of my own. It's a terrible and beautiful thing to make iron. It's honest work, too, work the world needs. They should honor us, Stefan. Sometimes when the bosses bring their friends through the mill they watch us make a cast and when the iron pours out of the furnace, you know how wonderful it is, especially at night, I feel big and strong with pride. I hope the visitors get afraid, I hope they're admiring us. I know when I saw my first cast, I was only a boy, the men working with that burning iron seemed like heroes to me."

It was unlikely that Bodnar was listening to him or that Mike cared, for each was now isolated in the third and final stage of his inebriety, Mike in a world-encompassing despair, Bodnar in the silence of brooding frustration.

"I don't mind work. But a man should be allowed to love his work and take pride in it. There's good in all of us that would make our lives happier and the world a better place for everybody. But it's never asked for. We're only Hunkies."

Bodnar's breathing was almost regular and heavy enough to be a snore.

"Once I had an idea, I thought to myself: If we were to sing some of our songs and explain what they were about — would it surprise them to learn that we sang about such things and had such feelings? If we told them how we lived in the old country, how we worked the land, the crops we grew, the little money we saw from one year's end to another, our holidays and festivals — would they realize that even though we spoke different languages we were still men like themselves, with the same troubles, the same hopes and dreams? I hoped that we might learn to respect one another, that we might even become friends. And once we were friends it shouldn't take us long to discover that we had the same enemies."

The German band had moved out of hearing, it was probably in front of Dzmura's saloon now, and the boys and girls on the corner were having trouble finding another song to sing; nobody liked what anybody else suggested.

"I used to have such ideas, make such great plans. No more. Once I used to ask myself, Is this what the good God put me on earth for, to work my life away in Carnegie's blast furnaces, to live and die in Braddock's alleys? I couldn't believe it. Now I know that God had nothing to do with it. Chance rules the world. I was born a carpenter's son but I might as easily have been the son of a millionaire or a prince. I remember wondering when I was a boy in the old country if my father was really my father, God forgive me. I pretended that maybe an archduke or somebody of that sort had begot me and hidden me with a village carpenter for reasons of state, as they say, and that shortly men in uniform would be along to reclaim me, take me in a gilt coach to Vienna or Budapest."

The young people on the corner had agreed on "Sweet Genevieve," and their young voices were making the song lovely and heart-breakingly poignant with melancholy. Mike huddled on the doorstep with his face buried in his arms like a man overcome by despair.

"All a man can be sure of is what he gets here on earth. He gets it here or he never gets it at all. Don't comfort yourself that what you have to bear with in life will be made up by felicity in heaven, or that the enemy who harms you will be fittingly punished in hell, for what you get here on earth, whether it's riches or poverty, happiness or sorrow, is all you ever get, and what you want or have merited has nothing to do with it. The pleasant days, the quiet places; the money jingling in the pocket, the cities and countries you would like to see, the things you would like to do — all this you enjoy here on earth or forever go without. There's no making up what you missed, no going back; no triumphs for the long-suffering, no fiery torments for the evil-doers. Nobody keeps accounts, and once the worms have finished with them the murderer rests as peacefully as his victim. For there is no God and it doesn't matter how we live or when we die. Our work and our dreams, the good we did, the evil we suffered, the hope we kept alive in our hearts — none of it matters, and our laughter and tears and prayers alike come to no more than the howl of a dog in the night, heard for a moment and then heard no more."

"O Genevieve, sweet Genevieve, The days may come, the day-ays may go . . ."

"Hey you!"

She repeated the call before Bodnar snorted awake and looked up. A woman, her fat arms and shoulders bare, was leaning out of a window directly above them.

"Go home, bums! Get off my stoop before I empty a slop jar over you! You're keeping us all awake with your drunken jabbering!"

Bodnar said, "Mrs. Cibula, that's no way to talk to us."

She cocked her head at him like a startled hen. "Who is it? Bodnar? And I suppose that's Dobrejcak with you. And both stinking drunk. Shame on you!"

Bodnar had risen. "So, so. You've had your say; now go back to bed before you awaken the whole street."

"Shame on you both! A fine thing for men of your age, rolling around in the gutters while your poor wives wait for you at home!"

"At least," Bodnar retorted testily, "they're not showing themselves half-naked at their windows to every passer-by!"

He ignored her indignant sputters, stooped to pull Mike to his feet. "Come, great thinker."

Arm in arm they rolled down Thirteenth Street to Talbot and then along Talbot to Bodnar's house, which was across the street from the school. They parted at the door; then Mike went home through the echoing, deserted streets, stumbling now and then as though he were still drunk. Never in his life had he felt so alone.

He had hated poverty and ugliness; he had resented injustice and cried out against that sin of sins, the degradation of man by man, believing the world held few things more precious than human dignity. He had never looked on work and food as more than the beginning of living, matters a man took in his stride as he went gathering life's richer fruits, love and pride, laughter, accomplishment, the things of the heart and the head that lifted man above the brute. He had felt that no human being need go without his portion of comfort and beauty and quietness; the world held enough for all and if some had less than others it was because men had ordered it so and it lay in men's hands to order differently. It had seemed to him that men needed only to have this explained to them and they'd rise and do what was necessary; and when they didn't he felt angry and bewildered. Out of sloth or fear or stupidity they did nothing, they appeared content with little, whom injustice did not seem to burn nor denial embitter.

Yet he clung to his belief that the mass of men were in their hearts good, preferring the excellent to the shoddy, the true to the false, striving for all their blunders toward worthy goals and failing most often when they put their trust in leaders rather than themselves. Unless this was so he felt there was no use going on. Unless this could be proved true here and now, today, in the teeming alleys and courtyards and kitchens of the First Ward, it was true nowhere, never. And unless it was true there was no hope.

It never entered his mind that he himself was all the proof and hope he needed.

14

THE new year had brought little change. The railroads' dissatisfaction with Bessemer steel rails, their insistence on rails low in phosphorus content, had forced the company to begin construction of a basic open hearth plant. Work on it went forward during the spring and summer and there was hope that when it began operating things would pick up. The rail mills' attempts to diversify their output with tie plates, billets and sheet bars had not proved conspicuously successful. An immense, quarter-mile long building at the upper end of the company's property, the open hearth was finished and the first heat tapped in August, but times were so bad that it was two years before the gas was turned on in the last of its hundred-ton furnaces.

Eventually Kracha drew attention to himself by fracturing his arm while piling scrap at the skull-cracker. His daughters first learned about it when he appeared in Braddock, his arm in a sling. He exhibited it in most of the saloons along Washington and then returned to Homestead to enjoy his accident compensation and the sympathy of his latest boarding missus, a Mrs. Lizka. She was a middle-aged widow with three nearly grown children, and to hear her tell it Kracha was, in his habits and mannerisms, her late husband to the life. Kracha could hardly belch without reminding her of the dear departed. He sensed which way the wind was blowing with her but since he was still, so far as he knew, married to Zuska, he accepted the widow's tributes of special attentions and extra tidbits in his lunch bucket without trepidation.

He was back in Braddock for the christening of Anna's second baby, another boy. He came into the kitchen at the dusk end of a March afternoon, just as Mary was placing the lamp on the table, and waved a Slovak newspaper under Mike's nose. Mike was in his undershirt and still rubbing sleep out of his eyes.

"Look at this! What do you think of this? After all these years of wondering where she was and what she was doing! Devil take me if I could have imagined anything like this!"

"What are you talking about?"

"Read it. You know how to read. Right there."

He spread the paper on the table. Mary lingered beside Mike, her hand on his shoulder. There was a brief news item reporting the ordination at St. Vincent's in Latrobe of one Joseph Mihula, of Johnstown, and the accompanying photograph was a picture of Zuska's eldest son. There could be no doubt about it; even in the wretched halftone one could detect the relationship. He had his mother's full lips and smooth, bland face.

"Oh, that."

"You know about it?"

"Fecik gets the paper."

"Everybody I know has been asking me if I saw it," Mary said. Kracha relaxed visibly.

"It may not be the same Mihula," Mary suggested.

"How can you say that? Look at his picture. He's his mother all over again."

"It's her son, all right," Mike said. He chuckled. "So we have a priest in the family now. We're getting on."

"A fine priest he'll make if he's anything like her."

Mary stared at the paper.

"I wonder where she ever got the money to send him through school."

She should have known better. Kracha exclaimed, "Where would she get it? It's my money that made him a priest, money she stole from me!"

"*Ach!* How long do you think money lasts in this world?"

"If it's true she's been living with this storekeeper it's easy to see where she got the money."

"And how did they get the store? With my money!"

"Oh, good God, the way you talk one would think she had stolen thousands from you!"

"It's funny he should turn out to be a priest," Mike said. "You remember what they used to say: she'd have to pay God for the money she took from you."

Kracha grunted, nursing his arm. "I don't call making her son a priest paying God for what she did to me. She'll probably keep house for him; and if I know her she is through speaking to anyone below the rank of archangel."

Mike grinned.

The kitchen was aromatic; Mary was baking a cake for Johnny, whose eleventh birthday the day was.

"Are you working tonight?"

Mike rose, stretching. "Five turns this week."

"You're doing better than Homestead."

"They said things would pick up when the open hearth was finished but so far there's no sign of it."

"We've had an open hearth in Homestead for years and it never made any difference that I could see."

"How is Sedlar doing?"

"He's working but the two boys have been laid off. Young Andy bought himself a bicycle and now Francka has to keep up the payments on it."

"I can imagine how she likes that." Mike pawed at the clothes hanging behind the door. "Do I get a clean shirt?"

"Mihal, you know I wasn't able to wash this week. Wear your old shirt and I'll wash the first thing Monday morning."

The door burst open and Johnny came in, chunky, big-footed, mottled pink from the wind.

"Don't walk so heavy!" Mary exclaimed. "I have cakes in the oven."

"Hello, Dzedo," Johnny said. "Mamma, can I have a piece of bread and butter?"

"No. How did you get your shoes so wet?"

"We were down in Pustinger's stable. They had that man that drowned himself and Herman was washing him off with a hose."

"Good God!"

"I wasn't scared. Pauline wouldn't look at him but me and Mikie did. He was in a basket and Herman was washing the mud off of him with a hose. He was all swelled up."

"They must have found Rakovich," Mike said.

"I should think they'd know better than to let young children watch such things. And you — do you have to go sticking your nose into everything?"

"I wasn't scared. Honest. Can I have the end of the rye bread?"

"Get out of that bread box! How can you even think of eating after seeing such things? Go and call Pauline and Mikie. Supper will be ready in a minute. Go on!"

"But I'm hungry!"

"You heard what your mother said," Mike said.

"Oh, gee whiz!" He went out.

The kitchen seemed oddly quiet after he'd gone.

Mary got a straw from the broom and tested her cakes, two layers in separate pans. "I guess they're about done," she murmured. She drew them out, upset them onto plates and set about making the icing.

Rich with chocolate, blazing with pink candles — eleven and one to grow on — she set the cake in the center of a table cleared of most of the supper dishes. The children's eyes shone with candlelight.

"Can I blow now?"

"Oh, let it burn some more," Pauline said.

"You shut up. It's my cake."

"Now, now!"

"I never saw a prettier cake," Mike said. "Did you give your mother a kiss for making it for you?"

Johnny leaned toward his mother and kissed her cheek.

"Now kiss your father. And Dzedo, too."

He had to get up from his chair to do that. Then he sat down again. "Now can I blow?"

"All right. But all at once, remember."

He drew in his breath till his eyes bulged, and the blast he let loose flattened Kracha's mustache against his face.

"I did it! I blew them all out! Pauline had to blow twice to blow all hers out!"

"Well why shouldn't you? You're bigger than she is, and you're a boy."

"But I had more candles on mine too, didn't I?"

"He thinks he's so wonderful," Pauline said wearily.

"Stop it! Take off the candles and cut the first piece; your father has to go to work."

Pauline was, after some discussion, conceded the right to help pull off the candles; Johnny had, she pointed out, pulled candles off hers. Mikie took no part in this squabble over trifles; he kept his eyes fixed on the cake, his mouth half open.

Johnny cut his own first piece; Mary served the rest. She examined the grain of it with professional detachment. "I used a little more butter this time," she said. "Mrs. Fecik can't understand how I get such good results; she thinks it's my stove. But the real reason is she's afraid to use enough eggs and butter."

"It tastes very good," Mike said.

"I'll put a piece in your bucket."

The smoke of the candles hung like incense in the air.

"Did you stop in to see Baraj?" Mike asked.

Kracha had, of course. Why have a bartender son-in-law if one didn't drop in on him occasionally, and especially when he was the father of a new son?

"Anna's feeling much better," Mary said. "You can stay here tonight if you like, as long as Mihal is working. It will save you a trip to Homestead and back."

"I was going to ask you," Kracha said.

"You can sleep with Johnny and Mikie in the front room. I'll give you a key so you don't have to wake me when you come in, though I'll probably be up late ironing."

"Never mind that," Mike said.

"I have to get the children's clothes ready."

"I hear Koval is out of the hospital."

"Since Sunday."

"Has the company given him anything?"

"Nine months' wages, they say."

"That's a nice piece of money."

"What good's the money? He'll limp till the day he dies."

"What good's the money? A few years ago he would have got exactly nothing."

"They need it," Mary said. "They owe the store and the butcher for all the time he's been in the hospital. And the rent."

Mike got his pipe and tobacco and sat down again. "He's talking of putting the money into a farm in Michigan somewhere."

"What kind of farm can he get for that money?"

"Wold says it will be enough for the down-payment. Frank is willing to help with the interest and taxes and when the old man has things running well he may join him. He was hoping to get one of the cranes in the new open hearth but they all went to the bosses' friends and relations and now Frank is looking for a job in the Westinghouse, he doesn't want to work in the mill any more."

Kracha grunted. "I told him he was crazy to think they'd give him a crane. But you can't talk to him."

Mary glanced at the clock. "It's getting late, Mihal."

He rose and began to dress leisurely, a sweater, a jacket, an overcoat, all old and worn and work-stained, while Mary finished packing his bucket. There was a button missing from his overcoat. He planted himself in front of Mary and pointed to it in silent reproof. She exclaimed, "Oh, I forgot again!" and began rummaging through the drawers of the sewing machine.

"How are you getting along with your widow?"

"What widow?"

Mike chuckled. Mary dropped into a chair and pulled him toward her. Mike said, "Have you told her you've got a priest for a stepson now?"

"I don't know what you're talking about."

"Listen to him," Mary said, and shook her head despairingly. "Who do you think you're fooling?"

Mike stared down at her bent head. "What have you done to your hair?"

She glanced up, her needle motionless. "My hair? Nothing. I washed it for the christening tomorrow. Why?"

"It looks nice." He touched its softness with his hand. "The lamp makes it shine."

"I only washed it for Anna's christening. Maybe because I used rain water." But she looked pleased. She had drawn the lamp near her to sew by. For all its glistening chimney and full measure of pink kerosene its light was the yellow, inadequate light of an oil lamp, and because it stood well below eye level it was prolific of shadows; but it was kind to Mary, finding gleams in her hair, touching her skin with softness, making her face the brightest thing in the room.

"She looks better since you got rid of the boarders," Kracha said. "Even Francka says so."

"I feel better," Mary said. She bit off the thread. "There."

"*Dzekujem,* missus."

Mary went with him to the door.

It was already quite dark. The evening was mild, springlike. In the street men passed on their way to work; beyond Eleventh Street the stores and saloons were bright with Saturday night lamplight.

"It will rain before morning," Mike said.

"Don't say that. After Anna's gone to so much trouble."

"Well —" He kissed her. "*S Bohom.*"

"*S Bohom.*"

He went down the street, across Eleventh. Passing Perovsky's saloon he met an acquaintance and they went down Washington together, to where the mill gate was a black hole in the wall.

Kracha returned around midnight. It took him some time to find the keyhole, and once in the kitchen he stumbled against most of the furniture it contained. He could feel the stove's dying warmth in the darkness. He went upstairs feeling his way like a blind man, remembered that the children slept in the room to the left, at the front of the house — the bedroom facing the back yard was quieter, better suited for a man who had to sleep daytimes every other week — and entered, closing the door softly behind him.

He lit the lamp and sat down on the bed to undress. Mikie and Johnny slept like children, sprawling, uncovered, their faces flushed. Kracha, handicapped as much by a swimming head as by his injured arm, cursed under his breath as he pulled off his shoes.

He remembered that Mary had asked him to wake one of the boys when he came in because occasionally, especially after such excitement as a birthday party, he was apt to wet the bed. But which one? Kracha stared at the boys drearily, then woke Johnny, hoping for the best. Luck seemed to be with him; without being told the boy got up, padded to the corner, lifted the lid off the chamber pot and stood above it, swaying sleepily, skinny legs bent, the cover he held threatening to unbalance him at any moment. Then he replaced the cover with a hideous crash and staggered back to bed. He was sound asleep the minute his face touched the pillow, though it was doubtful if he had been awake at all.

All this had plunged Kracha into a thoughtful stupor. Now he shook himself out of it and unbuttoned his trousers. As he rose to slide them off he heard a dull knocking. He listened, heard it again and went to the window. Opening it, he looked out.

A man was standing directly below, knocking on the kitchen door.

"Well?" Kracha said.

The man looked up. "Is this where Mrs. Dobrejcak lives?"

"Yes. What do you want?"

"Who are you?"

"Her father."

The man murmured something under his breath. Then he told Kracha what he had been sent to say, and after a while he went away.

Kracha had sunk down on his knees beside the window. Now, chilled, he raised his head heavily. The night was quiet, the street empty. The air was thick with smoke and fog; a little way in either direction street and houses faded into nothingness. It was silent and motionless, sharp in the throat, something that came with the night and would be gone with sunrise, as though the lack of people in the street gave it an opportunity to gather, just as in the morning people moving about would stir it and make it disappear.

Kracha got slowly to his feet, dust on the window sill dry against the palms of his hands. He lowered the window most of the way; then he went out of the room and across the landing to Mary's. She was asleep. She had left the lamp burning low, no doubt because Agnes might awaken during the night, and the dim light threw shadows across the walls, the bed. Kracha looked down at his daughter. She was lying on her side, her lashes shadowy against her cheeks, her hair loose around her face. The lamplight found dull gleams in it.

He let out his breath in a shuddering sigh, wondering why God had chosen him to do this dreadful thing to her. Then he put out his hand to touch her shoulder, to wake her and tell her that Mike was dead.

Part Three
MARY

1

THEY brought him home, his face peaceful, the shattered skull and the burns on his body mercifully concealed, and for a while he lay in the children's bedroom upstairs. Then they took him away. The day was wintry, a dark, angry day with the wind scattering dry snow like dust across the face of the hill. They buried her heart with him. She couldn't imagine wanting to go on living, yet this is the way it was: after the return from the cemetery, after the last friend had gone, she had to cook supper for the children and put them to bed; and in the morning she had to get up and make the fire and send the children off to school. Nor could the washing be put off a day longer.

The company had her sign a release in full and gave her a check for thirteen hundred dollars. Joe, trying to recall the exact terms of the company's accident compensation plan, thought she should have received more. Mike's lodge paid a five-hundred-dollar death benefit, all of which went for funeral expenses, masses for the dead and a four-grave plot excellently situated (near the chapel) in a newly opened section of the cemetery. The gravestone she chose was a granite column surmounted by the triple cross of the

Greek Catholic Church. On it was carved: MICHAEL L. DOBREJCAK. *Born December 8 1875, died March 7 1914.* The L was for Ludwig, after an uncle who had died in some forgotten war.

She moved before the month was up, unable to remain in rooms that had known Mike's living presence. His clothes she gave to strangers, less in charity than to save herself further pain. Someone had brought his lunch bucket and overcoat home from the mill; the bucket still held the sandwiches, fruit, and the piece of Johnny's birthday cake she had packed in it. But that was the first morning, when she was still too stunned to feel anything. Later, cleaning the closets, going through pockets, she found the overcoat again, and when she touched the button she had replaced for him that last evening it had seemed more than she could bear. She put the coat with the other things; then, taking down his good Sunday hat, she caught the scent of his hair, like the scent that had always clung to his pillow, and before the rush of memory, the realization of her loss, she broke down.

Grief had its way with her and left her empty.

She found two rooms on Robinson Street, near the Pennsylvania tracks and around the corner from Wood Way, where Anna and the Barajs still lived. Their nearness was comforting. Her two rooms were a tiny house in themselves, nestled against a larger one overflowing with children and boarders but separate from it, with its own porch and outhouse. Perhaps owing to the slope of Robinson Street the bedroom was two steps below the level of the kitchen. The children found this, and the bedroom's open grate, enchanting. It was an odd little house but it was old, too, badly in need of paint and repairs and impossible to keep warm in winter.

She was at this time a few months past thirty. She had four children, the oldest eleven, the youngest not yet two. She had something over a thousand dollars in the bank, a knowledge of housework and dressmaking, and her two hands. Thus equipped she took up where Mike had left off.

Because of the children she couldn't accept a job which would keep her away from home overmuch, but that necessity never arose. Times were bad. She got a day's washing here, a day's sewing there, and toward the summer's end, as the newspapers discovered war in Europe, a Jewish dentist whose wife was pregnant gave her two days' work a week — washing, ironing, cleaning his home and office. On those days she left Mikie and Agnes with Anna. Johnny and Pauline got their own lunch, boloney sandwiches and coffee or a can of baked beans, and after school Johnny got meat and made soup. She taught him how, recalling how Mr. Dexter had once scolded her for skimming the brown, curdled blood off the soup; it was a waste of good nourishment, he said. But she always skimmed her own.

She couldn't hope to live on what she earned, only to make the money in the bank last as long as possible. What she would do when that was gone she didn't know, and it was going week by week for food, rent, clothes, coal. She had already learned how quickly people could get used to another's tragedy, how easily they accepted the change that had broken another's life in two. No one was ever unkind but they all had their own troubles, their own problems of living. And a year after Mike's death she sensed that they were still thinking of her as the recipient of thirteen hundred dollars, more money than most of them had ever dreamed of having at one time.

Johnny had always collected bottles, bones, rags and old iron for the junkman; now the pennies he got he gave to his mother. Every Saturday he took his homemade wagon and went for wood, scouring the alleys back of the Main Street stores for boxes. A house under construction drew him as the flower draws the bee, and a carpenter needed only to reach for his saw to have him at his side, ready to snatch up ends and scraps of wood. His mother forbade him to walk the railroad tracks for coal but he wouldn't have anyway, the pickings were too poor. He preferred to hang around when the wagons brought loads of coal to the schoolhouse or to buildings along Main Street; it was a rare driver who, properly approached, wouldn't throw a shovelful his way. The wireworks' barges at the foot of Eleventh Street were another source of supply. The procedure was to get aboard a barge and throw the biggest lumps he could manage ashore. He risked falling into the river and being chased by a watchman, and occasionally the coal hoist operator would scoop up a bucketful of river water instead of coal and shower him with it, but that hardly detracted from the sport. It was less adventurous, but surer, to go down to the Water Works, where there was a huge, lovely pile of coal right out in the open, protected only by a wire mesh fence eight feet high.

The second summer after his father's death Johnny got a job selling papers. The boy who had the Sixth Street corner, which was good, also had an equity in the Corey Avenue corner a block west, which wasn't. He stationed Johnny in front of the drugstore there — the only other corner was occupied by the Corey Avenue school — paying him half the profits to yell, *"Press, Telly, Sun* and *Leader!"* from midafternoon until seven every day but Sunday. Johnny yelled himself hoarse and at every opportunity boarded the passing street cars; by custom newsboys were permitted to ride free. He liked that. He liked it even better in summer, when he could go swinging magnificently along the outsides of the open cars, but he was wise enough to keep that a secret from his mother.

Papers sold for a cent and cost the boys half that; to make a dime for himself Johnny had to sell forty papers. There were many nights when he failed to do so by a respectable margin; there were nights, as when the *Lusitania* was torpedoed, on which he did better. There were occasional windfalls; once a man gave him a nickel and told him to keep the change, and once a woman asked him if he was hungry. He answered truthfully that he was; and scenting largesse and anxious to give her her money's worth he added that his father had been killed in the mill, leaving four orphan children, his mother had to go out washing, and there was nothing to eat in the house. He had never felt especially sorry for himself but this time he almost made himself cry. The woman took him across the street to a quick lunch and bought him a bowl of bean soup.

Another night a man came out of the drugstore as a streetcar approached; buying a paper he dropped a coin to the sidewalk. Johnny all but dislocated his neck with helpfulness, but was careful not to move his left foot until the man, swearing disgustedly, had boarded the car and the car was out of sight. Then he picked up the coin, a dime. It was exactly the price of the swimming trunks he needed; his mother had offered to get him a ticket to the pool in the Carnegie Library building as soon as school was out if he promised not to go swimming in the river and furnished his own trunks. But when he got home that night the wish to surprise and please his mother impelled him to put both dimes, the one he'd earned and the one he'd found under his shoe, into her hand. Her praise was sufficient recompense for his sacrifice, and the next day, on his way to work, he stopped off in the five-and-ten at the foot of Library Street and stole a pair of trunks.

He did it almost without thinking — it was to his credit that he hadn't had such a plan in mind when he gave his mother the money — and it cannot be said that his conscience ever troubled him. There were few boys in the First Ward who didn't look upon the five-and-ten as a happy hunting ground and themselves entitled to whatever they could steal without being caught. That the five-and-ten could afford it was justification enough, if any was needed.

On the other hand:

A Western Union messenger boy parked his bicycle outside the drugstore one Saturday afternoon, a beautiful, sunny day, and while he was abovestairs a boy who must have been trailing him appeared, took out a jackknife and slashed both tires, utterly ruining them. Johnny watched, horrified. The boy said threateningly, "You keep your mouth shut or I'll fix you." "I won't say anything." "He took my job," the vandal explained, and fled. When the messenger boy returned and saw what had happened he sat down and cried. He was a fairly big boy, too, but then it was his own bicycle, the company didn't supply bicycles in Braddock. After a while he went away, pushing his crippled bicycle, his face tear-stained, without even asking Johnny if he'd seen anything. And though he felt relieved Johnny knew by the scared, sickish feeling in his stomach that what he had witnessed was evil, not merely a criminal or heartless thing but evil itself. It was many years before he understood why.

"People get used to it sooner than you yourself," Dorta was saying. She had grown heavier with the years; in the semi-twilight of Mary's kitchen she seemed to be sitting very stiffly erect, her head set far back on her shoulders. A solid block of a woman. Speech did not disturb her immobility. "Do you think I've forgotten? For a few days everybody is sorry for you; after that you're just another widow. And a widow — there are hundreds of widows. Widows are nothing."

"Sometimes I think the world has no place for me. Everybody has a place, everybody has something to do, but me. A widow is outside everything. Even work is given to her more out of charity than because people want something done."

"I know how you feel. It's been twenty years but it all comes back. *Bohze moj,* how did I ever live through it?" For a moment she was silent. "I know how you feel. And I know how little good my saying so does. When Joe died people talked to me the way I'm talking to you. They meant well but all I could think of was that Joe was dead. What good was all their talk? I wanted my husband alive again."

Johnny thundered up the steps of the porch outside, yelled to someone in the street and then pounded off again, leaving the little house quivering on its foundations.

"Don't expect too much from people. How much thought did you ever give to the widows you've seen made? Everybody has his own troubles to think about. Keep yourself busy and remember you have your children to live for. Johnny will be going to work in a few years. How old is he now, thirteen, fourteen?"

"Thirteen in March."

"My Joie had his own lunch bucket when he was fourteen. Of course they're stricter now."

From the deep shadows of the corner which he was making fragrant with pipe smoke Joe said, "Mary, have you thought of taking in boarders again?"

Dorta answered for her. "Keeping boarders isn't what it was when you came to America. Then they were coming by the boatload; you could put six in a room, feed them pork chops and *halushki,* and make a little money. But now with this war going on not so many are coming, and those who do come board with their relations. And even they want carpets and lace curtains in their rooms, a different dish at every meal and God knows what else." Dorta snorted. "Instead of boarders, you might consider marrying again. You could do worse."

"I've thought of it," Mary admitted, "just as I've thought of boarders and a dozen other things. Joe tells me that a man he knows — " She didn't finish.

Dorta's head swiveled majestically on her shoulders. "Who?"

"I don't think you know him," Joe murmured.

"I know everybody."

"Czudek, Paul Czudek. His wife died last year and left him with two small children. He used to be one of my boarders. Mike knew him. He has a good job in the foundry down 8th street and if Mary will marry him he'll buy a house."

Dorta's hands moved in her lap and made the beads of her rosary rattle. Mary had met her on the sidewalk outside St. Michael's and was subjected to a scolding for keeping so much to herself. Then Dorta had invited herself to Mary's house for a little talk. Their progress up Robinson Street had been a series of reunions; it seemed as though every other doorstep was occupied by one of Dorta's former boarders or his wife. They had reached Mary's kitchen finally, and Dorta had no more than made herself comfortable when they had heard Joe outside, asking Pauline if her mother was home. He too had just come from Sunday vespers.

"I hear you're thinking of buying a house yourself," Dorta said.

Joe struck a match and for a moment his face was distinct, the firm mouth, the eyelids lowered, intent on the little flame. Then he blew out the match. "If Wold makes me a good price I'm willing to talk business."

"In North Braddock?"

"That place of his back of Dooker's Hollow."

"My sons' wives are always after me, they tell me everybody is moving to North Braddock, but I'm getting too old to change. I've lived in my house since the day it was finished. Why should I leave now?"

"You've paid for it twice over, too."

Dorta shrugged. She turned to Mary. "Well, here is your chance to get your own house."

Mary shook her head. "I can't marry again. Not yet. I have nothing against him but — "

"Well, you're still young. You have time."

Joe stirred. "I hope you won't mind my saying this, Mary. It's for your own sake. Don't go looking for another Mike. You know what I mean. Mike was — well, I don't have to tell you the kind of man he was."

"He was the best man I ever knew," Mary said. "In all the years we were together I never knew him to do an unkind thing. He was always good to me. No woman could have asked for a better husband. Do you know, Dorta," she said, turning her face a little toward her, "we never had a fight. Never. Oh, a quarrel now and then about nothing. But never so bad that we hated each other, that we wanted to hurt each other."

"Well," Joe said, "it takes two to make a good marriage, though one can spoil the best."

"Any woman could have gotten along with him."

Joe made doubting noises in his throat.

"I remember he said to me once — it was that time Grancik came home drunk and gave his wife such a beating. You remember, Dorta. It was while we were living in Twelfth Street. Mike said to me, 'Marcha, always remember this: People are born good, they want to be good. But there is something in the world that makes them bad, something that is always trying to keep them from being good.' That's what he told me."

"It sounds like him," Joe admitted. "Was that the time he emptied a bucket of water over Grancik?"

"Yes. They were living next door. Her screaming, the children crying, Grancik yelling — at one in the morning, think of it. Mike put a stop to it; everybody else was afraid to interfere. Then when he came back to bed and I started talking against Grancik he told me what I've just told you, about people wanting to be good."

"After nearly drowning Grancik."

"Yes."

Joe chuckled. "Nobody else in the world."

Boys were yelling faintly in the street.

"I don't dream about him so much any more," Mary said slowly. "I used to, almost every night. In a way I'm glad; I don't think I could have stood it. For a while after he died I wanted to die too. Now and then during the day I forget he is dead. I'm working or I think of something and for a moment it's as though nothing had ever happened. I feel so light and unburdened that it surprises me. Then I remember."

"It takes a long time for the dead to die."

"Sometimes I think of him and I always see him the same way. He's looking at me and laughing. Not saying anything, just standing there and laughing at me, the way he used to do when he had made some joke, when he was feeling good. You remember how his eyes used to crinkle. Looking at me and laughing."

2

THE former bartender, a man named Timko, whose job John
Barry had inherited when Timko left to open his own saloon in
Donora, unexpectedly offered John a job as head bartender at his
place, and they moved almost at once. Donora was twenty miles
up the river from Braddock, one of the newer steel towns, the site
of a steel mill, a wire mill and one of the corporation's two zinc
smelting works. It wasn't as big as Braddock but, as Anna pointed
out, it wasn't as old and dirty either. Her departure left Mary
feeling more alone than ever.

While Anna was still boring the Barajs with her breathless trips
to Donora, her reports of the housing situation there, Mary had
suggested to her father that she move to Homestead and he come
to live with her. Kracha objected so forcefully, made himself so
downright unpleasant about it, that she abandoned the idea. Alice
was convinced his widow had enslaved Kracha body and soul.
By spring, however, Mary could no longer hope to go on without
help. Hard with desperation, prepared to defy the widow in her
own kitchen if necessary, she made a second trip to Homestead;
and this time Kracha was not listened to or pleaded with. He was
told. The widow wasn't mentioned.

She found a small house in Munhall Hollow, not far from
Francka, but put off moving until after the school picnic so that
the children wouldn't be cheated of their day in Kennywood. One
horse and wagon was enough to move all her goods; when something broke or wore out now it was seldom that she could replace
it. After the rooms were empty she gave the key to a neighbor and
then she and Johnny went down Robinson Street for the last time,
in the warm sunshine of a June morning. The other children had

spent the night with Francka. While they waited for the car she asked, "Are you sorry you're leaving Braddock?" and Johnny shook his head. "Only on account of my job." "Oh, you'll find something in Homestead. Better than selling papers." The children liked Munhall's hills and creek but leaving Braddock made her feel how greatly her way of living had changed. There had been a time when moving from one street to another was something to be discussed for months ahead. Now she had no ties; one place was like another and nowhere would she be missed. "The first thing we've got to do is set up the stove so we can eat tonight."

The car slid through Braddock. Storekeepers were sweeping sidewalks and washing windows. The motorman banged his bell and a wagon, piled with secondhand furniture, junk, swerved out of the way with the delayed abruptness of wagon wheels jerking loose from car tracks. Johnny exclaimed, "Mamma, look! There's the wagon!" and she saw that it was her own rolled-up mattress that looked so shameless in the street's sunlight. The driver and his helper must have stopped in some saloon for a drink. The backs of their blue work shirts were dark with sweat. She shushed Johnny, and then they were going by the hospital. One shiny yellow brick wing was already up and a second was building; the house on the crest of the slope that had been the Dexters' home was now the nurses' dormitory. She often wondered how it looked inside, whether she would still recognize it.

Kracha joined her a few days later, getting off the Homeville car with his suitcase one evening when the Hollow was a smoky blue with twilight. Mary heard the children greeting him and got up from her sewing machine. He came across the yard, stooping under the limp clothes lines and looking about him disapprovingly. The houses on either side seemed buried in trees and vegetation because Mary's yard was bare, with hardly a blade of grass showing. When it rained half the water that fell on the hill coursed like a flood through her yard; because it had no back fence traffic between the hillside and the road, children, chickens, even an occasional cow, used it for a thoroughfare. The outhouse was a skinny booth set in the most conspicuous position on the slope back of the house. House and outhouse sat naked on naked ground, everything exposed, ugly and bare.

"So this is where you live," Kracha said.

"It needs a little fixing," she admitted. "But if it was in perfect condition I wouldn't be getting it for ten dollars a month."

He grunted. "When I first came to America," he said, shaking the porch rail to test it and stopping almost at once because it threatened to come loose in his hand, "the railroad gave us better houses than this for nothing."

"You haven't seen the inside yet and you're finding fault already. Come in and look at your room."

He was to have a bedroom to himself while she and the children shared the other. His held a bed, a chair and an old washstand. On the wall was a picture of the Holy Family, on the floor a rag rug. The sharp slope of the hill darkened the room and kept it cool.

Kracha put his suitcase on the bed without comment.

"Well? Can't you say something? I tried to fix it nice for you."

"What do you want me to say?"

"*Ach!*"

She asked him what time he had to be at work in the morning.

"Seven. I've been getting up at six but I see now I'll have to get up a good half-hour earlier." He said it like a man looking for an argument.

Mary did not intend to give him one. "Do you work night turn?"

"No."

She felt relieved. Night turns would have made it next to impossible for her to accept outside work.

They didn't discuss what board he should pay. When payday came he had his supper and dressed; as he was leaving he put a ten-dollar bill on the table. "Here."

She looked at it and then at him. "What's that for?"

"My board. Two weeks' board."

She stared at him, her hands quiet in the dishpan. "Is that what you intend giving me? Twenty dollars a month?"

"That's what I've been paying in Homestead."

"I don't believe it."

Shrugging, "Go and ask her."

Her anger rose. "Do you expect me to feed you and pack your bucket and do all your washing for twenty dollars a month?"

"Don't you want the money?"

"I want more than twenty dollars. This isn't 1900. Everything costs more, prices are going up all the time. It cost me money to move. I can't keep you for twenty dollars a month. Nobody could."

He gestured impatiently. "If you don't want the money, say so."

He was, she felt, only looking for an excuse to pack up and leave. Her body lost its angry tenseness, her shoulders slumped wearily. "How can you treat your own flesh and blood like this? Have you no feelings?"

He went out without replying. He came home drunk.

When Francka was told about it she said, "Don't argue with him. Take what he gives you and when he comes home drunk go through his pockets."

Mary shook her head. "I don't like that. Why should I have to steal? I'm not asking for anything but what he owes me."

"Then it won't be stealing if you take it."

"But he should give it to me himself. After all, I'm his daughter, it's for his own grandchildren. Has he no feelings toward us? Even an animal will take care of its own."

"He was never much of a father and he stopped being one altogether twenty years ago. Nobody should know that better than you. Did he worry about you after your poor mother died? A fine father. Forget he's your father and be hard with him. Treat him like any other boarder."

"He's only waiting for an excuse to leave."

"You make it harder for yourself by showing you're afraid of him. Tell him you'll have him taken before the squire. Don't give him an inch. It's the only way you'll get anything. I know him, the old devil."

"When people treat me like that I can't do anything. I feel sick. I only want to get away."

"You can't afford to have such feelings. Learn to fight. If you don't fight people think you're afraid and walk on you twice as hard. You have no husband to fight for you now so you've got to learn to do it yourself."

"But why should people be like that?"

Francka threw up her hands impatiently. "Why, why? Why is anything in this world the way it is?"

Mary couldn't keep Kracha for twenty dollars a month and that hard fact drove her to having it out with him, whatever the risk. "It's no use staying here if you won't give me more money. I can't keep you for twenty dollars a month. I may as well go back to Braddock. I don't want to fight with you. I'm not asking you to support us. All I want is the regular board that everybody pays. Thirty dollars a month at least."

When he made no comment — he was looking over a pair of shoes before resoling them — she repeated in a flat voice an old saying: "Widows are beggars and orphans are scum. Every day I learn how true that is."

He sputtered, "What are you talking about, what are you talking about?"

"You heard me. I must have thirty dollars a month at least."

Kracha slipped the shoe over the iron last. "Thirty dollars is a lot of money."

Her heart lifted; the money was as good as hers. She hadn't expected him to give in so quickly.

As a boarder he was no particular trouble. He was easy to cook for; he wanted steak or pork chops for breakfast and noodle soup for supper. On Fridays of course he did without meat. When Mary tried to vary his diet he protested, so for the two years he lived with her she fried steak or pork chops every morning and made soup in the evening, every day, winter and summer. He was usually

in bed by nine. Saturday nights and pay nights he went to Homestead and got drunk.

It was summer when they came, and for all its ugliness the Hollow was a pleasanter place for children than the streets of the First
Ward. Across the road was the creek, little better than an open
sewer but possessing some of the eternal fascination of running
streams. On the hillsides were space, wind for kites, thorny shrubs
bearing a tiny fruit called haws, holes in the ground obviously made
by wild animals, and a shallow cavity under a ledge of rock waiting to be named Indian Cave. Over the hill's rim was a cemetery,
and beyond the cemetery the far outskirts of Homestead, a winding
macadam road and a deep ravine. There an incinerator smoldered
and stank sporadically at the brink of an avalanche of rubbish, the
refuse of three boroughs; thence the children were always returning laden with treasure, parts of baby carriages, leaky pots, picture
frames, chairs without legs — it was amazing what people threw
away.

When the lovely summer was over Johnny and Pauline attended
school in Munhall proper, climbing the hill by a long, slanting path
to the paved streets and dull frame houses where the "Americans"
lived and looked down, in more senses than one, on the Hunkies
in the hollow. Johnny was in the Eighth Grade and Pauline, a sickly
intense child with bad teeth and a vivid imagination, in the Seventh.
Francka disapproved of keeping Johnny in school instead of sending him out to work and brushed aside Mary's protests that she
had no choice, the boy was only thirteen. She was somewhat mol-
lified when Johnny got a job delivering wallpaper for a Homestead
store. Working after school and Saturdays, he earned three dollars
and fifty cents plus infrequent tips and what carfare he could save
by hitching rides.

He quit the wallpaper store when school ended and got a real
job, a lunch bucket and work clothes job, in a glass factory, a
glass "house" as it was called, on the edge of Swissvale. With the
chain mill in Braddock it was the largest employer of child labor

in the vicinity, a sort of preparatory school for future employees of the steel mills and the Westinghouse. At that time it was producing mostly lampshades and reflectors and automobile headlight lenses, an old ruin of a place which made up for antiquated methods and equipment by an abnormally low wage scale.

Johnny was put to work in the grinding department, introduced to the knack of roughing off the jagged edges of lampshades with a tool like a ten-inch bolt without a head and threaded its whole length, after which girls ground the edges smooth, on horizontally revolving stones flowing with sand and water. The fact that glass could be rasped like so much wood or metal, the chips flying from under one's tool, was something Johnny had to see to believe it possible. It was also a skill which had to be acquired. The first day he cracked the beginner's normal quota of lamp shades and went home with all ten fingers bandaged. His mother was watching out the window for him and when she saw his hands she exclaimed, "My God! What's happened to you?" He said it was nothing, only a few scratches, and felt flattered by her anxiety.

He and the foreman and the assistant foreman were the only males in the department; the rest were girls and women, twenty or thirty of them. A number were from Braddock and two sisters who knew his family undertook to look after him. He resented their solicitude, and with equal intensity was puzzled by the questions young men from the other, less feminine, departments asked him. They seemed to have queer ideas of what was going on. The girls alternately petted and fought with him, used him to carry notes, told him jokes whose points escaped him and became morbidly excited, it seemed to him, because one girl was going to have a baby. He himself had known that a girl could have a baby without being married for quite a while.

He was paid fifteen cents an hour. "That's five cents an hour more than I got when I first came to America," his grandfather told him. "And I was a full grown man."

"When you came to America everything was different," Mary said.

"Ten cents an hour on the railroad. And I worked for every penny I got."

He seemed to think that Johnny didn't. Annoyed, Johnny said, "What year did you come to America?"

Kracha had no memory for dates. He made the surface of his soup black with pepper. "The year Garfield was shot. You've heard of President Garfield, haven't you? The year he was shot. Almost the very month."

"Yes, but what year was it?"

"You went to school. Look it up. If you couldn't learn a little thing like that why did you go to school?"

Mary interrupted. "Eat your supper, both of you! *Bohze moj*, you're as bad as he is, and you're four times his age."

Johnny worked in the glass house all summer and for a month after school began, quitting only when the foreman said he couldn't keep him any longer unless he got his working papers. He returned to school a month late — nobody seemed to have noticed his absence — and never quite caught up with the others. Algebra, for instance, remained an incomprehensible mystery, and the arbitrariness of its rules, *a* plus *b* was whatever it was, because the book said so, take it or leave it, never ceased to offend him.

And in high school he found himself more than ever a Hunky.

3

SHE used to watch them go off in the morning together, the grandfather and the grandson, the thick-backed, plodding man and the boy with his clean neck and buoyant gait and no more behind to him than a broomstick. At that hour of the morning the hollow was dewy, cool and fragrant. In the evening Kracha was home first; Johnny had to come by car from Swissvale, with a change of cars at the Braddock end of the bridge, so it was for him that supper waited. When Kracha grumbled he was fed, but since he disliked to eat alone his grumbles continued.

The money Johnny brought home from the glass house every two weeks put an end to the dollars she had been wheedling out of Kracha over and above his board. This didn't matter while Johnny was working; but when he went back to school it became serious, and Kracha's scornful, "Go ask your son for money," hardly amusing. The war was raising prices to fantastic heights. Sugar rose to twenty-five cents a pound, potatoes to seventy-five cents a peck; and when the Government paused in its inventing of meatless, heatless and wheatless days to recommend rice, as a substitute for potatoes, then rice immediately tripled in price. Three or four days after a payday she'd be asking Kracha for money, and nagging him until she got it, but she never learned to enjoy it as some women seemed able to; the constant squabbling exhausted her. Unlike many others Kracha worked overtime and Sundays only when he couldn't avoid it; even so, he was earning twenty-five to thirty dollars a week and he never spent money on anything but work clothes and whisky. When she asked him, out of a simple inability to understand, how he could begrudge her a few dollars for food and clothes and then spend ten or fifteen dollars in a saloon, she was told it was his money and he had a right to do what he liked with it.

He was prickly with grievances. He resented having to get up half an hour earlier in the morning, he resented the long walk down the Hollow to the mill — few Hollow residents ever used the car — he resented it when supper was late because Mary hadn't been able to get away from her washtubs and ironing board in time. He resented the fact that when one moved to Munhall Hollow the crowds and saloons of Homestead's Eighth Avenue were no longer around the corner, and he resented the fact that, after being a bachelor so long, his own man, coming and going as he pleased, he was now reduced to a householder trudging back and forth to work, a member of the family expected to put up with inconveniences instead of a guest whose whims were catered to. Kracha behaved, in short, like a man determined to make people suffer because his accustomed way of living had been so changed that he was one quivering bundle of outraged habits, and because he was getting to the age when it is harder to change one's habits than to die.

So he was at times unkind, foolish and cruel; but not more so, in all likelihood, than Francka and the rest would have become under the same stresses. It may be that he would have helped Mary with better grace if it hadn't been so obviously his duty, so obviously what was expected of him. On the other hand, none of them was especially endowed with benevolence; with them all it was at best an impulse rather than a trait, and certainly never meant for the wear and tear of daily use.

On Christmas Eve Mary was waiting for him to come home. A week out of bed and still shaky — Mrs. Patterson's damp basement and windy yard had laid her low with a bad cold — she was planning to go shopping in Homestead as soon as Kracha paid his board. At ten o'clock, however, he was still missing.

Impatience had given way to anger, anger to fear and — though she kept telling herself that it was Christmas Eve and even he couldn't be thoughtless enough to spoil it, heaven itself wouldn't let him — fear gave way to a sickening presentiment of disaster.

She sent Johnny to Francka's for news. While he was gone a neighbor mounted the porch and stood, embarrassed and pitying and blinking with curiosity, in the light from the open door. "Mrs. Dobrejcak. No, no, I must get back, I only threw on my shawl to tell you something. My husband just got back from Homestead and he says your father has been arrested. It's none of my business but you know how the police are, they'll let a man spend Christmas Day in jail before they'll take the trouble to find out where he lives. My husband didn't want me to say anything, he said it's none of our business, but I thought — "

Mary heard her out and thanked her and closed the door. Her

chest felt tight. The children stared at her. "Did she say Dzedo was in jail?" "Yes." She told Mikie and Agnes to start undressing. "You better go to bed too," she said to Pauline. "I don't know what time we'll get home." She put on her hat and coat and when Johnny returned — he said only Aunt Francka was home and she didn't know anything about Dzedo — they left at once.

She had no money for carfare so they went to Homestead the back way, up over the dark hillside. Johnny led the way, warning her about rocks and gullies, pausing until she caught up with him and then going ahead. He was all feet and clumsiness at home, in the house, but on this dreary hillside he made her realize how old and tired she was. (Yet she could remember playing on the cinder dump, running over North Braddock's hills, as young and tireless as Johnny, and it wasn't so long ago either; lord, lord, what had time done to her?) His voice made the darkness vaster, space emptier. Though it was a cold night, not windy, the air a heavy, raw coldness that penetrated clothing and sank into one's bones, she was warm and perspiring when they reached the top of the hill. She gasped, "Let me catch my breath, I'm not as used to this as you!" and they stood for a moment in the lee of someone's back yard fence. The hollow lay below them, dotted with pale rooftops and lamplit windows, the street lights winding to the Junction where the end of the hollow was like an open door, lit up by the glare from the mills. Johnny tried to find their house for her but the darkness hid it. She recognized the distant, querulous bark of a neighbor's dog.

She shivered, and they climbed a rubbish-littered slope to street level and hastened through Munhall's quiet streets, past houses in which people were trimming Christmas trees, past the school and the Carnegie library and the mill Superintendent's great mansion and the Slovak church, its stained-glass windows glowing, where people were gathering for midnight mass, into Homestead and the police station on Ninth Avenue.

Kracha was there. They brought him out, still carrying his lunch bucket, and Mary said, "Yes, that's my father." He was sodden, dirty, bleary-eyed. And penniless. He'd been paid that day but his pockets were empty; what money he hadn't spent had been lost or stolen.

Trembling with weariness and despair, Mary pleaded with the officer behind the high, varnished desk, and he agreed to waive the usual fine. Because it was Christmas Eve. But he warned them that next time Kracha would go to the workhouse, money or no money. He lectured Kracha on the evils of drink, mentioned the war, used the phrase, "You Hunkies" once, and by inference blamed Kracha for the Prohibition Amendment which Congress had approved the week before. Then he yelled, "Hey you, where do you think you're going?" just as Johnny was about to see for himself what a real jail looked like inside, and let them go.

She had walked out of a police station with him once before, on a flag-decked summer afternoon years and years ago.

They went back to Munhall the long way, in the shadow of the mill wall to the Junction and then up the Hollow. It was nearly midnight when they reached the house. The children were in bed. Kracha went to his room; since leaving the police station he hadn't opened his mouth. Exhausted, Mary dropped into a chair. Johnny poked at the stove; Pauline had put in too much coal and the fire was nearly out. Four black stockings, long and skinny, were hanging from nails back of the stove. Mary stared at them. "Johnny, what are we going to do? Tomorrow's Christmas and we haven't got anything." She put her hands to her face and began to cry.

Johnny tried to comfort her — "Don't cry, Mamma. Please don't cry. It's all right, it ain't anything to cry about" — and that calmed her a little. She sent him to the store for oranges, mixed nuts and candy, and they put some in each stocking. Johnny reminded her of the buffalo nickels in the desk and she decided the emergency justified using them. They weren't as shiny as when Mike had first dropped them into the little drawer, for no reason except that they were new and pretty and uncommon, but the children wouldn't mind. She put one in each stocking and then they sat

down and between them concocted a letter, Mary disguising her
hand to write it:

Dear Children:

On account of the war I couldn't bring you anything this time but I
will be back on Greek Christmas, as that is your Christmas anyway, and
I will try and bring you some nice presents. So be good children and I
will try and come back Greek Christmas.

Your friend,

SANTA CLAUS.

Johnny, delighted with his role of conspirator, was confident it
would do. Pauline wouldn't believe Santa Claus had actually written it but Mikie and Agnes would. And anyway they were used
to having Christmas in January, it was only since Papa died that
they'd been celebrating it in December. They tacked the note
above the stockings and then they went to bed, Mary wondering
if she would ever be able to get up again.

Francka shrugged. Andrej shook his head and had a profane
half-hour with Kracha, after which he loaned him enough money
to pay his board. More sobered by the loss of his pay than anything
else, Kracha behaved himself and Greek Christmas was a tolerably
joyous occasion. But Mary was beginning to feel that she couldn't
go on with him much longer, and looked forward to summer, when
Johnny would be working again.

She didn't have to wait that long. Early in April Pauline reported that Johnny had had a fight in the school yard. He evaded
questions but his unhappiness was evident, his attitude toward
school increasingly bitter. She gathered that he was spending whole
days in the study hall because he had stopped attending some
classes and had been asked to remove himself from others. During
the Easter holidays he looked for a job, but his youth was against
him. One day he came home and said he'd asked a lawyer in Homestead and the lawyer had told him that if his mother was willing
to swear to it he could get an affidavit saying he was sixteen years
old, for two dollars. Unable to withstand his pleas she accompanied

him to Homestead. His lawyer turned out to be a real estate and insurance agent who was also a notary public, a gross, heavy-breathing man suffering audibly under his burden of flesh. His air of large good humor may not have been, as with most fat persons, spurious. He stared at Mary and asked her if she was willing to swear the boy was sixteen. She said she was, but when he held out a small Bible and asked her to repeat after him a long and impressive oath ending with a solemn, "So help me God Almighty and His Son Jesus Christ!" she faltered. She couldn't blacken her soul with such a dreadful sin. Somehow they got out. On the street Johnny exclaimed, "Why didn't you swear? He only said it like that to scare you. He knew I wasn't sixteen, if I was sixteen we wouldn't have to come to him, the dirty crook! You should've swore! Tomorrow I would've been able to get a job if you would've swore!"

"I know. I know how you feel. But I couldn't. It would have been too big of a sin."

"Oh!" He kicked at something in his path. "Well, I ain't going back to school. I won't go back even if they arrest me. I'm through with school. They only make fun of me because I'm a Hunky anyway."

"You have to go to school, Johnny."

"I'll find a way."

He did, too. Since they put such store by an affidavit, a paper, a paper he would get. He went next day, a Saturday, to the home of the school principal's secretary and told her some story of a lost birth certificate and a trust fund in the bank which she may or may not have believed. At any rate she took him into the house — she'd been drying her hair in the back yard when he came — and typed a note to the effect that the bearer, John J. Dobrejcak, was according to the school records born on March 7, 1903. Signed, H. Matthews, Secretary to the Principal. Thanking her extravagantly, he sped to a schoolmate whose father owned a typewriter, and not too skillfully — the type faces were unlike — they changed 1903 to 1902.

Mary was surprised at his ingenuity and doubtful of the paper's value, but Johnny was not to be discouraged. Because he felt the paper would be more impressive and the danger of exposure less likely at a distance, he went to Braddock Monday morning, wearing overalls in lieu of long pants, a paper bag of lunch under his arm.

He returned that night triumphant, an apprentice armature winder with a brass check to prove it. "I told them I wanted a job where I could learn to be an electrician and have a chance for advancement, so they put me in the electric shop. Mamma, I've got to get some tools."

"What's an armature?" Mary asked.

"It's part of a motor, the part that goes around."

"Is there any danger of getting hurt by electricity or something?"

"Oh, Mamma, what danger? What kind of a place do you think it is? I'll bet you have an awful funny idea of what it's like."

"I just want you to be sure and take care of yourself."

"Are we going to move now?"

"It would be nice if we could stay. The money you make added to Dzedo's board would be nice."

"But you said you didn't want to stay with Dzedo any more, you were going to move as soon as I got a job. Besides, we've got to move. If the school finds out I'm working they're liable to make trouble. We've got to move, Mamma."

She sighed. "I suppose so."

Alice and Frank Koval were living on Franklin Avenue in North Braddock, and toward the end of the month she found three rooms near them, a stone's throw across the Pennsylvania tracks from Wood Way and her old place on Robinson Street. It was an elongated shell of a house, unpainted and ugly, sitting on a bald hump of ground beside the tracks. It reminded her of the old company houses on the cinder dump.

The war ended in November. Johnny worked overtime on the second, the true, Armistice eve.

4

THE war was over but prices stayed high and the mills continued running full time. Though Johnny had been given a raise — to twenty-five cents an hour — it had been wiped out before he got it by deductions for the Liberty Bond and War Savings Stamps he had to buy. (He sold them during the depression of 1921 at a heavy discount.) His wages and the little she was able to earn did no more than keep them housed and fed. Rent and food took every penny yet they needed new clothes, insurance premiums had to be paid and it was impossible to deny the children an occasional movie, an occasional bag of candy. And it seemed that everything she owned started to wear out at the same time. Struggling for cleanliness and decency with a ramshackle, vermin-ridden house, with sheets and curtains that ripped at a touch, with chairs that fell apart, broken dishes which couldn't be replaced, a stove that seemed bent on consuming its own vitals, she sometimes didn't know whether to laugh or cry.

She could have used help, but in those from whom alone she could have asked it she felt an apprehension that she might do just that — which kept her still. She had her pride.

On a morning shortly after New Year's she got up and made Johnny's breakfast, packed his bucket, and after he'd gone to work she went back to bed. She couldn't get up to make supper that night. Next morning she felt so ill that she yielded to Pauline's entreaties and let her go for Dr. Kralik. He came and told her she had Spanish influenza. There had been epidemics of it for two years and thousands of people had died all over the country; movies had closed, schools shut down and people went around with gauze masks over their faces. In the mill the company had given the men free injections which made some of them sick, though Johnny wasn't affected one way or another. The popular preventative and cure was whisky in quantities.

She was in bed for nearly two weeks. She arose thinner than ever, very weak, and with a cough that no gargle or cough medicine seemed able to cure. Dr. Kralik shook his head when he came and found her up. "Mrs. Dobrejcak, if you won't stay in bed I can't tie you. But you're not doing yourself any good by getting up." He told her to rest all she could and to eat lots of milk and eggs. Eggs were seventy cents a dozen.

One evening, early, she was brought out of a tired doze by voices outside, on the railroad. She had left Pauline and Mikie in the kitchen doing the supper dishes; Johnny had gone to a high school basket-ball game. She sat up in bed and raised the shade. A passenger train's bright-windowed cars were halted before the house. It was an express train for she could see the towels on the seats which identified Pullman cars for her, and one car was a diner. A white-jacketed porter was leaning out of a door and people at tables were peering out into what must have seemed to them a dismal and impenetrable darkness. Men with lanterns and flashlights were moving back and forth along the train's length, and there was a good deal of confused yelling. She hoped there hadn't been an accident and lifted the window as Mikie clumped down the porch steps and crossed the yard.

"Mikie! Don't you go on the tracks."

At the sound of her voice the porter looked around too. "I won't," Mikie said. He stopped at the edge of the ditch.

"What's the matter with the train?"

"I don't know. I guess they got a hotbox."

The children had explained to her what a hotbox was. "Well, you keep off the tracks."

Cold air was drenching her and she lowered the window, coughing. She kept coughing, deep, wracking convulsions that shook her, shook the bed, threw her clawing helplessly against the wall. And then, as though what had been making her cough, the irritant, had finally torn loose, she felt her mouth fill. Even before she took her handkerchief away from her mouth she knew it was blood.

The engineer blew four blasts on his whistle.

She lived through the night somehow, death a shadow beside her, waiting. That dreadful presence accompanied her to Dr. Kralik's office on Talbot Avenue the next morning. He didn't seem surprised to see her. She told him about the blood and he looked grave and told her not to think too much about it, such things happened sometimes. "By itself it means nothing." He used his stethoscope and thumped her back and chest and asked questions. Then:

"What you need, Mrs. Dobrejcak, is rest and fresh air and good, nourishing food to build you up."

"Doctor, tell me. Have I got consumption?"

He answered with obvious reluctance. "Your lungs are touched. Yes."

Mary didn't move. "I knew it," she said in a flat voice. "I knew it as soon as I tasted the blood."

"And I suppose you saw yourself already in your grave. Well, Mrs. Dobrejcak, it's not going to be like that. We're catching it in time and before we're through we'll have you as good as new."

"Do you really think so?"

"Why should I lie to you? But we can't do it all. You have to help us." He paused. "I want you to go to a sanitarium. It will cost you nothing and it's the best place in the world for you. The only place."

"A sanitarium? You mean away from Braddock? Oh, I couldn't do that."

"Mrs. Dobrejcak, you're a sick woman, and unless you get the care you need you'll keep getting sicker and one of these days it will take more than rest and fresh air to fix you up."

She explained patiently, "How can I think of going, Doctor? I can't leave my children. Who would look after them if I went?"

Apparently he hadn't thought of that because he didn't say anything.

"You tell me what to do and I'll take care of myself here, I'll do everything you say. Why it would be worse for me if I went away, I'd be so worried about the children all the time. Don't you see?"

He shook his head. "You can't stay at home, Mrs. Dobrejcak. It's foolish to think you could take care of yourself. You'll have to go, not only for your own sake but for the children's." He stared at her, compassion in his eyes. "If you go, Pauline will have to go with you."

"Pauline?"

"I didn't like the way she looked while you were sick and I examined her. Her lungs are touched too."

"Pauline? Oh, dear God." It was like a sigh.

"You see now why you have to go. If you stay, you and Pauline may infect the others."

She put her hands to her face. "Oh God, what have I done, why must You do these things to me?"

"It was nothing you did, Mrs. Dobrejcak. Don't say things like that."

Mary cried silently.

After a while the doctor said: "It will take me a month, maybe longer, to arrange things. You'll have people coming to see you, state doctors and inspectors; they don't take my word in these things, you understand." He drummed his finger tips on the desk. "I've been thinking about you even before you came here today and I'll tell you my idea. I'm going to see if we can't have all the children sent along with you. Not the oldest boy; he looks too healthy. But it's just possible we may be able to slip the others in. God bless us all, Mrs. Dobrejcak, you couldn't ask for much more than that. You'll have your children with you and you'll all live like kings, I give you my word. The best of food, the best of care. If they so much as sneeze a dozen doctors and nurses will pounce on them as though they'd committed a crime. And a whole mountain to run around on, trees, grass, fresh air — you never smelled such air in your life."

He made it sound almost exciting.

"Where is the sanitarium?"

"There are several in Pennsylvania and you may be sent to any one of them but I'm pretty sure you'll go to Cresson. It's about seventy-five miles from here, the other side of Johnstown. They have another one in Mt. Alto and I think a small one in White Haven."

Mary looked up. "White Haven? White Haven, Pa.?"

"Yes."

"Why, I was born in White Haven." She stared at him. "Oh, don't let them send me there." She couldn't voice what chilling thought had struck her but no doubt he guessed.

"You'll probably go to Cresson. It's the nearest and not too far away for people to visit you. Don't forget, this isn't a jail, Mrs. Dobrejcak. People can come to see you almost any time."

"If I go how long do you think I'll have to stay?"

"Mrs. Dobrejcak." He sounded patient. "Understand this: You can leave any time you like. I told you it's not a jail. But if you're smart you'll stay until they tell you you can go. How long that will be nobody can say."

"But — "

"At least a year. Don't count on less than a year. But I warn you that once you get there you won't want to leave. Meanwhile I want you to take good care of yourself. I have a little pamphlet here somewhere. I want you to read it and do exactly as it says, especially about towels and your coughing and such things." He began pawing through the drawers of his desk.

She said nothing to anyone but after several people, including a brisk, spinsterish woman from some charitable organization, had been to the house she couldn't keep it a secret. Later, she and the children, including Johnny, went to a clinic in Pittsburgh and were examined. When the nurse came back with Johnny she patted him on the back and said, "There's nothing the matter with this young man. He's got a fine pair of lungs." Mary beamed. "Oh, he's always had a big chest. When he was born I thought he had something the matter with him because his chest stuck out so much." Johnny, getting into his shirt, exclaimed, "Oh, Mamma, she ain't interested in what I looked like when I was born!"

Word came, late in April, that the sanitarium would accept them all.

She had been given a list of things to buy, bathrobes, toothbrushes and so on, and one morning she went down street to the jewelry store where, years before, Mike had bought her engagement ring. To the man behind the glass display case she explained, "My husband bought this ring here a long time ago and when he bought it you told him it was a real diamond and he could always get his money back. I don't want to sell the whole ring, just the diamond. I want to keep the gold part."

The jeweler hemmed and hawed, said he wasn't running a pawnshop, peered at the stone through what looked like a telephone mouthpiece, reminded her that the war was over and finally offered her thirty dollars. Mike had paid seventy-five for it, on time. She got him up to thirty-five and he agreed to make the gold setting into a signet ring free. She had the ring engraved with Johnny's initials; when she gave it to him she said she'd found it and had had it fixed up for him. He believed her. No one missed her ring.

She was carrying two insurance policies on herself, one for five hundred and one for seven hundred and fifty. She told the agent to make the smaller one over to Anna. The other she instructed should be paid, in the event of her death (which the agent poohpoohed with professional scorn) to the bank, and held in trust for Agnes until she was twenty-one. "Boys can take care of themselves better than girls," she said.

The agent agreed, scribbling. "When will she be twenty-one?"

"She was born in 1912."

"Ah. 1933. That's a long time away."

Johnny was to move in with Alice and Frank in North Braddock. With him went her bedroom set, Mike's desk, her sewing machine and a few odds and ends. The rest — there wasn't much — she gave away after the secondhand man turned his nose up at it. She felt, in those closing days, as though all the evidence that she had lived, all that had made her a person, an individual, was being stripped from her bit by bit.

She had a final errand. She went alone to the cemetery one afternoon and sat on the grass beside Mike's grave. It was spring and the world had never seemed lovelier.

They left the first week in May.

5

IN the second letter Johnny wrote to his mother after she'd gone to the sanitarium he mentioned the possibility that there might be a strike in the mill. This was in May. The previous year's A.F.L. Convention, after authorizing an organizational drive in steel, had apparently regretted it at once. There was no other ready explanation for its giving Foster a dozen organizers and $2400 — he had asked for $250,000 — to organize the most powerful open shop industry in America.

Foster had begun the campaign in Gary and the Chicago district, and the measure of his effectiveness there was the company's announcement of its "basic eight-hour day," involving no reduction of hours actually worked but paying time-and-a-half after the first eight. Johnny, like the majority of workers, believed the change had been ordered by the Government, but Frank told him that was exactly what the company wanted him to think. "The only reason they started paying time-and-a-half was because they're afraid of the union, and don't let anybody tell you different. The Govern-

ment — hah! When the company starts letting the Government tell
it what to do . . ." He didn't finish.

"The Government's stronger than the company, ain't it?"

"Listen, Johnny. You're just a kid yet. You have a lot to learn."

Nothing annoyed him more than to be spoken to like that.

He wasn't really interested anyway. His world was filled at the moment by a bicycle which a Main Street hardware store was willing
to sell him for five dollars down and five dollars a month for five
months, plus war tax. He would have been completely ignorant of
what was going on if Frank, periodically roweled by the viciously
anti-labor stand of the Pittsburgh newspapers, hadn't felt the need
of an audience. He was too young and inexperienced to have acquired interests, political, cultural, domestic, which clashed with
the company's — to be allowed to earn money was still something
of a privilege — and the atmosphere of secrecy and suppression
so characteristic of the mill had never oppressed him. It was part
of working in the mill, like the cement walls, the cops at the gates
and being bawled out by the foreman. He sympathized with the
union, when he thought about it at all, because Frank did and
because it seemed to be scaring the pants off the company. That
delighted him.

He was a child of the steel towns long before he realized it himself.

The union had drawn up a list of twelve points for discussion
with the company, the most important of them being the right of
collective bargaining, a wage increase (unskilled labor had reached
a wartime peak of forty-two cents an hour), an eight-hour day, no
more twenty-four–hour long turns, and one day off in every seven.

Organizers appeared and several meetings were held in Braddock and McKeesport. In July, after Gary refused to meet with
the union and a strike vote had been authorized, union meetings
were outlawed in steel towns up and down the valley and union
organizers were arrested almost on sight. (The president of Homestead's borough council was also chief of the mill's mechanical department. The Burgess of Munhall was a mill department head.

The Burgess of Clairton was a mill machinist. The Burgess of Wilson was a mill cop.)

In Braddock, Father Kazincy, who had been urging his parishioners to join the union, allowed the men to meet in the church basement, and when veiled threats to foreclose on the church mortgage reached him he replied that he'd hang a sign across the front of it: "This Church of Christ closed by the United States Steel Corporation."

The company went ahead with its preparations for the strike. It built kitchens and bunkhouses inside the mill — Johnny helped wire them — and put up searchlights along the riverfront, on shop roofs and at the wide break in the wall where the B. and O. tracks entered the mill. Truckloads of stores were shipped in, mostly at night. State troopers in dark gray uniforms and potlike helmets, riding beautiful horses, appeared out of nowhere and within a week became the most hated human beings ever to be seen in the steel towns. Fannie Sellens was murdered by deputies in a Brackenridge alley; in Clairton a meeting outside the town limits was attacked by state troopers and scores of men clubbed and arrested. The Sheriff of Allegheny County swore in deputies by the thousand.

Meanwhile Johnny had got his bicycle and was going traveling every fine Sunday, to Kennywood, Munhall, Homestead, Duquesne, and once into Pittsburgh as far as Schenley Park and the paintings and plaster casts of the Carnegie Museum.

On the Sunday morning before the strike started people coming out of St. Michael's after mass lingered on the sidewalk and a state trooper rode into them, ordering them to move on. Father Kazincy came out of the church and protested, a tall, gray-haired man in priestly robes standing beside the trooper's restless horse, his face uplifted, alight with indignation. Meanwhile, the pastor of St. Brendan's on Holland Avenue, not far from the Dexters' old home in the "good" part of town, was preaching a sermon. In it this man of God said, among other things, "This strike is not being brought about by intelligent, English-speaking workmen. . . . You can't reason with these people. Don't reason with them. You can't, any more than you can with a cow or a horse. . . . And that's the only way you can reason with these people: knock them down!" He was commended by Governor Sproul for the "very good judgment expressed."

Later, a committee of Catholic delegates tried to see Bishop Canavan in Pittsburgh, tried to get from him some expression of sympathy with the strikers, most of whom were Catholics. They failed; and not long after that the Pittsburgh Catholic Charities received a check for twenty-five thousand dollars from the Carnegie Steel Company.

The morning of the strike was foggy. Frank and Johnny left the house at the usual time but wearing their second-best, week-night clothes and not carrying lunch buckets. At Thirteenth Street a dozen men were standing on the railroad overpass looking down at the mill. From their height it lay exposed, the wall around it become a decorative border, blast furnaces, rooftops and stacks filling the valley as far as the eye could see. The long row of open hearth stacks were smoking and there was a billow of steam above the blooming mill, but even Johnny could see that the smoke was the wrong color and the steam wasn't the puffing exhaust of a working engine. "What the hell are they burning in the open hearth, for God's sake?" "Tar paper, I guess. Don't let it worry you. From now on all they're goin' to produce is noise, smoke and scrap." Number 2 gate, near the corner of Thirteenth, was open; now and then a man would go in. There were no picket lines, of course. A state trooper came out of the end of Main Street and rode slowly up toward Number 1 gate. Their eyes never left him. Someone muttered, "Son of a bitch," and Johnny, the metal of the overpass cool under his chin, someone's pipe smoke brushing his face, wished fleetingly for superhuman powers so he could astonish his companions by destroying the state trooper at a quarter of a mile merely by pointing his finger.

A second trooper appeared. He glanced up toward the men on the overpass and turned his horse.

"Here he comes."

The men scattered.

The Pittsburgh newspapers began publishing a series of full-page advertisements; one portrayed Uncle Sam telling the strikers in six or seven languages to go back to work, the strike was a failure. The news stories and editorials played infinite variations on that same theme. To the strikers' demands for collective bargaining, for an eight-hour day, for one day's rest in seven, the newspapers retorted that the strikers were foreigners and anarchists and America would never stand for the red rule of Bolshevism. The strike was the work of Huns and radicals, a diabolical attempt to seize industry and establish Bolshevism in America. The steel workers weren't underpaid; some of them made twenty-five and thirty-five dollars a day. The strike was doomed to fail, like all unpatriotic movements. The union leaders expected to make five hundred thousand dollars for themselves out of initiation fees and dues. The strike was a failure. The mills were running full time, men were flocking back to work, the strike was crumbling, the strike had failed, the strike had failed. . . .

After that first morning Johnny didn't go near the mill, and the second Saturday after the strike started he pedaled twenty-five miles up the river to Donora. Nobody bothered him as he went through the mill towns. It was his first long trip and he enjoyed it. He took sandwiches along and at an open space between Glassport and Elizabeth he sat on the grass and lunched, the river and the Clairton mill on its other side spread out before him. It was a warm, hazy day; the air was very still, the river sparkled with sunlight and autumn had set the hills flaming. He felt a little like a world traveler and a little like Daniel Boone, and longed for a camera to capture something of the moment forever.

In Donora his Aunt Anna went about getting rid of a headache while he told her about the strike and Father Kazincy's commissary. Anna filled a glass with water, bunched three matches in her hand and struck them at once, let them burn for a moment and then doused them in the water. Then, murmuring under her breath, she sprinkled a little at each of the room's four corners and drank the water without swallowing any of the floating cinder.

She wiped her mouth. "When did you hear from your mother?"

"Last week. They let her get out of bed so I guess she's feeling better. I was going to bring her letter so you could read it but I forgot."

"I'm still trying to find time to answer the last one she sent me. How is Pauline?"

"I guess she's still in bed. Mikie and Agnes are up; they only kept them in bed when they first came. Mamma wants me to come up and see them but I can't until I'm working again. Maybe I'll go Christmas, if I'm working. My foreman saw me on the street and asked me why I didn't come back to work so I said I was afraid. He told me there wasn't anything to be afraid of, but I don't want to go back as long as there's a strike. The foreman thinks I don't want to come back because Uncle Frank won't let me, I guess, from the way he talked."

"Well, don't you pay too much attention to what your Uncle Frank says. If you lose your job he won't be able to get you another one. He'll be lucky if he can get one for himself. Is he in the union?"

"I guess so. He says he ain't going back unless the union wins."

"He's crazy. That's what he said when the Westinghouse went on strike. He got a job in the mill then but where will he go now? They probably won't take him back in the Westinghouse."

"He hasn't said anything about what he'll do. Aunt Alice is pretty worried."

"She has a right to be. Well, she wanted him, she couldn't live without him. Now she's got him."

"Aunt Annie, I want to ask you something. Do you think I could get a job of some kind here in Donora? Maybe Uncle John knows somebody. I don't mean in the mill. Any kind of job, just so I can keep up the payments on my bike."

"That's what you get for buying it. What did you need with a bicycle? You're getting too big for such things."

"I wanted it. I wanted it for a long time."

"Do you have to get everything you want? I wish I could get half of what I wanted."

Stubbornly, "It was my own money. I didn't take money from anything else. After I pay Aunt Alice and send Mamma ten dollars I only have sometimes five or seven and a half for myself to buy clothes and things. What's the use of working if I can't buy something for myself once in a while?"

"Well, I don't know of any jobs in Donora."

"I'll ask Uncle John. Maybe he knows somebody."

"Don't go bothering your Uncle John. He's got enough worries of his own."

Uncle John, it turned out, knew a Dr. Knight, a big, handsome man, descendant of an old Pennsylvania family, who was, for reasons of his own, drinking himself to death. More to the point, he was a Councilman and on the Republican county executive committee. A local contractor was putting down a new concrete road for the county outside Donora, and some days later Johnny was put in the road gang as a laborer, his wages forty cents an hour, four dollars a day.

It wasn't a bad job, as jobs went. Johnny liked working in the open air, outside mill walls. He shoveled cinder, wheeled sand and gravel and ate prodigious lunches sitting at the side of the road. Men made idle by the strike used to come and watch them at work; on the horizon the air above the mills was only faintly soiled.

Payday was Saturday. At noon the men put away their shovels and wheelbarrows and lined up at the shanty. Inside it there was a little counter; the paymaster and the big boss — he went around in khaki riding breeches and high laced boots and may have been an engineer — were standing behind it. On the counter were a tin box and a long-bladed butcher knife. Johnny blinked at the knife as he showed his brass check. He was given an envelope. He had worked three-and-a-half days and had earned fourteen dollars. The figures on the envelope showed that two dollars had been deducted for "purchases."

He said, "There's something wrong, mister. What's this two dollars for purchases?"

"You can read. That's for the stuff you bought."

"What stuff? I didn't buy anything."

"Listen, I ain't got any time to argue with you. Get going. You ain't the only one that wants to get paid."

Johnny went outside and lingered uncertainly for a minute, wondering what to do. The man who had been immediately behind him came out of the shanty, glanced at him and murmured, "It's no use hanging around, bud. You ain't the only one."

They went up the road toward town together. Johnny said, "I didn't buy anything."

"Neither did I, but they took two bucks out of my pay just the same. It's their graft."

"But that ain't right. I worked for the money."

"Sure you did."

"It's the county that's payin' for the road, ain't it? Couldn't we put in a complaint?"

"Who you going to complain to? The cops would laugh at you. How do you think the contractor got this job? He's in with all the politicians. Look at the road he's buildin'. It won't last five years. But you can bet your boots he's getting paid for a good road."

"Do they take off two dollars every week?"

"Yeah. If it means that much to you just don't bother coming back Monday."

"I need the job."

"Don't take it too hard, bud. Just figure you're workin' for two dollars less a week."

He told his uncle about it. "That's a damn shame," John said. But he didn't know what could be done about it.

"Well," Johnny said, "I ain't goin' to stand for it."

"What can you do? Quit? That won't get you anywhere. And don't forget Dr. Knight got you this job as a favor to me."

"I'll do something. Nobody can do things like that to me and get away with it."

During the following week he approached the foreman one noon hour. "Mr. Crombie, I want to buy a pair of work gloves."

The foreman squinted up at him, his jaws working. "Why bother me? They sell them up at the crossroads."

"I mean from the company."

The foreman studied him. "You tryin' to be funny?"

"Nossir. They been taking two bucks out of my pay every week for stuff I never bought, so — "

"Listen, kid. You want to keep this job?"

"Sure. I have to have work."

"All right then. Don't try to act too smart. It's all right to be smart but not too smart, understand? Now beat it."

Perhaps the foreman assumed that settled it. It didn't. His third week on the job the contractor himself made one of his infrequent visits and Johnny was assigned to wipe off his car, a Packard twin-six, while the contractor and the engineer strolled up toward where the cement mixer was rumbling. Johnny polished off the car and while he was about it he drove a nail part way into a rear tire. His first idea had been to pour sand into the gas tank and crankcase, but he couldn't bring himself to injure a piece of machinery.

He worked in the road gang until the end of November. Bad weather began cutting into his earnings, and as more and more strikers returned to work he started worrying about his job.

He left Donora after Thanksgiving. In Braddock, Frank had little to say when he told him he was going back to work; even he could no longer pretend that there was still hope for the strikers. He seemed to be taking it hard; he brooded a good deal and there was a beaten sag to his shoulders. He insisted it wasn't the company alone that had licked the union but the company plus the Government, plus the newspapers, plus the A.F.L. itself. When he spoke about the Pittsburgh newspapers there was an indescribable bitterness in his voice. "The lies they told, Johnny. Every day lies, lies, lies. I tell you I began to feel myself going crazy."

But he brightened a little when Johnny said he hadn't heard about Blackjack. All the state troopers followed what seemed to be a planned and systematic program of terrorism against the strikers, but one, whose talents had won him the nickname Blackjack, surpassed the rest for violence and cruelty. Where the others ordered men and women along if they lingered on a street corner, he rode his horse on them; if he saw a man sitting on his front porch he chased him inside. He had invaded a Washington Street house and beaten a man because he claimed the man had laughed at him from his window, and another time he had ridden his horse right into a Halket Avenue kitchen. One night, however, on Talbot Avenue, a striker called him a son of a bitch, added a corrosively insulting phrase in Slovak, and ran. Blackjack spurred his horse and followed. The striker fled into the maze of alleyways and courtyards between Talbot and Washington, and in that maze Blackjack was ambushed, pulled off his horse and all but beaten to death.

"It will be a long time before he hits anybody else over the head with his club," Frank said, looking pleased. Nobody knew exactly who had taken part in the affair; the men themselves weren't boasting, naturally.

Johnny went down to River Street a few evenings later, gave Dorta the latest news about his mother and on the way back inspected the courtyard in which Blackjack had been ambushed. He met several boys he knew and one of them claimed his brother had just about managed the whole business, but nobody believed him. Johnny returned by way of Thirteenth Street; at the B. and O. tracks the searchlights in the mill were pouring a flood of bluish light through the break in the wall, and in this light, as on a spotlighted stage, children were strutting and gesturing, making grotesque shadows, and a little girl, humming some song, her skirt spread, was dancing gravely, lost in a world of her own.

He went back to work Monday, showing his check as he went through the gate. His drawer, his tools, were untouched. When the foreman saw him he grunted but made no comment. About half the shop's original force never returned to work, a surprising proportion because most of them were English-speaking men and from the beginning the strike had been labeled a "Hunky" strike in an attempt — largely successful — to keep the "American" workers on the job. Two apprentices didn't return because they'd got better jobs elsewhere, and Johnny found himself advanced two places. At the back of the shop, where miscellaneous repairs were done, all the faces were strange, but as time went on they disappeared one by one; a queer sort of men who seemed to have worked in hundreds of different places.

The union called the strike off in January and the company announced a ten per cent wage increase. About the same time one of the state troopers quit his job and came to work in the shop. He said his time in the troopers was up and the company had offered him a job so he had taken it because he wanted to get married and settle down. He never did much work and he talked a lot but the foreman didn't seem to mind. After a month or so of this he apparently decided to take up the machinist trade because he left the electric shop and the next time Johnny saw him he was lounging around the machine shop, as gabby and simple-minded as ever.

Frank, who by that time had got a job, not a very good job but the best he could get, in the boiler house in the Pennsylvania railroad shops at Pitcairn, said the company had put the trooper in the shop to make sure the men didn't try to start up the union again. Later he changed his mind and decided the trooper was trying to find out who had been mixed up in the Blackjack affair. He couldn't have learned much because nobody spoke to him unless he had to.

Johnny went to see his mother at Christmas. She was up and seemed to be feeling well. She scolded him for kissing her on the mouth. He brought presents and received some in return; his mother had knitted him a sleeveless sweater and Mikie had made him a bead watch fob with his initials in red, white and blue beads worked into the design. Agnes liked the doll he brought her. Pauline, thin, big-eyed, strangely well-mannered, her bed strewn with novels and love story magazines, seemed to be getting neither better nor worse. He spent most of the day outdoors, with Mikie. He let him take several puffs on his pipe once they were deep in the woods, and while he was inspecting the ruins of an old sawmill Mikie had discovered he said casually, "Listen, don't call me Johnny any more. Call me Dobie, like the fellas in the shop." Mikie nodded, stricken dumb with embarrassment. He hadn't grown much, he was still a skinny kid, but he was as brown as an Indian and as tough as a fence rail. He had been made Ward Captain, a position to which he added the authority derived from the circumstance that, as the only healthy, untubercular boy in the ward, he could lick kids twice his size, and did.

In the spring Johnny's — Dobie's — mother wrote that she had caught a slight cold and the doctor had ordered her back to bed again. She promised to be up and around when he came to see them on Decoration Day. But she was still in bed when he came; and some weeks later she wrote that they had put her into a small, semiprivate room off the end of the ward, because it was quieter there.

6

HER bed faced the windows. Nearest were the tops of some trees, forever in motion; beyond them space and sky and the rolling hills composed so wide a view that she could follow a cloud's shadow as it slid across the earth. The hills had been a deep green at first; now they were turning brown, and square-cornered farmlands, like patches against the hills' smooth flanks, were a bright gold. The windows were kept open except in the very worst of weathers and the sounds of the outside world entered, the wind in the trees, birdsong, the distance-softened tumult of the children's playground.

Mikie and Agnes came to see her every day and seemed to fill the little room with noise and bursting energy even while they

were motionless. Pauline sent long notes. Every two weeks there
was a letter and a money order from Johnny, and less frequently
a letter from Anna. No one else ever wrote, and only Johnny ever
came to see her.

Dr. Kralik's year had come and gone. She seldom asked the
doctors, the nurses, when she would be well enough to go home. At
best she got a stock response: "What's the matter, Mary, don't you
like us any more?" At other times her questions, however timid,
seemed to annoy them. She never doubted that someday she would
leave, as healthy and strong as ever. Almost from the day of her
arrival she had ceased to think of herself as doomed; here, one
among many, her illness didn't set her apart, here she could feel
that every breath she drew was like another spoonful of medicine.
She no longer felt a sense of guilt — accentuated when the scrub-
woman or the window cleaner came around — at lying in bed daytimes, doing nothing; to be waited on no longer embarrassed her
and after receiving several scoldings she had given up trying to save
the nurses trouble (and herself mortification) about bedpans. She
was content to lie still, to feel clean and rested and cared for.
Mealtimes, rest periods, the doctor's visits, the children's invasions
— these and her thoughts filled her days, and one day was like
another.

The other bed in the room was occupied by a fragile, rather
homely girl from Uniontown. Her name was Agatha Holloway
and she had been a schoolteacher, engaged to be married, until a
haemorrhage had brought her to the sanitarium. Her intended husband was a pleasant, ordinary young man whose last name was the
most remarkable thing — to Mary — about him. It was Button:
Walt Button. An old American name, Agatha assured her. He
was a partner in an automobile agency and garage in Uniontown.
Lately he had been talking about buying his partner out. He came
to see Agatha regularly once a month. Mary tried to give them
privacy by turning on her side and pretending to go to sleep but
the ruse was never very successful. In between his visits Agatha
would talk for hours on end about him, from the time they'd met

at a church picnic to the time they'd picked out the kind of house they were going to build someday. She asked Mary all sorts of questions about married life and Mary answered them as well as she could, feeling a little tug at her heart and wondering if she herself had seemed as young and absurd and touching when she was looking forward to marriage with Mike.

At the moment Agatha was reading, for the third or fourth time, a letter from Walt. Outside the open door, in the ward, the murmur of voices which the distribution of mail had temporarily silenced, was beginning to rise again. Agatha looked up as Mary poured herself a glass of water.

"Walt's coming next week."

Mary replaced the glass and wiped her mouth. "That's nice."

"He says he has a surprise for me but I'll bet I know what it is. Father's loaned him the money and he's bought out Mr. Marinello." She glanced down at the letter, a smile trembling on her lips. "If he has, you know what he'll want to do. I don't know how I'll ever be able to talk him out of it now."

Walt wanted to marry Agatha right away and take her home, hire a nurse to look after her.

"It *is* a crazy idea, isn't it, Mary?"

"I don't want to say anything, Agatha." She had, once, and it had ended with Agatha in tears.

"Oh, you. You don't think I ought to let him, do you? But we'd be married and in our own home, seeing each other every day. I really think it would do me good. I'm so sick and tired of this place." Her cheeks were flushed. "Anyway, it's what Walt wants."

"There's more to being married than just seeing your husband every day," Mary said cautiously.

"There you go. Of course I wouldn't be much help to him at first. I know that. But don't you think it would make a difference to him if he could come home at night to his own house and be able to talk things over with somebody who sympathized with him and encouraged him? Especially now, when he'll have the responsibility of the whole business on his shoulders."

Mary sighed. Presumably Walt knew what he was doing, and why. As for Agatha, Mary hadn't yet determined whether it was from ignorance or delicacy that she had never once referred to the more intimate aspects of marriage. Nor did she care. She felt tired. She wanted to close her eyes and lie still and let her thoughts murmur her to sleep.

A nurse paused in the doorway. "Did you get a nice letter, Mary?"

Mary smiled, turning her head on the pillow. "It's from my sister."

"Walt's coming next week," Agatha said.

"Oh dear!" The nurse made a face and left the doorway. She and Agatha didn't get along too well.

"Walt says that for a while he didn't know when he'd be able to come because it looked as though there was going to be another coal strike. His Legion post was getting ready to help the police but it seems to be all settled now."

"I'm glad of that."

"So am I. It would've been just like him to get hurt and not tell me. They have so much trouble with those miners. Walt says it seems as though every time business begins to get a little better they start making trouble. They're all foreigners and he says most of them are nothing but Bolsheviks."

"I wouldn't say that," Mary murmured.

"What's worrying me," Agatha said, "is what I'm going to tell him if he wants to take me home." She sighed and settled herself more comfortably to think the matter over.

Mary didn't reply. Her finger tips rested on Anna's letter. John Barry was still working in the saloon — it was a speakeasy now, of course — but Anna wanted him to quit and get a job in the mill before something happened. Francka's Andy had got some girl into trouble and had had to marry her. They were living in Homestead and — Mary's eyes had widened as she read this — Francka had somehow persuaded Kracha to come to board with her. "After the way he used to kick about living in Munhall with me," she thought tiredly. But Prohibition had lifted whisky prices sky-high, and that Francka was making her own moonshine and home brew Kracha must have found an irresistible inducement. Lad Dexter had been killed during the war in an airplane crash in Florida. Anna had first learned about it when she read that Mr. and Mrs. Dexter had given the Braddock Hospital a memorial operating room or X-ray machine or something of the sort. Johnny had been in Donora for the Fourth of July and had taken some pictures with his new camera. He said he was intending to go to the sanitarium the Sunday before Labor Day. "I'd like to come myself and bring the boys but I don't see how I can. Helen Strojni expects her baby about that time and wants me to be godmother. Best regards and love from your sister, Ann."

Mary closed her eyes. So Lad was dead. She remembered the brilliance of sunlight on white beach, miles and miles of it, and Lad a brown, half-naked little animal tumbling in the surf. Now he was dead. God give him peace, and his mother too. . . . But for Mary it was the young man who had gone to college and was going to be a lawyer, the young man she had never known, who had died. The boy on the beach was as alive as ever. She had only to close her eyes to see him.

The human mind was a queer thing. There were times when she recalled Mike, something he had said or done, the way he'd looked, so vividly that it seemed unjust, a needless cruelty; times when she almost wished that the dead could take with them the memories of the living. Mike going to work in the morning, turning to wave a hand at the corner of Twelfth Street; Mike washing in the yard, stripped to the waist and exchanging pleasantries with Mrs. Slema or whoever; Mike sitting across the supper table from her, the lamplight modeling his face, the muscles in his temples and jaw, as he ate. Mike's voice in the darkness outside the door, discussing the obscure, absurd matters men took so seriously; Mike asleep, the afternoon's heat dampening his hair into curls, awakening reluctantly at her touch, her voice: "Mihal, it's getting late." Mike watching the children at his feet or solemnly examining a school report card; Mike holding her arm as they went up the steps of Turner Hall, their faces lifted to the lights and music. Mike angry and Mike sad, Mike tired, tired, and Mike gay and unable to keep his hands off her. The exciting, frightening look in his eyes as he watched her step naked into the washtub by the kitchen stove of a Saturday night, and the lifted blanket, the waiting arm and shoulder, as she crept into bed beside him. Mike with his restless inability to be satisfied, to accept the inevitable, with his queer way of looking at things and the queer things he said, the impression he sometimes gave of being larger than ordinary men, of one who had looked at the world as at a globe held in his hand.

She never doubted that someday, maybe soon, maybe late, but as surely as there was a God in heaven, she would see him again. It would be like him not to say anything for a minute after he first saw her, she reflected, but just stand there looking at her, his eyes crinkling with a secret amusement. She had once asked him, "Why do you always look at me like that?" "Like what? Can't a man look at his own wife? Good God!" "Yes, but not the way you do, as though you were thinking of something funny." "I can't help it. Every time I look at you I want to laugh. I look at you and it makes me feel good and I want to laugh."

Someone went past on the walk below the windows, heels tapping, fading.

Yet it would be hard to die, she thought, and felt a chill touch her lightly. Perhaps this was her appointed end, here in this bed, in this strange world of the sanitarium. But she couldn't believe it. It wouldn't be right. It didn't make sense to think that the baby whom Andrej had carried to White Haven on a bitter December morning, the child who had played in Homestead's alleys and across Braddock's cinder dumps, the girl who had gone to work for the Dexters, married Mike, borne his children, buried him, — all those years, all that living and working, taking the good with the bad and always doing one's best, never giving up hope, — had been destined for no better end than a pointless death among strangers. It wouldn't make sense. It would make living sheer waste, without meaning; and God didn't play tricks like that on people.

I don't want to die, she thought. I'm too young to die, I'll only be thirty-seven years old in December. What would become of my children? The youngest is only nine years old, practically a baby. They still need me. I can't die. Not yet. When the children are old enough to take care of themselves it will be different. And by that time . . .

By that time Johnny and Mikie would be young men coming home from work in the evening, tall, handsome young men with good jobs — not necessarily in the mill — coming home to a house something like Joe's, away from the mill where there was grass and trees. They'd fill it with noise and movement, clumping in and out of rooms, yelling downstairs, Where's my this, where's my that? *"Bohze moj,* the house was so nice and quiet until you two came home!" Pauline — she'd never be very pretty, Mary reflected with a sigh, but good looks weren't everything — would help with the housework and keep her company except on the nights she had a date. The girls Johnny and Mikie would be going around with troubled her with their vagueness, she found it impossible to visualize them, but she had Pauline's wedding pretty well planned. As for Johnny, his first baby would be a boy; the Dobrejcaks ran to boys. She tried to imagine herself with a grandchild in her arms. "Me a grandmother!" she thought. It was too silly for words. Why she could still remember herself playing, a dirty-faced brat, around the stables on the cinder dump. Of course by that time she'd be a lot older and no doubt it would feel perfectly natural to be a grand- mother; and by that time she would have forgotten all about dying.

She intended to tell the children all she could about their father. Mikie and Agnes hardly remembered him. Where he had been born, how his father had lost his life winning a bet, how he had come to America a mere boy, — "He walked across Europe, imagine!" — how he had learned to read and write English, things he had said and done. He had never liked being called Mizhu, a variant of Mihal. "Mizhu, Mizhu! What am I, a cat?" It was the popular name for toms. And she would play his game with her grandchildren when they were getting their baths. "Did you know that when you were born you had a chicken tattooed on your belly?" And then, while the wet and naked child peered down over its round belly she would touch its navel and exclaim, "Oh, what do you know about that, it's all faded away, nothing's left but the behind!"

The girls, she suspected, would be more interested in how she and Mike had met. "Of course he knew me a long time before that, but he never paid any attention to me, I was just a neighbor's girl. The first time he ever looked at me twice was when I came back to Braddock after being away with the Dexters all summer. I was all in white."

Far in the distance, but not as far as it seemed to her, a truck labored up the hill from town, the whine of its motor easing as it entered the sanitarium grounds.

She didn't know what she'd say if the girls wanted to know how Mike had proposed because he had never asked her to marry him in so many words, they'd just gone along and somehow it became understood between them that they were going to be married. "The funny part was that he was just as good as going steady with another girl but after he met me he dropped her like a hot potato. She wouldn't speak to him for the longest time. I invited her to our wedding but she wouldn't come. She got married herself about a year later. Of course you know her. She's Mrs. Ocenik that used to have the store on Talbot Avenue." "Mrs. Ocenik! You mean Papa almost married her?" She could picture the girls' amazement. It would be so hard for them to imagine Mrs. Ocenik as a young and rather pretty girl.

She wondered if she should mention the ring Mike had given her. They'd want to know where it was and maybe they wouldn't forgive her for having sold it. "After we'd decided to get married we made a promise not to give each other any presents that Christmas, to save money. But I guess neither one of us meant to keep the promise, because I got him a watch chain made out of my own hair — that's right, that's the same one — and he gave me my engagement ring. Oh, I don't remember what we said. How do you expect me to remember something like that? Wait till you get your ring and see how much you remember."

The nearest thing to a proposal that she could recall was the time Mike had seemed so impressed by the Dexters' house. He'd stood in the living room and observed that this was the way a man should live. And then he'd asked her if she thought they would ever have anything like it.

She couldn't remember her reply. But she did remember how he had put his arm around her waist and smiled down at her. "Well, who knows what may happen? I'm still young. We'll work hard, save our money. One of these days . . ." Standing there in that overfurnished room, the cold sunshine of a winter afternoon flooding the street outside, he had been quite confident, quite sure that heaven wouldn't deny so little to two young people whose intentions were so fine, who had never done anyone any harm, who were ready to work hard for what they wanted. "I want a good life for us, Marcha. For you, for me, for our children . . ."

She moved her head on the pillow as though to get away from the memory, sudden tears stinging her eyes. He had asked for so little. And as so often before, the contrast between what she and Mike had been and what they had become, between the dreams of their youth and the hard reality the years had brought them, bewildered her. Why did such things have to happen? What had gone wrong, what had they done? She felt lost. The girl who had stood beside her lover that Sunday afternoon — what was she doing in this bed, among strangers?

This isn't where I belong, she thought, this isn't me.

And for a moment everything that had happened since Mike's death became a bad dream which she needn't take seriously any more because it was only a dream and all she had to do was turn in her sleep, as she always did when a nightmare became unbearable, and she'd awaken and find herself safe in her own bed, with Mike warm beside her.

She started to turn, so vivid was the thought, a faint smile on her lips; and when the nurse noticed her the smile was still there.

Part Four
DOBIE

1

DOBIE came through the gate, said "So long" to Hagerty, and crossed the street, lively with traffic and home-going men. Except where the posters and banners announcing a new model car made one corner gay, Thirteenth Street looked shabbier than usual, perhaps because it was in shadow. Afternoon sunshine flooded the General Office building's ordered brick and limestone, its green lawn and white parking lines; above and beyond it the hills of North Braddock were a dusty brown. It had been a dry September. Mr. Flack, the General Superintendent, was standing on the steps of the building's main entrance, listening to some minor boss but not looking at him. He was a shortish, thick-bodied man with a close-cropped mustache and a funereal taste in haberdashery — he favored black silk neckties and a pearl stickpin — which impressed people almost as much as his bursts of temper and his very real power.

Someone yelled and Dobie looked around. A car disgorged Mikie and Chuck, Alice's son, and looked no emptier. They slammed the door, swaggered for the benefit of some girls who were waiting for the Dooker's Hollow bus and in time remembered Dobie. They crossed, still swaggering. Mikie was sixteen but his years in the sanitarium were beginning to have an effect: he was already as tall as Dobie and still growing, a lean, bony, ingratiating youth. Chuck was shorter and heavier, and his curly hair, the dimple in his chin, didn't save him from a certain homeliness. Both were apprentice machinists in the Westinghouse and both were, beside Dobie's workday neatness, indescribably filthy.

As they went up Thirteenth toward the railroad overpass Dobie said, "Why you guys can't clean up a little before you come home beats me. What's the matter, you afraid the gals'll think you're still going to school if you wash your faces?"

"We'd only have to wash them again when we got home."

"All you do is show you're apprentices. You never saw a mechanic going home looking like that."

"I've saw plenty," Mikie said.

They reached the steps of the overpass and started up, the sun warm on their backs. At the top they paused. Below them Thirteenth Street sloped in a straight line to the pumping station at the river's edge; over to the left the crowded rooftops of the mill looked hot and dusty. The railroad tracks curved out of sight in each direction, to Pittsburgh and to Philadelphia.

"Well," Dobie said, "I asked for my time today."

"The foreman have anything to say?"

"He said I'd be back."

"Did you tell him you were going to Detroit?"

"I guess he knows. I've been talking about it long enough."

They turned and went on toward Franklin.

"I wouldn't mind going to Detroit myself," Mikie said. "Or somewhere."

"You stay right where you are until you've learned your trade. You only have three years more and once you have your trade you can go where you like. You don't want to turn into one of these 'anything' fellas that goes around looking for a job and when they ask him what he can do he says 'anything.' That's just another way of saying he can't do nothing. Yeah, and don't get the idea that drinking moony and gambling and tom-cattin' around makes you a man either."

"Look who's talking."

"All right. But you're just a snotnose kid yet and you have a lot to learn."

"When are you figurin' on leaving?" Chuck asked.

"I think there's an excursion Saturday night."

"Well, maybe this'll get my old man off his behind and looking for work."

"Your old man's forgotten what it is to work."

They opened the rickety gate and went around to the back of the house. Frank was sitting on the porch, his feet on the rail, spitting tobacco juice into the withering morning-glory vines. He'd been sitting pretty much like that for several years now.

Pauline had died, as quietly and inconspicuously as she had lived, a year after her mother. Like Mary she was buried from Alice's house, but this time, because Francka and Alice had resented Anna's complete control over the funeral arrangements and the insurance money, — they were still inclined to brood over the fact that there hadn't been enough money left to buy a marker for Mary's grave, — Pauline's insurance money was paid directly to Dobie. He spent three hundred dollars in a single day and wondered if he would ever be the same again. The usual family squabble enlivened the wake. The sanitarium had sent Mikie and Agnes home, unwilling to keep them any longer; too many children who were really sick were waiting for admission. The elders' deliberations were edifying. Nobody wanted the children but only Francka was outspokenly in favor of sending them to an orphanage. Dobie watched and listened. In the end Anna took Agnes with her to Donora and Mikie stayed with Dobie in Alice's house on Franklin Avenue.

That was the year Dobie completed his apprenticeship and after hounding the foreman for a month was grudgingly given an armature winder's rating. He had been doing winder's work for a year. The following July the railroad shopmen went on strike and

Frank, who was then working in the Pennsylvania shops at Pitcairn, once more found himself jobless. He looked for work but his repeated failures to get anything in the mill or the Westinghouse — he tried Homestead and Duquesne, too, and even Donora, where John Barry had given up tending bar for a job in the rod mill — convinced him he was black-listed.

Perhaps he was; in six years he'd participated in three major strikes. The toll of his misfortunes, however, wasn't finished. Alice gave birth to and buried another baby, — ultimately she was to bear twelve, of whom nine died, — and several weeks after the funeral Frank and another man who was out of work hitch-hiked to Michigan. His friend went along for the trip, but Frank planned to visit his parents and see about bringing Alice and the children to live on the farm. They returned with an amazing story. Frank's father, a limping maniac, had driven them off the farm at the point of a shotgun. He didn't want Frank or his friend around, he wouldn't even let them stay overnight. When Frank reminded him of the money he had been sending through the years the old man behaved as though he hadn't heard. Frank's mother, so aged and shrunken that he hardly recognized her, never opened her mouth. Frank was sure the old man had gone crazy. The farm itself looked run-down and the house wasn't much more than a shack.

Since then Frank had worked only at odd jobs. John's ex-soldier brother, who'd got in with the Republicans and had some kind of court job in Pittsburgh, once got him a summer's work with an ice company. Frank said the dampness gave him rheumatism and when he was laid off took to sitting on the porch or near the kitchen stove and complaining about the pains in his legs. He also claimed to be chronically constipated and chewed a tablespoonful of dry Epsom salts every morning before breakfast without seeming to do himself any good — or any harm either, for that matter. The family lived on what Dobie gave them. When Chuck went to work Frank ceased even to talk about looking for a job.

Dobie's somewhat truculent announcement that he was going to

Detroit was received in silence, though Alice cried the night he left. A month after his departure Mikie wrote that he had moved to Uncle Joe's in Wolftown. "Aunt Alice cried again and I felt sorry for her but what could I do? I would have stayed because I know she needs the money but Chuck and the old man fight all the time and the grub isn't as good as it used to be. I left most of the furniture but I took the desk and I gave Agnes the Bible and that box of pictures and some other stuff. Let me know if there's anything special you want me to save. Your letter sounds as though you're doing all right. I guess Chuck would get out tomorrow if it wasn't for Aunt Alice. Frank keeps telling him that he kept him for sixteen years so now he can keep him for a while and things like that. I'm still waiting for the snapshots."

Dobie worked in Detroit for five years, living for most of that time with a Canadian couple who bore the slightly unbelievable name of Younglove. They lived in the Fairview section near the Chrysler plant, where Dobie got his first job, roughing pistons on a multi-cut machine. Its chuck, operated by compressed air, fascinated him. He moved from one plant to another for little or no reason, even sojourning unharmed one winter in Boggs's Body — it had a notoriously bad safety record and the advice, "If poison fails, try Boggs's," was to be found scrawled on most toilet walls — and once quitting a job at Ford's the same day he got it.

Detroit was flooding the world with cars, Detroit was booming, Detroit was full of young men away from home for the first time. Dobie enjoyed himself. He made good money and he spent it almost as fast as he made it. He went to Windsor and sent postcards to everybody he knew to prove that he had been in Canada, duly noting that at this point Canada was south of the United States. He picked up girls on Belle Isle, went boating on its canals in summer and skating on them in winter. Once he went skating with a drawling, hill-billy sort of young man from Kentucky whose wife had left him; the forsaken one sang "Melancholy Baby" with tears flowing down his cheeks until he ran into a low footbridge over the canal and knocked himself unconscious. He developed a collector's passion for suits, shirts and neckties and learned to eat in good restaurants. He went to burlesque shows at the Cadillac until he discovered that the touring New York revues provided better music, funnier comedians and nuder choruses. He argued their superiority with his burlesque-loving companions, but when they learned his seat had cost $5.50 they told him he had no sense, and when he paid sixty dollars for a tweed suit and fifteen for a pair of shoes they were sure of it. Yet they often gambled away whole pays and considered it almost a privilege to lose money at Johnny Bryan's place in the Grosse Pointe section. Dobie went there once to see what it was like and found the elaborate precautions, the concealed machine gunners, free food and gambling equipment reminiscent of a movie about racketeers. He lost five dollars at blackjack. He made several trips to Braddock, once to see Mikie before he left for New York and once to see Agnes graduate from high school, and never failed to be gratified by the effect his clothes, his stories about Detroit, and his easy way with a dollar created.

His last job in Detroit wasn't a good job but it was the best he could get; he had been on the point of returning to Braddock when he heard they were hiring at Budd Wheel. He worked the night shift, twelve hours on his feet on brake band assembly, riveting the lining to brake bands for Fords. The floor was cement and every morning at four the big doors at the end of the shop were opened to let in a line of freight cars, and along with them a wind that came straight from the frozen wastes of northern Canada.

On payday he and the other men in line discovered shortages in their envelopes. They made out shortage claim slips and saw the foreman toss them into the wastebasket. The rates had been changed, he said. When they protested that nobody had told them anything about a change, he shrugged. He didn't make the rates.

Going out, somebody said, "The hell with this. I'm quitting."

"That won't do you no good. It's getting hard to find a job and it looks like a cold winter."

"Yeah, but if we stay how do we know they won't change the rates again without saying anything?"

Dobie said, "Let's wait till we see the big shot tonight. If he don't give us no satisfaction we won't work."

"You mean quit?"

"No. Just refuse to work until they give us our old rates back."

"Oh — a strike."

Dobie shrugged. "The point is to make a stink. If we take this without making a stink about it, why next week or next month they'll do it again."

In the winter twilight that evening they gathered again, and most of them, by the clothes they had chosen to wear, showed small expectation of doing any work that night. One who had come in working clothes, a young, curly-haired Jew, asked, "Where you fellas think you're going all dressed up like that?" When he was told about their plan he became indignant. "Hell's fire, why didn't you guys say something? Listen, don't do anything till I get back. Promise you won't start anything till I get back."

"Where you going?"

"Home and change my clothes. I want to be in on this too."

He got back in time to be thrown out with the rest, after they had brought work in the shop to a standstill by yelling "Strike! Strike!", by throwing things at the men who refused to join them, and by cutting a few transmission belts. Guards and bosses were summoned from other departments and the rebels were herded out of the plant. Feeling, on the whole, well pleased with themselves, they ate a victory supper of pie and coffee in a lunch wagon and then scattered, some to their homes, some to the downtown movies and burlesque shows. They, and the evening, and the depression, were still young.

Dobie remained in Detroit for another week; then an opportunity to drive to Pittsburgh presented itself and seemed too good to refuse. He packed his things and told Mrs. Younglove that he'd return soon, never doubting that he would. But he was back at his old job in the electric shop and boarding in Perovsky's hotel in

East Pittsburgh a few days after he reached Braddock. McLaughlin, the foreman, swore incredulously when he saw him. "By God, if you don't pick your time!" Later, Dobie learned that two winders had quit the week before, one to go on a farm and one to go into the garage business with his brother-in-law.

As time passed, as the machinery of the country slowed down and the streets darkened with unemployed and it became plain that something was wrong, and even plainer that no one knew what to do about it, Dobie occasionally wondered about those two with a certain grim amusement. Still, they couldn't have done much better by staying.

2

THE depression deepened to the sound of voices chanting that prosperity was just around the corner, the country was fundamentally sound. In the face of unparalleled catastrophe the rich and powerful lacked even the decency to keep silent. Blind, ignorant, obsessed with the myth of their own infallibility — they had been obeyed longer than was good for any human being — they drooled their obscene mumbo-jumbo, witch doctors without faith in their own magic imploring the betrayed to have confidence, the penniless to put their money into circulation, the despoiled to take pride in an America plundered, gutted and laid waste. Silence would have become them more and proved wiser, for there must have been many like Dobie whom their stupidities shook out of bewilderment, goaded to anger.

The company cut wages ten per cent in October and an additional fifteen per cent the following May. By that time it hardly mattered; under the company's work-spreading scheme Dobie was getting only two days' work a month. Perovsky's hotel emptied. The one-time saloonkeeper and politician had been a minor casualty of the 1919 steel strike. Torn between conflicting interests he had eventually sided with the company, splitting with Father Kazincy, who was throughout vigorous in support of the strikers. The decision cost Perovsky votes and influence and ended his usefulness to the company, which unsentimentally backed an ambitious real estate and insurance broker, Andy Malko, in the next election. Malko had won, in the Harding landslide. By that time Braddock had adjusted itself to Prohibition and most of its former saloonkeepers were operating speakeasies. Perovsky's place now began to be raided regularly, the police charging that he permitted gambling — and Malko was heard to say that the raids would continue until Perovsky closed up or got out of town, preferably both. Perovsky said he was being persecuted because he had threatened to run against Malko again and because the other speakeasy owners wanted competition reduced. He began to drink heavily and his wife chose this time to resent his chronic association with other women; she left him, taking the children. Perovsky aged ten years. Even the men who during the strike had sworn never to have anything to do with him again felt sorry for him, but he made politeness embarrassing: five minutes after one greeted him on the street he was as likely as not to be clinging to one's lapel, crying drunkenly. Kracha, remembering the past, made a special trip to Braddock to view the spectacle.

After a year or so Perovsky had confessed defeat. He bought an old frame hotel in East Pittsburgh, near the Westinghouse, and opened a speakeasy there, putting the latest of his mistresses, a slatternly widow, in charge of the boarders.

From the beginning he was his own best customer, but young men seeking greater freedom of action than they were permitted at home filled his rooms and kept him from bankruptcy. "I like to see boys and girls have good time, Johnny," he told Dobie; and as long as they paid their rent and didn't set fire to the place they could do as they pleased. With bad times, however, the young men drifted away and the girls stopped coming around; there were no more parties, no more singing and dancing and naked girls stuck in transoms, and no one regretted it more than Perovsky himself.

Dobie found him a gabby old rumpot, made less sport of him than most and occasionally found his talk of ancient political chicaneries worth listening to. When the mill all but shut down only he and one other roomer remained. Dobie let two weeks go by without paying his rent. Then:

"Well, I guess I'll have to be leaving you, Joe. I'm only getting two days a month and even that's liable to end any time. No work, no money."

Perovsky mumbled, "No work, no pork, no money, no boloney." He spoke English nowadays with a steadily thicker accent. He was fat, unshaven and not overclean; and it was years since he had been completely sober.

"Unless you want to let me stay here on tick. How about it?"

Perovsky blinked at him. "Where you go?"

"I don't want to go anywhere, you ol' bastard. I want to stay right here. If you throw me out I guess I'll go to my uncle's in Wolftown, if he'll take me. I hate to ask him, though; they're just living on his pension and what his girl makes cashierin' for that movie in Braddock."

Perovsky didn't seem to have heard. It was cool and damp in the barroom and heavy green curtains on the front windows kept it dim, though blazing sunlight was beating against the street outside.

"How about it? You want to let me stay here on tick for a while? You have a dozen rooms that ain't workin' anyway; you may as well let me have a place to sleep."

Perovsky's head swiveled on its thick neck. "You want to stay, stay."

"I'll pay you when work picks up. If the lousy mill ever gets going again."

Perovsky merely stared at him. Dobie studied him for a moment and then shook his head. "Boy, you're all right, you are. You don't look out you'll end up cutting out paper dolls. But thanks anyway."

The mills lay silent month after month, under a sky that had never been so clean and blue before. After a while it was hard to remember what it had been like when they were working, the smoke and dust, the glare in the sky at night, the men streaming in and out. Going into the mill was like entering a deserted city. There was no movement, no sound. Men worked joylessly at little tasks that had no meaning. The open hearth and the rail mills were vast, echoing caverns with a single light here and there and a man, sometimes two, puttering around the still machines, the dead furnaces. They looked up eagerly at the sound of a footstep; when they spoke they kept their voices low. But not even the silence and the emptiness were as profoundly disturbing as the all-pervading cold, the strange, unnatural chill of these places of iron and flame. Leaving them was like coming out of a tomb.

Outside the walls idle men lingered like ghosts, staring at the quiet buildings, the vacant roadways, the weeds showing green against a pile of metal rusting in the yard.

The wire mill shut down and when some of its men were transferred to other mills the word went around that it would never run again. Nor did it. Bad times finished what the construction of new, automatic mills, like the one in Donora in which John worked, had begun. The chain mill shut down. The Eighth Street foundry shut down. The Westinghouse laid off all five-year men, all ten-year men, and shortly thereafter Frank and Alice were evicted for nonpayment of rent. Their furniture was sold by the sheriff; Dobie saw his mother's bedroom set and sewing machine, all that he recognized as once hers, go for a few dollars. "I was born in that bed," he thought. "We all were. Made and born." He felt that it should have seemed more important than it did. Chuck went to stay with his girl's family; they had been waiting to marry for two years. Alice went to Homestead, where her daughter was living with a man separated from his wife; he was a former automobile salesman but people had stopped buying cars and he had turned to writing numbers, the daily lottery brought to the steel towns by the Negroes and become almost a mania with the coming of bad times. Frank disappeared into the First Ward. Frankie, the younger son, was somewhere on his way to California.

In Donora John was, like Dobie, getting two days' work a month; the rest of the time he and the boys — they hadn't had steady work since they'd graduated from high school — sat around at home while Anna reverted to the past and did housework by the day, competing with Negro women whose menfolk the company had imported as strikebreakers in 1919. Agnes was working in a chain store, but her wages had been cut to the vanishing point.

An air of listlessness and decay settled over the steel towns; along their ever-shabbier Main Streets empty stores multiplied. People lost their businesses, their cars, their homes, their furniture. Families broke up, young men took to the roads. Tax receipts dropped, and the town sent its men around shutting off water until the danger of disease penetrated even their stupidity and compelled them to be generous. When the public utilities cut off their services people found ways of getting what they needed for nothing; gas and electric lines were tapped and the illegal wires and pipes replaced as fast as they were torn out. Dobie fed and smoked for weeks on his skill at by-passing electric meters and constructing long, wired poles to be hooked over the nearest power line. Movies cost him nothing; Helen Dobrejcak let him in free. Depression gardens scratched the hillsides; underneath them men pecked at long-exhausted coal veins. Here and there, in Pittsburgh, in McKeesport, Homestead, Turtle Creek, groups of people organized Unemployment Councils and marched on borough halls, shocking the newspapers and the well-fed not merely with their bad manners but with their fantastic demands for adequate relief, for unemployment insurance, old age pensions and what not. They were instantly identified as Communists and dealt with accordingly. The utterly defeated gathered with unconscious symbolism on wastelands and garbage dumps, and ramshackle "Hoovervilles" immortalized a President who refused to undermine American self-reliance by feeding the hungry and clothing the naked. The mill began distributing food boxes, forbidding its employees to seek relief from charitable organizations. People starved slowly.

And Dobie fell in love.

Agnes was engaged and planning to marry when she came of age, when she got the insurance money the bank in Braddock was holding in trust for her. Her young man was at the moment unemployed. He had worked in an office in Pittsburgh and still talked of becoming an accountant. His name was George Hornyak but he called himself Horne, pretended he couldn't understand Slovak and seemed more anxious than most of his contemporaries to forget his ancestry. He forced on Dobie some moments of rueful self-examination. He dressed well, his manners were obtrusively correct and his interests those of the prosperous young businessman — university graduate, with an office in the city, a home in a fashionable suburb — upon whom he was so obviously modeling himself. He was absurd and pathetic. It was his misfortune, Dobie reflected, to have been born just about ten years too late.

He could find no fault, however, with the girl Agnes had chosen to be her maid of honor. Julie was lean and long-legged, with a bony frame that gave her a loose, adolescent look and a stomach so flat that her hipbones made small bumps under her dress. She had a wide mouth, high cheekbones, a windblown mop of light brown hair and gray eyes that seemed forever dancing with laughter. She was the gayest thing Dobie had looked upon for longer than he cared to remember; and five months after he first set eyes on her his Aunt Anna and Agnes and the rest stopped asking him when he was going to get married because it wasn't a joking matter any more.

3

HE hitch-hiked the twenty-five miles to Donora the Sunday before Election Day and found his Uncle John watching a roast in the oven. It was his usual Sunday morning task while Anna, Agnes and the boys went to High Mass. In good times a pint of moonshine kept him company and mellowed him for dinner. This bright, crisp forenoon, however, he was cold sober, even subdued.

"It's too bad you didn't get here a little sooner," he said, as Dobie got out of his overcoat. After twelve years in the rod mill he still looked more like a bartender — a heavy-set, pink-faced, gray-haired bartender — than a millworker. He was wearing his best trousers and a white shirt open at the throat. "O'Rourke just left."

"What did he want?"

"He wanted to know what your Aunt Annie was up to. He said the office heard she was working for the Democrats and they didn't like it."

"Oh, they didn't."

"I told him I don't know what she's doing. I said Don't come to me, she's got a mind of her own and I never try to tell her what to do. If the office wants to try let them go ahead, I says. You know, joking."

Dobie sat down and stretched out his legs. He hadn't had any breakfast and the roast smelled good. "They must be plenty worried. I thought they gave up that kind of small-time stuff years ago."

"I told him to go talk to her if he wanted to. I said, That's what you get for giving women the vote. You know, kidding. Don't blame me, I says, it wasn't my idea to give women the vote."

"Well, I wouldn't let it worry me. There won't be any Republicans left after Election Day."

Anna came home ahead of the others. She was thinner and more energetic than ever, a sharp-nosed, quick-moving little woman in a neat black dress and the homeliest of hats. She sat by the table, her gloves and rosary in front of her, and listened to John's account of O'Rourke's visit.

"I passed it off as jokingly as I could. There was no use making him mad."

Anna's lips thinned. "Well, they're not going to stop me. This isn't 1900 and if they think people are going to jump any time they feel like saying Boo, they have another think coming. The Democrats asked me to work for them and I'm going to and I don't care if I don't get anything out of it, I'll do it just for the satisfaction of beating the Republicans."

"Attagirl, Aunt Annie."

"What did they ever do for the working people? All through the depression they haven't done anything to help anybody except the big banks and corporations. What good did voting Republican do John when he was getting dollar-fifty pays and taking money down to the mill on paydays to keep his insurance in force because they weren't even giving him enough work to pay for his insurance? He had to take from our few dollars in the bank and pay it to the mill on paydays instead of them paying him. I owe four months' rent and I've got a store bill that scares me when I think of it. Do they think we're all greenhorns and they can rub our faces in the dirt forever?"

"What's all the excitement about?"

Agnes had come in the front way. She was not as tall or as slim as Julie — by whom Dobie now judged all womankind — but most people thought her much prettier. She had a round, babyish face, a pink-and-white skin and pale blond hair. She was told a little of what had happened, and when the boys strolled in with the Sunday paper the story was repeated.

"I just told him, Well, I says, that's what you get for giving women the vote. Don't blame me, I says, it wasn't my idea to give women the vote."

"All right," Anna said, "all right."

Agnes began to set the table.

After dinner Dobie went up the hill to see Julie. She lived with her parents and a younger sister in an old frame house a block or so back of the Greek Catholic Church, which crowned the steep rise of Fifth Street and spilled the chime of its bells, its clock, over the dingy town. She was watching for him and opened the front door as he came through the gate. The house and the picket fence in front of it needed painting; the yard was untidy with dead vegetation.

"Hi, sweetheart."

"Hello, John."

She closed the door and kept her hand lightly pressed against it while he kissed her. Then he kissed her again; she'd put perfume behind her ears. "That's for last Sunday."

He took off his overcoat and dropped into the sofa. Its springs creaked and its dark green upholstery was old and worn, like the rest of the room, like the carpet, the repainted floor lamp with its dime store shade, the primitive radio. The room was clean and orderly; but ever since the previous autumn, when Julie's older sister had married, it had looked bare. Marion had taken a lot of things with her that she'd bought from time to time while she was working, to help fill her own two rooms.

Julie settled beside him. He smiled at her. "Well, how's everything?"

"All right. How're you?"

"Okay." His eyes swept her. "You're looking good."

"Thank you."

"Your mother home?"

"She's lying down. Papa went to the Slovak club and Cissy's over Marion's."

"That's good. I've got something I want to talk to you about."

He felt his pockets, then rose to get tobacco and papers from his overcoat. Julie said, "I wish you'd put on some weight."

"You never saw me any fatter."

"I have so, and so has Agnes and your aunt. You never had those lines in your face before. And look at the way your clothes hang on you."

"What's the matter with my clothes? I bought this suit in Detroit and I'd hate to tell you what I paid for it. Maybe a tailor could've pressed the pants better but it's still a good suit. Imported tweed."

"I'm talking about you, not your suit. I wish you'd take better care of yourself."

He grinned down at her over his cigarette, his fingers busy. "I took care of myself for a long time before I met you and I did all right. And while we're on the subject of puttin' on weight, how about yourself?"

"Mamma says I'm the kind that puts it on after she gets married. What did you want to talk to me about?"

Dobie made himself comfortable and beneath him a spring let go with a small thump. The couch awakened to activity when people sat on it and kept up a continuous and somewhat disconcerting barrage against their flinching posteriors as long as they remained. But Dobie was used to it.

"I don't know how much you know about Dzedo," he said. "That's my grandfather, my mother's father."

"Isn't he the one that's in a home or something?"

"He was. But I'd better begin at the beginning. He'd been living in Munhall with Francka, that's his sister, since away back, before my mother died. Then about 1927, '28, I don't remember exactly, he got laid off from the mill for good. He was pretty old; he must be close to seventy now. Well, he'd been saving money with Francka all the time he'd been working so he didn't worry; he figured he had enough to take care of him."

Julie leaped ahead of his story. "Why didn't he put it in a bank?"

"He didn't trust banks. None of them old-timers had much use for banks and the way they've been blowing up lately I'm beginning to think they weren't so dumb at that. Anyway, he stayed with Francka and everything was fine until about three years ago, just about the time I came back from Detroit, I remember. Francka said his money was all used up and if he wanted her to keep him he'd have to pay board."

Julie shook her head. "Her own brother."

"Wait. Well, Dzedo told her she was crazy, he claims he gave her damn near three thousand all told to save for him and he'd expected it would last just about as long as he did. But Francka said it was all gone for his board and spending money and the white mule he drank. She makes her own stuff. He didn't have any proof that he'd given her the money even if he had been able to go to a lawyer or something, so there he was. I remember there was quite a stink about it at the time but I didn't pay much attention; those old-timers were always scrapping about something and when it comes to my relations I gave up trying to keep track of who ain't talking to who long ago."

He reached a hand toward the ash tray in Julie's lap.

"Andrej, that's Francka's husband, was on a pension from the mill and Dzedo tried to get one too but they claimed he hadn't put in enough time, though Dzedo claims he did. Well, Francka didn't throw him out exactly but she made him sleep in the coal shed. He fixed up a cot and made a stove out of some junk he picked up to keep warm in winter."

"How could a woman treat her own brother like that?" Julie demanded in a shocked voice.

Dobie shrugged. "There's plenty people living a lot worse right now. And he was too damn drunk most of the time to care anyway. Fact is, Francka kept him drunk. I have an idea all this was after she found out he couldn't get a pension. She gave him all he wanted, just kept pouring it into him as fast as he could swallow it, I guess, and why that didn't make him suspicious I'll never know, because Francka ain't the kind that gives things away for the fun of it. I don't know what the record for being drunk is but I'll bet Dzedo broke it. He had a stew on you could've framed."

"It's a wonder it didn't kill him."

Dobie cocked an eyebrow at her. "Let me tell this. I remember just before she had him taken away, I went there once and he didn't know me. He used to go around talking to himself and picking up scraps of paper and saying it was money. He had his pockets full of paper. Francka said he was crazy and she had him sent to this Woodville place. I don't know much about it. After she sent him away she told Aunt Annie that she'd confessed to the priest what she had done. She'd kept Dzedo full of white mule on purpose so he'd die soon because he wasn't much use any more and he'd be better off dead."

Julie gasped.

Dobie smiled crookedly. "Yeah. And to meet her you'd figure she was just an ordinary old Hunky woman. She still goes around in her bare feet and can hardly talk English. When I was a kid I used to like to go to her place. She always fried me three eggs. I never got more than two at home. Not that I couldn't have got more, but you understand. I guess I had an idea two eggs to a person was in the Bible or something."

"Why, if he had died it would have been just as good as murder!"

"You would've had a tough time proving it. Anyway, Woodville fixed him up. I saw him Sunday and he looks swell. He knew me right off and talked sense; I guess he's in better shape now than he was ten years ago. But all he could talk about was getting away from Francka. He doesn't want to stay with her."

"I don't blame him."

"After I left I got to thinking about him and next day I went back to Munhall and took him to the mill office. I had a talk with the pension officer and he still claimed Dzedo hadn't put in enough time. Dzedo said when he first came he worked in Homestead, and then in Braddock until he went into business for himself. He used to own a butcher shop. After he lost the butcher shop — I'll have to tell you about that sometime, that's a good story too, and shows you the kind of luck Dzedo's had with women — he went back to Homestead and worked there until he was laid off. Well, the pension guy said the Homestead record was all right, but they didn't have any record of him working in Braddock. And that was that."

Dobie rolled another cigarette. Driven to rolling them by necessity, he had grown to like his own better than the manufactured brands.

Julie said, "You're smoking too much."

"Yeah, I guess I am. Well, I figured we might have better luck by going direct to Braddock so I took Dzedo there." Dobie grinned. "He thinks hitch-hiking is a swell way to get around. But it was the same story in Braddock. No record. So I just about gave it up. I took Dzedo with me to Perovsky's and he treated us to a couple of beers; he knows Dzedo from away back. I told him what we were up against but he wasn't much help. In a couple years he'll be as bad as Dzedo was before he went to Woodville if he don't lay off that paint remover he sells."

"John, be careful! You'll burn my dress."

"Sorry. Well, Perovsky said it would be all right for Dzedo to stay overnight with me and that night we got to talking and I had him go over the whole story, step by step. And guess what I found out."

"What?"

"The reason Dzedo had moved to Braddock in the first place was on account of the Homestead strike, see? And he was afraid they might not give him a job if they knew he came from Homestead so he gave a phony name."

"He did? No wonder they couldn't find any record!"

"That's right. Only trouble was, Dzedo couldn't remember what name he'd used."

"Oh, for heaven's sake!"

"Yeah, I felt like that too. We stayed up half the night trying to remember the name. I guess we thought of every Slovak name there ever was. But none of them was the one."

"What did you do?"

"Well, next morning he still couldn't remember. He wanted to see some old friends of his before he went back to Munhall and I went up to Wolftown. When I came back to the hotel Dzedo was parked in my room and the first thing he said when he saw me was 'Lupcha.' "

"Was that the name?"

"Uh-huh. He'd been down to River Street to see this old friend of his, Mrs. Radilla, and he asked her. She told him right off. She even remembered he picked the name because of some gal in Homestead."

"Did you go back to the office?"

"Sure. But on the way I thought of something else. If they did have Dzedo's record as Lupcha how was he going to prove it was him?"

Julie looked worried. "What happened?"

"They looked it up and found it all right. And right alongside his name as Lupcha they had the name Kracha in parentheses."

"What do you know about that!"

"I guess that was some company spy work. Dzedo hadn't been kidding them a bit. Anyway, I think he's all set now."

"You mean he'll get his pension?"

"I think so. It'll take a couple months but I'm pretty sure he'll get it. I don't know how much it'll be. Andrej gets around thirty-five dollars a month but the last ten years he worked he had a pretty good job on the pouring platform in the open hearth. You know, pouring the steel into the ingot molds. Dzedo never was anything but a laborer."

"I'm glad it came out all right."

"So am I."

"I suppose he'll leave Francka as soon as he gets it."

"He's left already."

"He has?"

Dobie grinned. "He's moved in with me. He packed up and hitch-hiked over the next day. Said he didn't have a bit of trouble; just stood at the Junction and waved his thumb and the

second car came along picked him up. Said he's never going to
pay for a ride again. So far Perovsky hasn't said anything.
Maybe he thinks Dzedo's been there all the time. I wouldn't be
surprised."

On the street a girl called, "May — ree! Ask your mother if you
can . . ." The rest was gibberish. The sun had shifted away from
the front of the house. Julie, still holding the ash tray, her legs
drawn up under her, sat relaxed, facing Dobie.

After a while she said, "What are you thinking about?"

"You. And me." He scratched at a spot on his crumpled vest
front. "Look, Julie. If the mills opened up and I began working
again, even if I only got three turns a week, there's people living
on less than that. Hell, it's got to open up sometime. Things can't
go on like this." He leaned toward her and put out his cigarette.
"What would your mother say if we sort of started planning to
make it soon? Provided the mills opened up, of course." He eyed
her hopefully.

Julie said gravely, "She wouldn't care. She says I'm over twenty-
one and it's entirely up to me."

"June?"

"June! But how could we? We haven't got furniture, we haven't
got anything."

"We could get enough to start with on time. And Dzedo's
pension would help out."

"Oh. Would you have him come to live with us?"

"Unless you didn't want him. But he's all right, Julie. He wouldn't
be any trouble."

"How do you know he'd want to come?"

"I asked him."

"Oh, you did."

"The thing is, I can't go on like this. If I keep on I'll turn into
a regular bum. Never mind, I see it going on all around me and
I ain't so different that I couldn't turn into as big a moocher as
any of them, sponging on people and grubbing my meals and

my smokes anywhere I could, and perfectly satisfied, too. You think I like going around like this? You think I like bumming my breakfast in Wolftown and my supper in Munhall and my Sunday dinner in Donora, never having any dough in my pocket, washing my own socks and shirts and being nice to an old bar rag like Perovsky so he won't throw me out on my can? I've taken care of myself practically since I was fifteen and I'm used to paying my own way and not asking favors off of anybody. Furthermore, I'll be thirty years old next March and you'll be — what is it, twenty-three? And finally — well, never mind that."

"Never mind what?"

He stared at her glumly. "You. The gal with the perfume behind her ears and the lipstick on her mouth and the silk stockings on her legs. The gal that keeps me awake at night."

"Do I keep you awake?"

"You don't put me to sleep."

"Poor John." But she looked rather pleased.

He dipped two fingers into a vest pocket and brought out a small gold signet ring. Its initials were almost obliterated. "It isn't much of an engagement ring for a man to give his best girl but maybe it will do until I can get you a real one. My mother had it made for me out of a ring she found just before she went to the sanitarium. Say — "

Julie glanced at him. "What?"

"Funny I never thought of it before. I remember now at the funeral Aunt Annie and the rest wondered what she'd done with her engagement ring. I'll bet that's exactly what happened. We were pretty hard up at the time and if she really had found a ring she'd been more likely to sell it than lay out good money to fix it up for me." He stared at Julie. "I'll bet this is my mother's engagement ring. What's left of it. She must've sold the diamond and had a ring made for me out of the rest of it."

Julie had leaned toward him until her head touched his, and they looked down at the little gold circlet in his palm. Julie's voice was soft with sympathy. "Poor woman. It must have broken her heart to sell it."

"Yeah, it must've been tough. Well, let's see if it fits."

It did, snugly.

After a while she said, "I want to show Mamma." She pushed her legs off the couch.

Dobie sat up. "As long as you're going upstairs get your hat and coat and we'll go for a walk. Maybe I'll treat you to a hot chocolate or something."

"You save your money. If we're going to get married in June we'll need every penny."

"I'm rich this week." He jingled some coins in his pocket. "I did a wiring job for Perovsky and knocked down a little on the supplies."

Julie went upstairs and Dobie rose, releasing a series of muffled explosions in the couch. He stretched lazily. He could hear Julie talking, the excitement in her voice carrying all the way, and her mother's drowsy responses. He got into his overcoat and then stood at the foot of the stairs and watched Julie come down them, her fur-collared coat open, a bright scarf flying at her throat, her knees rhythmic. When she reached him he said, "You're the prettiest damn thing I've ever seen," and kissed her.

Then Julie wiped lipstick off his lips and then they went out; and had they been married twenty years Dobie couldn't have shut the gate behind them more sedately — he fairly creaked — or Julie slipped her arm through his with a more wifely authority.

4

TOWARD the end of that bitter winter, one of the coldest and snowiest in years, he and Julie took to walking along McKean Avenue, inspecting furniture displays, looking at stoves and blankets and dishes. It cost nothing to look, to make lists. Julie didn't think they should count on many wedding presents. Dobie said his Uncle Joe in Wolftown had told him he could have his father's old desk any time he wanted it; it still looked good and it would help fill the room. They'd need at least three rooms, Julie said, if Kracha was going to live with them. Her mother was willing to give them Cissy's daybed for Kracha, and there was an old icebox in the cellar they could have; all it needed was a coat of paint.

"But it's so hard to make plans when you're not sure. Sometimes I don't know what to do. Pretty soon we'll have only three months left and we're still not sure about anything."

"Well, lots of things can happen in three months."

"Marion wants to give me a shower when we're surer, and I think Agnes will give me one. Don't you ever breathe a word that I said so."

"I won't."

"I've only told a few people but everybody in town seems to know it already, and they all take it for granted we're going to get married in June. I keep telling them it isn't sure, it all depends on how you're working. Oh, I hope it turns out all right. Do you think it will?"

"I think so."

But after he left her he'd stand waiting for a hitch beside the road at the edge of the town, the road he himself had helped build during the 1919 strike — it had long since crumbled to near-impassability but the contractor was still in business, still a respected citizen — and look up at the darkening sky and wonder whether to shake his fist at it or to pray.

A lot, he had assured Julie, could happen in three months. Agnes, for one, didn't have to wait that long. Two or three days before Dobie's thirtieth birthday the new President closed every bank in the country, and not all reopened. Among those which didn't was the Braddock bank that, ever since Mary's death, had been keeping her insurance money in trust for Agnes; with compound interest it had grown to nearly eleven hundred dollars.

She couldn't believe it at first. For her as for most people a bank had always been the very symbol of strength and security, partaking of the Government's own indestructibility. And for a while even Dobie believed the carefully phrased newspaper stories, the grimly optimistic statements of bank officials. Then a letter came: liquidation of the bank's affairs was in progress and all depositors would be kept informed of developments.

"Not a word about when they'll pay or even if I'll ever get anything at all," Agnes said, as Dobie gave her back the letter. It was the Saturday afternoon of Marion's shower for Julie and he had stopped in at the store on his way to the house.

He leaned on the counter. "It takes time."

"Well, they'd better hurry up and do something. They can't just tell people they haven't got the money. Where's it gone? They were supposed to hold it for me until I was twenty-one. They can't take money from people and then just say they haven't got it any more. Somebody must have it. Money doesn't evaporate into thin air."

"I guess they invested it and made loans and things like that and now they can't get it back."

Agnes looked surprised. "Are they allowed to do that with people's money?"

"Sure."

"But that's not right. I didn't tell them they could loan out my money. They were supposed to hold it for me."

"I know, but that ain't the way banks work. Cheer up. The State's taken it over and maybe they'll pay off soon."

"Yes, but when? I'm supposed to get married in September."

Dobie grunted. "Think of the people that worked for years and put in their money a dollar at a time. At least you didn't have to work for yours."

"Mamma did. In a way."

"Yeah, but you don't realize what it's done to some people. I know a couple men in Braddock, they're going around now as though somebody'd been hitting them over the head with a club for a week."

She left him to serve a customer who wanted a pound of coffee, percolator grind. Dobie propped himself on his elbows and stared vacantly at a sign above the cash register announcing that the chain store company had signed the President's recovery agreement. When Agnes came back he said, "You working tonight?"

She nodded. "I won't be able to get there till after the store closes."

"I'm taking her to a movie in Charleroi. Marion said not to come back before ten. Do you think she suspects anything?"

"I don't think so, but naturally even if she did she wouldn't let on. How's Dzedo?"

"Fine. Oh, between my three days a week and his pension we're getting along swell. All he's worried about is that the banks don't close down again when he gets his next pension check. We had to wait nearly a week before we could cash the first one."

Dobie lifted himself from the counter. "Well, I guess I'll go on up to the house. Did I tell you Chuck got a letter from Frankie?"

"It was about time. Where is he, California?"

"Iowa, working on a farm. He says it stinks. But he went up to Michigan to see how the old folks were getting along and found out they lost the farm a couple of years ago. The old lady's in the poorhouse and as far as he could make out the old man is in a sort of combination hospital and nut-house."

"For God's sake!"

"He didn't see them, it was just what people around there told him."

Agnes shook her head despairingly. "That family!"

Another customer entered and Dobie left. And if he swaggered a little, brave in a new hat and necktie, he had some reason to. The country was still stagnant with distress but a fresh wind was rising. Following Roosevelt's inauguration Washington had exploded into activity, with Congress passing laws and establishing bureaus, FERA's, NRA's, CCC's, AAA's, apparently as fast as new combinations of letters could be devised. The Government took over relief activities, putting an end to the mill's food boxes and the unspeakable poorhouse charity of the local authorities. The mills came to life with a rush; by the middle of May, Dobie was getting three days' work a week and the valley was filling with smoke. Julie had decided on a maple bedroom, and set her wedding for the third Sunday in June, and Dobie had put a deposit on a four-room house on Summer Street in North Braddock.

When he called for Julie that night he gave her a kiss and smacked her behind. "Well, Missus-pretty-soon-Dobrejcak, how are you?"

"I wish you'd learn to be more gentle," Julie said, rubbing. "That hurt."

"Wait'll we're married. I'll beat you three times a week and twice on paydays, and you'll get fat on it." He held her close, his hands clasped in the small of her back, so that she had to lean away to look at him.

"Have you heard from Mikie?" she asked.

"He won't be able to come. He's working again but I guess he hasn't been making out so good. He tells me that now, after it's all over. Not that I could have helped him any," he added ruefully.

"Who will you get — Chuck?"

"He's willing, if he can scrape up enough dough for a new suit. He says it'll be good practice for when he gets married. I wish it could be Mikie though; if I had the money I'd send him the fare myself. Well, no use thinking about it. Sweetheart," he went on, giving her a squeeze, "have you got a couple rocks under your girdle or is them your hip-bones?"

"Then don't hold me so tight."

"Can't help it. Listen, how about getting married next Thursday?"

"Next Thursday?"

"Aunt Annie says it's my mother's wedding anniversary. They would've been married thirty-one years if they'd lived."

"We'll wait till June."

He rubbed noses with her. "If I keep seeing you I won't be able to wait."

Then Cissy came in to see what was going on.

They were married in the Greek Catholic church on a brilliantly hot Sunday. The rooftops of the town and the mill were shimmering with heat as they came out of the church. Kracha stayed sober; John got drunk. Agnes was a pretty maid of honor and a poor wedding guest. A few days before she had received a second letter from the bank receivers. This one enclosed a check for $53.25, five per cent of her account. The receivers said they hoped to be able to make an additional payment in the near future but Dobie read in the financial pages — something else the depression had taught him to do — that there was little likelihood of the bank's depositors' ever getting more than a third or so of their money. Agnes was sick with fear.

Some weeks later, when Julie, Dobie and Kracha were well settled in the house on Summer Street, they heard that George Horn-

yak had gone to Cleveland on the vague promise of a job. Agnes
never saw him again.

5

THE NIRA with its controversial Section 7(A) affirming the
right of workers to collective bargaining through representatives of
their own choosing — this was inserted largely to head off a
thirty-hour work-week bill then before Congress — was passed, and
assorted master minds began the preparation of a code for the steel
industry. Two days earlier, in the same week that Dobie married,
the company posted announcements of its Employee Representa-
tion Plan "in compliance with the principles of the National Recovery Act as sponsored by the President and passed by the Congress of the United States." Such eager, even precipitant, deference
to civil law was touching, but when the election of representatives
was held, in the millennial atmosphere of bosses turned labor organizers and the company flinging money around in a fifteen
per cent wage increase, Dobie refused to vote; and he was not
alone. "We need a union all right," he told Julie, "but not that
kind. It's a company union and I don't intend to have anything to
do with it."

When McLaughlin, the foreman, came around for the second
time to tell him pointedly that Todd wanted a one hundred per cent
vote in the department, Dobie said: "No law says I have to vote, is
there?"

McLaughlin grunted. Loyalty to the company during the 1919
strike had made him a foreman but he would have been a happier
man, Dobie suspected, if he had refused the promotion. A good

mechanic, he was better at doing a job of work than at carrying out Todd's more unpleasant orders. Of late years, moreover, the foremen's importance had been steadily declining, and the fear and respect they had once inspired declined too; some were little better than pushers or straw bosses. McLaughlin was neither better nor worse than the average, a lean, worried-looking man with thinning gray hair and loose-fitting glasses, a home partly paid for and a son in Carnegie Tech.

He said, "For a man that just got married you ain't acting very smart."

Dobie swung the flame of his blowtorch off the commutator — he was stripping an armature — and pushed his safety goggles up on his forehead. "Meaning what?"

"Just what I said." The foreman walked away.

Later that afternoon Todd, the departmental superintendent, stopped beside Dobie, who had the armature stripped and was straddling one end of it, cleaning the slots of the commutator with a hacksaw blade.

"Did you vote yet?"

Dobie looked down at him from his perch. "Nossir."

"The polls are still open."

"I ain't voting."

Todd stared at him impassively for a moment, then went on. Dobie bent to his work again. Six feet away Ziggy looked up from the tangle of wires that made his partly wound armature resemble a frightened porcupine. "Now why didn't he ask me whether I voted? I was all set to tell him."

Dobie grinned. "Maybe that's what he was afraid of."

Of the fifteen men in the shop four refused to vote at all. The proportion was typical of the plant as a whole, despite pressure and thinly disguised threats by foremen and superintendents. Those who for one reason or another did vote were silent or cynical or inclined to boast that they had dropped unmarked ballots into the boxes.

"What would you have told him if he'd asked you why you didn't want to vote?" Julie asked, and Dobie shrugged. "I don't know. Maybe that I didn't like company unions. Or that I already had a union."

For the A.F.L.'s Amalgamated Association, jolted out of its senile coma by the march of events, had sent organizers into the steel towns; and when they distributed literature announcing a meeting in Homestead, Dobie accepted a card — purposely made small so as to be inconspicuous — with the remark, "We've been wondering when you guys were going to show up." He attended the meeting, recognized a number of men from Braddock, and after the speech-making was over they approached the organizer. "When are you going to do something like this in Braddock?"

"When enough men over there sign up."

"How many you need to start?"

"About five hundred."

The men from Braddock glanced at one another. Then, "Okay. Give us five hundred cards and we'll see what we can do."

They returned the following week and dropped a package before the startled organizer. "There's your five hundred cards. All signed. We could've used a couple hundred more if we'd had them."

And that was how, after fifty years, the union came back to Braddock. As simply as that.

Meanwhile the company union, the E.R.P., opened its inglorious career with a characteristic meeting. The elected representatives were nearly all hand-picked company men, though the Maintenance Department, of which the electric shop was a part, had chosen Bill Hagerty as one of its two representatives — a big, middle-aged Irish lineman with a reputation for pugnacity and outspokenness. He had once worked in the shop but had abandoned it for the line gang; and there was something about him that suggested he had been drawn by the job's dramatic possibilities, the danger, the clinging to high places, the swaggering about belted with tools. His work took him all over the plant and everybody knew him. He was not an easily overlooked figure in any company: good-looking, colorful, gifted with ready speech. He was married and the father of nine children, all living.

From him Dobie learned most of whatever went on at the E.R.P. meetings that didn't get into the minutes as posted — though after the first two meetings little happened that even a born actor like Hagerty could make worth recounting.

The first meeting was held some weeks after the election in the Electric Department storeroom inside the mill. The representatives gathered after the quitting whistle blew, had a group picture taken, and then Flack, the General Superintendent, read a speech which Hagerty was sure had been written for him in the City Office. Later reports from other mills seemed to bear him out. The speech glowed with good feeling and high purpose, heralding a new era in industrial relationships and ringing with calls to new responsibilities, new opportunities. It was a fine speech but its effect was somewhat marred when Flack produced a list of the men he wanted the assembled representatives to choose for officers. When they objected — "We figure we ought to get to know each other better first" — Flack told them they wouldn't be permitted to leave the mill until the officers he wanted had been elected; and he did keep them there, chaperoned by a mill cop, until nearly nine that night. Meanwhile he kept telephoning at frequent intervals and at last returned in person to send them home after delivering an angry speech which was probably not written for him in the City Office.

At the second meeting some days later Hagerty was elected chairman and immediately offered a resolution asking for a general ten per cent wage increase and vacations with pay. The resolution was defeated, the Superintendent of Industrial Relations, as the management's representative at the meeting, pointing out that the constitution of the E.R.P. gave them no authority to consider plant-wide questions of wages and hours. "Then what the hell good is it?" "Who the hell ever said it was any good?" None of all this, however, got into the published minutes that, sometimes weeks later, carefully edited, mimeographed in a pale violet ink which

faded to invisibility when exposed to light, the company posted
at frequently unreadable altitudes on the bulletin boards.

It was almost, but not quite, funny. As a labor union the E.R.P.
was a joke but the company wasn't going to trouble and expense to
provide laughs for anyone. Its purpose clearly was to circumvent
the law and to hamstring genuine organization by splitting the men,
supplying an approved refuge for the timid and the servile, isolating
the recalcitrant.

In this it was only partly successful. The very fact that the company had established the E.R.P. at all was a break with tradition,
a retreat, and as such the steel towns evaluated it. "The only reason
they started the company union was to keep the real union out,"
Dobie argued. "That shows they're afraid of it." Moreover, the doc-
trine that the Government was behind all workers, protecting them
— "You can't be fired for joining the union!" the leaflets exclaimed
challengingly — had not yet been disproved, and there were only a
few skeptics to observe that it hadn't been proved yet, either.

All this helped to break down the fear of unionism the company
had built up through decades of merciless repression, a fear so
deep-seated that when the Amalgamated opened an office in Braddock people went out of their way to look at it, to see it with their
own eyes. There were few who didn't find something brave and
hopeful in its mere presence, the soiled curtains across the windows
of what had been a vacant store as heart-lifting as a flag in the wind.
Yet the decisive factor was the tireless work of men like Dobie,
who joined the union and got others to join, who talked and argued
and gave up evenings to go calling on men they knew, visiting at
their homes with pockets filled with leaflets and application cards.
Fear alone kept many from joining, yet the membership grew,
the meetings in little, out of the way halls drew ever larger audi-
ences.

"It's taking hold, Julie, it's taking hold," he said exultantly. "The
meeting we had tonight was a pip. You ought to see the way some of
them old-timers get up and talk. You couldn't pay one of them to
go on the platform and make a speech but they'll stand up and say

what's on their minds. And nobody has any trouble understanding them either, even if they can't always talk good English."

Dobie himself, at a meeting in old Turner Hall alongside the B. and O. — the Poles had taken the building over and renamed it Falcon Hall — had risen to make a point about the food boxes the mill had distributed during the worst of the depression, and found himself making a speech. "I just wanted to say that I've been going around and most of the people I talk to are Slovaks and I found out that a lot of them aren't sure about the food boxes the company handed out last year. If it's all right with the rest of you I'd like to say something about that for the benefit of the people who don't understand English very good."

At a nod from the chairman he continued in Slovak:

"I just wanted to say that nobody who works in the mill should fool themselves about the food boxes. Many people I've talked to think the company has forgotten all about them, but that . . ." He fumbled for the word. "That is a mistake." He paused, shrugged apologetically and added, "For the first time in my life I wish I had listened to my father when he used to tell me not to forget my own language. My grandfather still says I talk like a gipsy."

There were a few smiles.

"But I think you understand me. The company made you sign cards saying they could deduct from your wages for the boxes, and when they are ready to do it they will. Mark my words. And you won't be able to do anything about it. If you have a good strong union, yes; but if you think the company union will ever do anything you're crazy." He paused again. "I guess that's all."

He sat down, not a little surprised at himself, to murmurs of *"Pravdu, pravdu,"* and of "Who was that?" And then he had to get up again at the chairman's request to repeat what he'd said in English.

Julie complained a little at first and taught him he was married. "I don't mind one or two evenings a week but this week you've been out nearly every night. I wouldn't mind so much if we were living in Donora but here I don't really know anybody and when you go out I have to stay home. After all, I deserve a little consideration, don't I? Let some of the other men do a little work too."

So he kissed her and promised not to leave her more than two evenings a week and to let her know beforehand when he expected to stop off somewhere after work, because she worried when he didn't get home on time. "This won't last," he assured her. "It's just while we're getting started. Once it gets going good I'll say the hell with it. I'll just pay my dues and go to a meeting once in a while."

Julie looked doubtful. "If I could believe that. First you were just going out for an hour to see some man and now you're making speeches."

He grinned. "It wasn't really a speech. I just stood up from my seat and said a few things. My old man should've seen me," he added reflectively. "I'll bet when he used to take us kids to balls at Turner Hall he never thought that someday I'd be making union speeches right in the same place. For that matter I never thought so either."

"You're enjoying yourself, aren't you?"

He grinned again. "I guess I am at that. Yeah, in a way I guess I am. And I'll tell you why, Mrs. Dobrejcak. Because I got so God damn' fed up doing nothing during the depression. I don't mean work. I mean not being able to do anything about it. The whole country was going to hell and the fat boys that were supposed to know it all just made a lot of noise and looked out for themselves. The rest of us sat around watching our jobs and everything we had getting shot out from under us without being able to do anything. On the level, I think that used to get me down more than anything else. But now we ain't waiting for anybody and anything that happens from now on we're going to have plenty to say about."

"Well, all I ask is that you remember you've got a wife at home once in a while."

Julie's forebodings were well-founded; when the Braddock lodge was chartered Dobie was elected secretary. He got home late that night, tired, proud and a little apprehensive. "I guess the main reason they picked me was they heard I had a writing desk at home," he said deprecatingly, after he'd told Julie what had happened at the meeting.

That was far from the truth, and Julie sat up in bed to tell him so. "I wish you wouldn't say things like that. They elected you because you're one of the best men they have in the union and you know it."

It was a warm night and she was wearing her thinnest nightgown. Dobie eyed her appreciatively as he lifted a hand to the light switch. "Clock set?"

"Yes."

He climbed into bed. "Got a pretty good opinion of your husband, haven't you?"

"I certainly have."

"Well, I didn't go looking for the job but when they asked me I said all right, if they wanted to elect me go ahead."

"I knew something had happened as soon as I saw your face. You looked so pleased." She kissed his ear. "Weren't you proud? I am. After all, it shows what they think of you."

"I suppose it does."

"Just wait till Donora hears about this."

"It won't mean anything to them."

"You leave that to me." She made herself comfortable against him. "Maybe I'm dumb but what does a secretary do?"

"Oh, he takes down the minutes of the meetings and sends out notices and takes care of the mail. Walsh will do most of it for a while, I guess." The organizer from Pittsburgh was a middle-aged, rather pompous man whom Braddock's blithe ignorance of union regulations and of Robert's *Rules of Order* perpetually fretted. He maintained an almost complete control over the lodge's affairs, and Dobie and the other officers — Burke, the president, a heater in the open hearth, and Gralji, the treasurer — willingly yielded to his presumably superior knowledge and wider experience.

Though every effort was made to keep the membership a secret the honor that had come to Dobie could not be hidden. McLaughlin commented, "I hear you're getting to be a big shot down the other end of town."

Dobie eyed him blandly. "No furshtay."

"You furshtay, all right."

Dobie picked up a coil and tapped it into the armature slot. "Look, Mac. Why don't you let Todd take care of his own dirty work?"

"Getting pretty cocky, ain't you?"

Dobie fitted the coil leads into the commutator, then straightened. "Nope. Just standing on my feet again instead of crawling around on my knees, that's all." He was tempted to suggest that Mc-Laughlin himself try it sometime but refrained. The foreman wasn't a young man any more and had to think about the pension he'd be applying for in a few years.

Dobie knew, if McLaughlin didn't, that close to half the men in the mill were union members; and he suspected that, despite the elaborate system of code numbers and double files which Walsh spent his days concocting, the company knew it too. That, even more than the obligation to live up to his new position, made him confident. Their strength was his; and when Todd sent for him he strolled into the dusty office, his muscles loose. His heart was beating a bit faster than usual but fortunately that didn't show.

"Mac said you wanted to see me."

Grizzled, paunchy, Todd made his chair creak as he leaned back, one hand resting on his desk. He had the mottled face and hoarse voice of a heavy drinker, the big fists, short temper and overbearing manner of the old school of bosses. He said, "You've worked here a pretty long time, haven't you?"

"Since 1918, except for a couple years in Detroit."

"Like your job?"

"Yessir."

"I just wondered."

Dobie waited.

"That's all," Todd said.

Outside the office door Dobie took a long drink of water, then returned to his armature, wiping his mouth. Every eye in the shop was on him.

"What's up?" Ziggy whispered.

"He wanted to know if I liked my job."

Ziggy whistled softly. "Putting on the pressure, hey?"

"Looks like it."

"Don't let it scare you."

"It don't. Much."

By the end of the week it seemed that most of the mill knew Dobie had been asked if he liked his job; and Burke and Gralji reported somewhat similar experiences. Yet if a number of men made it a point thereafter to avoid his company, at least as many who had never noticed him before waved to him as he went through the yard or spoke to him; and the burden of their low-voiced greetings was, "Don't let them scare you, Dobie."

"Hell," he told Julie, "that kind of thing would make any man feel good. Sure I'm worried. A little. But if they do try something we won't take it lying down."

"I certainly hope they don't."

"They won't. You can bet your boots they have a pretty good idea of how many men we got in the union, and they'll think twice before they start anything. Anyway, I'm making damn' sure not to give them an excuse. Johnny-on-the-job from now on, that's me."

He wiped a pot carefully. "You know, I never realized what this business of feeling you've got a lot of men behind you could do to a man. Or even having them come up and slap you on the back and all. It sort of makes you feel you can't back down no matter what happens. And if something does happen to you, well, it may be tough but it ain't important. What happens to one man, I mean." He paused, frowning. "It's hard to explain."

"Did you ask Walsh what you could do if they tried anything?"

"Oh, that guy. He's a dope and one of these days I'm going to tell him so."

"Now what's happened?"

"Nothing special. It's just the way he talks and acts sometimes. You remember I told you about the union in Clairton writing us a letter. Well, he won't do anything about it. Says it ain't any of our business because it's an outlaw strike and stuff like that. Same with the Ambridge and Weirton strikes. Now you know that ain't right. I don't suppose we could do much to help them but at least we could write them a letter saying we were on their side. That's what a union's for, the way I see it. Suppose we got into a spot where we needed help."

"Well, he's had more experience with unions than you so he ought to know what he's doing."

"He ought to. And I hope to hell he does."

Julie wiped the inside of the dishpan and then tipped the water out. "I don't think it would hurt to ask him, though. About what you could do."

"I don't have to ask him. We couldn't do anything, except maybe appeal to the Labor Board."

"Is that all?"

"Don't be in such a rush. We haven't even asked for recognition yet. When we're strong enough to get recognition it'll be different."

"Suppose you don't get it. What'll the union do, strike?"

Dobie shrugged. "Maybe. But it's too early to worry about that yet."

Outside they could hear Kracha pumping water for his hillside garden and complaining to their neighbor, old Peg-leg Cassidy, about the lack of rain.

6

HIS coat slung over his shoulder, Dobie went up Thirteenth Street from the railroad overpass, past Franklin, Bell, Kirkpatrick, until he came to where it ended, looking less like a street than a neglected building lot between backyard fences. Picking his way through weeds and rubbish he followed a path that led up across the face of the hill, scraggly with clumps of harsh grass, milkweed, ragweed, thistle. It wasn't a pretty hill. Most of its topsoil had been washed away and its face was scarred with gullies, pitted with holes where people had scratched for coal; in the very center of the hill's side was a large, scooped-out depression where a mine dating from the middle of the previous century had caved in years before. Yet old Peg-leg Cassidy said he could remember when the hill was lovely with trees, when there was a picnic grove on its top with tables and benches under the trees and a pavilion for dancing, as good as Kenny's Grove if not better, and the people coming down off the hill late at night, carrying lanterns and singing, was (Peg-leg said) a sight to remember. The trees and the dance pavilion had long since disappeared, the lanterns and the songs alike extinguished. Even the hawthorn and elderberry bushes of Dobie's boyhood were gone. There may have been giants in the old days, he reflected, but sometimes it seemed that the world would have been a better place if they had never lived. In fairy tales, he remembered, giants had always been the destroyers. And dwarfs, little people, the workers and builders.

As he climbed the town flattened, fell away, to his left. There was a blur of heat and smoke above the rooftops which grew thicker with distance; toward Rankin and Homestead it was an impenetrable discoloration against the sky. As a child playing on Washington Street Dobie had believed that was where the world ended. The huge, flat-sided hill on the other side of the river was acquiring its autumnal look of a shaggy bearskin. The river's surface was flat and dull.

His house was one of two which sat on the open hillside fifty yards beyond the end of Summer Street; farther on the hill was too steep for even the most intrepid of builders. His neighbors were a numerous and noisy family of Irish. The patriarch of the clan, who had lost a leg in the mill years before, was sitting on his lofty front porch as Dobie came by. He waved his pipe at him. "Pretty hot in the mill today?"

"It's cooler up here."

"It is that."

Dobie went on to his own gate and to the kitchen in the back. His house was set into the hill rather than on it, like the Cassidy's, which was reached by a long, skinny flight of wooden steps. Thus overshadowed, it looked even smaller than it was. But it had gas and electricity and a bathroom which the landlord was going to tile one of these days, and from its front porch one got as fine a view as one could want: Braddock and North Braddock spread out before one, the river, the hills, and on summer evenings the lights of Kennywood Park winking through the smoke above the blast furnaces.

He saw Kracha and his dog brooding on the hillside back of the house. Julie, looking clean, smiled at him through the screen door and then waved a dish towel to keep out the flies as she opened it for him. "I heard you talking to Mr. Cassidy."

"Oh, you did."

He kissed her.

The kitchen looked as cool and clean as Julie herself. Tomatoes were ripening on the window sill and there was a handful of flowers in a glass on the table. The green and white checked oilcloth on the floor was spotless; the stove, its sliding top lowered over the burners — Kracha had never ceased to marvel that a stove could be so beautiful — was bare of pots, glistening and immaculate.

Dobie hung his coat and battered felt hat back of the door; a moment later his shirt joined them.

"Did you work hard today?"

"No harder than usual."

As he moved to the icebox for a bottle of beer Julie said, "You got a letter from your sister. It was addressed to both of us so I opened it."

"Uh-huh. What she have to say?"

"Read it," Julie said, like a wife who has already made up her mind but wants her husband to prove his mettle by reaching the same conclusion unaided. "It's on the table."

The beer bottle was cold in his hand. "Where's the opener?"

"I'll get it."

Her legs, brown from Sundays beside the Kennywood pool, were bare, and her dress was blue scattered with small white flowers. She wasn't wearing much under it; her hipbones were prominent and her breasts shook gently when she moved. The sense of intimacy produced by her casual apparel was strong, making him realize all over again that she was here to stay, that she was his.

He accepted the opener. "Seems to me you're looking extra special today."

She examined herself interestedly, fingering her dress. "I didn't do anything except take a bath after I finished ironing. And fix my hair and put on a clean dress. I always like to look nice when you come home."

"I guess that's why I like to come home."

"The least a woman can do," Julie said with a trace of self-righteousness, "is make herself look nice for her husband when he gets home from work."

"Mrs. Dobrejcak, you are not only the prettiest girl in North Braddock, which has more pretty girls than Braddock, Rankin and East Pittsburgh put together, but you are also the smartest." He kissed her nose.

"You always say the nicest things. Give me a real kiss."

"Wait till I've cleaned up, I'm all crummy. Did you light the hot water?"

"Yes." She was still holding up her face.

He put his arms around her and pulled her close and gave her a real kiss.

"That's better," Julie said. "Now sit down and I won't bother you any more."

She stood near him, one hand on the back of his chair, while he read Agnes' letter. They had decided not to wait too long, Agnes wrote, after the usual preliminaries. Martin wanted to get married as soon as possible and so did she. It would be just a small wedding, probably in December. Aunt Annie was having a few people in on Sunday after next and she hoped Dobie and Julie could come, and to bring Dzedo with them. Aunt Annie wanted them to come for dinner, unless Julie would rather go to her mother's. She hoped they were getting along all right. Larry was going to a CCC camp. Uncle John was working steady. Aunt Annie was going to make tomato butter and if Dobie still wanted some for himself she'd get extra tomatoes; let her know. And so on.

Dobie looked up. "So she's going to marry him."

"It looks like it."

He grunted, his hand absently sliding up and down the back of Julie's legs. "You say I've met this guy?"

"He was at our wedding."

"Sweetheart, you'd be surprised how much I don't remember about our wedding."

"He's a little, skinny shrimp. Very dark." Julie paused. "He's a widower."

"A widower? For God's sake, how old a man is she marrying?"

"See? You never listen when I tell you anything. I told you he was a widower when Agnes first started going with him. He's not old. He's younger than you. He married some girl from Charleroi about two years ago and she died having a baby. The baby died too. He was all broken up about it; anyway, he acted as though he was."

"What kind of a fella is he? To know, I mean."

"He's all right, I guess," Julie said with a marked lack of enthusiasm. "I was never very friendly with him. I really never noticed him much until his wife died and he started going around like a I don't know what. I mean it's all right to feel bad because your wife's died but I always thought he put it on too thick. He'd sit with the old people all the time and never drink or dance and when he smiled it was such a sad, sweet smile." Julie grimaced. "He made me sick."

"Well, if she wants to marry him I don't know anything we can do to stop her."

"She's all mixed up. First the bank and then George running out on her two months before they're supposed to get married — my goodness, that's enough to upset any girl. Of course it may turn out all right. You can't tell. He hasn't got any bad habits that I know of and he has a steady job in the nail mill. His father owns their house but it's a pretty big family. And he still has all the furniture and things from when his wife died. You can't tell."

"Uh-huh."

"It's funny the way it's turning out, isn't it? I mean Agnes was going to buy furniture and set up housekeeping with the money from the bank and now she's lost it but she's getting furniture anyway. I don't suppose she'll want all new things. Where would they get the money?"

"Well, I certainly ain't going to try to stop her. She's over twenty-one."

They heard Kracha's heavy footsteps outside. "Wipe your feet!" Julie called, as Dobie gave her a final pat and withdrew his hand. They could hear Kracha muttering under his breath; then the door squeaked open and he entered. He sat down carefully, feet planted solidly, resting his gnarled hands on his knees. His dog peered in through the screen door after him, then collapsed tiredly on the porch.

"Well, what have you been doing today?" Dobie asked in Slovak.

"I manage to keep myself busy. When your *Rusnačka* here lets me."

"If I didn't keep after you my house would look like a pigsty," Julie retorted.

He blinked at her. "When you've lived as long as I you won't be so afraid of a little dirt."

"Never mind. It's hard enough to keep this place clean without you and that flounder-footed dog of yours dragging in dirt from all over the hill."

Kracha glanced at Dobie and shrugged hopelessly, as one man to another, before the unreasonableness of woman. Dobie grinned. "Fight it out between yourselves. I'm going to take a bath."

He went upstairs, leaving Julie to start supper and Kracha sitting by the door, an old man in baggy trousers and a shapeless hat. The years had bowed his shoulders — Dobie was a good head taller — and he moved deliberately, carefully, but his eyes were clear and his face almost free of wrinkles. There was remarkably little gray in his hair, and his mustache was still luxuriant.

They had settled into living together with less friction than Dobie, in spite of his assurances to Julie, had expected. Perhaps most of the credit for this belonged to Kracha; he was used to living with people as only the old can be. By nine in the evening he was in bed; by six in the morning he was in the kitchen, banging pots and brewing coffee of a heroic strength and blackness. In between times, he was quarreling with Julie because she wouldn't give him steak for breakfast oftener, — oatmeal was for children and eggs you ate on Fridays from necessity; he wanted steak or, better still, pork chops, — or contemplating his garden's superiority to Peg-leg Cassidy's miserable patch of clay and weeds, or berating his hens for not laying more eggs, or sawing and hammering at something, or putting on his best black suit and going visiting, or looking forward to Saturday when Julie gave him fifty cents' spending money, or to every third month, when his pension check came and Dobie bought him a pint of moonshine. The check was for around seventy-eight dollars, three months' pension. Dobie charged him a reasonable twenty dollars a month board and Julie bought him socks and shirts as he needed them.

He never went out at night though he insisted that his eyes were as good as ever. He'd picked himself a pair of glasses out of a tray in the five-and-ten but he seldom wore them. When the mood was on him he liked to talk and bit by bit Julie had learned all about his coming to America, his years on the railroad, his butcher shop, Zuska, Francka, Dobie's father and mother. He ate well, slept well and took an unbounded interest in the Cassidy girls. The two fought like cats over clothes, boy friends and housework; once the elder had thrown the younger out of the house and locked the door — kept her yelling and banging on the back porch in nothing but her pants and a brassière for fifteen minutes of a March morning. Kracha still pitied Dobie for having been at work and missing that.

He got along well with old Peg-leg — though, like Uncle John and Uncle Joe and most of the older people Dobie knew, he had no high regard for the Irish.

Kracha still hoped Julie would relent and let him keep a pig. You got a small one in the spring, fed it garbage all summer and when you slaughtered it you had enough ham and bacon to last all winter. It wouldn't cost her a penny; he'd butcher it himself. Did she think he'd forgotten how to cut up a hog? Hah! And why let that shanty on the hill stand empty and unused?

But Julie remained adamant. Then he'd come home one day and said a man in Dooker's Hollow, a man he'd known for years, as fine a man as you'd ever want to meet, well this man was willing to sell him a nanny goat for next to nothing. A goat was even less trouble than a pig; you let her out on the hill in the morning and forgot about her until milking time. And goat's milk was good for you, better than this cow's milk you got at the store, which was full of chemicals anyway.

Julie had put her foot down on the nanny goat too. They had compromised on a few chickens. Kracha considered chickens brainless nuisances but they were better than nothing; you got an egg or two every day and a chicken for Sunday dinner now and then.

Dobie said, "He just wants something to feed."

Not long after he got his chickens he came home with a puppy. He said it was for Julie if she wanted it — he must have known that she'd yield helplessly once she had the fat, squirming, face-licking ball of fur in her hands — but long before the hound was half grown he was as much a part of Kracha as his shadow. Kracha named him Hussar and argued with him in Slovak.

7

AS the year drew to a close there was a growing demand from within the ranks that the union seek recognition. Warnings by the union's executives — each one more like a rebuke than the last — that the time wasn't propitious only added to the rising discontent. Production in the mills, lifted in anticipation of price rises under the code, had fallen sharply, and in apportioning work the company was using a certain discrimination. "Since work fell off," Dobie said, one leg hoisted over a corner of the organizer's desk, "company men are getting full time and men right alongside of them are lucky to get two, three turns a week. If a union man just stops to light a cigarette the boss is right on top of him. You know the men ain't goin' to stand for that. In the rail mill they practically tell a man he's loafing if he stops to eat his lunch. Right, Steve?"

Gralji, his arms folded across his chest — a favorite pose — lifted his head and the others waited for him to speak. He was a few inches shorter than Dobie and a few years older, a stocky, almost completely humorless man with an angular face, all planes and corners in the extreme Slav manner, and a grave, careful way of speaking, as though he was choosing one word at a time. He worked in Number 3 rail mill, most of which he had organized single-handed, and had a wife and two children.

"The men keep asking me when is the union going to ask for recognition," he said. "They say what's the use of having a union if we don't get any protection? They say if we get recognition, good. If we don't, they say we ought to go on strike. But as long as we don't have recognition we can't do anything."

Walsh, the organizer, looked annoyed. "It's easy to talk strike. The trouble with most of the men around here is they don't use their heads. They think all we need to do is walk in and ask for recognition. The steel corporation's been fighting the unions for forty years and yet a lot of men around here join the union and a week later they want to know why the company doesn't recognize the union. If they knew a little more about it they wouldn't be so impatient. Rome," he added sententiously, "wasn't built in a day."

Burke, his chair tilted against the wall under a poster announcing a union meeting, drawled, "The building trades were probably battling over jurisdiction." He was a lean, handsome Irishman, a widower and for all the gray in his wavy hair a startlingly youthful grandfather.

"The thing is," Dobie said, "the company's putting on pressure and if the union don't go into action pretty soon there's liable to be trouble. The men maybe don't say much while they're in here paying their dues but you talk to them on the street or in their houses and you'll hear plenty."

"It might be a good idea," Walsh said, "if they let Pittsburgh run the union. They've been doing it for a long time."

Burke murmured, "If Pittsburgh don't look out it won't have any union to run. It's a lot easier for a man to stop paying dues than it is to get him started in the first place."

"Let them stop," Walsh exclaimed testily. "The union will be better off without them."

"Christ, Walsh, talk sense."

"Pittsburgh knows what it's doing," Walsh went on, "and the sooner a lot of the men around here realize it the better it'll be for all concerned. They only think about what's going on here, but Pittsburgh has to go by what's going on all over."

Burke let his chair drop with a thump, rose slowly to his feet. "I think I'll go home."

Dobie and Gralji left with him. The day had been cool and sunny; the winter twilight, deepening almost as one watched, promised a fine, crisp night.

Beyond Sixth, easily the widest street in town, Braddock Avenue —a civic campaign some years earlier had discouraged the use of

the old-fashioned and provincial "Main Street" — was lined solidly
with stores. Their windows, brightly lighted, were gaudy with
Christmas trappings, the sidewalks populous with shoppers.

Nearing Library Street Dobie said, "You know what I've been
thinking? It wouldn't hurt if we knew a lot more about unions
than we do. I mean how they're supposed to be run and the right
way to deal with the company and so on. Then we wouldn't have
to depend so much on dopes like our pal back there with his Rome
wasn't built in a day. Jesus! If we had the experience and knew all
the ins and outs we could get a lot more done. It makes me sore to
think how much a guy like Walsh knows that we could use. As
it is, we've got to take his word for everything."

"If you got rid of him," Burke said, "you'd still have Pittsburgh
around your neck. And if you think Walsh is a dope wait till you
see what Pittsburgh can do without half trying."

"I even went to the library but they ain't got anything. For that
matter, I don't even know if there is such a book."

"They probably wouldn't carry it if there was."

"The only trouble with books," Gralji said, "is they're written
by writers."

"Well, it was just an idea I had. Wait a minute, I want to take
a look at something."

He edged between pedestrians to the window of a jewelry store
in which chromium cocktail shakers, toasters, waffle irons, silver
salt-and-pepper sets and candlesticks were artistically distributed
over tinsel-scattered cotton. "My sister's getting married next Sunday," he explained, "and we still haven't got her a present. Trouble
is, she's marrying a guy who's got a houseful of stuff from when
his first wife died and we don't know what in the hell to get her.
How you like that tray over there, the one with the glass dish in
the middle?"

They stared at the hammered silver and crystal tray. "That looks
nice."

"I don't know what she'd use it for, but at least it looks like a
wedding present."

"It's pretty, all right."

Dobie inspected the rest of the display. "Money sure can buy nice stuff, can't it? Boy, if you had the dough you sure could fix up a swell house for yourself."

"It takes money."

"You're telling me. That's where all my dough goes nowadays," Dobie said, as they moved away from the window. "Into the house. I give the wife my pay envelope and that's the last I see of it. Not that I mind," he added honestly. "Fact is, I guess I get almost as much kick out of buying a new lamp or something for the house as she does."

"You're only starting," Gralji said. "Wait till you have a couple kids."

"Oh, we'll get them. We're just waiting till we're caught up a little. We both want kids. Though sometimes I wonder if it ain't playing a pretty dirty trick on a kid to bring him into the world right now. The way things are."

They parted at Library.

The vote in February on the revised E.R.P. indicated a growing militancy which the announcement of a general ten per cent wage-increase merely encouraged. Of the changes in the plan, the one that aroused the most excited discussion was that which permitted any person, whether employed in the mill or not, to be elected a representative. Hagerty scornfully brushed aside the more imaginative possibilities of this and insisted that another amendment, the one in which the company waived its right to terminate the plan at any time, was more important. "They don't know it yet," he said, "but what they're doing is grabbing a bear by the tail." His optimism seemed unjustified to Dobie. The E.R.P., amendments and all, seemed likely to go on as before, puttering futilely with safety rules, complaints about toilets and plans for bowling tournaments.

Meanwhile, conditions in the Amalgamated reached the exploding point when Tighe, the ancient president of the A.A., perhaps smarting because the big, unorganized mills were now paying higher

wages than the two-bit stove-lid factories with which he had con-
tracts, and apparently determined to show he was still a force to
be reckoned with, advanced the cause of unionism by forthrightly
expelling the striking Weirton lodges — a stupidity so breath-taking
it made Dobie's head swim.

He dropped that morning's paper — Pittsburgh had only one, of
which it might be said that it was printed in black ink on white
newsprint by union labor — on the organizer's desk. "What the
hell's got into them bastards in Pittsburgh?" he demanded. "Are
they out of their heads? It's bad enough the Government's stooges
do all they can to break strikes without the union chipping in to
help."

Walsh lifted his nose and looked at the paper through the lower
half of his glasses. "They know what they're doing," he said shortly.

"It don't look like it. Fighting their own men! Of all the God-
damned — "

"Suppose you let them handle it," Walsh suggested. Seated at his
desk, eyes blinking behind his rimless glasses, vest pockets filled
with pencils, he looked more like a small businessman than a labor
leader. His round face bore a petulant expression as he stared at
Dobie, confronting him from the other side of the desk in a hat
and overcoat spotted with rain. The dank little office smelled of
gas; outside the February afternoon was wet and unpleasant. "Suppose you let them handle it," he repeated. "That's their job and in
case you don't know it they were at it a long time before you ever
heard of unions. While you were still dirtying your diapers."

"Yeah? Well, I wear long pants now and I don't like the kind
of work they're turning out and what do you think of that? If they
can pull stuff like this in Weirton they can pull it in Braddock or
anywhere else. It's all right for you to talk. What the hell are you
risking? If this lodge folds up you'll go plant your fat ass somewhere else and your pay will go right on. But we're in the mills.
We're the ones that'll get fired and black-listed if the union don't
back us up, not you!"

"That kind of talk won't get you anywhere, mister."

"Maybe not. But there's a hell of a lot more like me thinking and saying the same thing. And if them fatheads in Pittsburgh don't wake up they'll find it out when it blows up in their faces!"

Steve Gralji shifted unhappily from one foot to another.

The organizer tapped his fingers against the desk. "They don't need you to tell them their business, young feller. You're like a lot of other smart alecks I've run into. You join a union and right away you think you know it all."

"I know stinking dirty work when I smell it and this smells a mile away. It's no God-damn' wonder you guys were never able to organize anything bigger than a peanut stand!"

"If I were you I'd watch your mouth. I don't have to take that kind of talk from anybody."

"What are you trying to do, scare me? Jesus!" Dobie stared down at the man contemptuously. Then he put his hands on the desk and leaned toward him, his chin thrust out belligerently. "Let me tell you something, mister. You've been around unions so long maybe you've forgotten what they're for. But we haven't. And we ain't going to stand for what's going on much longer, whether it's in the mill or in the union. There's men being spied on and passed over for turns and laid off and transferred from one lousy job to another, just because they had the guts to join the union. How long do you think they're going to stand for that? And how long do you think they're going to stand for the union doing nothing about it? They ain't paying initiation fees and dues just so you can have a place to keep out of the rain in, and don't you forget it!"

He straightened abruptly. "Come on, Steve. Let's get the hell outa here."

He strode out of the office. Gralji, after a moment of indecision, followed.

They were nearing Corey Avenue before either spoke. Then Dobie said, "Well, I'm glad I got that off my chest."

"You shouldn't let yourself get so sore. He'll have it in for you now."

"He's had it in for me ever since he found out I liked to ask

questions, so a little more won't matter. And I've been wanting to
tell that guy a few things for a long time."

"He thinks you're a Communist."

"I wouldn't be surprised." Dobie turned up his coat collar against
the drizzling rain and tugged at his hat brim. "I used to sell papers
on that corner over there when I was a kid. Used to be a drugstore
where that poolroom is now."

Gralji murmured vaguely.

For a while they walked in silence. Then, "I didn't say anything
that wasn't the truth, did I?" Dobie demanded. "If this dope don't
realize what's going on it's time somebody told him."

"It's no use getting mad at him," Gralji said. "He can't do anything. It's up to the Executive Council."

"I'm getting tired of hearing that, too. It's as bad as the E.R.P.
Anytime they ask for something that might cost the company a
dollar Flack just shrugs and says it's up to the City Office. With us
it's the Executive Council."

"It don't do any good to get sore."

"I feel better."

They parted in front of the five-and-ten at the foot of Library
Street, in the very heart of town, Gralji going on to Ninth and
Dobie turning moodily up Library. Beyond the Pennsylvania Railroad underpass, a gloomy stone tunnel with the station on its top-
side, it was Jones Avenue; farther along the mill superintendent's
mansion, a large, ugly pile with a covered carriage entrance and a
glass conservatory in the back, squatted amid leafless shrubbery and
black, dripping trees. Dobie turned right at Summer Street, glancing into the windows of the police station as he passed and as usual
seeing nothing of interest. He followed the street to its end, a street
of shabby frame houses and wet, vacant porches. Past the pavement's
end the earth underfoot was spongy; down the hillside to his right
lights gleamed in the mist above the town. He closed the gate behind him and strode toward the kitchen. Inside it, Julie's voice
stopped suddenly; and Dobie knew she had heard his footsteps on
the walk.

8

IN THE face of the union heads' continuing refusal to act, the rank and file, exposed to all the varieties of intimidation and persecution in the company's repertoire, moved to force a decision. Under the leadership of a group of men which included the veterans of the Weirton and Clairton strikes, two hundred and fifty rank-and-file delegates representing fifty lodges met to formulate a program to be presented to the Amalgamated convention in April. Tighe sputtered in vain. The delegates approved a program whose heart was the demand that the convention authorize all lodges to ask for recognition simultaneously, and to set a strike date if recognition was refused.

Burke attended both the rank-and-file conference and the convention as delegate from Braddock. He had no more trouble getting time off than he had expected. The first time, he told his superintendent that an uncle had died in Cleveland. When the convention opened and he asked for time off again the superintendent wanted to know if another uncle had died on him. Burke said no, it was his aunt this time. The death of her husband had apparently been too much for her. The superintendent said he'd heard of such cases but he didn't see how he could let Burke go; he needed every man. All the mills had stepped up production as the strike threat grew. Burke replied that it was a hell of a note when a man couldn't get time off to attend his own aunt's funeral and — this tickled everyone who heard about it — threatened to appeal to his Employee Representative.

When blank form letters requesting a conference with the mill management arrived from Amalgamated headquarters, Dobie turned to Walsh. "What do we do with this? Mail it to Flack or take it in person or what?"

Walsh all but smirked. "Don't ask me, mister. This ain't my party."

"What d'you mean, this ain't your party?"

"Just what I said. I'm leaving the end of this week."

"Oh. Well, ain't Pittsburgh sending somebody to take your place?"

"I wouldn't count on it. You guys have been wanting to run things so long that Pittsburgh's finally decided to give you the chance."

Tighe, it developed, was withdrawing every organizer and letting the rebellious lodges shift for themselves. Desperate as was their need of experienced leadership, most of them called it good riddance and went ahead with the business of seeking conferences with mill superintendents. In Braddock, Dobie made a fair copy of the form letter on the lodge's antique typewriter — "The undersigned are the collective bargaining committee elected by a self-organization of a large number of your employees," it began — and mailed it to Flack. "This ought to start something," he reflected as he dropped it into the mailbox.

May twenty-first came and went. They heard that the Duquesne Superintendent had returned the union's letter unopened; from other mills came reports that the letter had been completely ignored, or that the committee had been refused admission to the Super- intendent's office, or that in the rare instances where a conference had been granted the union men came out as empty-handed as they went in.

After some discussion Dobie filled out and sent Flack a second letter, this time in a plain envelope, by registered mail, with a return receipt requested. The receipt arrived signed by Flack's secre- tary. While Dobie was examining it Burke came into the office and said that Flack had stopped him in the mill yard and asked him what the hell was the idea of sending him registered letters. "I told him he didn't answer the first one we sent him and we wanted to make sure he got it. He was pretty sore."

Two days later Dobie got a letter addressed to him at his home.

Evidently Flack didn't propose to recognize the existence of the union even as an address. In his letter Flack noted the receipt of a communication asking for a conference, and since it was the management's policy to recognize any individual or organization as the spokesman for those employees whom they represented, he would be pleased to see them in his office on May 26, at 4 P.M.

Burke and the other committeemen received identical letters.

"He must've heard from Pittsburgh," Burke said.

"They're scared of a strike."

"You see what it says about recognizing any individual or organization?"

"Yeah, I saw it. Don't start getting excited."

"All I'm really worried about," Dobie said, "is what we'll say to him. You'd better do most of the talking."

"Getting nervous?"

"It's just the idea."

On the appointed day, a Saturday, the committee met on the steps of the General Office building. There were six of them, all in their Sunday best and none comfortable. Burke had brought a woman friend along to take down a record of the conference. She didn't know shorthand but she could use a typewriter and thought she'd manage all right if too many people didn't start talking at once.

While they were waiting in Flack's outer office Dobie could feel the excitement their presence aroused permeating the building. One departmental superintendent after another discovered he had business with Flack's secretary, or disdaining subterfuge paused in the doorway to stare at them in silence, with particularly lingering glances for the hapless committeeman from his own department. Out in the hall, meanwhile, a whole procession of minor bosses and clerical workers was going up and down, eyes goggling.

"Looks like we're upsetting the routine," Burke said.

Dobie whispered, "This is the first time in my life I ever really wanted a drink."

"Cheer up. Maybe Flack will offer us a shot."

"If he does I'll drop dead."

The secretary appeared. "You can come in now."

Flack was seated at his desk; near him sat an elderly, well-dressed man Dobie had never seen before. Neither rose. Flack glanced inquiringly at the woman.

"This is Miss Morrison," Burke explained. "She's going to be our stenographer."

"I see." He arranged with his secretary for a typewriter and paper. The secretary then settled himself near Flack, notebook and pencil poised.

Unexpectedly, Flack pointed a finger at Fred Stephens, the tall, mild-voiced Negro — he was a preacher, Sundays — whom the blast furnace department had chosen as its committeeman. "Where do you work?"

"Blast furnace, suh."

The finger shifted. "And you?"

"Transportation."

The secretary's pencil began to twitch. Miss Morrison, until that moment an interested spectator, looked surprised and turned hastily to her typewriter.

"And you?"

"Number 3 rail mill."

"And you?"

" 'lectric shop."

"And you?"

"Splice bar."

He didn't ask Burke where he worked; presumably he knew. His reason for asking at all wasn't clear and he offered no explanation. He inclined his head toward his companion. "This is Mr. Forbes from the City Office."

Mr. Forbes nodded gravely.

Their chairs faced Flack's desk and the windows that looked out on the mill, though all Dobie could see was the roof of the machine shop and the stacks of the open hearth. The office was simply furnished, framed portraits of Braddock notables, beginning with Carnegie and Captain Jones, and several mounted trout — Flack was reputed to be something of an angler — were its sole decorative notes.

Mr. Forbes cleared his throat. "You sent Mr. Flack a letter requesting a conference."

Burke crossed his legs. "That's right."

"You claim to represent a number of our employees?"

"The ones that are in the union. Yessir."

Mr. Forbes leaned back and clasped his hands and bent his head toward them thoughtfully. "Now as you probably know," he said, "it is the policy of the management to recognize any individual or organization as the spokesman for the employees they represent."

Dobie felt like saying that that was news to him, but didn't. Burke said, "That's all right with us."

"However," Mr. Forbes continued, the thumbs of his clasped hands fondling his chin, "I think you will agree that we must exercise a little discrimination. In other words, we must have proof that the spokesmen really do represent the employees they say they do and that those employees have authorized the spokesmen to speak for them. Otherwise anyone could walk in here and claim they represented so many of our employees and we'd have nothing but confusion."

"That's what I call really going out of your way to think up trouble," Burke said. "But I don't think there's much danger of it happening."

"We must be prepared for everything, Mr. Burke. Have you any proof that you represent a number of our employees?"

"We've got our membership list and dues book. That ought to be proof enough."

"Do you have them with you?"

"What, the membership list?"

"Yes."

"No, we haven't."

"Can you arrange to let us examine it and check the names with our payroll?"

"I don't see how. The membership list is supposed to be confidential."

Mr. Forbes glanced at Flack and shrugged ever so slightly. "Then what proof have we," he asked, "that you do actually represent the employees you claim to?"

"We've got proof. We know how many men we've got in the union."

"But we don't. We don't know how many employees you represent or which ones, and until we have figures and proof there's not much that we can do."

There was a brief silence. A streetcar clanged on Braddock Avenue.

Burke sat up. "Look here, Mr. Forbes. Our request was for a conference with Mr. Flack. We know him and he knows us. We don't know you. When it comes to proof, what the hell proof have we got that you have a right to ask us questions?"

"Mr. Forbes," Flack said coldly, "is here as a representative of the City Office, with full authority."

Burke ignored him. "And since when does a union have to show its books to an employer? The only reason you brought that up was to have an excuse for not recognizing the union, because you know damn well no union is going to expose its membership. If you want to know whether we really represent the men just ask Flack there. He knows damn well we represent them. And he's the man we came here for a conference with, not you."

Mr. Forbes was gently waving Flack back into his chair. "Let me handle this, John." It looked as though more strenuous methods might be necessary —Flack's forefinger had already begun to waggle — but at that moment a small electric clock on Flack's desk burst into a subdued thrumming, the most discreet and musical alarm Dobie had ever heard a clock give forth. Flack murmured, "Excuse me," to Mr. Forbes, and all the committeemen watched while he put two pills into the palm of his hand and his secretary filled a glass from a shiny silver carafe that Dobie had been coveting ever since they'd entered.

"Now, sir," Mr. Forbes said, turning to Burke. "Your grievance seems to be, as well as I can understand it, that you came here for a conference and that in some way I'm keeping you from having it. Well sir, what are we doing now? Aren't we conferring? Just what did you think a conference was?"

"We came here to discuss matters that affected the men we represent. That's what we asked for a conference for, not to argue whether we have a right to be here or not."

"Very well. What are the matters which affect the men you say you represent?"

"We don't just say we represent them. We do. We've been instructed by our membership to ask that the company recognize their union, the Amalgamated Association, and to confer with you about signing a contract covering wages, hours, vacations with pay, and seniority."

"I'm afraid you're laboring under a misapprehension." Mr. Forbes's thumbs were playing with his chin again. "Even if Mr. Flack or I wanted to, we have no authority to sign a contract. That's something you'll have to take up with the City Office. As for recognizing your organization, I told you before it is the policy of the company to recognize any group or individual — "

"I know. I heard you before."

Mr. Forbes's lips thinned. "Then I have no more to say."

There was a brief silence.

Dobie moved forward in his chair. "Look, Mr. Forbes. We've got to make a report to our membership of what took place here. As the secretary I'll have to read them that record." He inclined his head to Miss Morrison. "How do you think the men are going to feel when I read what you've been saying? Believe me, Mr. Forbes, it's going to sound a lot different from the way it does in here."

Mr. Forbes glanced at Flack. Flack glanced at a paper on his desk. "Dobberjack. Electric shop."

"Well, Mr. Dobberjack," Mr. Forbes said, "I appreciate your thoughtfulness, but what use you make of your transcript is, of course, entirely up to you."

The mispronunciation of his name annoyed Dobie only a little; he'd long since discovered that the solid, mouth-filling vowels and ripping *r*'s of the correct "Dough-BRAY-chuck" were beyond the average Anglo-Saxon larynx.

"Okay," he said, "I just thought I'd tell you in case you hadn't thought of it yourself."

Again there was a brief silence. Then Burke said, "So the answer is No?"

Mr. Forbes's eyebrows rose. "What was the question?"

"No recognition, no contract?"

"We've recognized you, haven't we, in granting this conference? And I repeat, neither Mr. Flack nor I has the authority to sign a contract. As you probably know, it's been a consistent policy of the corporation not to — "

"All right, all right. I guess there's no use keeping this up." He rose. "Let's go, boys."

But they had to wait until Miss Morrison finished typing and gathered her things together. No parting remarks were exchanged as they filed out.

As they went down the steps outside Dobie took a deep breath. "That was as nifty a run-around as I ever saw."

Burke grunted. "I should've known they'd ring in a lawyer on us."

"You did all right."

"Who gets these papers?" Miss Morrison asked.

"Give them to Dobie. He's going to have to make the report."

They got into Burke's car and drove Miss Morrison home, then went down to the union office where Gralji and a number of others were waiting for them.

Dobie got home in time for supper. He told Julie what had happened. Worried, she asked, "Does that mean there will be a strike?"

He threw up his hands. "Jesus, I don't know, and that's a fact. A week ago I would've said 'Sure.' But when it starts staring you in the face you begin to get a little scared — which is more than I'd admit to anybody but you. But I ain't the only one. Nobody's saying anything but it's there. And when you figure what a lousy deal we're getting from Pittsburgh — "

"Sit down and eat."

After a while she said, "Well, it's not just up to you."

"How do you think that gang's going to feel after we report the kind of run-around we got? The trouble is, it takes more than just being sore to win a strike. You need experienced men that know what they're doing, you need a good, tight organization with everybody working together, you need dough for strike relief and leaflets and radio time, you need men to make speeches and write handouts for the papers telling our side of the story — Christ, what don't you need!"

Kracha looked up from his plate. "Well, did you see the Super'-tendent?"

Dobie filled his mouth and stared at him, his jaws working. "By God, I don't think he believes me yet." He swallowed. "I showed you the letter he sent me," he went on in Slovak. "Where do you think I've been all afternoon?"

"And you talked to him about the union?"

"That's what we went there for."

"With the Super'tendent?"

"Two hours ago I was sitting in his office. He was no farther away from me than you are now."

Kracha waggled his head from side to side.

Dobie's smile held a touch of complacence. "We've come a long way, eh? When somebody like me can walk into the Superintendent's office and talk about unions. They didn't do such things when you were in the mills. But times have changed." He added in English, "It's too much for him."

"Never mind, never mind! You and your English! As though I was a greenhorn just off the boat." Kracha snorted. "You think you know everything. Tell me something, mister smart aleck. Was there ever a union in Braddock with a contract with the company? Yes, and with the eight-hour day, too? You're so smart, tell me."

"In Braddock?"

"In this very mill."

"I never heard of it. A union contract and an eight-hour day in Braddock?"

"Hah! Before you were born, before your father even came to America!"

"Don't argue, eat," Julie said. She helped herself to more salad, lettuce dressed with a hot bacon-and-vinegar sauce. "One of these days I'd like to eat just one meal without you two getting into an argument."

"I'll admit it's a new one on me," Dobie said.

"Then don't talk to me any more as though you had invented unions last Monday between breakfast and supper."

And Kracha cut into his steak, his mustache fairly bristling with triumph, while Dobie stared at him thoughtfully. It wasn't the first time Kracha had startled his grandson with glimpses of the past that clashed sharply with Dobie's conception of it.

Preparations for the strike, now seemingly inevitable, intensified. There were rumors that the company was buying arms and ammunition, hiring strikebreakers and guards, dusting off the cots and commissary equipment left over from the 1919 strike. Foremen went around asking their men whether they would be loyal to the company in the event of a strike and got the only answers they should have expected. Flack organized a Committee of One Hundred, the usual business and professional men, and addressed meeting after meeting, warning all that a strike would plunge the country into another depression, damning the Communists in the Amalgamated and predicting that the strike was doomed to fail. Newspaper headlines were blacker every day and editorial pages lectured the union men on their duty to the country.

The strike committee went to Washington to ask for Presidential intervention, to demand that the President arrange a conference between the union and the Iron and Steel Institute. The President, they were told, had gone cruising. They returned empty-handed to Pittsburgh, to a special convention called by Tighe in a last effort to head off the strike. Green, President of the A.F.L., spoke; that he came to kill the strike movement, no one listening to him, no one in all the tense, waiting steel towns, doubted. "I come," he began, "as a miner speaking to steelworkers." He came to warn them not to play into the hands of the "autocratic barons" of steel, to use "strategy," to convince them that this was not the time for a strike. He came bearing a proposal for a special Steel Labor Board to receive complaints and hold elections.

Inexperienced, their own union officials openly hostile, without a treasury, the press yapping hysterically at their heels, the rank and file leaders yielded.

Dobie and a few others were in a speakeasy near the union office — it had been a legal bar and grill ever since Repeal but one still thought of it as a speakeasy — drinking beer and waiting for a news broadcast, when the word came. The music — an orchestra was playing "The Continental" — faded. "We interrupt our program to bring you a special news bulletin. Pittsburgh. There will be no strike in the steel industry. The Amalgamated Association convention voted this afternoon to accept William Green's proposal, which it is understood has the approval of President Roosevelt and the NRA, for a special Labor Board. In his speech Mr. Green said, and I quote . . ."

The voice went on, and ended, and the music came up again. Dobie, hunched over his beer, swore softly. "I don't believe it," he said to no one in particular. But he knew it was true. And he thought of Julie with her plans to stock up on flour and canned stuff while their credit was still good; she could forget that now, and their first wedding anniversary might turn out to be a joyous occasion after all, and he could fall asleep without wondering what he would do when he didn't have a job — no job, no money, maybe their furniture going one way and Julie another and he somewhere else. He had been prepared to face all that, fighting back the fear and the sickish feeling in his stomach, but now that he needn't think about it any more relief was beginning to rise in his throat like an impulse to gurgle. He suppressed it and was ashamed of himself. "I'm a fine union man," he thought wryly.

Farther down the bar a man Dobie knew only as a union member lifted his voice above the arguments the radio bulletin had loosed. "Hey secretary! Look!"

Dobie turned his head and watched while the man held up a union card and carefully tore it to pieces.

He didn't say anything.

The man threw the pieces away from him with the exaggerated gestures of the stewed. "That's what I think of the union now."

Dobie licked his lips. "Okay. This is a free country."

"You God-damn' right." The drunk seemed somewhat disappointed. "You God-damn' right," he repeated.

Gralji touched Dobie's elbow. "Come on. There's no use getting into an argument with him."

In the union office Dobie dropped into the organizer's chair and lifted his feet to the desk. "I don't get it, Steve," he said. "I just don't get it. They know what to expect from a Labor Board."

Gralji shrugged. "Maybe it's better this way. A strike is no joke."

"I can't say I'm sorry there ain't going to be a strike. But I hate to think what it's going to do to the union. That stewpot in there won't be the only one tearing up his card."

"The ones that stick will be worth three of the ones that drop out," Gralji said hopefully.

"The company won't figure it that way." He tilted his hat forward over his eyes. "And can you imagine what it'll be like in the mill now? Jesus!"

Burke came back from the convention and reported that they'd simply decided it was no use trying to fight the whole world. "The company was against us, the Government was against us, the A.F.L. was against us, our own union was against us, the papers were against us — I'm telling you, boys, I found out what it feels like to have the whole God-damn' world against you. And you can take my word for it it's one hell of a feeling."

It was something workers all over the country learned that crowded summer. While a great drought turned whole states into dusty wastelands, the hundreds of thousands to whom Section 7 (A) had been quite literally a promise of freedom learned the true value of that promise. The San Francisco longshoremen, the Minneapolis truckmen, the Milwaukee utility workers, the Kohler workers, the textile workers — strike after strike was systematically sabotaged by Government officials or broken by troops until Dobie found himself wincing whenever he picked up a newspaper, until he sometimes wondered how men could have the heart ever to hope and fight again.

9

KRACHA was mending a pair of shoes on the side porch — it was hardly larger than a good-sized stoop — as Dobie came up the walk, slapping a folded newspaper against his leg. Two lines of wash crowded the walled-in little yard behind the house. From within the kitchen Julie called, "Don't come in. I'm wiping up the floor."

He looked in and saw her on her hands and knees. "Need any help?"

She smiled at him over a shoulder. She had a bright-colored kerchief around her hair and she looked warm. "I'll be through in a minute."

"Why did you wash today for? You knew I was off the rest of the week."

"The radio said rain so I decided not to wait."

He settled down on the edge of the porch. It didn't look like rain; the October afternoon was clear and cool and the night would be frosty. A good night, he reflected with pleasurable anticipation, to stay at home. He hoped Julie wouldn't want to go to a movie. "Were you figuring on going anywhere tonight?"

"Not especially. Why?"

"I just wondered."

"Did you want to go somewhere?"

"Nope. Not me."

"Dzedo's the one that's going out. That's why he's fixing his shoes."

"What, tonight?"

"Tomorrow. He's going to see Mrs. Radilla."

"Oh." He glanced at Kracha. "Last week Munhall and Homestead, tomorrow River Street — you're getting to be a regular gadabout."

Kracha studied a run-down heel. "You could do worse than come with me tomorrow."

"What do I want to go there for?"

"*Ach!* She was like another mother to your father and you ask me that."

Kracha slipped the shoe he was mending over the iron last between his knees. Dobie, rolling a cigarette, watched his hands. They moved slowly and a little stiffly and they were as wrinkled and lumpy as the shoe. He wasn't a very good shoemaker but, it had taken Dobie some time to realize, Kracha didn't mend his own shoes merely to save a few nickels. An old man had to keep himself busy, too busy to die.

"I suppose we could go and see her."

"I know she'd be glad to see you," Julie said.

"You come too."

"I'll have to press my black dress."

Nearly finished, she was backing out of the door, still on her hands and knees. Each time she stretched forward to swish the rag around, Dobie observed interestedly, her dress pulled up, exposing the back of her legs and thighs.

He drawled, "If old Peg-leg falls off his porch and breaks his neck one of these days I'll know the reason why."

"What are you talking about?" She peered around a shoulder at him. "Nosey! Who told you to look?"

"When I have to be told to look at your legs, sweetheart, you can start getting a grave ready for me." He reached out a hand and patted her.

"Don't, I'm all perspired. I can't wait to climb into the bathtub." She was clean and pretty when they called on Dorta the next afternoon. It was a fine day. Julie said, "Will you look at that weather! And the radio said rain." "It'll rain yet. If it doesn't, I guess we'll have to get you another radio." "I suppose so," she murmured absently; and then, "Oh, you." Overnight it had turned unseasonably warm; the afternoon was soft with hazy sunshine that seemed even warmer once they were down off the hill, walking between the grimy mill wall and the wretched hovels of lower Thirteenth Street.

The company had put a coating of cement over the old stone wall and filled in the Washington Street tunnel. A comparatively new enginehouse towered above the wall and made the houses in the street look diminutive. There was hardly any noise from the mill.

"This place never changes," Dobie said. "It just gets older and dirtier."

"It's dirty all right." The uneven pavement had never been meant for high heels. "I don't know why Mrs. Radilla doesn't move."

"She's lived in the same house on River Street for the last forty years and I guess she'll die there."

"She ought to own it by now."

"She does."

At Washington some very dirty children, Negro and white, were playing on the empty corner lot where once Wold's saloon had stood in all its glory. Wold had died some years before, very rich, people said.

"I bet you wish you had half the money you spent in the saloon that used to be here."

Kracha grunted.

Dobie glanced down the length of Washington Street. There weren't many people about; it had, like most of the First Ward, a vacant, forgotten look. "My old home town. We'll have to go back through Twelfth Street and I'll show you where we used to live. Last time I passed it was full of shines."

"Get Dzedo to show us where his butcher shop used to be."

"I know it was in one of them little wooden buildings the other side of Gyurik's saloon. That's closed up too. Wold's torn down, Gyurik gone, Spetz gone, Dzmura, Veroskey, Finish's grocery, Froelich's dry goods, Pustinger the undertaker — they're all gone now, hey Dzedo? All the old-timers."

"All dead or moved away," Kracha said. "Now there is nobody here but niggers."

"You can blame the company for that. It was the company brought them here to break the strike."

They turned right into River Street. People sitting on doorsteps watched them pass; none of the white faces looked familiar. Poverty had laid a heavy hand on everything, neglect a heavier. The world had been here for a while, crowded, busy, full of life, and then had moved on; now the people, the street, the dreadful houses, seemed to be waiting for the end without complaint, in the pleasant sunshine.

"It sure has changed. This didn't used to be such a bad place. I know I had some pretty good times on Washington. Though I guess a kid can have a good time anywhere. But it was different. There was more life to it then."

Dorta agreed. She didn't look like a woman who was having trouble with her heart or her blood pressure, Dobie couldn't remember which. She had lost weight but the effect was to make her seem smaller and more compact than he remembered her, and by now he was used to that. The big, loud-voiced men he had known as a boy, the broad-hipped, maternally bosomed women, had a queer way of turning into small, mild people who treated him with unexpected deference and reminded him almost apologetically when he couldn't remember their names.

"Nobody wants to live here any more," Dorta said. "People have automobiles and the farther away they can get from the mills the better. Who can blame them? I don't. It's not like the old days when a man worked twelve hours a day and had to live close to his work. Now because it's near the mill you can't give away a house that has electricity and gas and a bathroom."

"You'll never get back what you paid for this house," Kracha said solemnly. "Unless you find a rich nigger."

"After I'm dead my children can do what they like with it." She sighed. "It used to be a good place to live. So many people wanted to live here there were never enough houses to go around. As fast as they built them they filled up. People used to buy out a family, furniture and all, just to get their rooms. Remember, Djuro? And people coming over from the old country every day — so much excitement!"

"And every Sunday two or three weddings," Kracha said. "Every Sunday without fail. All you had to do was walk along the street until you heard the gipsies playing and there was your wedding."

"In the yard," Dobie added for Julie's benefit. "They'd start it in the house but it always ended up in the yard. I remember I used to go around and collect beer-bottle caps. You were supposed to be able to get something for them but I never found out what. I must've collected a bushel of them."

"Did you used to stick them on your shirt?"

"Uh-huh. Did you ever take evaporated-milk cans, the big ones, and stamp your heels into them until they stuck to your shoes and then go clattering all over the street?"

"No, I don't remember ever doing that."

"You could make one hell of a racket with them. Every house you passed a woman would stick her head out and yell at you for waking up her boarders."

"Everybody kept boarders," Dorta said.

"You saw how dead Washington is now. You should've seen it twenty years ago when it was full of stores. On payday nights it was almost as crowded as Main Street."

"Main Street!" Kracha exclaimed. "It was better than Main Street. People used to come from Homestead and Duquesne just to walk along Washington Street."

"Everybody knew everybody else in those days," Dorta said. "It's not like that now anywhere, North Braddock or East Pittsburgh or anywhere. There was more friendliness. You know how it was, Djuro. Nobody was a stranger. At first, when there were still a lot of Irish living here, we kept together because we had to. But when the Irish got out it was all our own people. It was good then."

"Remember the balls at Turner Hall?"

"We had good times," Kracha said, sucking on his pipe. "Good times."

"So it goes. It's too bad the niggers had to come. They never bother me, but some of my neighbors have moved, especially the ones with daughters. The men are always getting drunk and fighting, and you hear women screaming during the night. They all live together like so many animals. And so dirty!"

"They're poor," Dobie said.

"How much does soap and water cost?"

"I know. But I was just thinking that once it was the Irish looking down on the Hunkies and now it's the Hunkies looking down on the niggers. The very things the Irish used to say about the Hunkies the Hunkies now say about the niggers. And for no better reason."

Dorta shrugged but didn't say anything.

Kracha asked, "Where is your husband?"

"He went for a walk upstreet. Julie, take some more cake." She apologized again because it was store cake; she didn't do much baking nowadays.

"When we used to live on Washington," Dobie said, his mouth full, "I generally managed to get around here every Saturday. She used to do her baking on Saturday and I'd sit here and grub *kreple*. You know, raised doughnuts. Remember that, Mrs. Radilla?"

Dorta smiled. "First he would ask me, Mrs. Radilla, do you want anything from the store, Mrs. Radilla, do you want me to chop some wood? But it was the *kreple* he came for. He was always hungry."

"He still is," Julie said.

"I don't bake much now. Christmas and Easter a little; the rest of the time I don't bother. Who will I bake for?"

They had accepted cake and coffee — with evaporated milk, which Dobie detested — to be polite, though they'd just finished lunch. Kracha allowed himself to be coaxed into pouring another glass of whisky. Outside, the back yards were quiet; during the two hours they sat in Dorta's kitchen not one train went by. The railroad tracks, the river, the looming hill, dozed in the sunshine. On the land between the tracks and the river the mill had stored great piles of scrap and pig iron. The crane that loaded the stuff into cars for the open hearth stood idle, loose cables drooping to its magnet. Over to the right, toward Eleventh Street, what had been the wire works was now a ruin. It had never reopened; some of its workers, including Dorta's younger son, had been transferred to other mills but most had simply been turned loose, with little likelihood of ever finding work again. The wrecking crews had moved in and now only two or three gaunt structures remained, and they were without walls, without roofs, iron skeletons picked clean in the midst of desolation.

"Are you working, Johnny?"

"Three days a week." Production had dropped abruptly after the strike threat passed and work had been slow all summer.

"Well, it's better than nothing. I saw your Aunt Alice the other day. She says Frank's eyes are very bad."

They were living around Ninth Street somewhere, Dobie knew, and on relief. Kracha sometimes went to see them.

Julie mentioned that Agnes was going to have a baby in April or May and the inevitable question followed. "When are you two going to have some children?"

"Pretty soon, I hope. When things get a little better."

"*Ach!* If people waited until things were better nobody would ever have children."

"We will."

"Are you still secretary of the union?"

Dobie nodded. "But I don't have much to do nowadays. We lost a good many members this summer."

"So I heard. My Joe —" Her Joe was a grizzled grandfather in his own right — "said they got mad at the union for not going on strike. As though a strike was a picnic!"

Dobie spread his hands. "They got mad at the union, they got scared of the company — each one had his own reason. It was mostly the younger men who quit. The older men like your Joe still pay dues when they can. But the younger ones who were always loudest for the strike were the first to quit."

"Oh, my Joe is still strong for the union. You should hear him sometimes."

Dobie leaned forward, his elbows on his knees. "The men who quit the union will come back. I can understand how they felt. Our own union's officials were against us, and still are. We got a dirty deal from everybody, including the Government. Oh, a dirty deal! It was enough to take the heart out of any man. More than once I've felt like telling the whole business to go to hell. But then I think of what happened and I get mad. Nobody can do things like that to me and get away with it. So I stay. Just because there are a few bastard union officials doesn't mean the union itself is no good. The union is our only hope, and the men will realize it when they find out that the company doesn't intend to treat them any better just because they tore up their union cards. They'll come back. The company is our best organizer."

Kracha took his pipe out of his mouth. "Mike should be sitting here listening to him, eh?"

Dorta smiled. "What did I say when Joe told me he had been elected secretary of the union? Mike, *neboščik,* should be alive today."

"If he was," Dobie said, "he'd probably be secretary instead of me."

"He was always saying there ought to be a union. He nearly got into trouble more than once. He was never one for keeping quiet. But he used to say, If I don't speak out it will poison me."

"Yeah, I can understand that."

"Your mother used to worry so about him. He wasn't like other men."

"They were married from your house, Mrs. Radilla?" Julie asked.

"We set up the tables in this very kitchen."

"And the way I got it," Dobie said, "he threw over some gal to marry Mamma."

Julie brightened.

Dorta said, "Oh, yes. What was her name, Djuro? She married some man and they had this little store on Talbot for the longest time. Helen — Mary — "

Kracha gestured. "How should I remember? Every time you turned around he was going with a different girl."

"Say, I'm learning a lot about my old man that I never knew before."

"Anna Kovac," Dorta said triumphantly. "She married Ocenik, the one who got hurt in the mill. Remember, Djuro?"

Kracha nodded.

"I don't know where she is now," Dorta said. "She may be dead, *Bohze zavaruj*. Your mother invited her to the wedding but she refused to come."

Julie said she didn't blame her much.

Dobie rolled another cigarette. Licking it, he stared at the ruin of the wire mill. "They sure made a wreck of the wire mill, didn't they?"

They all looked at it. Dorta said, "My George was lucky. They gave him a job in Rankin. But so many others will never work again."

"Yeah, there's a lot of good jobs buried over there. And there's going to be a lot more if they keep on building these new automatic mills."

"I watched them build it," Dorta said, "and I watched them tear it down. They made almost as much noise tearing it down as they did building it."

"You're thinking of the blast furnaces," Kracha said.

"No, the wire mill. Do you think I can't remember any more?"
Dobie stared at her. "Do you remember when the wire mill was
built? I thought it was a lot older than that."

"You were still in Homestead," Dorta said, continuing to address
Kracha. "Do you think I forget so easily? We were living on the
cinder dump, where we moved after the fire."

Kracha nodded. *"Pravdu, pravdu.* It was I who had forgotten."

"What cinder dump?" Dobie demanded. "What fire?"

Before they'd finished telling him it was time to leave.

10

WORK picked up in the late fall and stayed reasonably constant through the winter; by spring they were able to make the last
payment on their furniture. They celebrated, not without misgiv-
ings, by returning into debt for a washing machine. They discussed
it for weeks ahead and inspected machines each time they went to
make a payment on their furniture; now they stood outside the
store and pretended to look at a bedroom display while the Saturday night crowd surged past them.

The window, thriftily combining an appeal to spring brides with
a bow to the approach of Easter, was adorned with silver bells,
paper lilies and a cardboard bride peering raptly into a cedar chest.
The furniture was a cheap and showy modern, and when Julie
sniffed at it Dobie observed that somebody must like the stuff or
they wouldn't keep making it.

"What I was really wondering," he went on, "is how you manage
to stay on a bed like that. Especially when you start fooling around."

"I'll keep my maple. I'm so glad I didn't get a vanity. Practically
every girl buys one when she gets married and none of them ever

really uses it. At least a dresser has drawers that you can put things in."

"They probably picture themselves sitting in front of it in a fancy negligee while their husbands gaze at them longingly."

"They get over that."

"Trouble with you is you're too practical. Well, shall we go in and get it over with?"

Her eyes rose to meet his.

"Oh, come on. It doesn't cost anything to look."

"Do you think we should? It won't kill me to do the washing a little longer. Until we can really afford it."

"Don't back down on me now. Just when I was figuring I wouldn't have to rinse clothes or crank that damn wringer any more." He took her arm. "Come on. We'll just look at it."

When they came out Julie said, "I've got a funny feeling inside. I'm beginning to wish we hadn't."

"You needed a washing machine, didn't you? All right, now you've got it."

"Yes, but all that money."

"We managed to get the furniture paid for and that was a lot more. Anyway, I was getting fed up seeing you wear yourself out over a washboard."

"It *will* be a big help. Do you think we could've done any better in Pittsburgh?"

"Probably, if we'd had the cash." He steered her toward a drugstore. "How about a soda? Spending all that money made me thirsty."

"It's funny. Buying the furniture didn't bother me a bit. But now it scares me to owe money."

He patted her hand. "That's because you're an old married woman now."

They had sodas in the chain store which had taken over one of the oldest drugstores in Braddock and then they went out into the crowded street again. It was a fine spring night, so warm that the storekeepers had left their doors open, so windless that traffic exhaust was a haze in the air. High above the street a movie theater's sign spelled out its name one letter at a time; as they passed under the brilliance of its canopy they waved to Helen Dobrejcak, but didn't stop because she looked busy. A baby spotlight set into the booth above her — this was the enamored manager's idea and had won him a paragraph in an exhibitors' trade journal — made her red hair flame.

Julie said, "Do you think he's serious about wanting to marry her?"

"Don't ask me. Last I heard, he was, as soon as his wife gave him a divorce. Trouble is, he claims she don't want to."

"Maybe that's just what he tells Helen."

Dobie shrugged. "She's old enough to know what she's doing."

Near Library Street they ran into Bill Hagerty and an assortment of his children. Dobie introduced him to Julie and inquired after his wife, who was at home with a new baby.

"That makes ten now, don't it Bill?"

"Yep. Six boys and four girls."

Julie was staring at him without saying anything.

"I don't know how you do it," Dobie said.

Hagerty grinned. "Son, there ain't nothing to it once you get the knack." It was his stock reply.

They had just come from the supermarket on Eighth Street and even the smallest child had a bundle to carry. It took, Hagerty admitted, a lot of food to fill twelve stomachs, and then they both agreed that the supermarket had knocked hell out of a lot of stores around town.

As they moved with the crowd again Julie said, "Ten children! My goodness! And he's the only one working?"

"I think the oldest kid has a job after school."

"I don't see how they ever manage."

They stopped to look at the dresses and coats in The Famous's windows and then they turned up Library Street, leaving the lights and crowds of Braddock Avenue behind. There was an orange moon high above them.

"In a way," Julie said meditatively, "we'll really save money. Our clothes will last longer."

"And so will you, which is the main thing."

"It *is* a beautiful machine. When it comes you give it a good going-over."

"Uh-huh."

"It's only when I think of owing all that money . . . But I'll see if I can't economize a little, and if you keep working we shouldn't have any trouble."

"We'll make out all right."

For a while they walked in step, in silence. The slope of the street was just enough to make leisurely walking automatic.

"Do you think I ought to spend money for an Easter outfit now?"

"You need clothes, don't you?"

"Yes, but — "

"You get what you need as soon as Dzedo's check comes. All I want out of it is a pair of shoes and a hat."

"If I had a sewing machine I could make a lot of my own clothes."

"I'd rather we got an electric refrigerator first."

Julie sighed. "We need so many things. Refrigerator, sewing machine, vacuum cleaner, good silverware — "

"Sure takes a lot of machinery to keep house nowadays, don't it?"

"If you want to live nice."

"We'll get them. It just takes time. Look at what we've managed to get already and we ain't married two years yet. Nice furniture, a radio, and now a washing machine. I think we're doing pretty good."

"Do you think we'll ever have a house of our own?"

"I don't see why not. Lots of other people manage it."

"That's when we can really plan. Of course we'll be able to use most of the things we're buying now; that's the reason I'd rather do without than buy cheap stuff. But when you have your own place you can make every room just perfect because you know you're going to be there for the rest of your life. A long time, anyway." She slipped an arm through his. "Wouldn't it be nice to have a little house back in the hills somewhere? Of course you'd have to have a car, unless it was near a bus line or something."

"Well, if we could afford to buy a house I guess we could squeeze out enough extra for a secondhand tin can."

"Just so it got you back and forth from work. It would be so nice. A house with trees and flowers around it, and a nice big kitchen with those built-in cabinets and a linoleum floor like you see in the magazines. I'd love to have copper pots. And a nice big living room with a fireplace and those windows you can walk through; and upstairs a tiled bathroom and our bedroom and two rooms for the children. They'd have to have separate rooms after they got big."

They passed the mill superintendent's mansion, dark and massive among its trees. A Bell Avenue car swung around the corner and headed toward Pittsburgh, the grind of its motors, the whine of its trolley, fading into the night. Between street lamps the moonlight was bright enough to cast shadows.

"You'd rather the first one was a boy, wouldn't you?"

"I don't think I care much one way or another, to tell you the truth."

"I'd rather have a girl first. You can have more fun with a girl. Boys you can't do anything with; no matter how you dress them and fuss over them they still look homely. But they make such cute things for girls, they look perfectly darling. And girls are much more satisfying, they help around the house and don't forget you when they get married, the way boys do."

"That's what I call looking ahead."

"You think I'm silly, don't you? I suppose men never think about things like that."

"Oh, I don't know. I've thought about it off and on though I always have a tough time trying to imagine what it'll feel like to be a papa."

"You'll make a wonderful father. I can just see you." She squeezed his arm.

"Well, I'll do my best but all my kids better expect from me is food and clothes. I'll try to see that they grow up strong and healthy and put them through high school but after that they'll be on their own."

"You just say that now."

They turned up Summer Street, darker even than Library-Jones; at their end of it a solitary street lamp splashed shadows over the quiet house-fronts, attenuated the scrawny trees. Its light went only a little way into the darkness that shrouded the hillside beyond the pavement's end; their shadows lengthened grotesquely ahead of them.

As they reached their gate one of the younger Cassidy children exclaimed, "Here they are, Mamma. Julie, something's happened — "

"Keep your trap shut there!"

Julie said, "What on earth — "

Mrs. Cassidy appeared in the kitchen doorway. Inside it Dobie saw old Peg-leg and the younger of the Cassidy girls. He asked, "What's happened?"

"It's nothing, Dobie. Don't get excited. It's your grandfather."

The kitchen looked strange with the Cassidys in it.

"Where is he? What happened?"

He was lying on the couch in the parlor, his eyes closed, his face drawn. Julie dropped to her knees beside him. "Dzedo, are you all right?"

He opened his eyes. When he spoke one side of his face seemed queerly stiff. "Why shouldn't I be all right?"

Between them the Cassidys explained that they'd heard the dog barking so much old Peg-leg had gone out to yell at him and had seen Kracha sprawled out on the kitchen doorstep, half in the house and half out. They hurried down and put him on the couch and splashed him with water and gave him a shot of whisky. About half an hour ago, this was. Just after nine o'clock, the Cassidy girl added, pulling up her stockings with a fine disregard for the amount of leg she exposed; the radio program had just changed.

They'd thought of calling a doctor but Kracha had indicated he didn't want any.

"It was blessed luck Gran'pap went out to see what was the matter with the dog," Mrs. Cassidy said. "He might have been laying there yet."

"At first I thought he was down on his hand and knees looking for something," Peg-leg said. "That's the first thought that entered me mind."

"Well, I'm certainly glad you found him when you did."

"Did he ever have anything like this happen to him before?"

"Not as far as I know."

"He's had a stroke, if you want my opinion," Peg-leg said.

Kracha said, "Get these people out of here."

That took some doing.

When the door had closed on them Kracha sighed. Julie felt his forehead. "He hasn't got a fever. Do you think we ought to get the doctor?"

"What for? Do I look as though I was dying?"

"What happened?" Dobie asked. "Did you faint or stumble or what?"

Kracha said slowly, "I was just coming in the door and it was as though something had hit me on the back of the head. I went down and I couldn't get up, that's all. I didn't faint. I heard the dog barking and I saw the Cassidys come. Only they seemed far away, and I couldn't move."

"How do you feel now?"

"Weaker than I want to admit." His eye gleamed hopefully. "Do you have a bit of whisky hidden somewhere?"

"You know I haven't. I'll get some tomorrow."

Kracha sighed. "I always told you to keep some around. You never know when you're going to need it."

"I'm willing to keep it but where would I hide it so you wouldn't find it?"

"He must be feeling better," Julie said, "if he can think about whisky."

They helped him upstairs — his whole left side seemed half-paralyzed — and Dobie undressed him while Julie got a hot-water bottle ready. Kracha complained that his left side felt numb. He lifted his arm off the bed and let it drop and it fell like a stick of wood. "It's the arm I broke in the mill years ago," he muttered. "I was carrying it in a sling the night your father was killed."

They made him comfortable. "Try to sleep. We'll leave the door open and if you want anything during the night, call us. In the morning if you're not feeling better I'll get the doctor."

"I want no doctors practising on me."

"Good night." Dobie said. Then he added, somewhat awkwardly, *"S Bohom."*

"S Bohom."

Kracha got out of bed in the morning at his usual hour, and though his arm and leg were stiffer than they should have been he had no trouble getting around. The stiffness was a week or two leaving him, but the attack, stroke, or whatever it was didn't recur. Dobie got him a pint of whisky and by the time it was gone Kracha was almost his old self again, yet it was noticeable that he walked a little more carefully when he went abroad, and neither so far nor so often; and as the spring days grew warmer he seemed content to sit in the sun for hours on end, doing nothing but sitting in the sun with the dog at his feet.

11

IN every steel town union membership had fallen off disastrously; following the collapse of the strike movement Tighe had reported to the A.F.L. convention in October that only some five thousand steelworkers still paid dues. The cold figures were disheartening in themselves, and a withering indictment of the man who revealed them; behind them, unexpressed, was the plight of the men in the mills, stripped defenseless by the union's defection. The tale of union men hounded and discriminated against by their superiors never ended. During the slack of that summer and fall Dobie had been cut to two and three days a week while known company men were getting full time — something he hadn't told Julie. But he wondered when something would happen that he wouldn't be able to keep from her.

Encouraged by the A.F.L.'s promise of aid, four hundred rank-and-file delegates met in February to make plans for a new campaign to organize the steel industry. Tighe promptly revoked their charters. Before he rested he had thrown seventy-five per cent of the organized steelworkers out of the union — a lunacy comparable with a man's kicking himself out of his own house. Then, like a steel plant manager threatened with collective bargaining, he summoned police to protect Amalgamated headquarters.

A committee went to Washington and secured a hearing before the A.F.L. Executive Council; it was obvious that no attempt to organize the steelworkers could possibly be successful until the fantastic and intolerable warfare Tighe was waging on his own membership was terminated. The Executive Council took up the problem with little enthusiasm. Tighe discovered "proof" that the rank-and-file movement was a Bolshevik plot to destroy the A.F.L., and the dismal farce was capped once and for all when a committee named by the council to consider ways and means of aiding the steelworkers masochistically dismembered itself over the craft issue. John L. Lewis expressed his disgust and hinted darkly of a new federation.

And then, in May, the Supreme Court declared the NRA unconstitutional.

It was every man for himself now, Dobie reflected; and one pleasant spring afternoon Gralji climbed the hill to Dobie's house and they sat on the front porch and talked, their feet propped up on the railing.

"Well," Dobie said after a long pause, "what do you think of the idea?"

Gralji shrugged slightly. "It sounds all right. If you can get away with it."

"We can try. Hell, we've got to do something. We can't just sit around and trust to luck."

"How about this National Emergency Council or whatever it is the expelled lodges have? They've taken it to court and if it goes against Tighe they might be able to do something. That Irwin who's the head of it is a damn good man."

"Sure, and look what happened to him. And Moore in Weirton. Fired as soon as the NRA was killed. And compared to us they're big shots, at least people have heard about them. The point is, we can't afford to wait. There's nothing to hold the company back now from doing anything it likes. We can't expect any protection from the union or the Government. The union will be lucky if it don't have to go underground. And I need my job."

"Who doesn't?"

Gralji stared at the rooftops spread out below them. In the immediate foreground they were brightened by patches of green where trees were leafing, by the clean freshness of a newly painted house or garage. The flatter expanse of Braddock lower down was a uniform, soiled colorlessness. Eleventh Street was a straight, wide scar on this dingy plain, the spire of St. Michael's at its head, the glintless river at its foot and the long roof of the First Ward school near its middle. The flat-sided hill was still brown; because it was a Saturday the sky above the blast furnaces was fairly clean.

"You sure get a nice view from up here," Gralji said.

Dobie contemplated it possessively. "That's one reason we took this house."

"I wouldn't mind moving up around here somewhere myself."

"I can let you know if I hear of anybody moving."

"It wouldn't be much use right now."

Julie appeared in the doorway to the parlor. She was fresh and clean from a bath and she was wearing a starched apron over her dress. "I'm going to make some coffee," she announced. "You'll have coffee and cake before you go."

She lingered in the doorway for a moment, gossiping, then left them.

Afternoon sunshine filled the porch, shining almost into their faces; it was warm and not too bright and as the sun sank toward Homestead it was growing larger and redder.

"Well," Dobie said, "getting back to what we were talking about. I think we have a damn good chance. The men know us. And there's still plenty of good union men in that mill even if they have stopped paying their dues. Enough to elect us. Without counting the ones that would vote for us just because it would be a slap at the company."

The lump in Gralji's cheek moved; he leaned forward, spat across the porch railing past his shoes and then settled back again. "It would be one of the God-damnedest things ever heard of if we got away with it."

"It does sort of hit you between the eyes at first, don't it?" Dobie brushed tobacco off his trousers and felt pleased. "We ought to be able to raise plenty hell. Me, you and Burke, plus Hagerty, Smolinski, Ragalyi — Jesus! If we worked together we'd have Flack and the rest of them running around in circles. And they wouldn't be able to do a thing to us. That's the beauty of it. We'd be perfectly safe."

"If you got elected. Flack ain't going to sit on his hands."

"I don't expect him to. But I figure that anything he does ought to work for us."

Half a dozen children and a dog marched past the house and continued on to the open hillside. The children were laden with wood, paper and raw potatoes.

"At first," Dobie said, "I thought it would simply be a good way to protect ourselves. Then I thought that if we did get in there was no reason why we couldn't raise hell and maybe get some benefits out of it for the men. If enough of us got in we could just about take the damn thing right over."

"You wouldn't have a hell of a lot if you did. Not the set-up they got there now."

"I don't know. Suppose a lot of guys in the other mills did the same. Suppose we figured out a way to get together. We could take over the whole E.R.P., Pittsburgh district, Gary, Youngstown, Birmingham, and by the time we were through I'll bet the company would be wishing to God it'd never thought of it."

"It's a crazy idea."

"Crazy enough to work."

"Have you said anything to anybody yet?"

"You're the first one. If you're willing, we can talk it over with Burke and see what he says. Then we can see Hagerty. And once we're in we want to keep hammering away for things that count. The hell with this crap about bowling leagues and more toilets. Keep hammering away for raises and vacations and no favoritism on turns. Act as though the E.R.P. was an honest-to-God union. Make a stink every time a foreman looks at a man cross-eyed. And never let up."

"If we can get elected."

"We stand a damn good chance. How's your department?"

"It's hard to say now. Most of the men stopped paying dues but as far as I can tell they're still strong for a real union. I don't know what they'll say when I tell them we're going to run for representatives, though."

"Just tell them that as long as the Amalgamated is shot to hell we want to go into the E.R.P. and see what we can do there. They know we're good union men and it's a cinch they'll be better off having us in there than the company stooges they got now."

"Would you resign from the union?"

"What for? The whole idea is we're going in as union men. I looked up the constitution of the E.R.P. and it says they can't discriminate or abridge anybody for belonging to a union, society, fraternity or anything like that. You know the kind of language they use."

After a while Gralji said, "We'll have to work pretty fast."

"We can see Burke next week and if he's willing we'll get hold of Hagerty. Then if it's okay we'll start the ball rolling. I know we won't have any trouble getting nominated. How many names we need, ten? Whatever it is." He chuckled. "I'd give ten bucks to be in Flack's office when he finds out our names have been put up."

Dobie was rolling another cigarette when Julie called that the coffee was ready.

They saw Burke Tuesday. He had to be argued into the wisdom of consulting Hagerty. "Why drag him into it? We don't need his permission."

"We ain't asking his permission. We're going through with it regardless and we're going to tell him so. But if we got into it without saying anything to him he might get sore. Let me finish, will you? Look at it this way: Up to now he's been more or less the big shot in the E.R.P. and he's liable to figure that if we get in he might not look so big any more. Which, if you ask me, he won't. But we can't lose anything by going to see him. That's what you call diplomacy."

Hagerty was on his back porch in his undershirt, a can of beer in his fist, when they called on him. If their plan startled him he didn't show it. He said he didn't see any reason why they shouldn't run if they wanted to. "I can't stop you."

"We know that," Dobie said. "The point is we'd rather have you with us. And if we get in — well, just figure out for yourself what we could do if we worked together."

Perhaps he was flattered because they had come to him; at any rate, he agreed to do what he could to help them.

Walking down the street from Hagerty's house Burke said, "As long as we're doing this we may as well do it right. I got an estimate on those cards they pass around election time. You know. Vote for Joe Shitheel, the people's friend. Only we could say vote for us and have real union men represent you in the E.R.P. or something like that. We could figure out the exact words."

"That sounds like a good idea."

"They'd only cost us a couple of bucks apiece and they'll show we mean business. Put some life into the election."

"There ought to be plenty as it is."

The announcement that the three leading officers of the union were going to run for election as Employee Representatives created a minor sensation; the appearance of their campaign cards, bearing their names and check numbers, another. Flack immediately summoned them to his office, pointed out that the cards were a violation of company rules, and asked them to stop distributing them. Since practically their entire supply had already been distributed they agreed readily.

They were all nominated, and a week later all elected.

At the first meeting after the election, Flack appeared and made a short speech. "You've been elected by the employees to represent them under this plan," he said in part. "I'd like to say that your personal opinions, or what your opinions may have been in the past about this plan, should not be allowed to interfere with your obligations as Employee Representatives. If you'll all co-operate I think you'll find that this plan can be made to work with everybody benefiting."

After he left Hagerty, as chairman, asked, "Any new business?"

Dobie and Gralji looked at Burke. He glanced at a slip of paper in his hand and cleared his throat. "I make a motion that we appoint a committee to see Mr. Flack at once and present demands for a twenty per cent wage increase, vacations with pay, cancellation of food box debts and — " He paused for breath. "And an Employee Representative on the board of the United States Steel Corporation."

Somebody chuckled.

"I second the motion," Gralji said.

It was put to a vote and, with the newly elected representatives voting like one man, passed. A committee of three was appointed and departed to see Flack.

While they were gone Hagerty said, "You guys ain't losing any time, are you?"

Dobie grinned.

The committee returned.

"Your committee begs to report," Burke said, "that Flack told us to get the hell out and stay out."

The meeting then adjourned.

12

*F*ROM *the minutes of the regular meeting of the Employee Representatives, Edgar Thomson Works, August 25:* —

MR. BURKE: "I have received a written answer from Mr. Walling concerning the request from the dinkey men. Mr. Walling says he does not feel he can recommend the rate adjustment at the present time. The men aren't satisfied. They want an equalized rate with Homestead or a flat rate of 70 cents an hour for engineers and 58 cents for hookers-on. These men are underpaid for the work they're doing. There are some days when they work for 8 hours straight without stopping. They neglect to eat their lunches because they want to get the work out, that is, they want to get the heats up and the steel up to the strippers. But every request we put in where it concerns two or more men there is no favorable action. It's always turned down."

MR. GORDON (*Management's Representative at the meeting*): "As I've explained before, it is not the corporation's policy to handle rate adjustments involving large numbers of men in this manner."

Mr. Hagerty stated that a time study had been received on open hearth stockhouse cranemen and a meeting will be held by these men to decide what they are going to do. A time study was shown to the soaking pit cranemen and they are very dissatisfied with it.

A discussion was held on the subject of men who have less than 5 years service holding steady jobs while men with 15 years or more are on the extra list, getting just a few turns a month. This committee feels that the 5-years rule should be enforced for all with no favoritism by foremen or superintendents.

Mr. Dobrejcak asked if any more had been heard from the City Office about pensioners being paid once a month instead of every three months as at present. The Chair said no answer had been received.

A general discussion was held on the proposed new insurance plan to take the place of the old one which was recently canceled.

Meeting adjourned 3:30 P.M.

From the minutes, September 29: —

This was a special meeting called by the Chairman of this committee at the request of several hundred employees of this plant to consider what action may be taken either to defer or reduce deductions or make cancellations of the entire indebtedness which was contracted by employees during the depression for material relief.

Before the meeting began the Chair remarked that Mr. Walling, Supt. of Open Hearth and Bessemer Departments, was present at the meeting in order to straighten out a matter that concerned himself and Mr. Frank Davis, one of the representatives of his department.

Mr. Davis stated: "When I was elected to represent the workers I realized it was to bargain with the company on a give-and-take basis, which is collective bargaining and that is what I tried to do. This morning Mr. Walling called me to the office and told me I was not on the job. He said I was in the Open Hearth Department yesterday for three hours. That is wrong. I was in the Open Hearth from 1:20 P.M. to 2:15 P.M. and came back to the Bessemer and we shut down at 3 P.M. My business in the Open Hearth Department yesterday afternoon was a petition for the men which they signed, asking the company to wait until the men are working more steady before they make the deductions for food and supplies. I was asked to go to the Open Hearth and was only performing my duties as representative. Mr. Walling told me if I did not stay in the Bessemer Department I would be fired, saying that I had no business in the Open Hearth and if the men want they can come over to the Bessemer and see me. I don't want to be fired by Mr. Walling or anyone else for representative duties which are given me. If they don't want this plan carried out let us know. They don't put pressure on any representative who is doing what the company wants, only on the ones that are trying to help the men."

Mr. WALLING: "Mr. Davis has confused the issue somewhat. Three or four days ago I received this note from a maintenance foreman: 'For your information we find that repairs are large on the Bessemer cinder cars due to the packing burnt out of the journal boxes and no oil in the same. Cars are run dry, cutting bearings and in some cases cutting axles so they have to be replaced with new axles.' As Mr. Davis said, he was in the Open Hearth and spent some time there yesterday. Until he told me I did not know he was there with a petition. His failure to do his work brought censure and not his duties as representative. If I fail to do my work I expect to be censured. He must put in more time on the buggies, oiling them. As regards the petition, I knew nothing about it until he told me, but I do not feel it was his duty to invite complaints."

Mr. DAVIS: "I object to your statement that I invite complaints. I have never went around to dig up any complaints from the men."

Mr. BURKE: "I see no reason why a representative should not ask the men in his department if they have any complaints."

Mr. DOBREJCAK: "You can't tell, he's liable to run across a man that's perfectly satisfied."

THE CHAIR (to Mr. Davis): "Do you have any orders as to how much time a representative is to spend on his job?"

Mr. DAVIS: "No. Do you mean representative duties? Nobody ever said anything to me about how much time."

Mr. GRALJI: "Some superintendents have been telling the men in their departments not to go to their representatives."

Mr. GORDON: "There seems to be a misunderstanding about that. I have investigated the charge and the Superintendents have simply told their employees that it isn't necessary to take every little grievance or request to the representative because many of these things can be settled without much trouble. However, some employees misunderstood and thought the Superintendent was advising them against going to their representative. This is not so. The Superintendents simply ask that the men have enough confidence in them to come to them first. However there is no rule that compels an employee to go to his Superintendent if he does not wish to do so."

After some discussion about the food box debts, Mr. Dobrejcak made a motion, which was seconded by Mr. Gralji and adopted, that the following be inserted in the minutes:

"The following are some of the reasons advanced by Edgar Thomson employees as sufficient reasons for these representatives to ask cancellation of all the credit extended from Sept. 1932 to July 1933.

"That employees signed for these items knowing there was no other way to take care of their families, as they were forbidden by the company to apply for outside relief which would not have cost them anything.

"That employees were forced to take the grocery orders as they were not eligible for outside relief, yet they were granted no choice in the matter of selecting items they were charged for. This resulted in an over-supply of many items and insufficient or none at all of needed food items, especially for young children. The oversupply was in most cases given to others to help them out.

"That some of the food received was in a spoiled condition and was thus wasted yet it has to be paid for now.

"That there was no way for the employees to check the correct cost of the items they were charged with.

"That work in this plant, the wages for which are to be used to pay off the credit thus extended, is being given to many employees who are not indebted to the company and even to men newly hired.

"That the U. S. Steel Corporation took credit in the public prints for taking care of their employees and that the costs were charged to welfare and credited as such in reduced taxation and reports to stockholders, some of whom were the same employees who are now being asked to pay for the welfare thus extended."

Meeting adjourned 4:15 P.M.

From the minutes, November 21: —

Mr. Burke stated that he has not received an answer on the four hours pay his men are to get after being called out and then sent home. Mr. Gordon, Management's Representative, said that as far as notifying the men not to come out, that is being done.

MR. BURKE: "Yes, they are told not to show up until they're sent for and the men who get the turns aren't entitled to them. There is too much discrimination."

It was asked if the schedule for paydays in the coming year was ready yet and Mr. Gordon said it was expected soon. The first submitted schedule was rejected by this committee (see Minutes Nov. 3) on the ground that there was too many paydays too far apart.

Mr. Hagerty: "This committee has requested that paydays come every ten days."

Mr. Gordon: "Paydays every ten days, for various reasons, cannot be handled satisfactorily."

Mr. Hagerty: "They can do it in other plants, why can't they do it at Edgar Thomson?"

Mr. Burke: "How about the older men laid off?"

Mr. Gordon: "No answer yet."

Mr. Burke: "It's a —— shame the way they're being treated."

Mr. Dobrejcak: "I would like to ask Mr. Gordon, officially, what has happened to the cranemen's requests?"

Mr. Gordon: "I can tell you. City Office."

Mr. Dobrejcak: "How about the motor inspectors?"

Mr. Gordon: "City Office."

Mr. Dobrejcak: "The men say they'll walk off the job."

Mr. Davis: "The heaters and bottom makers are still waiting for an answer to their request for a minimum rate of 900 tons when the mill rolls less than that amount."

Mr. Gordon: "That's in the City Office."

Mr. Burke: "The Superintendent has something to do with granting rates, hasn't he?"

Mr. Gordon: "He can recommend."

Mr. Smolinski: "I got an answer about Number 2 mill men being put on tonnage. The men don't want tonnage. They say the hell with tonnage. What they want is an increase in rate."

Mr. Gralji: "Number 3 pilers and gaggers are not satisfied with the answer they received. They feel they are not being paid enough and want an increase."

Mr. Gordon: "It will have to be referred to the City Office."

The meeting adjourned 3:30 P.M.

"And that," Dobie said to Julie — he usually brought a copy of the minutes home, his desk was slowly filling with such literature — "ought to give you an idea."

"I think it's a shame," Julie said.

"Oh, you've got to give them credit. It's a honey of a system and it works like a clock. We figured that by going into the E.R.P. we could raise enough hell to get something done but the way it's worked out we can raise all the hell we like and it don't get us any-where. We sign petitions and pass resolutions and it don't mean a thing."

"Well, at least you're proving it's no good."

"Yeah, but we knew that before we started."

The efficiency of the system was undeniable. A "request" faced a succession of hurdles: unfriendly Superintendents, Gordon's cita-tions from the constitution of the E.R.P., Flack himself, and the ever-dependable "corporation policy"; while for those that sur-mounted all these there waited at the end the bottomless pit of the City Office, whence none returned recognizable, if any returned at all.

"Maybe this central committee they've started will be able to do something but I doubt it. Gary's had one for nearly two years and they're no better off than we are. It'll be the E.R.P. all over again. You watch. They'll ask for a raise or something and the com-pany'll say, No, you can't have it because it's against corporation policy and Article 99 Section XYZ and who the hell's running this company anyway? And there you are."

"Well, don't get discouraged."

"I'm not discouraged. Only thing is, I don't see how we can do much more from the inside than we've already done. Not with the set-up they've got now. What we need is some outside help, and I only hope Lewis means what he says about organizing the steel mills."

While making a plea for industrial unionism before the A.F.L. convention in Atlantic City John L. Lewis had been interrupted, to put it mildly, by Hutcheson, president of the carpenters' union and embodiment of all that was most reactionary in the Federation. When the two men were pulled apart Lewis had a torn shirt and Hutcheson was nursing a smashed mouth. The clash was symbolic. Some weeks later, Lewis announced the formation of a Committee for Industrial Organization "for the purpose of encouraging and promoting the organization of the unorganized workers in mass production and other industries on an industrial basis," and the

C.I.O. was started on its way, destined to earn the hatred of its enemies and to enlist the loyalty of millions on whose lips three letters, three initials — "C.I.O.! C.I.O.! C.I.O.!" — were to become a chant, a battle cry shaking the country from coast to coast.

13

T HE visitor from Uniontown leaned against the refrigerator in Anna's kitchen and talked about politics. He was a big, homely man, prematurely bald, his expression jovial and shrewd. He said, "If you spend a dollar on cars you're crazy. You've got dealers in this town, haven't you? Sure they're Republicans. But most of their customers are Democrats and if they start forgetting it you remind them. I went to Walt Button last election, one of the biggest agencies in Uniontown and a black-hearted Republican if there ever was one. He's in the Chamber of Commerce, he's in the Elks, he's in the Legion, he was in the Ku Klux, he's a son of a bitch from the word go. I told him, Walt, I want four cars from you on Election Day. And I got them."

He let that sink in.

"If we had somebody like you . . ." Anna said with a sigh. "There's only a few here who really want to work. We don't get much co-operation from the committee. They have dinners all the time in Little Washington and make speeches but they expect you to do the work. And with what?"

"Somebody's getting the money." He — his name was Steve something, a long Slovak name that Dobie hadn't heard clearly — sipped beer. "You ain't got the right kind of people. It takes time to train experienced workers and build up a good organization, especially in a town like this where the steel company has been God Almighty since the Indians cleared out. But we had the coal companies to fight, don't forget that."

He looked pleased. "Before the primaries last year we went to the committee and said we wanted two of our men put in. Their slate was lousy with businessmen and lawyers. How about our people, we said. How about all them miners back in the hills. They said nothing doing. We said all right, you bastards, and we got together with the Mine Workers and put up a whole opposition slate. Then we went to work in every coal patch in the county, places them God-damn' committeemen never even heard of and wouldn't go if they did because they might get their shoes muddy. Don't vote for this guy, we said, he don't like unions. Don't vote for this other guy, he's been a lawyer for the coal company in compensation cases. Another guy is a big property owner and wants the Coal and Iron Police back. Down with so-and-so — he's a Ku Klux." Steve drew his finger across his throat expressively. "We went right down the line, turning them inside out."

He sipped beer. "Well, we licked them. We didn't get just the two places we asked for. We got eight out of twelve. Day after the primaries I walked into headquarters and the county chairman says to me, Steve, you're a son of a bitch. I says, Fred, you're twenty years behind the times. You ain't got a bunch of Hunky greenhorns back in the hills there any more. They've been educated, I says. The coal companies have spent thousands and thousands of dollars educating them with tear gas and machine guns. And then you come along with your lousy crew of shysters and real-estate dealers. Get smart, I says. And next time a union man walks in here you listen to him."

"You couldn't do anything like that here."

"You could if there was a union in the mill," Dobie said.

Steve swirled the beer in his glass and chuckled throatily. "I sent my wife around. One old Hunky *baba* said she couldn't go to register, she didn't have a pair of stockings to her name. My wife goes out and buys her a pair, how much, fifty, seventy-five cents, and the old *baba* almost cried on her shoulder." He changed to fluent Slovak with hardly a pause: "My dear, my darling, I voted so many times and this is the first time I ever got anything. The men get drinks and cigars but never a present for the women. Now I don't have to wear my husband's socks when I go to church."

He emptied his glass and set it on top of the refrigerator. Dobie said, "That's the next move, all right. If a union ever gets into the mills it'll have to go into politics. It'll have to. Look what happened in Germany."

"Let me tell you something." Steve's forefinger came out. "What's your name, Dobrejcak? Let me tell you something a lot of people never realize. If you're making a living in this country you're in politics whether you think so or not. People who never vote or say it's a racket and things like that are simply getting the other guy's politics, that's all. The smart people go out and make their own."

"Yeah, I guess you're right."

"I know I'm right." He turned to Anna. "Well, I'd better be going. My wife's probably wondering what happened to me."

"I'm glad you dropped in," Anna said, rising. She looked tiny beside him. "I told Helen if she saw you that the next time you came to Donora, if you could drop in, I wanted your advice."

"Any time you think I can help you let me know. But as I say, the organization in this county . . ." His voice merged with the murmur of voices from the parlor as he and Anna went into the hall.

Dobie and Julie, with Kracha, left a bit later. Marion and her husband drove them to the Webster station, across the river from Donora and on the same side as Braddock. It was still early in the evening and the sky was so luminous that the smoke from the zinc works was a pale shadow against it. Freshly charged, the zinc smelting furnaces, crawling with thousands of small flames, yellow, blue, green, filled the valley with smoke. Acrid and poisonous, worse than anything a steel mill belched forth, it penetrated everywhere, making automobile headlights necessary in Webster's streets, setting the river-boat pilots to cursing God, and destroying every living thing on the hills. Webster lay directly in its path, and in its streets children played, in its dreadful little houses men and women ate and slept, made love and died, perpetually enveloped in smoke. Sometimes the wind shifted and blew it back the other way, over lower Donora where another Webster was in the making, no less dreadful, no less hideous; and then Webster's stricken earth, like a scabrous body, lay bared to the clean light of day until the smoke returned and shrouded it.

But tonight the smoke was light and what there was of it stayed on the far side of the rigid black pattern that was the bridge — boys and girls still strolled over it on a Sunday evening, Julie observed sentimentally — and the air was clean enough to carry the smell of new vegetation from the hills. After the car had gone, its lights climbing the ramp to the bridge, they stood outside the shabby, neglected station looking at the quiet river, the black mills on its other side, the lights of Donora beginning to shine in the dusk. There was a Sunday stillness in the air.

Kracha said the train was coming.

Julie's dress slid revealingly up her leg as she mounted the steps. "It's something when you can still pop an eye at your own wife's leg," Dobie murmured, dropping into the seat beside her. He explained, and she said, "I'll begin to worry when you stop. Put your arm around me." The conductor gave them a fatherly smile in exchange for their tickets; perhaps he thought they were lovers. Kracha dozed in the seat ahead of them.

When they got home he said "Good night" and went upstairs, his shoes rustling the Sunday paper scattered over the parlor floor. Dobie opened his shirt. "We got anything to eat in the house?"

"Don't touch that ham; I'm saving it for your lunch."

He was peering into the lower half of the icebox. "I'm hungry. What's this?" He uncovered a saucer containing a pork chop, breaded and fried.

"I was saving that for Dzedo."

"Anything around here you ain't saving?" He put the saucer on the table and got out a loaf of rye bread. "How about making some tea?"

"I suppose I'd better. You'll only fill up on beer and if there's one thing I can't stand it's when you come to bed smelling of beer. I'll be right down."

She gathered their things together, her own coat and bag, Dobie's jacket and tie, and went upstairs. She returned in a few minutes saying Dzedo was getting ready for bed and didn't want anything. "I guess he's pretty tired. But you can't very well leave him behind." She put water on for tea.

Dobie, elbows on the table, smeared mustard on the chop and bit into it. "Want some?"

"Ugh! Cold pork at this time of night."

"Put steam in your whistle, as the dinkey men say."

She had changed to a flowered housecoat that reached to her bare ankles. Dobie eyed her. "Come here a minute."

"What for?"

"Never mind. Come over here."

She approached suspiciously. When she was close enough Dobie reached out and pulled the zipper of her housecoat open.

"Ah. Just as I suspected."

She didn't move. "Are you satisfied?"

"Mrs. Dobrejcak, you're lucky I got my hands full of pork chop. Better close that before I forget."

"I wasn't the one who opened it."

He slid the zipper shut. "You don't know how I hate to do this. But it's for your own good. Lots of gals get pneumonia and die going around bare-naked like that."

"I know one who never will." She moved back to the stove and folded her arms across her chest. "Remember that skinny girl in the skinny little black dress? She came in while we were at Agnes'. The one with the mouth." Julie contorted her face and pursed her lips unappetizingly and looked absurd. "She's been married over a year and her husband hasn't seen her undressed once."

"How do you know?"

"Agnes told me. They're friends of Martin's."

"They would be. What's the matter with them?"

"Don't ask me. I guess she thinks she's being modest. They're very religious."

Dobie grunted.

Julie dropped tea leaves into bubbling water and shut off the gas. Upstairs Kracha loosed a rush of water in the bathroom and thumped solidly to bed. The tick of the clock on the stove seemed to grow louder. There was no other sound anywhere.

They had their tea and Dobie rolled a final cigarette and then they went upstairs. He pulled shut the door to Kracha's room and undressed while Julie stood before her dresser and fixed her hair. A small lamp made shadowy hollows under her cheekbones, shone through her hair. Dobie's eyes met hers in the mirror and he grinned. Julie smiled, her face framed by her uplifted arms.

He rose and stood close behind her. "Make yourself real beautiful, sweetheart."

"I suppose you think I'm going to bed with you."

"If you don't you'll break my heart and that's no lie." His arms went around her. She threw her head back and he kissed her throat.

She murmured, "After nearly two years. It's about time we were settling down."

"It's all your fault."

She sighed. "I hope it'll always be like this."

His fingers found the zipper and opened it. "You won't need this." He pushed the housecoat off her shoulders and down until it crumpled against the swell of her hips. Her skin glowed richly in the lamplight. "There. That's the way I like to see you."

"When am I going to put on some weight? Look at me."

"I am."

"I'll never get my hair fixed this way."

"Who cares?"

"I'll only be a minute. Though I don't know why I bother; it's worse than when I started after you get through with me. Let me go."

He kissed her once more and smacked her behind and then lay in bed watching her, watching the play of light on her face, her body, until she turned off the lamp. She had one knee on the bed when she exclaimed, "Oh, I forgot!" She returned to the dresser and busied herself there, ignoring his questions, his protests. "Don't be so impatient! My goodness, I'm only trying to make myself a little seductive." She giggled.

She returned and bent over him, shadowy, warm with life. The tips of her breasts brushed his face and the darkness suddenly filled with fragrance. Dobie chuckled. "Mrs. Dobrejcak, you're a whore in your heart, but don't you ever change."

He lifted his arms and drew her down.

She was shaking his arm. "John. Wake up. John. Wake up." He opened his eyes. It was still dark. "What's the matter?"

"*Shh!* Listen."

He was awake at once. He heard nothing for a moment; then there was a dull thump somewhere.

"Hear it?"

It came again. Dobie felt his nerves tighten.

"I thought at first it was old Peg-leg going up the wooden steps. But so slow. And at this hour."

He twisted in bed and pulled the blind aside. The Cassidy house was completely darkened and over the hillside, the sleeping town, lay the mist and stillness of a late hour. The wooden steps were empty. As he looked the thump recurred, a weird, ghostly sound.

"It's in the house." He swung his legs out of bed and stood hesitating, remembering the room's contents, choosing a weapon. He picked Julie's hand mirror off her dresser, a heavy, silver plated thing she'd got for a wedding present.

"John, be careful. Put something on."

The thump came again and this time he felt it with his heels. He murmured, "Hell," and strode to Kracha's door and threw it open. For a moment he couldn't see much; then he saw Kracha on the floor, the bedclothes partly pulled down over him. As Dobie stared Kracha lifted himself on one arm, straining as though he had a whole world on his back, and then he dropped heavily, his elbow thumping against the floor.

Dobie bent over him as Julie appeared in the doorway. She gasped.

"Give me a hand. It looks like he's had another stroke."

He turned Kracha over and they lifted him back into bed. Julie said, "His underwear's all wet."

"He must've started for the bathroom. Go back and put some clothes on; I'll change him. Fill a hot-water bottle. And bring the whisky; you know where it is."

It was getting light before he spoke. Julie had made some hot tea with whisky and lemon and was kneeling beside the bed. "Dzedo. Drink this. It will make you feel better."

His eyes opened and he looked at her. His face twisted queerly; perhaps he was trying to smile. "*Vnučka moja,*" he whispered, "granddaughter mine, you will surely go to heaven, you're always on your knees."

But when she held the cup to his mouth he choked, as though his throat was closed.

He spoke once more, after the doctor had visited him for the second time that day, and while Dobie was out getting Father Kazincy and sending telegrams to Donora, to Munhall, to New York. All he said then, to no one in particular, was, "My children, my children . . ." After that he just lay quiet, his eyes closed.

Kracha died at a quarter to five that afternoon. Dobie was sitting near the bed while Julie moved around the kitchen downstairs, getting supper. An odd sound from Kracha, as though he was trying to clear his throat, brought Dobie to the bedside. A moment later he had stopped breathing.

Dobie stared down at him. He had never seen anyone die. Once in the mill a crane had pinned a man against a girder and by the time the craneman had sent his crane shuddering into reverse the man had stopped screaming; and Dobie, doing a repair job on an adjoining crane, had felt sick as he watched the body drop to the open hearth floor. But that wasn't like seeing your own grandfather die in bed before your eyes. He felt frightened and alone. He tried to remember a prayer and all he could think of were the first few words of Our Father: *Oče nas, i se jesi, na nebesci* . . .

He covered the dead man's face — he didn't know why exactly but it seemed the proper thing to do — and pulled down the blinds and closed the door and went downstairs. Julie was cleaning soup greens. She looked around and he said, "He's gone. I didn't have a chance to call you."

"Oh," Julie said. "Oh, the poor man, the poor man." She bent her head and began to cry softly.

"He went easy. He put up a pretty good fight but the end was easy. He just stopped breathing."

"I'll miss him. And the way I used to yell at him. But I never really meant it. Honest I didn't."

Dobie patted her shoulder. "That's all right. I guess he understood."

He blew his nose and then put on his coat and hat and went out to phone the undertaker. From the porch of the Cassidy house, which had been unnaturally quiet all day, old Peg-leg asked him how his grandfather was, and Dobie told him. Peg-leg said, "God rest him," and stamped into the house with the news. Dobie went on down the street. It was a fine, sunny day.

14

ANNA and John were the first to arrive, an hour after the undertaker had come and gone. They had received Dobie's telegram around noon but John was working until three and there was no train scheduled anyway; bad times and the automobile had cut railroad services in the valley to a minimum. Anna had finally persuaded her butcher's son to drive them down. After them came the rest: Anna's gangling sons; Martin, Agnes and the baby; Julie's father and mother; Joe, Elena, Helen, Joie and his Polish wife and several children, Steve and Kitty; Alice, Frank — his eyesight so bad he had to be led to a chair in the darkened parlor; with Chuck and his wife and baby, and their daughter Florence — without her married automobile salesman, who was a process server now; Radilla, Dorta, her sons and grandchildren; Francka, Andrej and their sons, now middle-aged, the one who had never married and the one whose wife had left him; and out of the depths of Homestead, Borka, a shriveled mummy of a woman whom Dobie hadn't seen since his mother's funeral sixteen years before. And people Dobie didn't know or had forgotten: Bodnars, Novotnys, Feciks, Slemas, Martineks — an endless stream of people for three exhausting days.

Mikie got in from New York the morning of the funeral. His train didn't stop in Braddock so Steve, Joe's youngest son, and Dobie drove to the East Liberty station to meet him. He got off the train carrying a small bag, a topcoat over one arm, a leather case slung from his shoulder. He was as tall as Dobie but pounds leaner, his clothes impressive, his grin as infectious as ever under a thin mustache.

The brothers shook hands. "It's been a long time," Dobie said.

"Six years."

"You don't look any different. Except for that thing on your lip."

Mikie grinned. "The gals like it."

They got into the car. "How's everything?"

"All right. Julie's pretty well fagged-out. You can imagine what it's been like the last couple days. I've seen people I didn't know were still living."

"There's nothing like a funeral to bring them out."

Steve started the car. "Did you come by Pullman?"

"Where would I get the dough to ride Pullman?"

"I just asked. I've always wondered what it's like to sleep in one of them berths. Especially the upper ones."

"I pulled a couple seats apart and got a little sleep. They turn down the lights and you can rent a pillow for two bits. But I feel like I could stand a good wash."

"You look all right. What've you got in that case, a camera?"

"Uh-huh."

He exhibited it with obvious pride. Dobie whistled. "That's a camera, all right. Let's have a look at it."

Mikie's hands let it go reluctantly. "Just don't let it drop. Put the strap around your neck."

It was unexpectedly heavy. Dobie examined it enviously, put it to his eye and tried to focus the coupled range finder, admired the shining lens.

"I've only had it a couple months," Mikie said. "I was going to get an enlarger but this trip's taking all the money I had saved."

"What's a thing like this cost?"

"Hundred bucks. It's a refugee job. You know, people who can't take money out of Germany buy cameras and stuff and then sell them over here."

"It sure is a beauty. Makes mine look like a hunk of junk."

He gave it back. "I wouldn't mind owning a good camera. Like you said, an enlarger and all. But where would I get a hundred bucks?"

"That kind of money," Steve said, "I'd rather put on a car."

"Oh, you can have a lot of fun with a good camera," Dobie said. "It's the only hobby I ever really liked."

A descending trolley passenger leaped for the sidewalk as Steve stepped on the gas. "You must be working steady."

"I am. We're doing nothing but Navy work now and it's piling up faster than we can turn it out. I got a raise in March; making eighty an hour now."

"Hell," Dobie said, "you're making eight an hour more than me. Forty hours?"

Mikie nodded.

"It's the no layoffs that count," Steve said.

He drove through Swissvale, through Rankin, swung the car around a corner and plunged down a steep, winding street. Mikie said, "I've been pushing my feet through the floorboards ever since I got into this car. Where did this guy learn to drive?"

"He just picked it up."

"What's the matter with my driving? Your grandpap used to like to ride with me."

They dropped out of Rankin onto the edge of Braddock, the end of Braddock Avenue. Driving into town Dobie pointed out the union office and Mikie mentioned changes he noticed, a new movie, new store fronts, new traffic lights. "But it's still as dirty as ever. Christ, but it's dirty."

"The mills are all working pretty good right now."

"Even without the mills. I'd forgotten just how lousy this place really was."

"Where we live it isn't so bad."

Where they lived several people watched from the front porch as they got out of the car. Mikie glanced at the wreath on the door. "My flowers get here?"

"Yeah."

He lowered his voice as they went through the gate. "What'll I do, go right in?"

"You'd better. Just kneel down for a minute."

"I haven't prayed since Mamma died."

When he came out of the dim, flower-scented parlor he was engulfed by relatives. He kissed a few and shook hands with the rest, said he was working steady, said he wasn't thinking of getting married, admitted he'd rather live in New York than in Braddock, and then expressed a desire to wash up. Dobie and Julie accompanied him upstairs. Agnes' baby was asleep on the bed and there were two slightly older children sprawled on what had been Kracha's bed. The bathroom was hung with diapers.

"You have a pretty nice place."

"It's a mess right now," Julie said. She spoke tiredly.

"They sure take over a place when something like this happens, don't they? Move right in."

Dobie shrugged. "You've got to expect that. Did you bring a black tie?"

He had. The funeral, Dobie said, was at one; Father Kazincy had a wedding at twelve.

Outside there was a burst of voices. Dobie went to the window and saw Francka's two sons, both drunk, fighting clumsily in the roadway. Some men separated them. Dobie grunted and turned away. "Between the kids and the drunks this sure is a funeral."

"That's what you get for having liquor around."

"What I had went the first day. They're buying their own now."

"Well, Dzedo got stewed at more than one wake so I guess he won't mind people getting stewed at his. Just as long as they don't get so drunk they take him out of his coffin. A fella from my shop went to a wake like that. They got pie-eyed and started arguing about how it felt to lay in a coffin and finally they stood the corpse in a corner and took turns climbing into the coffin. And while the corpse was standing in his corner somebody stuck a cigarette in his mouth and damn near set fire to his mustache."

"Listen to the way he talks," Julie said. "Like a regular New Yorker. Why don't you pronounce your *r*'s?"

Mikie threw up his hands. "And in New York they keep telling me I still talk like a farmer!"

He washed and shaved and put on a clean shirt and the black tie. Julie said, "That's a nice suit."

"When you're single you can afford to wear suits like that," Dobie said. "You see his camera?"

"Is it the kind you'd like to get?"

"Better."

They showed her the camera and then locked it in a dresser drawer — Dobie thought that, on the whole, it would be better if Mikie didn't take pictures at the cemetery — and went downstairs.

Anna was making coffee. The table was littered with food and dirty dishes, there were empty beer bottles on the window sill and cigarette butts in the sink. A baby was wailing and someone was shushing it; men were arguing in the little yard and children yelled from the upper hillside. Francka, Borka and Alice sat quietly in the parlor; in the kitchen Dorta was talking with a woman Dobie didn't know, a heavy, old woman whose hands lay lifelessly in her lap, whose feet looked like misshapen lumps. She was saying in Slovak, "Who knows better than I? Look at me, look at my hands, look at my feet. That is what America did for me. My husband sent for me and put me in a house and filled it with boarders, and for thirty years that's all I saw of America. Work, work, day and night, cooking, scrubbing, washing. And now I can hardly walk, I can hardly put a spoon to my own mouth. They told me, Oh, you're going to America, that's a fine place, you'll live enough for two lives there." Her face was old and tired and resigned. "And I have, I have."

Steve appeared at Dobie's side. "Listen, I think I'll go for the old man now."

"Okay. Don't take too long."

"Be right back."

He went out, Kitty at his heels. She was wearing a kerchief around her hair, and Dorta said, "Five years ago if you had asked a girl to wear a kerchief on her head she would have cried. Only old greenhorn *babas* wore such things. But now some moving picture actress wears it and it's all right."

"I hear you had a flood, Mrs. Radilla."

"Oh, *Bohze moj!*" She lifted her hands and burst into speech. There had been a flood in March, the worst the valley had ever known. Pittsburgh's pretentiously named Golden Triangle, its department stores and office buildings, disappeared under water to the ceilings of their street floors. Mills shut down, power and water services were cut off, and on St. Patrick's Day, the crest of the flood, Dobie had looked down from his front porch on a river grown monstrously wide. From the base of the opposite hill to the B. and O. railroad tracks lower Braddock was a single, glistening sheet of water out of which houses rose like blocks of wood. Dorta had fled to her son's house, her kitchen completely under water, but many people, including most of the Negroes, stayed where they were because they had no place else to go. They climbed to the upper floors and were photographed by the newspapers waving and grinning out of bedroom windows. Rowboats slid up and down Washington Street. Kracha said there had been a flood in 1907 but nothing like this. He and Dobie had gone down to Halket and a little beyond and stood there as at the shore of a lake, as before a second deluge which had obliterated a world. It seemed improbable that the First Ward would ever be the same again, but after the waters had receded and the muck had been washed off it was hard to see any change. One sagging hovel had collapsed and the others merely sagged a little more and everything looked a bit older and shabbier, that was all.

Julie began clearing the table. Dobie whispered, "Don't bother."

"I just want to clean up a little before Father Kazincy gets here." She sighed. "I'll be so glad when I have my house to myself again."

They buried Kracha beside Pauline. Dobie remembered the other times he had stood on that hillside beside an open grave, listening to the voice of a priest and to women crying: the scuttering snow and his mother's agonized sobs when they buried his father, and the gray, sunless day when they had laid her beside him. Pauline had been given a day much like this, clear and warm with white clouds lovely in a blue sky. But he found himself no longer resenting the extravagant grief of the old women, not even Francka's. "I'm getting old," he thought. Mikie whispered, "I should've brought my camera. Look at those clouds." Down the hill a piece a cemetery worker straightened to light his pipe.

Only a few people returned to the house and by late afternoon the last, the Donora contingent, had left. The house seemed cool and empty. Julie lifted blinds and opened windows, uncovered mirrors and pictures. The scent of flowers and incense was a long time fading.

There was nothing in the house for supper, Julie said. What would they like? Mikie, pressed, said steak and French-fried potatoes would be all right with him. Julie gave Dobie a dollar and they went out.

As they walked toward Jones Avenue Mikie said, "I guess you're glad it's over."

"I know I'll be glad to get back to work tomorrow. Julie's all worn out."

"She looks like a swell kid."

"She is."

"How's Agnes making out?"

Dobie shrugged. "She seems satisfied. Especially since she had the baby."

"Did that guy who scrammed out on her ever show up again?"

"He's been back for visits. I hear he's in Chicago now."

They walked around a group of small girls jumping rope. The housetops made a saw-tooth line on either side of the descending street. A man, still in work clothes, came out on a porch with a bucket of paint. He said, "Hi, Dobie," and Dobie replied, "Hi, Nick," as they passed.

"Those old-timers sure hang on, don't they?" Mikie said.

"They'll start going any day now, I guess. One goes, they all go. All except Francka. I don't think she'll ever die, unless she commits suicide. Like our grandmother in the old country."

"That what she did?"

"Couple years ago. Uncle Joe got a letter. She drowned herself in the *močila*, the place where they wash clothes or something. Must have been close to ninety."

"I only hope we inherit something from her."

"Yeah."

"Did you have any insurance on him?"

"Three hundred. That was the first thing the undertaker wanted to know. It was an old policy Mamma took out and when she died Aunt Annie kept up the payments. She gave it to me when Dzedo came to live with us. The cemetery didn't cost anything, of course. The lot's filled up now, though, so I guess me and you will have to find some place else to get buried in."

"I ain't worrying about it yet."

"It's lucky we had what we had. The only other insurance on him was in the mill and they stopped that last year. Francka was keeping up the payments on it and when they ended it she was fit to be tied. She heard I was a representative and came over to see if I could do anything. What could I do? We passed resolutions and signed petitions but it didn't do any good."

"You still a representative?"

"Yeah. How's your place, union?"

"Hell no. The A.F.L. tried to organize it during the NRA but they never got far."

"They stink."

They got meat and vegetables, milk, cake for dessert and fruit for Dobie's lunch, and started back. Mikie said, "I don't think I could ever come back here to live again. New York ain't the best place in the world but compared to Braddock, or even Pittsburgh — " He shook his head. "It's not only the dirt. It looks so damn poor and neglected, as though the people didn't give a damn what the place they lived in looked like. It must be one of the ugliest places in God's creation. Hell, I like to look at something nice once in a while even if I can't own it."

"I'm used to it, I guess."

"I suppose you're set here for good."

Dobie shrugged as well as he could, considering that his arms were laden with packages. "Where would I go? I've got a trade but I wouldn't be much good outside of a steel mill. And I've got nearly fifteen years' service in that mill. Fifteen more and I might get a pension, if you want to look at it that way."

"Provided they don't build an automatic mill somewhere and heave you out on your tail."

"I've thought of that. But I figure I have a pretty good chance even if they do. These new mills maybe can almost run themselves the way they say but just the same they can't fix themselves when they break down. And that's where I come in. It ain't as though I was in the production end. They've been cutting down on the

Production Departments right along but the Maintenance is as big as it ever was. Bigger. It's the biggest department in the mill right now."

"Still, it's not a hell of a bright future to look forward to, now is it?"

Dobie shrugged again. "You have to work no matter where you go. Here at least I'm more sure of a job than I would be somewhere else. The kind it is. And — well, I feel at home here. I remember how it struck me that time I got back from Detroit. It was like coming home again after living in a boarding house. I belonged here. When I looked around everything seemed to fit my eyes, if that makes sense. Everything was just where it belonged, the streets, the houses, the mill. It's hard to explain."

"I think I got a little of that feeling this morning," Mikie admitted. "But not enough to make me want to come back," he went on firmly. "All right, you have to work no matter where you go but some place else you can at least breathe clean air and get a look at some really bright sunshine once in a while. And water to drink that they don't have to load with chemicals to keep it from killing you."

The little girls were still jumping rope. The man with the paint was standing on the porch rail and jabbing his brush at the gingerbread under the eaves. He didn't see them pass.

"It's a lousy dump, I'll admit that," Dobie said. "But I suppose it's like being married to a homely wife. After a while you never notice whether she's homely or not; she's just your wife with the puss God gave her and if somebody remarks on how homely she is you sort of feel they're not being fair. What the hell, she's not claiming she's beautiful."

Mikie objected that that wasn't the same thing at all and Dobie agreed that perhaps it wasn't. "It doesn't matter. As far as that goes, we don't expect to live right in Braddock for the rest of our lives. If we ever get a break we'll have our own place back in the hills somewhere. You'd be surprised how it's building up."

"If you ever get a break."

"We'll have to take our chances. I don't think we've done so bad so far. The house is a mess right now but when it's fixed up its pretty nice. There's a kick in having your own place and buying stuff for it. Wait till you get married. And I couldn't ask for a better wife than Julie."

"She's a damn sight prettier gal than I ever thought you'd get."

"I'll have to tell her you said so."

After a while Dobie said, "I'm not having such a bad time. I mean being a representative and working with the union and all. I'm no big shot but you can ask practically any man in that mill and he knows who I am. And we're raising plenty hell. That company union's been nothing but a headache to them ever since we got in."

"At least you're doing something. It's guys like Larry and Steve that I can't understand. They're not married and the jobs they've got ain't anything to write home about but they don't seem to give a damn. I asked them why they didn't get out and they just looked at me and made some answer that didn't mean anything. They don't seem to have any push."

"They don't have much and that's the truth. I came across plenty like that when I was going around for the union. I gave them all up finally. If a person won't try to help themselves why the hell should I bother? They're the kind that as long as they've got some lousy job they work and if they're laid off they'll just loaf around until they're called back. Either way they're satisfied."

"I couldn't live like that," Mikie said, shaking his head. "I want too many things. I want good clothes and money in my pocket and I like to see good shows and fool around with pictures and if I ever get married I want a decent place to live in. And I'm willing to take chances to get them. But these guys don't even seem to want anything."

"They want cars."

"Yeah, I know that. Give them a tin can and they won't care if the seat's out of their pants and they eat nothing but bread and boloney three times a day. They even have the nerve to get married. Jesus, I make twice as much as most of them and I'd hesitate."

"A good many of them don't marry because they want to."

"I'd forgotten about that. The old Braddock system."

"I guess that's the only way Kitty will ever pin Steve down. I'm surprised it hasn't happened already. But there's one thing you've got to remember about guys like Larry and Steve," Dobie went on: "In a way they got a tough break. Don't forget you had a chance to learn your trade but when they came out of school where could they go? The mill's only starting to talk about taking on apprentices again, and these guys are past the age anyway. You have to figure on that, too."

They left the paved part of the street and started up the littered hillside. The sun was sliding into the murk above Homestead and there was a blue haze over the town; lights were already yellow in the mill. A day was ending.

Mikie said, "You get the feeling, all right. I'm nine years old and Mamma's making noodles down on Franklin and I'd better be getting off the hill before it gets dark." He shivered. "I'll be glad to get back to New York."

Dobie didn't say anything.

Mikie contemplated the scene broodingly. "You know, you really ought to be allowed to pick your own place to be born in. Considering how it gets into you."

"It's an idea," Dobie admitted.

They turned toward the gate.

As the screen door slammed behind them Hussar appeared from somewhere, looked in after them and then lay down, his paws over the edge of the porch.

"Poor mutt," Julie said. "I'll bet he's wondering what on earth's been going on around here."

"They say dogs know," Dobie said, "but there wasn't a sound out of him."

"I think maybe because it happened in the daytime." Julie was rustling bags and packages. "Do I get any change?"

"What change? I have to buy gloves and tobacco tomorrow."

"My goodness, when I give you a dollar I may as well kiss it good-by."

The Cassidy's radio blared triumphantly as Dobie settled into a chair. "Sounds like old times again," he commented. Mikie had dropped into the chair by the door, where Kracha had preferred to sit.

"Well," Dobie said, "I don't think anybody can say we didn't give him a nice funeral."

"You won't know what they thought of it for a while. Then it'll start getting back to you."

Mikie looked up. "Are they still like that?"

Dobie eyed him. "You've forgotten what it's like to have a lot of relations, haven't you? Yeah, they're still the same. I half expected them to ask me how much insurance money I had left and what I was going to do with it."

"They won't," Julie said. "They're afraid of you." She looked at him thoughtfully. "They really are. You don't realize how much they leave you alone. They'd be dragging you into all their squabbles if you let them. But he's got them scared," Julie said, smiling at Mikie.

"It's just as well. Cigarette?"

"No, thanks. I don't smoke."

"Won't your husband let you?"

"No, he wouldn't care. I just never got into the habit."

"If he smoked decent cigarettes you might."

"I started rolling my own during the depression and got to like them. Now tailormades hurt my throat."

"I almost wish he would," Julie said. "With these he drops tobacco and ashes everywhere. He's got holes burnt in every shirt he owns." She prodded the steak with a forefinger. "He gave you a good steak for once."

"I guess he felt sorry for me because my grandfather died."

Julie got a bag of potatoes and sat down across the table from Dobie. "Don't forget to take my knife into the mill tomorrow and sharpen it. What time does your train leave?" she asked Mikie.

"Ten o'clock, from Pittsburgh."

"Are you working tomorrow?"

"I'll just about have time to change my clothes and punch in." He looked diffident. "I thought I'd leave here about half-past eight, if it's all the same with you people. I'd like to take a mope around downtown and see what it looks like again."

"No burlesque shows open now," Dobie said.

"I can see all I want to in New York." He stretched toward the ash tray on the table. "Remember when you used to go?"

Dobie stared reminiscently at his shoes. "That was when I learned what a gal could do with her hips if she really set her mind to it. A snotnose kid watching the Oriental dancer and buying phony French postcards. But I thought I was a hell of a sport."

"You had me believing it, anyway. Ever take Julie?"

She nodded. "We haven't been for quite a while, though. Since last winter."

"You ought to take her to a real show sometime. A play or a musical comedy."

"Real shows cost money."

"I suppose you see a lot of shows in New York."

"I go about once a month."

"I'd like to see New York sometime. I don't think I'd want to live there but I'd like to see it."

"It's worth seeing."

"One of these days," Dobie said.

He was living in a furnished room, Mikie said, but he was planning to get an apartment soon. One room with a kitchenette and bath would cost him about thirty dollars a month. Julie exclaimed, "Thirty dollars for one room! My goodness, we pay only twenty-five for this whole house."

But this, Mikie pointed out, wasn't New York.

"You'd do better to stay where you are, and put the money in the bank," Julie said.

"No, it looks like I'll be working steady for a while yet and I'd like to have my own place."

"You can't bring gals into a furnished room, Julie," Dobie explained.

Mikie grinned. "It's been done. But I want my own place anyway."

"You ought to be ashamed of yourself," Julie said. "Don't you know any nice girls?"

"Say, all the girls I know are nice."

"I mean that you'd like to marry."

"Give me time. I'm only twenty-seven and my brother waited until he was thirty to get married."

"He'll get married when he starts having trouble getting gals to come up to his room and look at pictures," Dobie said.

"Or posing for them," Mikie added.

"You ought to be ashamed of yourself," Julie said.

"Reminds me." Mikie rose and went upstairs. He returned carrying his camera. "I want a couple pictures of you two."

"In here?"

"Sure. I'm using a fast film and I'll pull her wide open."

Dobie, a shade self-conscious, began rolling a cigarette. Mikie snapped him licking it. When he pointed the camera at Julie she exclaimed, "My goodness, I'll look terrible! At least let me take off this apron and get these potatoes out of the way."

"No no! You sit right there and peel potatoes. Only don't hold yourself so stiff. Smile. Think of something pleasant. Think of your wedding night or something."

"My wedding night! Whatever made you think of that?" She glanced at Dobie and burst into laughter, and Mikie got her with her head back, her mouth open, a potato in one hand and a paring knife in the other.

As he wound the film he asked, "What's so funny?" Then he glanced at Dobie and grinned. "Don't tell me she let you down."

Julie had the grace to blush.

The tall iron gates were locked for the night. The street lamps came on, illuminating the bare sidewalk and the granite stubble of a stonecutter's yard, but a little way beyond the gates the shadows, like the silence, were undisturbed. The wind moved gently through the trees and stirred the ribbon on a wreath, the petals of a flower. The last light died out of the west and then it was dark on the hill

where Kracha lay; only on the horizon's rim the Bessemers con-
tinued to flicker restlessly against the sky.

15

HE had felt a quiet excitement in her from the moment he got home. She was nearly always neat and presentable but this day she was wearing one of her better dresses and she seemed to have been more than usually particular about her hair. There was a glow about her that made him look at her twice. "Are we going out tonight?" he asked.

"No. Why?"

"You're all dressed up."

"Dressed up! This dress is two years old!"

"Okay, okay. I just asked."

During supper she asked him about the shop and the representatives' meeting he had attended and as he talked she nodded brightly and looked interested and didn't hear a word he said. Afterward, while he sat by the radio and read the paper she curled up on the couch. From behind his paper he was conscious that she couldn't seem to make herself comfortable, that she twisted and turned, that she sighed frequently, that whenever he turned a page and glanced at her he found her staring at him. He frowned at an editorial which conceded that the unemployed should not be allowed to starve but, on the other hand, the soldiers at Valley Forge hadn't had an easy time of it either. His conscience, being a married man's, frightened easily; the paper's date line, however, assured him it wasn't a birthday or anniversary, and he couldn't remember having done something, or having promised to do anything, which should have disturbed her.

He kept the paper between them. "You expecting company?"

"Company? Here, tonight? No. Are you?"

"Not me."

"I had enough company at the funeral to do me for a long time."

"Me too."

She hummed with the radio. She smiled to herself for no reason at all. She murmured under her breath and wet her finger tip and pressed it against her stocking. Then she sighed and folded her hands in her lap and stared at Dobie, a dreamy and somewhat vacant expression on her face.

Dobie lowered his paper. "You feel all right?"

"Who, me? Certainly. Why shouldn't I feel all right?"

"You're acting awful funny."

"I'm acting funny? Why I'm not doing a thing!"

"You've got something on your mind. I haven't been married to you two years for nothing."

"I don't know what ever gave you that idea. I'm just sitting here and listening to the radio. My goodness, a girl can't even sit quiet in her own house any more."

"Okay. I can't help it if you won't tell me."

The paper was a barrier between them again. Julie's voice came over it, dripping with injured innocence. "I don't know why you think I'm keeping something from you. I always tell you everything, don't I?"

"I guess so."

"You guess so! I like that."

Silence.

"John."

"Uh-huh."

"I want you to tell me something. Are you listening?"

"Sure."

"I want you to tell me the truth. Have you ever felt sorry you married me?"

The paper came down. "For God's sake, why should I feel sorry?"

"I don't know. Why do men feel sorry? I'm not very pretty or clever or anything."

"I told you what Mikie said about you."

"Well, naturally he wouldn't tell you he thought I was as homely as a mud fence."

"Why should he? You ain't."

Julie picked at the hem of her dress. "Before you met me," she said, "did you ever think about the kind of girl you'd like to marry?"

"Well — " He scratched his chin. "I suppose you could call it that. It never kept me awake at night, though."

"What was she like?"

Dobie gazed at her solemnly. "My dream gal," he said, "was a fat blonde who could play the piano."

Julie gaped at him open-mouthed. "A fat blonde who could play the piano? My goodness! and look what you got. I suppose you could call me a blonde. But I'm not fat and I can't play the piano."

"Nope."

"What ever made you pick on a girl like that?"

"Oh, I had good reasons. I figured a blonde would be nice because they have white skins and if their legs are hairy it don't show so much. And I wanted a fat one because in them days the more there was of a gal the better I liked her. And I wanted her to play the piano because I like piano music and I guess because in Detroit I happened to look in a window one time and saw a girl sitting at a piano in a negligee or a nightgown or something and playing. Boy, was that romantic!"

"You don't have to rub it in. It's not my fault my mother never gave me lessons. Though I don't suppose it would have done much good. You're always telling me I sing flat."

Callously, "You even gargle flat when you have a sore throat. I never heard anything like it."

"Well, I don't care if you are sorry you married me. You're stuck with me now and you may as well get used to it."

"I never said I was sorry I married you."

"You just as much. A fat blonde who could play the piano."

Julie sniffed. "She'd probably go around the house all day in a dirty old kimono and use perfume instead of taking a bath. And spend every cent you made on herself."

He was grinning broadly.

"I don't care," Julie said. "I'll go right on being my own sweet self and if you aren't satisfied it's just too bad. Anyway," she went on, hoisting her nose, "you're not the only one who had an ideal."

"He must be the one you were dreaming about last night."

Her nose came down.

"Was I talking in my sleep again?"

"I don't know what was going on, but you kept saying, No! No! You better not! So I said, Listen, sweetheart, it's all right to make him fight for it but I'd like to get some sleep."

"You never said anything of the kind. It was that banana cream pie we had for supper."

He merely grinned at her.

Julie sighed. "Just let a girl try and get a compliment around here. Just let her." Her finger was tracing the pattern in the couch's upholstery. "I don't think you love me any more."

"Nope, not any more. Just as much."

"See? That's what I mean. You always make a joke of it."

"Oh, now look. You know how I feel about you."

"You hardly ever tell me."

"That's where you're wrong. I'm always telling you. Every time I kiss you or smack you on the fanny or make some joke I'm telling you I love you."

"I know. But you could say it once in a while, too, couldn't you?"

He lifted himself out of his chair and crossed the room and dropped to the couch beside her. "Look, sweetheart. I love you. I think you're the swellest thing a man ever married. On the level, if I didn't have you I wouldn't be worth two cents." He turned her face to him and kissed her. "There."

She sighed, snuggling into the shelter of his arm. "You can be so sweet when you want to."

"Just because I don't go around all day saying I love you don't get the idea that I don't. I think you're pretty and smart and like I told Mikie I couldn't ask for a better wife." Her hair, brushed glossy, faintly fragrant, was tickling his cheek. "And it looks like you'll have to be better than ever from now on, Mrs. Dobrejcak. Dzedo's pension check wasn't much but we're going to miss it."

"You let me do the worrying about that. As soon as the washing machine's paid for I'm going to start putting money in the bank every payday."

"We could use an electric refrigerator."

"That can wait. We've got to think of other things, too. Suppose I got pregnant?"

"With the luck we've been having I'm beginning to wonder if you ever will. Hell, I always figured there was nothing to it. I remember when I was single it seemed too damned easy."

"Oh, you did."

"You think there might be something the matter with one of us?"

"Of course not."

"You can't tell. I had the mumps when I was a kid and that's supposed to play hell with a man sometimes."

Julie giggled.

"I don't think it's so funny. Suppose it turned out we couldn't have any."

"Would you be sorry?"

"Well, wouldn't you? After all, we've been planning on it."

"Would you divorce me if it turned out to be my fault?"

"No, but —"

"You wouldn't hold it against me?"

"Of course not. What the hell, you didn't have any kids when I married you, did you? Well."

"You're so funny." She giggled again.

Dobie stared down at her, puzzled by her manner. Her face was hidden from him against his chest, the part of her hair directly under his lips. Her hands were restless in her lap.

Then it hit him.

For a moment he didn't move. He continued to stare down at

her, his mind busy putting two and two together. Then he said, "Let me up a minute."

"What for?"

"I'm thirsty."

"I'll get it."

"No, you sit still."

He went into the kitchen. There was a grocery calendar near the sink and as he let the water run he examined the current month's tab and then the previous month's. What he learned, added to what he knew, convinced him. He murmured under his breath, "What do you know about that," and filled the glass and lifted it to the calendar in a silent and somewhat flabbergasted toast.

Julie was still sitting on the couch. He picked up his tobacco and papers on the way and stood before her. Rolling a cigarette he discovered that his fingers were trembling. It surprised him. "I know what's the matter with you," he said. His throat hurt.

She looked up. "With me?"

"I knew there was something." He held her eyes. "You're going to have a baby."

She didn't say anything. She continued to look up at him. Silently, without moving any other part of her, her eyes widened and her mouth went down and her face twisted childishly and she began to cry.

They found the spilled tobacco, the crumpled paper, on the floor later.

His arms folded her in. Her grief seemed uncontrollable. He held her like a baby and she sobbed against his chest while he stroked her hair and kissed her and murmured comfortingly. "Don't cry, sweetheart. It's nothing to cry about."

"I was going to make it so nice and surprise you."

"I know."

"I've been keeping it a secret since last month till I could be sure and surprise you. But you always guess everything. When I get you a Christmas present you always guess what it is before you open it."

"Sweetheart, if I'd known —"

But no defense, he realized, was possible. He got out a handkerchief and helped her blow her nose.

"I've been so excited. I kept hoping you wouldn't notice anything so I could surprise you when I was sure. It was all I could do to keep from telling you a dozen times."

"And then I had to go and spoil it."

"That's why I got dressed up and everything. I had it all planned to tell you tonight."

He kissed her ear. "Tell you what. On the second one don't you tell me anything until it's just about ready to pop. That'll make up for me guessing this one."

She smiled tearily.

After a while she said in a small voice, "Are you glad?"

"Sure I'm glad. And I want you to take extra good care of yourself from now on. You'd better go down to the doctor tomorrow and have him give you a diet and everything."

"You come with me. Tomorrow night."

"Okay." He sobered. "We're going to have to watch the pennies from now on, missus. Like we never watched them before."

Confidently, "We'll manage."

"I just hope I can keep working steady."

"I'm not going to tell anybody until I can't hide it any more." Her eyes searched his. "You're really glad about it, aren't you?"

He nodded. "It's beginning to sink in, sweetheart." His hand came to rest on her belly. "Can't feel anything."

"Of course not, silly. Not for months."

"When will it be?"

"March or April, I think. The doctor'll know."

"Bet you it's a boy."

"I don't care. Just so it's healthy and perfect." She nestled against him, utterly relaxed. "It's going to be so nice," she said.

16

THE C.I.O. swung into action. It formed the S.W.O.C., the Steel Workers' Organizing Committee, which took over the Amalgamated, lock, stock and barrel, and with half a million dollars behind it moved into the steel towns. The change, after the bumbling inefficiency of the old leadership, was startling. There had never been anyone to reply to the company, to newspaper publishers, to civic authorities, in their own language, which was the only language they understood, nobody to fight them in their own front yards, which was the only place where they could be licked. There was now.

By the summer's end a company spokesman could hardly comment on the weather without drawing a barrage of speeches and press releases; but it wasn't merely that. It was the way the C.I.O. men went about it. Out of the exhilarating turmoil of that summer and fall, out of the organizational work, the unslacking guerilla warfare inside the E.R.P. — passing resolutions for their publicity value in the minutes, belaboring the City Office with protests, straining the structure of the E.R.P. until it gave at the joints — perhaps this was what, in the end, meant most to Dobie. The way the C.I.O. men went about it.

Working with them, listening to them, — they had a fund of stories about company officials, New York finance and Washington politics which were like the stories a soldier brings back from a war in their unexpected revelations and complete irreverence, — he was conscious of this something about them that he couldn't place. It puzzled him until he realized why. They were all sorts of men, Scotch and Irish and Polish and Italian and Slovak and German and Jew, but they didn't talk and act the way the steel towns expected men who were Scotch and Irish and Polish and Italian and Slovak and German and Jew to talk and act.

They were outspoken, fearlessly so, as though they had never learned to glance around and see who might be listening before they spoke. They were obviously convinced that they were individually as good as any man alive, from Mill Superintendents up or down, as the case might be, and probably better. They assumed that there was one law for the rich and one for the poor, and that it was the same law; and they talked about newspapers and radio chains and law courts and legislative bodies as though these things could be used for the benefit of ordinary people as well as against them; and there was something almost fantastic in their easy, take-it-for-granted air that Braddock burgesses and Pittsburgh police chiefs and Washington congressmen were public servants. And nobody in the steel towns had ever been heard to talk the way they talked — without stumbling over the words, uttering them as though they meant something real right there in Braddock — about liberty and justice and freedom of speech.

It made the old distinctions meaningless but it didn't immediately suggest any other to Dobie, who had been born and raised in a steel town. For lack of a handier label he thought of them simply as good C.I.O. men.

Their campaign reached a sort of climax shortly after the November elections, when the company asked the representatives to sign a sliding scale wage agreement and the Labor Board issued a complaint against it for fostering a company union. The C.I.O. denounced the sliding scale agreement. A complicated gimmick of index numbers, percentages and dates, it gave the men very little and would have put the company in a position to say it already had a signed agreement with its employees, when the C.I.O. came seeking a contract. The Braddock representatives, among others, refused to have anything to do with it. Amid the ghostly fluttering of company chickens coming home to roost, they told Flack : —

"We're not signing. We can't. Every time we asked for a signed contract we were told it was against corporation policy and the constitution of the E.R.P. and Christ knows what else. Fairless told us that in Pittsburgh, and you've told us that right here in this room, and more than once. All right. We can't sign for the men. And we ain't signing for ourselves because we think the plan stinks."

Flack — that summer had made him a harried, desperate man — tried to get the defiant representatives removed by petition. Most of the mimeographed sheets ended in scrap boxes and toilets.

Dobie hardly cared. He was going into Pittsburgh several afternoons a week to talk with the investigators and lawyers of the Labor Board; and early in December he and Hagerty were subpoenaed to appear as witnesses from Braddock.

He had expected trouble when he came to tell McLaughlin that he wanted three or four days off, and he wasn't disappointed. The foreman replied noncommittally; later in the day he told Dobie that he'd have to work. Dobie grunted. There was no point in arguing with McLaughlin. "Okay. I'll ask Todd myself."

He went into Todd's office shortly before quitting time, first stopping at his locker for the subpoena. Todd was bent over the morning newspaper's sport pages.

"Mr. Todd, I told Mac I'd have to take a couple days off beginning Thursday and he said nothing doing. So I thought I'd ask you."

Todd looked up. "If he said you can't that ought to settle it."

"It's pretty important. I've got to go to Washington."

Todd's eyes flickered. "Yes, I know you representatives have been pretty busy lately."

Dobie didn't say anything.

Todd straightened and leaned back, his chair creaking. To Dobie the creak of that chair was as much a part of Todd as his red face and ponderous walk. And like the office itself, the piles of dusty blueprints and trade journals, the soiled windows facing the bleak wall of the machine shop across the roadway, it had held unpleasant associations for him ever since his apprentice days. But it wasn't a quaking apprentice, Dobie reflected, who stood beside Todd's desk now.

Todd said, "There happens to be a rule on the books that says any man who takes time off without permission can be fired."

Dobie nodded. "Yeah, I know. Flack sent us all a letter about it when Hagerty and Smolinski took time off to go to a meeting in Pittsburgh. Nobody ever heard of the rule till a couple weeks ago and it looks like the only people it applies to is the representatives."

"I didn't make the rule and I can't change it."

"You can give me time off."

"McLaughlin says you're needed here." He leaned toward the sports page again. "That'll be all."

Dobie stayed where he was. He took the subpoena out of his pocket. "Mr. Todd, this is what says I have to get time off. I've been subpoenaed as a Government witness."

The subpoena seemed to annoy Todd unreasonably. He snapped, "Don't wave your God-damn' paper in my face!"

"I ain't waving it, I'm just showing it to you."

"I'm not interested. You asked for time off and I said you can't have it, you're needed here. As far as I'm concerned that settles it. If you think other things are more important than your job that's up to you."

"So if I take time off I lose my job, is that it?"

"You know the rules."

A C.I.O. man in Pittsburgh had remarked, "If the company's smart it won't make any trouble for you boys. But it isn't. It's never had anything like the C.I.O. stand up to it before and instead of using its head it's losing it. Say —" self-approvingly, "that's not bad. Hey Vin, maybe you can use this." And he'd gone off to present his jewel to the ex-reporter who was now editing the S.W.O.C. paper.

"Mr. Todd," Dobie said, "I've told you I'm a Government witness. I've shown you my subpoena. Then you tell me if I take time off I'll lose my job. Well, I only hope you have your dicto-graph turned on."

"What dictograph? What the hell are you talking about?"

"The dictograph in that clock. I know the man who wired it for you. I only hope it's taking all this down because if I lose my job you and your dictograph's liable to be taking a trip to Wash-ington too. When you tell me I'll lose my job if I take time off you're trying to intimidate a Government witness, Mr. Todd, and that can get you in a lot of trouble."

"You'll get me in trouble? Why God damn you — "

Todd's face had a thick color in it. "If he makes a pass at you," Dobie thought swiftly, "get him in that fat gut and knock the wind out of him." He shifted his feet for balance.

But Todd stayed seated in his chair, gripping its arms and glar-ing up at Dobie. "Just who in hell do you think you're talking to? You ain't talking to Gordon now, mister, and I'd advise you to remember it. As far as I'm concerned you've gotten too God-damn smart for your size. But don't come into my office and try any of your smartness on me or by God I'll kick you out of here so fast — "

"You'll what?"

"If you're not on the job Thursday morning don't come back at all. Is that plain enough?"

"I think so."

"I'm glad you do. I never hung out much with lawyers so I wasn't sure I could make it plain enough for a smart guy like you to understand. Now get back to your work."

Dobie shrugged, put the subpoena back in his pocket and turned away. Todd's voice halted him. "And if you do go to Washington I'd advise you to be careful what you say."

"Whatever they ask me I'll tell them the truth, that's all."

Then he went out, wondering if it was for the last time.

He stopped off at the union office after work to report what had happened. The organizer told him not to worry. "The worst thing they could do right now is fire you and they know it. They'll try to throw a scare into you but they won't fire you."

"Yeah, but it sounds different when you hear it said right out. One thing I do know, I'm getting tired of being pushed around."

"Well, don't start anything now. 'Course if he takes a swing at you, that's different."

"The trouble with that loud-mouthed son of a bitch is he don't realize what he's up against," Hagerty said scornfully. "He needs educating. Wait'll I go in to see him tomorrow."

Hagerty came into the shop the following afternoon and leaned across the bench where Dobie was rebuilding a small transformer. McLaughlin was at the other end of the shop and stayed there. "How's it coming?"

"He hasn't said anything to me since yesterday. Say, what's got into Flack? He's been tearing around like a fart in a windstorm all day."

Hagerty grinned. "He thinks somebody's tapped his telephone line. Well, I guess I'll go in and tell Mr. Todd I don't want to be a foreman."

Dobie looked up, startled. "He offer you the job?"

"No, but he's going to. Flack didn't care much for the idea but Todd thinks it's worth trying. See you later."

He strode across the shop to the office, his tools clanking, safety belt swinging. At the door he paused to fill his cheek with tobacco, then went in. He left the door open but a moment later someone — it may have been Hagerty, it may have been Todd himself — closed it. Dobie waited expectantly for their combined roars — the two were out of the same mold — to splinter it. But the interview was comparatively brief and their voices never passed the door. Fifteen minutes after it had closed it opened and Hagerty came out. His face was too dirty for its color to show but his eyes were snapping fire. He waved to Dobie and went out. A few minutes later Todd also departed. He seemed to be in a hurry.

"I told him what he could do with his foreman's job," Hagerty said later, in the union office. "I reminded him he promised me a foreman's job eight years ago and that was all the good it ever did me, but now I wasn't interested any more. He must've fired me four or five times while I was in there but I just told him it would take a better man than him to fire me." Hagerty made a good story of it, and it got better as he went along, but Dobie left early; he wanted to spend the evening with Julie.

When the possibility that he might have to go to Washington had first been mentioned he hadn't objected strenuously. He had hoped they'd want him. He had worked faithfully with the Labor Board's investigators, who were preparing the case, emptying his desk of the Amalgamated and E.R.P. material he had accumulated and answering hundreds of questions. It seemed odd that so much trouble was necessary to prove the obvious fact that the E.R.P. was supported and dominated by the company; but that, he gathered, was how the law worked. When the lawyers said he and Hagerty — Hagerty because he'd been with the E.R.P. from the beginning and Dobie because he'd been with the Amalgamated — would be subpoenaed he had felt proud and important. But now, an hour or so before his train was to leave for Pittsburgh, he felt depressed.

"I hate to go and leave you like this."

They were in the bedroom. Dobie's old bag was open on the bed and Julie was making sure that he had everything, shirts and underwear and the new toothbrush.

"I don't know why," she said. "I'll be all right. Where's your razor? Oh. Better than if I stayed home because Mamma won't let me do a thing." She was going to stay with her mother while Dobie was away.

"I know, but just the same — "

"My goodness, it'll only be a few days." But she dropped the socks she'd been examining for holes and faced him. Her fingers straightened his tie. "Of course I'll miss you. It'll be the first time we've been separated. But don't you worry about me at all. You just concentrate on doing as good a job down there as you can."

"I ain't worrying about that. For that matter it's not even sure that they'll call me. It's just that it ain't going to be much fun for you."

"Oh, isn't it? What do you suppose I'm going to answer when people ask me where my husband is? *Hmm!*"

She didn't go to the station with him; they agreed that she shouldn't risk the climb back up the hill alone. "And I don't want to say good-by in front of a lot of strangers anyway."

They said good-by in the kitchen.

"Take good care of yourself, sweetheart."

She said, "You'd think we were just married. It's so silly." But her eyes were shining.

"I'll be back as soon as I can. If anything happens send me a telegram. I'll send you one as soon as I find out what hotel we're staying."

"Nothing will happen."

"I hope not." He kissed her. "Just take good care of yourself."

"I will."

He patted her belly. "And if this guy gets tough, sit on him."

She smiled.

He kissed her again and picked up his bag. At the gate he turned. Julie was standing in the lighted frame of the doorway. He lifted an arm. "So long."

"Good-by."

He was to meet with the others — several S.W.O.C. officials and a dozen or so witnesses from other mills — in Pittsburgh. He began enjoying himself from the moment he strode into the station. It was almost like being twenty-three again and going adventurously to Detroit for the first time. Like cities, railroad stations were most exciting at night; and beyond question the finest way to begin a journey was to board a midnight train. They followed porters down the frigid, shadowy platform and as Dobie entered his first Pullman he thought of the shining Limiteds which had used to roar past the house on Franklin Avenue and of the boy who had wondered what it was like to ride in them. The first moments were disappointing. The berths were already made up and the green-tunneled car had a funereal, stuffy look. But the lounge car was all he had expected, though he was suddenly conscious that his suit could have been newer and that his hands and nails would never be anything but a mechanic's. When the train swept through Braddock he pressed his face against the window and felt a sharp pang at the thought of Julie up on that dark hill alone. Then the train crossed Thirteenth Street — they were traveling by B. and O. — and plunged into the mill, whistling past the ore bridges and blast furnaces and men silhouetted in the glare of flowing metal.

They tossed coins for a choice of berths. Dobie won a lower and spent most of the night propped up on one elbow, watching the dark countryside, the sleeping towns, slide by. He found it almost impossible to sleep; obviously there were certain luxuries one had to get used to. The men who had drawn uppers were amused by the porter's ladder and proved to everyone's satisfaction that the dirty stories were false, there was no way of watching, from an upper berth, a beautiful blonde undress in the lower.

They got into Washington at seven in the morning of a gray, unpleasantly raw day. Taxis took them to a hotel where they breakfasted. (Because the train had carried no diner Dobie had been denied the experience of eating on a train, as he had been denied the pleasure of sitting in a seat with a white towel across the back because the porter hadn't bothered about closing the berths.) He sent a telegram to Julie and then they went to the C.I.O. offices, where they were presented to Lewis himself. He shook hands with them all and reduced most of them to a grinning inarticulateness that lasted until they were in taxis again, on their way to the Labor Board. Then it was agreed that he was a swell guy and that he looked just like his pictures.

As did the Capitol and the Washington Monument.

During the next six days Dobie got to know the inside of the trial chambers as well as he knew his own parlor, the plain walls, the lighting fixtures, the be-flagged portrait of Lincoln, the tall windows that someone was always opening or closing with a catarrhal rattle of chains. "Them damn windows make more noise than the stockyard cranes." There were a number of reporters and photographers present the first morning but only one or two after that. The company was represented by a dignified, elderly man, a former Governor of New York, Dobie was told, and by the only one-armed lawyer he had ever beheld. He'd lost the arm in the war, Dobie's informant thought. He opened the proceedings with motions to postpone the hearing until the constitutionality of the Wagner Act had been determined. The motion was denied and Maloy of Duquesne was called to the stand, to tell the story of the E.R.P. from the beginning. Philip Murray of the S.W.O.C. followed him.

It was not as exciting as Dobie had thought it would be. The law in action appeared to be largely a dull, plodding business of questions and answers, objections, conferences, recesses. Watching and listening he realized why the Board's investigators had gone to so much trouble to buttress the obvious. The company's lawyers were politely incredulous of everything and surprised or shocked at nothing. After a while it seemed almost like a game in which what was said was less important than how it was said. A sentence would be carefully set up, everyone stepped back to a safe distance, and the opposing lawyers then attempted to shoot holes through it while both sides watched with a sort of detached, professional interest. Between shots the company's lawyers appeared bored but unfailingly well-mannered, like men spending a few hours with their social inferiors for appearances' sake. Dobie learned a little about legal methods but not enough to like them any better and a little more about newspapers when he saw what they printed about the hearing and what they left out. Julie wrote from Donora that the Pittsburgh papers were printing long stories about it, on inside pages.

Familiar names, Braddock, Duquesne, the names of people, the names of jobs and things in the mill, took on an odd sound. The place and the listeners made them hardly more than words, stripped them of most of their meaning. Sometimes he felt heartsick and discouraged because so little of what should have been communicated was coming through. What could all this talk of company unions and intimidation mean to people who had never worked in a mill or lived in a steel town? The company's lawyers knew what they were defending but how could anyone here understand what the witnesses were fighting for? It wasn't a game to them. They were awkward, their clothes didn't fit, they perspired and used bad grammar; but sit one of those beautiful lawyers on a casting in the mill yard and surround him with steelworkers and how long would his starched linen stay unwilted? That was where a hearing of this kind should have been held, in the mill yard or in one of the First Ward's noisome alleys, where words and names were actual things and living people, beyond any lawyer's dismissal — smoke and machinery and blast furnaces, crumbling hovels and underfed children, and lives without beauty or peace. And not this or some other Government board, but a jury should have sat in judgment here, a jury of ghosts: Mike Dobrejcak and Mary and Pauline, Joe Dubik and Kracha — the maimed and the destroyed, the sickly who died young, the women worn out before their time with work and child-bearing, all the thousands of lives the mills had consumed as surely as they had consumed their tons of coke and ore. They would have known what the words meant. They would have known what was being fought for here.

Evenings and over the week-end he wrote to Julie, addressed postcards and went sight-seeing. One night the S.W.O.C. men took them to a night club. The food was comparable with a bad cafeteria's, the drinks expensive and the floor show proved that a fan dancer looked better when she wasn't so close that one could count the corns on her toes. There were no amusing drunks and no women in conspicuously low-necked dresses. It wasn't, in short, like the night clubs one saw in the movies. Perhaps Dobie would have enjoyed his first night club more if he hadn't kept wondering whether he'd have a job when he got back to Braddock; the hearing was to adjourn for the holidays two days before Christmas. The S.W.O.C. men were as confident as ever that no reprisals would be attempted but how could they know what Flack might do?

The sensation of the hearing was Hagerty's revelation that he had been asked to become a paid company spy while retaining his positions in the E.R.P. and the union. Dobie gathered that he hadn't said anything about this even to the S.W.O.C. men. They seemed annoyed but they shouldn't have been too surprised. It was the sort of dramatic gesture Hagerty liked to make. He was a colorful witness; from the moment he admitted that he was the father of ten children — "And another one on the way" — the reporters pricked up their ears.

After him no one could hope to shine. Dobie was the last witness called but one and he wasn't long on the stand. He had prepared a handful of notes but they stayed almost unused. He began, as had most of the others, by testifying that he had been threatened with discharge if he went to Washington. Then he was asked about the beginnings of the A.A. in Braddock and identified Miss Morrison's transcript of the conference with Flack. For the rest he did little more than confirm Hagerty's testimony about conditions inside the E.R.P., the futility of resolutions, the censorship of minutes, the food box affair and Flack's attempt to remove the representatives when they refused to sign the sliding scale agreement.

He received a poor press. The Washington papers didn't mention him — it was all Hagerty — but in one of the Pittsburgh clippings Julie showed him later he found a single sentence: "John Doberjack, an electrician in the Edgar Thomson plant, also testified."

They left Washington the following night.

17

HE came home on the day before Christmas. After Washington's marbled vistas Braddock looked mean and soiled; after the hotel's splendors, — its rugs, its carefully assembled furnishings, its Niagaras of hot water, — the house seemed cramped and a little shabby, Julie's modest attempts at elegance more heart-warming than successful. "The party's over," he reflected, conscious of a letdown. He lunched on scrambled eggs and wondered if he still had a job. Without Julie the house felt empty.

He was going to join her in Donora for Christmas with her family. On the way to the union office he phoned the grocery store near her mother's house. Their conversation was brief. "I couldn't talk with those people just dying to hear what I was saying," she explained later. Her voice over the phone took him back to the days when they were going together. "I bet you don't remember the last time I called you up."

"You called me? When?"

"The day we were married."

"Was that the last time? My goodness!" She paused, and Dobie could hear the store's doorbell tinkle as someone entered or departed. "Well, get here as soon as you can. Unless you'd rather have me come home."

"No, you stay right where you are. I'll be up on that train gets to Webster around seven."

"Can't you come any sooner?"

"No trains. Besides, I have to pick up my pay, missus. And I want to stop down the union."

"Well, all right. But don't be too late."

The house, he assured her, was undisturbed, and the Cassidys seemed to be taking care of the dog and the chickens satisfactorily.

As he entered the union office the organizer let his heels drop to the floor with a thump. "Well, it's about time! I was wondering when you'd show up." He shook hands as though he hadn't seen Dobie for months. "Where's Hagerty?"

"I left him in Pittsburgh. They wanted to have a talk with him about that spy business."

"I read about that." The organizer cocked an eyebrow. "It sounded a little fishy to me."

"Oh, I guess it was on the level all right. After all, he was under oath. I think Murray and the rest of them were sore, though. Because he didn't let them in on it beforehand."

"He didn't? Hell, I don't blame them. But it's just the kind of thing he'd do. He gets an idea and says it or does it without thinking and then he wonders why somebody's always jumping on him. He can't get it into his head that working with an organization isn't the same as being on your own."

He glanced at his watch. "Were you going anywhere right away?"

"I want to pick up my pay. Yesterday was payday, wasn't it?"

"Sure. Well listen. They're having a special meeting around ha' past-three. They figured you and Hagerty might show up in time and tell them all about it."

Dobie shifted Julie's Christmas present — a silver-boxed, tissue-wrapped nightgown that had cost him five dollars in Washington — under his arm and fumbled for his tobacco and papers. "Think the cop will let me in?"

"Why the hell not?"

"You know what Todd said before I left."

"I wouldn't let that worry me."

"No, but it won't be a hell of a merry Christmas for us if I find out he meant it."

"Your envelope ought to tell you."

"Yeah, I thought of that. Well, I may as well go down."

"If Hagerty shows up I'll send him right along."

"Okay."

Braddock Avenue was lively with Christmas crowds under a heavy, sunless sky. He was stopped twice by men who said they'd read about him in the papers and asked questions about Washington. At the general office building the guard on duty in the hall nodded as he came through the door. He said the meeting hadn't started yet but a couple of the boys were downstairs. Dobie went first to the cashier's window. The cashier nodded too and after the usual delay pushed an envelope toward him. Dobie glanced at the figures in one corner. They were for his regular two weeks' wages.

Feeling better, he went downstairs. The meeting room was a bare, cheerless place, plainly furnished with a battered table, chairs that didn't match and a ceiling radiator which periodically sprayed Employee and Management Representatives alike with boiling water. The view from the windows — the concrete retaining wall set into the railroad embankment back of the building — was uninspiring. Several men were already there and others kept coming; after the quitting whistle blew a whole group arrived in work clothes.

He told them about Washington.

Gralji said, "I hear you met Lewis."

"That's right. They took us to his office the first day."

"What kind of a guy is he?"

"He looks just like his pictures, if that's what you mean. He shook hands and talked for a while and then we went to the Labor Board."

"What did he have to say?"

"Oh, I don't remember. He asked us about the trip and how things were in the mills and stuff like that."

"Big bastard, ain't he?"

"He's big, all right."

They wanted to know about Hagerty and he told them what he knew. Opinion was divided. "What he should've done," someone said, "was like that fella in Clairton or Duquesne or wherever it was. The one that told the Swock" — he pronounced S.W.O.C. like a word — "about being offered a spy job and they said all right, take it, and he deposited the money he got with the Swock and made out phony reports."

"I'm only telling you what I know," Dobie said. "I didn't get much chance to talk to him. You'll have to wait till he gets here."

"We tried to get Carnegie Hall to hold a big meeting where you guys could make a report but they wouldn't let us have it. We're pretty sure that's some of Flack's work."

"I wouldn't be surprised. How's he been taking it?"

Gralji shrugged. Burke grinned. "I heard he's ordered another clock and is buying them pills of his by the barrel."

"He don't look so good and that's a fact."

Dobie rolled a cigarette. "Anybody heard anything about me and Hagerty getting fired?"

Nobody had.

"I just got my envelope and there's only my regular pay in it."

"If you were fired they would've paid you off."

"Yeah, but I'd like to know for sure. I won't enjoy my Christmas much if I have to keep wondering whether I still have a job."

"They won't fire you. They're in enough trouble now."

"The only way to make sure is go in and start to work. You'll have to wait till Monday, though. The mill shuts down tonight."

"Why don't you ask Flack?" Gralji suggested. "Just ask him straight out are you fired or ain't you?"

"Yeah, I could do that. Wonder if he's in."

He was saved the trip upstairs. The door opened and Flack strode in. Someone murmured, "Oh-oh! Fireworks," and then the room fell silent. Flack glanced around, his head moving jerkily. He barked, "Where's Hagerty?"

Dobie was sitting with one leg over a corner of the table, his foot swinging. It seemed to be up to him to reply. "I don't know, Mr. Flack. I haven't seen him since this morning."

Flack's spectacles caught the light and gave his expression a blank, cold stare. "Expect him here today?"

"He didn't say anything to me about coming."

Flack advanced farther into the room until he stood a few feet from Dobie. He was dressed in his usual dark suit, black necktie and pearl stickpin — a well-dressed, impressively neat man. And a thoroughly angry one. Anger radiated from him in waves that were almost visible. Dobie hadn't seen him so nearly beside himself since the day the defiant representatives had refused to sign the sliding scale agreement. "What the hell's eating him?" he wondered. Flack had been mentioned more than once in the Washington testimony and seldom flatteringly, but so had a dozen other Superintendents.

He stood slightly bowed, his hands twitching, his wrath all but lifting his heels off the floor. "I wanted to have a little heart-to-heart talk with Hagerty," he said. "With both of you." His speech was clipped and harsh. "I suppose you bastards are pretty proud of what you did down in Washington."

"I certainly ain't ashamed of it, Mr. Flack."

"Oh, you *ain't!*"

Dobie took a deep breath. "And I don't like to be called a bastard."

"I don't care whether you like it or not! Who in hell do you think you are?" His hand flew up. "I'll do the talking here! You're not in Washington now. Why did you lie about me?"

"I didn't lie about you."

"You're a God-damn' liar! You dragged my name through sweat and shit down there and by God I'll break you if it's the last thing I do! I'll show you!"

Dobie's lip curled. "You'll show me nothing. If you didn't like what was said about you in Washington that's too bad, but I didn't say anything that wasn't the truth. I was under oath and I didn't feel like going to jail for perjury."

Flack's sneer was monumental. "You've learned a lot since you've been hanging around with those Government bastards, haven't you?"

"I know I don't have to take this kind of crap from you or anybody else. You asked me who I thought I was. Well who the hell do you think you are, God? Listen, Mr. Flack: I don't like to be called names and I'm telling you for the last time I didn't lie about you; and if you keep saying I did I'll sue you for criminal libel, by Jesus I will!"

Flack turned purple. "Sue me? You'll sue me? Why you dumb Hunky son of a bitch I ought to ram this down your dirty throat!" His fist was six inches from Dobie's face.

Dobie slipped off the table. "Try it. Try it, you pot-bellied old bastard, and I'll knock you right through that door!"

The others surged between them, their voices a babble in Dobie's ears. He heard himself saying, "Oh, for Christ's sake let me go. I won't hurt the old bastard." The door opened and a guard stuck his head in. "What's going on in here?" he asked. Someone infected with the general belligerence snapped, "Nothing! Beat it!" and the guard withdrew his head in sheer astonishment. Flack was mopping his face, his hand shaking. Dobie glanced at Gralji. "Well, I guess that did it."

Then resentment stirred within him. "No, by God. I've been getting pushed around till I'm God-damn good and sick of it. We'll get this straightened out right now."

Men fell back as he approached Flack. The Superintendent looked up and for a moment there was something close to alarm in his eyes.

Dobie felt himself scowling. "We may as well finish this thing right now. Before I left Todd told me I'd be out of a job if I went to Washington. I want to know if that still goes." He paused. "I'm speaking as a representative, and as far as I'm concerned you can call in the stenographer and make it official."

Flack didn't reply. He kept mopping his face and it was hard to say whether he had understood.

"If I'm fired, all I want from you is a pass to get my tools and stuff out of the shop. If I ain't — well, that'll suit me fine."

Still Flack didn't reply. Dobie put one hand into his trousers' pocket. "I'll tell you this much, Mr. Flack. If you fire me that won't be the end of it. I ain't saying that to be tough or start an argument. It's just the plain fact."

Flack said hoarsely, "I think there has been too much arguing and trouble-making already." He cleared his throat. "We'd all be better off if we concentrated on doing our work as well as we could."

It was Dobie's turn to be silent.

Flack put his handkerchief away. When he spoke again his face was completely expressionless. "As to your — the matter you mentioned," he said, "there has never been any question of discharging anyone for activities outside working hours, and there won't be as long as I'm in charge here." His eyes swept the faces around him. "I want that clearly understood."

"That means I ain't fired, right?"

"I know of no reason why you shouldn't go to work as usual on Monday morning."

"Okay. That's fine. That's all I wanted to know."

Behind Dobie there was an approving murmur that made Flack lift his head. He couldn't have misunderstood it but perhaps he had been a steel mill Superintendent too long to value it. Imperceptibly he had resumed his usual manner. Now he stood erect and in the gaze he directed at Dobie there was most of the old arrogance, the cold impersonality of long-established authority.

"I should like to say this," he said, "speaking not as the Superintendent of this plant but personally. It has not been pleasant for myself or my family to have things published in the newspapers without being given an opportunity to reply. Not that I expect either your sympathy or your understanding. As for what happened here this afternoon, we were both excited and angry and may have said things we didn't really mean. I think the best thing we could all do is forget it."

Their eyes met. Dobie thought, "You meant every word of it, you bastard. And I don't forget that easy." And perhaps Flack's thoughts were not dissimilar. Aloud, Dobie said with a faint shrug, "That's okay with me, Mr. Flack."

For a second he wondered if Flack meant to offer his hand. He didn't; the movement of his hand was a gesture for room to pass. The circle of men broke.

No one spoke until the door had closed.

"What the hell did you guys say about him down there?" Burke demanded. "I didn't read anything in the papers that should've made him so sore."

Dobie shrugged. "I guess it was more the idea of having it said right out in court like that."

"You know what I think?" Gralji said. "I bet the big shots in New York and Pittsburgh never realized what was really going on and they've been raising hell with the Superintendents."

Dobie was getting into his coat. "Don't kid yourself. They knew, all right. If they're sore at him it's because he let it get as far as Washington."

Someone chuckled. "He sure was mad, wasn't he? Jesus, for a minute there I thought he'd bust. Especially when you started talking about suing him."

"Mad or not," Gralji said, "he didn't have any right to say some of the things he did."

"Dobie didn't do so bad himself, if you ask me."

"Where's my package? I don't want to lose that; it's my wife's Christmas present." He found it under a pile of coats, its silver bow somewhat discouraged. He slipped it under his arm and faced the others. His voice was edged with a sort of good-humored truculence. "Listen," he said: "I may be a Hunky but I ain't dumb and I ain't nobody's son of a bitch. Flack's just finding it out, that's all. Well, I got to catch a train. See you guys next week."

"Merry Christmas."

He paused at the door. "You're telling me. That's all I could think of, what a lousy Christmas we'd have if I was fired."

"How do you feel now?"

"Swell."

"Don't get into any more arguments."

He grinned. "Not me. I love peace. Well, so long."

"So long."

The guard looked his way as he came up the stairs; at the sound of his footsteps in the tiled hall faces were lifted from desk tops and the cashier's head swiveled slowly on his neck like some absurd puppet in a cage. He marched past them with an amused glint in his eyes. The guard wished him a merry Christmas and opened the door for him.

It was already dark outside. He halted for a moment on the steps, breathing in the cold, smoke-scented air. Someone came out of the gate across the way, moving up out of the darkness in the mill, passing briefly under the light swinging above the gate and then disappearing into the shadows of Thirteenth Street. People waited for a Dooker's Hollow bus on the corner. The windows of the automobile salesroom on the other corner — Dobie could remember when it was a car barn — were squares of bright light. Beyond them Braddock Avenue curved out of sight, its trolley tracks squeezed between lines of parked cars, its dreary buildings shabby even in the pink fog of its countless beer signs. He stood and contemplated it all, a lean, silent figure, his coat collar up, hands thrust in pockets, the frivolous package under his arm. And he felt good. The story of what had happened back there would be all over the mill in a week, and the farther it went the better it would get. It shouldn't do the membership campaign any harm, he reflected. But it wasn't of the union or even of Flack that he thought now.

He lifted his eyes to the dark sky. "We've come a long way, hey Pop?"

Then he went to join Julie.

18

THEY went to Washington again in January. It rained every day, and the newspapers, driven to hysteria by the Detroit sit-down strikers, paid little attention to the steel hearing. Dobie wasn't called to the stand. The hearing came to an uneventful end and they made an equally uneventful return to Braddock. They were still waiting for the Labor Board to announce its decision when, at the beginning of March, the steel corporation capitulated. It signed a contract with the S.W.O.C. and "the most important job ever undertaken by organized labor in America" ended with victory for the union.

It was, in spite of all that had gone before as well as because of it, stunningly unexpected. When Dobie got home that unforgettable

Monday, Julie looked at him and asked him if he was drunk. He grinned. "No, I ain't drunk but I ought to be. You realize what's happened?" She said she'd heard it over the radio but thought that maybe she hadn't heard right.

In that she wasn't alone. Even the Pittsburgh newspapers seemed to have trouble believing their own headlines. They burst into praise of the corporation's patriotism and social vision like a suddenly prodded chorus, and they lectured the S.W.O.C. on etiquette with the air of an old club member addressing a new and incompletely de-loused one, but their hearts weren't in it. Along with the smaller, independent steel companies they felt that the corporation had betrayed them. Contract or no contract, they didn't like labor unions, they had never liked them in the past and they weren't going to start liking them now.

After the first excitement, however, they recovered their poise and as the days passed Dobie was conscious of a growing irritation. Increasingly the newspapers' tone when they discussed the steel corporation's capitulation was that in which they customarily reported the philanthropies of the Mellon family. "You'd think the company signed because it suddenly got patriotic," Dobie grumbled, "or because Fairless got up that morning and said to himself, Well, I feel so good today I think I'll sign a contract with somebody. What the star-spangled hell do they think we were doing all this time, playing marbles?"

Julie, her lap full of yellow knitting, told him not to get excited.

"All right, but it's enough to make anybody sore. The company signed because they had to, because we were licking the pants off of them. But you'd never guess it from the papers."

The knitting was yellow because pink was for girls, and a girl was what Julie wanted, and blue was for boys, which was what Dobie said she'd have, because the Dobrejcaks ran to boys.

A few days after the contract went into effect all the Employee Representatives who were also union members turned in their resignations from the E.R.P. There was some discussion, in the stenographer's cherished phrase, about the future status of the E.R.P.

(It continued a ghostly sort of existence until April, when the Supreme Court upheld the Wagner Act.) Flack was called in and read a notice which had already appeared on the bulletin boards. The company would continue to recognize any individual or group or organization as the spokesman for those employees it represented, but would not recognize any single group or organization as the exclusive bargaining agency for all its employees. The status of the E.R.P. would remain unchanged. It would continue as the spokesman for those employees who preferred that method of collective bargaining, which — and Flack's voice never faltered — had proved so mutually satisfactory throughout its existence.

To questions about the use of bulletin boards, grievance committees and the like, Flack replied that he had received no instructions and could make no promises. His position as little more than an overseer for an absentee landlord had never been made so plain before. There were rumors that he was going to retire soon.

There was a brief flurry of activity by what was left of the District Council. The indomitable stooges who composed it denounced the C.I.O. and held conferences looking toward organizational aid and possible affiliation with the A.F.L. These conferences, with a sort of idiot fatality, duly collapsed over the craft issue. The Council then changed its name to the American Union of Steel Workers and quietly disappeared. In New York somebody named Matthew Woll stood up in public and said out loud before witnesses that credit for the victory in steel belonged to the A.F.L. None of his hearers seemed to feel it was his duty to enlighten the speaker, and the steelworkers themselves were too occupied joining the S.W.O.C. to attempt it; Pittsburgh headquarters reported that thirty-five thousand had joined in two weeks. Even Dobie's Uncle John had signed up.

The fifty-year struggle to free the steel towns was nearly over.

He couldn't sleep, and after a while he gave up trying. Carefully, so as not to disturb Julie, he got out of bed, put on his slippers and bathrobe and went downstairs. His tobacco and papers were on the radio where he'd left them. He rolled a cigarette in the dark and then stood by the window smoking it. There was a thin mist over the sleeping town. Street lights made a scrambled pattern that ended at the river's edge and other lights blinked through the murk that shrouded the blast furnaces. Over to the left, around the shoulder of the hill, the yellow glare of the Bessemers flickered against low-hanging clouds.

Men would soon be striding past the cops at the mill gates with union buttons on their caps, and no knightly plume had ever been worn more proudly or celebrated a greater victory; but the job wasn't finished. Exactly what that job was Dobie had never got clear in his mind. All sorts of things were involved in it and he wasn't sure that some of them belonged there. It wasn't worrying him. He felt good. He felt proud and confident and in no special hurry, the way he felt when he had a job of work to do that was a little out of the ordinary but that he knew exactly how to go about doing, the way he felt when he was changing into his work clothes and talking back and forth with the others and this job of work was waiting for him out on the floor.

For instance, the union had to grow until every man in the mill belonged, of course; but what good was your union if every so often you let bad times come along and knock everything to hell? Perhaps it wasn't part of a labor union's job to find a remedy for the fluctuations of the business cycle. But somebody ought to tackle it and it didn't seem possible that the unions could make a worse botch of solving it than the bankers and businessmen.

And there was the necessity of going into politics and making sure that the union, working people generally, didn't get their pockets picked by corporation lawyers disguised as Senators and Representatives.

And there was the problem posed by the existence of such newspapers as Pittsburgh was afflicted with, undeservedly surely, for no community could possibly deserve typographical calamities on such a scale. Self-preservation alone demanded that the unions do something about them, perhaps establish their own papers.

And there was the problem of technological unemployment. The company was making elaborate plans for a sixty-million-dollar continuous strip mill near Clairton, but no one had announced any plans for the thousands of men in the old sheet and tin mills which it would permanently displace. No nation could permit such waste of its human material any more than it could permit the waste of its substance in the eroded hills and poisoned rivers and blasted earth of the steel country; not if it wanted to survive. Why not put an end to both wastes at one stroke? Before Carnegie put up his blast furnaces Braddock had been a green and pleasant place; now Dobie felt that it would have profited America to have voted him his millions out of the public treasury rather than permit such waste and destruction as his mills had wrought. Nor were Carnegie and Braddock unique. All over America men had been permitted, as a matter of business, as a matter of dollars and cents, to destroy what neither money nor men could ever restore or replace. With this result: that America was no longer, except to a few of its people, a beautiful land. Where it wasn't blighted with slums its deforested hills were being washed into the sea, or the soil of its plains was being blown in clouds across the sky; until from someone like Mikie could be wrung the wish that he could have chosen his own birth-place, there were so few places left that one could love.

For a beginning, something might be done about the mills themselves. In the mass they had magnificence, the magnificence of size, of leaping flame, billowing clouds of smoke and an over-whelming suggestion of monstrous forces barely controlled. In their details they were ugly, clumsy, apparently built of cast-off odds and ends with an air of congenital inefficiency about them — slovenly workmen doing everything the hard way with the wrong tools. The clean and quiet, all-electric, plate-glassed, green-lawned steel mills of the future would probably not be built as far from the ore mines as Braddock was, but surely something could be done to make the present mills less of a menace to the public health, less of an affront to the eye.

And while they were about it, Dobie reflected, they might try finding a satisfactory substitute for bosses and bossism. An end to the intolerable state of affairs under which some men had virtual power of life and death over others was long overdue. Perhaps the best way to take care of that was to do something about work itself. At its best, work was fun. With millions unemployed (which wasn't necessarily unpleasant) and starving (which was), it had sunk to a privilege. Ultimately, of course, it would have to become an honor, bestowed by the community only on those citizens who had proved themselves worthy of it, and on those whose doctors prescribed it.

He grinned suddenly and murmured, "What are you trying to do, make the world over?"

Why not?

His cigarette had gone out. He relit it, a spur of scorched paper flaring up like a small torch and expiring as suddenly in a dribble of sparks. He crushed them under his slipper and then watched a Chevvy coupe grind up the roadway from the paved street. It halted in front of the Cassidy house. The engine died, the headlights went out, and the younger Cassidy girl — the older one's boy friend drove a Dodge — began to bid her escort good night.

We've come a long way, he thought. The unhappy kid in high school, the young man footloose in Detroit, calling himself "John Dobie" and nevertheless discovering that saying you were an American satisfied no one, — where did your father come from? — had become a man who had offered to knock a General Superintendent through a door of his own office building, a man who played with ideas for making the world over without feeling either presumptuous or absurd.

To the day of his death, no doubt, some nerve would twitch, some uncontrollable muscle flinch, at the word "Hunky" used as an epithet; to the day of his death certain graces, certain niceties of taste and manner and speech, would stay unknown to him or become him awkwardly, like borrowed garments. And by so much, in his own eyes at least, he would always be a poorer human being than he might have been.

Otherwise, it didn't seem to matter as much as it once had. The old heart-burnings, the miserable self-consciousness, even a good deal of the bitterness, were gone. In their place were pride of achievement, a growing self-assurance, a certain degree of understanding that "Hunky" was only one word in a whole disgraceful dictionary of epithets whose use would continue to spread humiliation and discord until society made that use as unprofitable as it was dangerous. Meanwhile, one was in duty bound to fight it wherever it appeared — under whatever guise, whether it sprang from ignorance or nastiness or a studied purpose. Cherishing freedom and decency, one could do no less.

And he realized now what it was that had once puzzled him about the C.I.O. men. Whatever their ancestry, they had felt the same way about certain things; and because Dobie had been born and raised in a steel town, where the word meant people who were white, Protestant, middle-class Anglo-Saxons, it hadn't occurred to him that the C.I.O. men were thinking and talking like Americans.

"Maybe not the kind of American that came over on the *Mayflower*," he reflected, "or the kind that's always shooting off their mouths about Americanism and patriotism, including some of the God-damnedest heels you'd ever want to see, but the kind that's got *Made in U.S.A.* stamped all over them, from the kind of grub they like to the things they wouldn't do for all the money in the world."

He stared down at the sleeping town without really seeing it.

"Made in the U.S.A.," he thought, "made in the First Ward. Mikie was right; it's too bad a person can't pick their own place to be born in, considering what it does to you. I'm almost as much a product of that mill down there as any rail or ingot they ever turned out. And maybe that's been part of the trouble. If I'm anything at all I'm an American, only I'm not the kind you read about in history books or that they make speeches about on the Fourth of July; anyway, not yet. And a lot of people don't know what to make of it and don't like it. Which is tough on me but is liable to be still tougher on them, because I at least don't have to be told that Braddock ain't Plymouth Rock and this ain't the year 1620."

The mist was thicker than it had been only a short while before. The night of a steel town was settling over the First Ward, veiling the street lamps, muffling sounds, swirling through the silent alleys and courtyards; the sort of night, mysterious and a little terrifying and occasionally beautiful, which he'd taken for granted until he'd gone to Detroit, where nightfall was hardly more than a simple, unimaginative withdrawal of sunlight. As he watched the rooftops disappear, the remembered taste and smell of it returned so vividly that for a moment he would have liked to be down there, striding along Washington or turning into Thirteenth, his coat collar up and hands in pockets, the night a dampness against his face, a smoky thickness in his throat.

Made in the U.S.A., he thought, made in the First Ward. But it wasn't where you were born or how you spelled your name or where your father had come from. It was the way you thought and felt about certain things. About freedom of speech and the equality of men and the importance of having one law — the same law — for rich and poor, for the people you liked and the people you didn't like. About the right of every man to live his life as he thought best, his right to defend it if anyone tried to change it and his right to change it himself if he decided he liked some other way of living better. About the uses to which wealth and power could honorably be put, and about honor itself, honor, integrity, self-respect, the whatever-you-wanted-to-call-it that determined for a man which things he couldn't say or do under any circumstances, not for all the money there was, not even to help his side win. About human dignity, which helped a man live proudly and distinguished his death from an animal's; and, finally, about the value to be put on a human life, one's enemy's no less than one's own.

"I hope it's all in the Declaration of Independence and the Bill of Rights," Dobie reflected, "though that never kept the company from pushing us around whenever it happened to feel like it. And they'd still be pushing us around and the Declaration of Independence and the Bill of Rights would still be nothing but a couple papers in a glass case down in Washington if a lot of us hadn't got together and started fighting for what we believed in. And maybe it'll always be like that. I don't know."

He lifted his head. "All I know is there's certain things I've got to have or I don't want to go on living. I want certain things bad enough to fight for them, bad enough to die for them. Patrick Henry, Junior — that's me. Give me liberty or give me death. But he meant every word of it and by God I think I do too."

Out of this furnace, this metal.

After a while he rolled another cigarette and went upstairs, Julie was snoring softly. She always slept on her back now. Her hospital bag was packed and ready but she wasn't, as far as he could tell, worried. Not about having the baby, at any rate. "I just hope I get most of my figure back. Do you really think I will?" The minute she got back from the hospital, she said, she was going right upstairs and try on her good black crepe.

There had been a time, before he'd married and even for a while afterward, when he wasn't sure that he'd ever want children. They hadn't seemed worth the trouble. Now he thought that having a couple kids around the house might be fun. A lot of worry and expense, no doubt, but a lot of fun too.

The only reason for not having children that still made a little sense was the kind of world they'd have to live in. "But what the hell," he thought, "I took my chances and my kids can do the same."

He put out his cigarette and got into bed. Julie's warmth enveloped him and made him realize how chilled he'd gotten, standing by the window. He felt suddenly tired, too; the excitement that had kept him wakeful was dying. He made himself comfortable, and yawned.

Still and all (his thoughts ran on) the world my kid grows up in ought to be a little better than the one I was born into, and if it is I think I'll have the right to say I had something to do with making it better. Of course it'll be just like the lousy brat to decide he don't think much of his old man's work. But that's all right. Just so he don't leave it at that. Just so he goes out and does something about it.

Under the covers his hand moved. He patted Julie's great belly.

"Okay, kid. Any time you're ready."

Then he turned over on his side and went to sleep.

THE END

AFTERWORD

THE Monongahela Cemetery spreads out across a hilltop a mile north of Braddock, Pennsylvania. Its lower ranges are dominated by Irish names, burials that date from the late nineteenth century. Near the lower gate is the Victorian mausoleum of Captain Bill Jones, Andrew Carnegie's first steelmaster, killed in a furnace accident in 1889. The lower ranges are orderly and well landscaped.

By contrast, near the top, on the cemetery's steepest slope, is a dense cluster of Slovak burials from the first decades of the twentieth century. The memorials are small and often homemade—concrete or wooden or steel-bar markers that erosion has tilted at crazy angles. Here a recurring icon is the triple cross of the Eastern-rite churches. These are the graves of immigrant steelworkers and their families, a visual record of the first generation's struggle to find a place in America.

About midpoint on the hillside, in a still Slovak but more prosperous-looking section, stands a Greek Catholic chapel. Near it is a stone that says unelaborately, "Michael Belejcak, 1875–1914, Father."

Thomas Bell's description in *Out of This Furnace* is calculated and exact:

Mike's lodge paid a five-hundred-dollar death benefit, all of which went for funeral expenses, masses for the dead and a four-grave plot excellently situated (near the chapel) in a newly opened section of the cemetery. The gravestone [Mary] chose was a granite column surmounted by the triple cross of the Greek Catholic Church. On it was carved: MICHAEL L. DOBREJCAK. *Born December 8 1875, died March 7 1914.*

*   *   *

Thomas Bell (christened Adalbert Thomas) was born in Braddock on March 7, 1903, the son of Michael and Mary Belejcak. His deliberate choice of his father's gravesite for that of his fictional character Mike Dobrejcak is only one of many instances in which he borrowed from his family background to create *Out of This Furnace*.

The family chronicle of the novel spans three generations. The blundering, ineffective career of George Kracha, who, in 1881, is the first in the family to migrate to America, dominates the first section; the better-ordered but work-exploited lives of Mike and Mary Dobrejcak in the early twentieth century are the subject of the middle of the book; finally there is the familiarly American life-style of Dobie Dobrejcak, who comes of age in the 1920s and is active in the successful unionizing of the mills in the 1930s. In its larger implications, *Out of This Furnace* is about the acculturation and evolving political consciousness of the immigrant workers of America's steel towns. It is a history of an important phase of the labor movement, a splendid memorial to a particular ethnic group.

An article in 1941 in *The Saturday Review of Literature* sums up Bell's achievement:

> Of all the writers who have come out of our so-called "new immigration," that from Southern and Southeastern Europe, none deserves more hearty acclamation than Thomas Bell, author of the novel "Out of This Furnace.". . . Reading this book enriches one's understanding of the America of Braddock, Homestead, Gary and other steel towns. . . . [It] portray[s] the America of the newcomer for those who sometimes forget that at one time they too were newcomers.

Out of This Furnace is painstakingly realistic, painstakingly accurate in fact and detail. The alleys and byways of Braddock's First Ward, fifty and seventy-five years ago, are recorded with a precision that could only come from being raised there. And behind the general themes, behind Kracha, Mike, Mary, and Dobie—the fictional characters—are Bell's own family, the Belejcaks.

*   *   *

Especially in the case of Mary and Michael Belejcak enough remains in memory and the public records to show some of the choices Bell made as he adapted autobiographic materials to his fictional purposes.

Like Mike Dobrejcak, Michael Belejcak migrated in 1890, a teen-ager, from the village of Tvarosc in the Slovakian (Austro-Hungarian) province of Sarisa. During the next decade, Michael's three younger brothers—Joseph, John, and Paul—followed him to Braddock, leaving behind a widowed mother but apparently no siblings. At least two Belejcak cousins in the village took the same route. Why so many in the same family chose to migrate—why so many others from Tvarosc and Sarisa found their way to Braddock—is a matter of speculation (Bell's guess in the novel is that an effective recruiting agent for the mill was at work).

What the historic record does make clear is that Bell did not have to invent hardships in order to dramatize the precariousness of life in the mill towns, for the Belejcak brothers paid a heavy price. Paul died on December 31, 1909, aged nineteen, his death certificate summarizing, "traumatic pneumonia following a fracture of the right side of skull (probably murder)." Thomas Bell's brother Anthony, who was born in 1909, fills in with detail that has passed down through the family: "Paul, the youngest, tallest and fairest of the brothers, got into a quarrel in the mill—I have the impression that he threw his weight around with one of the Irish or Scotch workers. He was found alongside the railroad tracks that night after work, his skull cracked with a piece of pipe." John Belejcak, married and the father of three young children, died at age thirty-two in 1912, accidentally asphyxiated by gas from a charged furnace in the Edgar Thomson Works. Of the four Belejcak brothers, only Joseph survived into middle and old age.

In adapting family materials, Thomas Bell had no need to exaggerate; his problem was the reverse—suppressing tragic coincidences that actually happened because they might seem implausible in the world of a novel. The real story of the brothers is deleted. The account of the death of Kracha's wife has been altered from its even more vivid real-life counterpart; again Anthony Bell: "My maternal grandmother committed suicide—that's Kracha's wife. The story is that she handed Aunt Bertha, a babe in arms at the time, to a friend and walked into the Monongahela River." In the novel Bell also changed the cause, though not the date, of his father's death. Michael Belejcak, like his wife five years later, died of tuberculosis. Bell doubtless chose the mill accident as the cause of Mike Dobrejcak's death for dramatic purposes, in full knowledge that the family history supported the plausibility of his decision.

In making Mike Dobrejcak a steelworker and thus assigning him the typical mill town occupation, Bell altered other external circumstances. The real-life Michael Belejcak turns up in Braddock directories in 1906 and 1911 as a bartender, in 1913 as the operator of a cigar store. Anthony Bell: "Judging from the well-turned out appearance in the pictures, my father must have been doing much better than a mill worker. His friends were the ones active in the business and social life of the Slovak community." If inference and fading memories can be trusted, Michael Belejcak began in Braddock as a steel worker. By the turn of the century, clearly he had moved into various retail roles. His career was a perhaps more successful version of the experience assigned to Kracha in the novel.

By virtue of his seriousness, responsibility, and idealism, by virtue of dramatic intensity, the hero of *Out of This Furnace* is Mike Dobrejcak (Bell signals as much with the name: Dobrejcak means "good man"). In the central qualities of character and mind, Michael Belejcak sounds like the fictional figure. Again Anthony Bell: "I would say that Mike Dobrejcak is Mike Belejcak seen by my brother through my mother's eyes. . . . The character is true. He dominated his brothers; was head of the family. . . . He wrote and spoke English quite well, I was told; and there were books in that break-front bookcase." Since so much of the power of the two central sections of the novel hinges on the love of Mary and Mike Dobrejcak, Anthony Bell's further comment is of interest: "The love story is true, complete with diamond engagement ring, watch chain woven of my mother's hair and a golden heartshaped locket with miniature photos." (The expensive gravestone on the hill, "in a newly opened section of the cemetery," reflected more than ritual extravagance.)

The facts behind Bell's portrait of the original migrant, George Kracha (in real life George Krachun), are hard to reconstruct from sources independent of the novel, but much of the early career appears true to events ("Black Susan" still has a reputation among those who have some memory of Braddock during the first decade of the century). A grandson, Raymond Shedlock, can recall that for a year, in the twenties or early thirties, Krachun worked at Homestead on the "cripples gang," a mill arrangement that allowed old-timers to finish out their service so they would be eligible for pension. Both Anthony Bell and Shedlock remember the family struggle to get the paycheck before "Gramps" got to the saloons.

*   *   *

The autobiographic background of *Out of This Furnace* underscores one of the novel's important overall qualities—its ethnicity. *Out of This Furnace* is about Slovaks; comments about other national groups are always made in passing and always from a Slovak point of view. In this context, the book's strong family feeling translates into ethnic pride, and the union triumph at the end celebrates, in part, the hard work, determination, and intelligence of a people who had been a rural peasantry less than fifty years before.

In a 1946 interview in the newspaper *Ludovy dennik*, Bell talked about the Slovak theme of *Out of This Furnace*. Thirty years later, in an era of perhaps more widespread ethnic consciousness, his words sound distinctly "modern":

My conscience dictated me to write [the novel]. I saw a people brought here by steel magnates from the old country and then exploited, ridiculed, and oppressed. None of my books contains such a hunk of my life as this book about my people. The life of a Slovak boy in Braddock 30–40 years ago was a bitter one. As a small boy I could not understand why I should be ashamed of the fact that I was Slovak. While Irish and German kids could boast of the history of their ancestors, I as a Slovak boy did not know anything about the history of my people. I made up my mind to write a history of the Braddock Slovaks in order to tell the world that the Slovaks with their blood and lives helped to build America, that the steel they produced changed the United States into the most industrialized nation in the world. My book *Out of This Furnace* is an answer to all those unthinking people who look down on the Slovaks. It was also my aim to strengthen in the Slovaks their pride in their origin. Finally, I wanted to make sure that the hardships my grandfather, my father, my mother, and my brother, sisters, and other relatives lived through would never be forgotten. (Translated by John Berko in his "Thomas Bell (1903–1961), Slovak-American Novelist," *Slovak Studies*, vol. 15)

The prejudice evinced toward "Hunkies" that Bell describes is amply documented in the attitudes of other writers—non-Slavs—who have dealt with the same era. An early biographer of Andrew Carnegie explained the violent antiunionism of H. C. Frick this way: "Frick had . . . been unfortunate in the type of workmen with whom he had previously dealt. The Hungarians, Slavs and Southern Europeans of Connellsville were a savage and undisciplined horde, with whom strong-arm methods seemed at times indispensable, and when strikes broke out murder and arson became their favorite persuasions" (Burton J. Henrick, *The Life of Andrew Carnegie*, vol. 1 [Garden City: Doubleday, Doran & Co., Inc., 1932], p. 378). Later, describing the attack on the Pinkertons in the 1892 Homestead strike, the same writer knew where to put the blame: "The chief offenders were women, the wives of Hungarians, Slavs and Italians; these cowardly amazons . . . beat the unarmed men with clubs, hurled stones and pieces of iron" (p. 396).

Bell's picture of the Slovak world, presented with an insider's knowledge, is starkly different: "In the old country the Slovaks had been an oppressed minority from the beginning of time, a simple, religious, unwarlike people, a nation of peasants and shepherds whom the centuries had taught patience and humility. In America they were all this and more, foreigners in a strange land, ignorant of its language and customs, fearful of authority in whatever guise."

In the portrayals of Joe and Dorta Dubik and in the two central sections of the novel devoted to Mike and Mary Dobrejcak, Bell dramatizes with special emphasis the virtues of "my people"—their determined willingness to work, devotion to family and home, disciplined effort to budget and save, plus a political idealism that waited a chance for expression. The Slovak community in Braddock at the turn of the century emerges as an intimate neighborhood of friends and acquaintances—people from the same provinces in the old country or those who had met on first arrival in America. (Marriage and birth records for the Belejcak family show the pattern in real life: names like Babej, Pustinger, and Andrejchak occur again and again as godparents or witnesses—all originally from Sarisa, many from the village of Tvarosc.) Bell's picture of Slovaks is balanced: there is no attempt to disguise the flaws in a man like Kracha. But overall *Out of This Furnace* argues that the central flaw was not in the people; it was in the brutal problems they had to confront in mill town America.

In the novel, Slovak women play a notable role. Against heavy odds, they struggle to hold their families together, to create a sense of "home." Dorta is an important character. A substitute mother for the young Mike, years later, near the end of the book, she is stubbornly maintaining her home in the old neighborhood when Dobie revisits her as he might a real grandmother. Outspoken, commonsensical, Dorta endures, symbolizing the strengths requisite to making the mill towns habitable. The central female characters of the early generations—Elena and Mary, as well as Dorta—all face a world in which much of the time they must "go it alone." Threatened or confronted by widowhood, separated from their husbands in the best of times by the long mill workday, they also have the burden of devising extra income for the family budget. Bell's account emphasizes their tragedy, their heroism —Elena is crushed by the mill town world; Mary wheedles and coerces her wayward father when Mike's death has left her alone to raise her family.

Speculating on family events that may have prompted Bell to write *Out of This Furnace*, Anthony Bell comments: "About my mother he said once that at the time it didn't make much impression on him, but that when he was in his late twenties he began to recall the years right after my father's death and agonized over the anguish and hardships she experienced in the few years she lasted." One of the novel's most moving passages is Mary's stream-of-consciousness reflection on her life with Mike: " 'I want a good life for us, Marcha. For you, for me, for our children . . .' What had gone wrong, what had they done?" Bell's tender portrait of Mary is at once a personal statement and a tribute to the generations of women who built homes in the mill town world. (An album picture shows Mary Belejcak, in black mourning dress, standing next to Michael's gravestone, her four young children sitting in front of her.)

Despite his intimate detailing of Slovak life, Bell plays down certain elements that another writer might have chosen to emphasize. One is the role of religion. Bell's deemphasis of religion marks another departure from the facts of his father's life. Anthony Bell states: "My father was very active in the church and related organizations. He attended gatherings all over the state and Ohio. Pictures I have seem to indicate he was in office in some of them." Perhaps partly because of his early observations that the churches did not predictably side with the workingman's desire to improve his lot, perhaps because he wished to make his fictional character into a more typical figure, Bell ignores his father's special religious commitments in his picture of Mike Dobrejcak.

Another facet of mill town life that Bell underplays is the importance of military service for many families of eastern European origin. As route to citizenship, service in the First World War was perceived as an Americanizing status symbol—a fact still attested to by family photos and, in the Pittsburgh area, by war memorials that are scattered through local neighborhoods. Bell, an antimilitarist, makes small mention (and no positive one) of this aspect of the Slovak experience in America.

*   *   *

Thomas Bell himself left Braddock in 1922, having worked several years, as eldest son, in the mills. As a teen-ager, he had also begun writing. His cousin, Raymond Shedlock, remembers how he would work the twelve-hour shift in the Donora mill, come home and pound the typewriter till four in the morning, sleep a couple of hours, and then go back to the mill. In the early twenties he was turning out a column for the Braddock *News-Herald*. But in the classic pattern of small-town Americans, apparently he had to get away. After a brief stint in the merchant marines, he made his home in New York City for the next thirty years, giving his attention more and more to his writing. When he left Braddock in the early twenties, his brother Anthony and two sisters stayed behind, the younger two being helped by various branches of the Belejcak and Krachun families. Pauline, the oldest of the three, married during the twenties (but died of TB in 1932); Tony and Evelyn were with Bell in New York by 1930.

The final section of *Out of This Furnace*, dominated by the unionizing theme, is thus in a sense more purely fictional than the earlier portions: no single figure, or combination of figures, in the Belejcak family directly points to Dobie Dobrejcak, the son of Mike and Mary who stays in Braddock on through the thirties. But even if there is less autobiography in the last section of the novel, Bell continues to work with documentary mill town facts. From the standpoint of the author's own life, Dobie Dobrejcak might be viewed as an imagined projection of what Bell himself would have wished to be had he remained in Braddock.

Bell's particular source for much of the novel's inside account of union activities in the thirties appears to have been Louis Smolinski, now retired from U.S. Steel, who in the early thirties was president of the Braddock local of the Amalgamated Association of Iron, Steel and Tin Workers and then a member of both the Employees Representatives at Edgar Thomson and the Steel Workers' Organizing Committee. Smolinski states that the novel's documentary materials concerning union activities—letters, memos, minutes—are essentially verbatim (with some changing of names), passed by Smolinski himself to Bell when he was researching the novel in Braddock in the late thirties. Smolinski still has copies of the letters exchanged between the Amalgamated Association and the mill superintendent (detailed on pages 314–15 in the novel). The shouting matches with Flack (in real life Frank F. Slick) are directly rendered by Bell from accounts supplied by Smolinski.

*   *   *

The documentary style used in much of the Dobie section underscores the fact that Bell varies his method of narration in *Out of This Furnace* to show the evolution of the family from one generation to the next. The Kracha section is notably episodic—the arrival in White Haven, the affair with Zuska, the deaths of Dubik and Elena. The section is held together by a summarizing narrative voice, the author's own commentary on the problems Kracha encounters. The effect is to characterize Kracha—a man not much in control of what happens to him, too pressured to pause and reflect; Kracha is a man more acted upon than acting. Then there is a shift. After the long historical summary at the start of the Mike Dobrejcak section, the author's own direct commentary becomes less and less intrusive; the scenes seem to lengthen and to become more intimate. This new narrative approach again characterizes the actors, the warm relationship of Mary and Mike. And in the drunk scene with Steve Bodnar, it is Mike—not the author—who reflects passionately on the need for social justice. Mike may not be in control of events, but he has achieved a somewhat settled style of life that was more elusive for his elders, the earlier migrants.

The Dobie section of *Out of This Furnace* has a certain flat, reportage quality relative to the exotic colorations of Kracha's early career or the dramatic intimacy of the Mike and Mary sections. Dobie is a member of the generation that comes of age in America, that has achieved sufficient confidence and knowledge to act effectively in its own behalf. The reportorial style dramatizes this: Dobie's style is familiar; he is a contemporary American.

The diverse sections of *Out of This Furnace* are tied together by evident cross-generational bonds. The real-life Krachun died in 1935, and Bell uses his long endurance symbolically in the novel. He is a measure, by contrast, of the distance that Dobie's generation has come since the "bad old days"; he suggests the toughness and luck necessary in his generation for survival. When he dies an era is over: *"The tall iron gates were locked for the night. . . . The last light died out of the west and then it was dark on the hill where Kracha lay."*

Kracha's death also symbolizes the birth of an era, allowing Bell to move to his optimistic close, the union success of 1937, the vision of enduring industrial democracy in America: *"Out of this furnace, this metal."* And as union organizer Dobie acts as his father's son—another cross-generational bond is established. In a midnight ramble through Braddock's First Ward, Mike Dobrejcak had summed up his own vision:

He had felt that no human being need go without his portion of comfort and beauty and quietness; the world held enough for all and if some had less than others it was because men had ordered it so and it lay in men's hands to order differently. It had seemed to him that men need only have this explained to them and they'd rise up and do what was necessary; and when they didn't he felt angry and bewildered.

Years later, when union success is in hand, Dobie remembers his father: "He lifted his eyes to the dark sky. 'We've come a long way, hey Pop?' "

The triumph of the Steel Workers' Organizing Committee at the close of *Out of This Furnace* is a fitting climax to a novel so centrally about industrial justice and injustice. Among its other achievements, *Out of This Furnace* is a history of the labor movement in steel.

*　　　*　　　*

Overall, Thomas Bell published six novels: *The Breed of Basil* (1930), *The Second Prince* (1935), *All Brides Are Beautiful* (1936), *Out of This Furnace* (1941), *Till I Come Back to You* (1943), and *There Comes a Time* (1946). In the last two years of his life, when he knew he had terminal cancer, he also wrote an autobiographic memoir, *In the Midst of Life* (published in 1961—the year of his death). Bell's reputation was at its height from 1936 till the mid-forties. *All Brides Are Beautiful, Out of This Furnace,* and *Till I Come Back to You* were all prominently reviewed; *Brides* went through several printings and became a movie in 1946 *(From This Day Forward)*; *Till I Come Back to You* briefly became a Broadway play.

The three central novels in Bell's career are all immersed in naturalistic detail, the commonplace, often minute data of proletariat life. *All Brides Are Beautiful* describes the lives of a Bronx couple during two years of the Great Depression; there is no pronounced structure or plot—the effect is almost like a daily journal. *Till I Come Back to You* focuses on a single day's visit with Brooklyn friends during the Second World War. The attention to realistic detail in *Out of This Furnace* is characteristic of Bell's mature work, while the historical purpose of the novel gives it firmer structure than the others.

Two themes dominate Bell's fiction. One is romantic—the centrality of a love story (in *In the Midst of Life*, addressing a letter to his wife, Bell comments: "Something of the best of [our years together] is in the books I wrote, just as is much of the best of me. I was always my own hero; and after my first book I never had a heroine who didn't have more of you in her than of herself"). The second theme is the argument for social justice, the critique of exploitative capitalism, and the support of unionism. Both *All Brides Are Beautiful* and *Till I Come Back to You* end, much like *Out of This Furnace*, with their heroes articulating political credos. The union theme is particularly effective in *Out of This Furnace* because it grows so logically out of prior circumstances, because Dobie can pick it up as such a natural fulfillment of his father's idealism.

In only one other novel, *The Second Prince*, does Bell use a mill town setting. There the angle of vision is startlingly different from *Out of This Furnace*, since the hero is an Anglo-Saxon from an "old money family" that lives in a mansion on the hills above a mill town. However, a Slovak steelworker, active in the union, is a secondary character. The details of his life are reminiscent of Bell's own Braddock background, and his views suggest he is a preliminary version of Mike and Dobie Dobrejcak.

*   *   *

Not much is left today of the Braddock First Ward that *Out of This Furnace* takes for a setting. The Edgar Thomson Works has appropriated whole blocks; others are crumbling from age and poverty. Most of the Slovaks, most of the steelworkers have moved up the hills and into the suburbs.

The most vivid memorial left is a hilltop cemetery—and Thomas Bell's novel.

DAVID P. DEMAREST, JR.

CARNEGIE-MELLON UNIVERSITY
PITTSBURGH, PA.

DISCARD

ACKNOWLEDGMENTS

I owe thanks to many individuals who shared with me their knowledge of Thomas Bell and *Out of This Furnace*. Marie Bell, Thomas Bell's widow, and Anthony Bell, his brother, corresponded at length and supplied a variety of family materials. Other members of the family were also helpful: Raymond and Frank Shedlock of Donora; Rosella Busko of North Braddock; Michael Belechak of Trafford, Pennsylvania. John Berko of Slovak Art International answered various questions and sent me a copy of his manuscript, "Thomas Bell (1903–1961), Slovak-American Novelist." Tom Walsh, Director of the Braddock Catholic Cemetery, Kenny Poeschel, Director of the Monongahela Cemetery, and Father Blaise Kovach of St. Peter and Paul's Church in Braddock provided information; Poeschel and Father Blaise had relevant early records that I was able to study. Louis Smolinski of Braddock shared with me his recollections of Thomas Bell's research in the late thirties and his detailed knowledge about the Steel Workers' Organizing Committee. John Elco, now of Fort Myers, Florida, talked with me about labor conditions in Donora in the post–First World War era. Mary Pastor of North Braddock recalled life on Washington Street in 1910.

Special thanks go to Marie Bell, whose cooperation made everything else possible.